CHRISSIE MANBY

A PROPER FAMILY ADVENTURE

First published in Great Britain in 2015 by Hodder & Stoughton
An Hachette UK company

1

A CIP catalogue record for this title is available from the British Library

Paperback ISBN 978 1 473 61536 6
Ebook ISBN 978 1 473 61535 9

Typeset in Sabon MT by Palimpsest Book Production Limited,
Falkirk, Stirlingshire

Printed and bound by Clays Ltd, St Ives plc

Hodder & Stoughton policy is to use papers that are natural, renewable and recyclable products and made from wood grown in sustainable forests. The logging and manufacturing processes are expected to conform to the environmental regulations of the country of origin.

Hodder & Stoughton Ltd
Carmelite House
50 Victoria Embankment
London EC4Y 0DZ

www.hodder.co.uk

To my nephews, Harrison and Lukas Arnold

Chapter One

Jack

'Happy birthday to you! Happy birthday to you! Happy *birrrrth*-day, dear Granddad Bill. You smell like a poo.'

'*Jack Benson-Edwards*!'

That rising tone. Jack knew he was in trouble.

'Don't be so bloody rude to your great-grandfather,' said his mother Ronnie.

'Don't say "bloody",' seven-year-old Jack countered.

'Why, you little . . .' Ronnie made a scary face at her beloved son. He ran for the cover of his Auntie Chelsea.

'I'm sorry, Granddad Bill,' said Jack from behind Chelsea's legs. 'You don't really smell like a poo.'

'He does a bit,' whispered Lily, daughter of Chelsea's boyfriend Adam. She was also seven years old.

Granddad Bill didn't care. He was turning eighty-seven that afternoon. His entire family had gathered at his eldest granddaughter Annabel's big house in the country to celebrate in style. The party comprised his son and daughter-in-law, Dave and Jacqui, his three granddaughters, Chelsea, Ronnie and Annabel, their partners, four great-grandchildren and Lily, who counted as one of the great-grandkids as far as everyone was concerned. Now Bill blew out the candles on his cake. Not eighty-seven of them, but twenty-two.

'You'll just have to multiply by four and minus one,'

said Annabel. 'If we'd gone the whole hog, we might have burned the house down.'

And that would have been a big disaster. Annabel's spectacular manor house was a listed building of special historical interest. During the English Civil War, two princes – the future Charles II and James II – had slept in the attic that was now Annabel's teenaged daughter's bedroom.

Annabel's younger sisters, Ronnie and Chelsea, were both quietly impressed by the cake, which was in the shape of a shield, bearing the Coventry City FC crest. It was the first time Annabel had taken on the role of family cake-maker, which usually fell to Ronnie or to their mother Jacqui. She'd done a good job despite her protestations that she really couldn't bake. Granddad Bill was delighted to see his beloved football team honoured in sky blue icing. He blew out the candles in just five breaths.

'He's full of wind, is Granddad Bill,' said Mark, Ronnie's husband.

'Three cheers for Granddad Bill,' suggested Annabel.

'Hooray! Hooray! Hooray!' yelled Jack without waiting for any 'hip hips'.

Jack and Lily leapt forward to have the chance to cut the first slice of cake, each placing a hand on Annabel's fancy silver cake knife like a pair of diminutive newly-weds. That afternoon, the two children were getting on famously. This was a huge relief to everyone, since, like a real married couple, Jack and Lily were usually more likely to be found bickering or plotting murder than playing nicely.

'And now for the presents!' Jack squealed, piling brightly wrapped packages into his great-grandfather's lap as the old man sat in his electric wheelchair. 'This is from Mummy and Daddy. This one is from Auntie Chelsea. This is from Cathy Next Door.'

Granddad Bill opened the gifts his family and friends had chosen so carefully. He was delighted with a CD of the greatest hits of Acker Bilk, that year's Coventry City FC away shirt and a new pair of velvet carpet slippers to replace the old ones he wore every day. Cathy Next Door had bought Bill a packet of the small cigars he was supposed to have given up in the 1980s (they were swiftly confiscated by Dave). But Jack was sure that his gift was going to be the best of all.

'Izzy and Sophie had to help me get it,' he said. 'Because it's illegal.'

Illegal? The adults wondered what on earth Jack had asked his sixteen-year-old sister Sophie and his cousin Izzy to buy. Jack's parents, Ronnie and Mark, shared worried glances. They had known Jack was planning something special for his great-grandfather's birthday – he'd asked for an advance on his pocket money – but they would never have guessed it was something outside the law.

'But I chose the numbers,' Jack continued.

Jack handed Granddad Bill an envelope, decorated with the slightly wonky smiley faces that were Jack's signature. Unfortunately Granddad Bill had trouble with envelopes and it wasn't long before Jack grew impatient and opened his special gift himself. He pulled out the card he'd made with much secrecy the previous afternoon and waved it under the old man's nose, far too close for Granddad Bill to focus on, even with his glasses.

'Do you like the picture?' Jack asked.

'That's a very fine Dalek,' said Bill, making an educated guess.

'It's not a Dalek,' Jack sighed. 'It's you in your wheelchair.'

'Oh yes,' said Bill. 'I see that now.'

'And look what's in here. Look!'

Jack opened the card with a showman's flourish. Stuck inside with a piece of sticky tape was . . .

'A lottery ticket!'

'Not a couple of spliffs after all,' said Mark.

'Mark,' Ronnie scolded her husband. 'Keep your voice down.'

'What a clever idea,' said Jacqui, Jack's maternal grandmother. 'How did you come up with that?'

'Well, Granddad Bill is always talking about the lottery so me and Sophie and Izzy all went to Tesco and I wrote the numbers down and they went up to the till to pay because you have to be sixteen.'

Ah. That's what he meant by illegal.

'But it was mostly my money. I put in twenty pee.'

'You're a very generous boy,' said Jacqui.

The other adults agreed.

'I've got a good feeling about this one,' said Bill, holding the card and the ticket so that he could read what was written on both. 'How did you know thirteen's my lucky number?'

'It's my lucky number too!' said Jack.

'Come here, lad.' Bill opened his arms and Jack climbed onto his lap for a cuddle. 'Whether it's lucky or not, with a family like you lot, I've already won the bloody lottery.'

Chapter Two

Bill

Granddad Bill lived with his son Dave and his daughter-in-law Jacqui in a terraced house near the centre of Coventry. He'd lived in Coventry for as long as he could remember, never moving more than two miles from the Coundon Road Stadium, which was where his second favourite team, Coventry RFC, used to play. Like the stadium, these days Bill could almost be counted as a landmark.

Bill lived in the city through the Coventry Blitz and joined the army as soon as he was able, fighting in France at the tail end of the Second World War. When he came back, he worked at Dunlop for a while and, at twenty, he married Jennifer – a proper Coventry girl. Seven years later, they welcomed baby David into their lives. They were blissfully happy but alas, Jennifer died young, while Dave was still at secondary school. Bill always said that Jennifer was irreplaceable and indeed he never remarried (though he came close at the age of eighty-six after meeting a gold-digger in Lanzarote, but that's another story).

Bill moved in with his son and daughter-in-law once all his grandchildren had flown the nest. It was ideal for everybody. Bill didn't need the space he had in his old house and Dave and Jacqui could use the help with the mortgage on theirs. And while Bill was still relatively able, he also helped out in the garden. He had green fingers and suddenly there were carrots where Dave had cultivated only weeds.

In recent years however Dave and Jacqui had converted the front room into a bedroom for Bill, who was not as good on his feet as he had been. Though, on a good day, he could still get around using sticks, most of the time he used a wheelchair. He wasn't great on stairs. He also suffered from dementia, which seemed to be much worse at some times than others. There were days – such as his birthday that year – when Bill seemed entirely 'with it': totally lucid and aware of what was going on. Other days he mistook his son for his brother and called Jacqui by his dead wife's name. There were days, too, when Bill seemed to be living in a completely different time from everyone else, like when he asked why Jacqui wasn't carrying her gas mask when they went out to the shops.

It could be hard work, caring for Bill, but Dave and Jacqui would not have had it any other way. Bill had always been so good to them. When they were first married and struggling to cope with the financial and psychological pressure of raising two small children, Bill was always there. He was forever pressing money for housekeeping into Jacqui's hand, or offering them a few quid so they could have a night out. Ronnie and Chelsea were thrilled whenever they heard Granddad Bill would be babysitting. Bill never tired of dolly tea parties or adjudicating endless rounds of Happy Families and Go Fish.

Bill was such an important part of the family, Jacqui and Dave were determined to keep him out of residential care for as long as humanly possible. They were fortunate to have the support of a fantastic GP, who had recently put Bill onto a new medication regime that seemed to be working well. At least they'd not had any major incidents since that afternoon before Christmas when Jack commandeered Bill and his electric wheelchair for a cross-country adventure that ended up involving the police.

So, Bill was at home with Dave and Jacqui when the lottery draw took place on the Saturday after his birthday. They always watched the lottery show, though they never usually bought tickets. Mark, husband of Bill's granddaughter Ronnie, bought a ticket every week and had only won about fifty quid in the sixteen years he'd been playing. Bill had once won thirty quid on the EuroMillions. But it was a mug's game. A tax on the poor, Jacqui told Mark every time he mentioned his 'investment strategy'. Even one ticket a week added up to a small fortune over the course of a year. And it wasn't as though any of the Bensons were made of money.

But they still liked to watch *Win Your Wish List* and the draw itself. It was good entertainment. They all liked Shane Richie. And secretly Jacqui rather liked to reassure herself that she wouldn't have chosen any of the winning numbers. As the draw was announced, she would put down her habitual Saturday night Sudoku for a moment and mentally check off the balls.

'Twenty-eight? No, I wouldn't have chosen that. Nobody's birthday is on the twenty-eighth. Thirty-two doesn't sound very lucky to me. Who'd pick thirty-two? Six? I might have chosen that last year because of Jack but now he's seven, I wouldn't have picked it this week.' And so on.

Deciding that she would have merely wasted two pounds gave Jacqui a very warm feeling inside. It was almost as good as actually winning.

However, everything was about to change because that week, Granddad Bill had a ticket, courtesy of his great-grandchildren, Jack, Sophie and Izzy. Oh, and six-month-old Baby Humfrey, who was included on the card (as were the family cat, Fishy, and Izzy's dog Leander). For once, the National Lottery show had altogether more meaning.

'Let's get that ticket out then,' said Jacqui, sitting down on the sofa between Bill and Dave. 'See how Jack did with his picks.' She took up her special Sudoku biro, ready to tick the numbers off. The familiar music began to play as the multicoloured bouncing balls tumbled into the machine on-screen.

'What are you going to buy us if you win, Dad?' Dave asked Bill.

'Don't get your hopes up,' Jacqui laughed. 'If there's even two numbers on here, I'll eat my Sudoku pen.'

In the end, thirteen – Bill's lucky number – was the only one of the numbers Jack had chosen that *didn't* come up. At least, not in the main draw. It came up as the bonus ball.

Chapter Three

The Bensons

Jacqui, Bill and Dave all stared at the pale red ticket.

'Time to eat your pen,' Dave told his wife.

'I feel a bit sick,' said Jacqui. 'Look!' She showed Dave the goosebumps on her arms.

'Did we win it?' asked Bill.

'We didn't get them all,' said Dave.

'No, but we got five numbers and the bonus ball,' said Jacqui. 'Five. You still get something for that. If you get twenty-five quid for three numbers you must get something for five. How much do you think it is?'

'I don't know,' said Dave. 'We better call Ronnie.'

Over at Ronnie's house, Mark was scrunching up yet another losing ticket. That week he'd managed to get just one number right. Hopeless.

'I should give this up,' said Mark. 'I'd be better off throwing the money down the drain.'

'Or down your neck,' said Ronnie. 'Think of the amount of beer you could have bought with all the money you've spent on lottery tickets over the years.'

'Don't,' said Mark, as Ronnie's mobile began to ring. 'I can't bear to think about it. And if that's your mother calling to crow about my 'investment strategy', you can tell her where to stick it and all.'

'Ssssh.' Ronnie put her finger to her husband's lips

as she answered the call. It *was* her mother. 'Hello, Mum. You all right?'

'Oh Ronnie,' said Jacqui, her voice shivering with something that sounded like distress over the bad mobile line. 'Something's happened.'

'What, Mum? What?'

'Are you sitting down, sweetheart?'

Ronnie, who had stood up to find her phone, quickly collapsed onto the sofa in preparation for the worst.

'You're not going to believe this.'

'I wish you'd just tell me so I could find out whether I believe it or not.'

'It's Granddad Bill . . .' Jacqui began.

'Oh no!' Ronnie cried. Since he had his pacemaker fitted, the Bensons were always waiting to hear bad news about Granddad Bill. Ronnie screwed her eyes tightly shut. She couldn't bear the thought of losing him.

'We think he's won the bloody lottery,' Jacqui continued.

'What?!'

Ronnie immediately handed over the phone to Mark, who, having put so much effort into trying to win over the years since he was old enough to start playing, was rightly considered the family expert.

'Tell me again what the numbers are,' said Mark, checking them off against the Lottery app on his own phone. 'And tell me what it says on the top of the ticket. We need to make sure it's the right date. There are draws on a Wednesday too.'

Jacqui read out all the information. It definitely sounded as though she might be right.

'Can you take a picture of it, Jacqui?' Mark asked. 'And send it to my mobile. That way we'll know for sure.'

When the photograph came through, Mark and Ronnie stared at the picture on the screen as though they were seeing a newly discovered Dead Sea Scroll. They looked at it from all angles. Mark zoomed in on the figures. They so wanted to believe . . .

Sophie, who had been in her bedroom, talking to her cousin Izzy on Skype, came downstairs to find her parents thus absorbed.

'What's going on?' she asked.

Ronnie pointed to the screen of Mark's phone.

'Five numbers,' she mouthed. 'Five. And the bonus ball.'

'So?' said Sophie.

'So, we think Granddad Bill's just won fifty thousand pounds. With that lottery ticket you all got him for his birthday.'

Sophie shrieked in surprise and delight.

Jack was in his room. He'd been playing up all day, whining from the moment he woke, and his bad behaviour had been rewarded with an early bedtime and no *Doctor Who*.

'We've got to get him up,' said Sophie. 'He chose the numbers. This is huge.'

They didn't need to wake Jack up. He had heard his sister shriek and was already standing at the top of the stairs, trying to work out whether the shriek was a good or a bad one and whether he needed to intervene with his Sonic Screwdriver. He was clutching it in his hand, already on high alert.

'Jack!' Ronnie called. 'Jack! Come down here quickly. We're going over to Grandma and Granddad's.'

'What? Now?' said Jack. 'It's nearly midnight.'

'Yes. Now. Hurry up.'

Ronnie didn't even change Jack out of his pyjamas. She just put his anorak over the top. The Benson-Edwards family then piled into Mark's old car and drove at high speed across town.

Fifty thousand pounds. Jack's carefully chosen numbers had won his great-grandfather fifty thousand pounds.

But of course, the money wasn't just for Granddad Bill. From the very beginning, the Bensons all talked of a communal win. That was the way it was in their family. All for one and one for all. It would have been the same if Mark's ticket had come up, or Dave's, or Jacqui's, or Ronnie's.

Indeed in the past, Jacqui and Ronnie had spent many a happy hour at the kitchen table, drinking tea and pondering how they would split a win on the premium bonds (though they only had fifty quid's worth of bonds between them and hadn't seen one win in thirty years). There was never any question that the person whose numbers came up would share the bounty with everyone else. If Jacqui won a million, she would pay off all her daughters' debts. If Ronnie won, she would share with Chelsea (keeping just a little behind for some Jimmy Choos). So Granddad Bill's sudden windfall was a windfall for them all.

When they got to Dave and Jacqui's house, the celebrations were already under way. Jacqui had been on the phone to the people at the Lottery and they'd confirmed that Granddad Bill's ticket was indeed a big winner. The holy ticket itself was in a biscuit tin between the mattress and box spring of Dave and Jacqui's bed – the most secure place they could think of – awaiting such time as it could be handed over safely in exchange for a cheque. With the ticket safely stowed, Jacqui and Dave had opened the cocktail cabinet. Bill was drinking a bottle of Spitfire, though these days they tried to keep him off the booze. Even one bottle might disturb his sleep (though Dave was convinced Bill was actually more lucid when he'd had alcohol).

Jack rang the doorbell to his grandparents' house. Having been briefed on what was happening during the car journey, he was fizzing with excitement. When Jacqui opened the door, he ran straight past her to find his great-granddad in his chair.

'You did it, Granddad Bill. You won the bloody lottery!'

'Don't say bloody,' Ronnie yelled from the hall.

'I think he can say bloody all he likes tonight,' said Dave.

'We've won the lottery! We've won the lottery!' Jack danced around the living room.

More alcohol was opened. There was a bottle of champagne left over from Christmas. It was a gift from the Bensons' eldest daughter Annabel, whose husband Richard was very much into his wine. Dave and Jacqui weren't so much into their wine and the champagne would probably have made it through the whole year unopened, but you can't celebrate a lottery win without bubbles. Everyone was agreed on that. Dave got the bottle down from the kitchen shelf. Jack wanted to shake it like a grand prix champion. Jacqui let him do it, which was a mistake. When Mark got the cork out, the champagne exploded with such force it soaked the living room carpet and the curtains.

'Never mind,' said Dave. 'You'll be getting some new curtains now.'

'New curtains! Can we? Oh, I can't believe it.'

Jacqui took Ronnie by the hands and they polkaed around the coffee table.

'Oh, Dave. Do you think we could get a new carpet too?' Jacqui sighed.

'I can get a new Sonic Screwdriver!' said Jack. 'Can I get it tomorrow?'

'I'm sure we can sort that out,' said Jacqui.

'Can I get a new phone?' Sophie asked.

'I'm sure that will be possible,' said Ronnie.

'But we need to have a proper family talk about the money before we all start spending like crazy,' Jacqui pointed out. 'It's got to be shared between everyone. Not just us lot here this evening but Chelsea and Annabel and Richard and their children too.'

'It's not as though Annabel needs any,' said Ronnie.

'No. But she's your sister. And her children Izzy and Humfrey have exactly the same status in this family as Sophie and Jack. It's what Granddad Bill wants, I'm sure.'

'Oh yes,' said Granddad Bill. 'Everybody must have something.'

In truth, Granddad Bill wanted nothing more right then than another bottle of Spitfire. The sudden activity was making him dizzy. As Bill was sitting in his special television chair, his electric wheelchair was empty. Jack jumped in and took hold of the controls. He jerked the chair forwards and backwards across the plastic mat that covered the carpet by the door to make moving the wheelchair easier. He put on a deep voice and pretended to be his great-grandfather.

'I've won the bloody lottery,' he intoned.

'Jack!' cried his mother, grandmother and sister in exasperation. But Jack's glee in that moment was something they would all remember for the rest of their lives. It was a truly wonderful night.

Chapter Four

Ronnie and Annabel

A year earlier, Ronnie would not have questioned for a second that the lottery win should be spread throughout the whole family. But then, a year earlier, Ronnie had not known she had more than one sister.

Not even twelve months had passed since the family holiday in Lanzarote, to celebrate Jacqui's sixtieth birthday, when the startling truth came out. Jacqui had admitted to Ronnie and her younger sister Chelsea that there was a third Benson girl.

Born when Jacqui and Dave were still teenagers, Annabel, the baby Jacqui had called Daisy, was given up for adoption at just a few days old. It seemed like the only thing to do at the time. Jacqui and Dave had been going out since they were fifteen but they were broken up when Jacqui discovered she was pregnant and Jacqui's old-fashioned parents encouraged her to give the child up and make a clean break with her past. The seventies were not as progressive as nostalgic television programmes would have us believe. Having a child out of wedlock and becoming a single mother was definitely not something nice girls did in 1971.

Jacqui didn't have the emotional strength or the financial ability to defy her parents. She had only just left school. Without their support she would not have been able to raise a child. There was no social security net to fall back on. As Jacqui would discover, having a baby was no guarantee of hand-outs and a free council house. Jacqui even had to find the money to pay for Daisy's foster care in the months it took for a permanent placement to be found. The whole experience was horrible and traumatising and of course the misery didn't end once Daisy had been handed over to her new family. Feeling she'd been forced to give up her child, Jacqui became estranged from her parents. She moved to Essex where she lived like a nun for the next ten years, punishing herself daily by refusing to enjoy life, until Dave came back into it.

Dave didn't blame Jacqui for what had happened in his absence. He was only sad and sorry that he'd not been there to support her. They married and went on to have two more children – Chelsea and Ronnie – but there was always a Daisy-shaped hole in Jacqui's heart. Jacqui was relieved when the secret was finally out.

Annabel was raised by Sarah and Humfrey Cartwright, a wealthy couple from Warwickshire. She had an idyllic childhood, full of the sort of privileges and treats that would be on any child's wish list. She went to private school. She had ballet and riding lessons. She was treasured and doted upon. Though she knew from an early age that she had been adopted, Annabel was certain she could not have grown up in a better family or been more loved. Daisy Benson seemed like some sort of ghost – nothing to do with her. Annabel felt every inch a Cartwright and later, after her marriage to Richard, a Buchanan.

Annabel might never have known the rest of the Benson family at all had her own daughter Izzy not fallen dangerously ill. Aged sixteen, Izzy had gone to a festival with friends from her smart private school. Once there, she'd taken some dodgy ecstasy that damaged her kidneys beyond repair. Unable to donate one of her own kidneys to her little girl because she was pregnant with Humfrey at the time, Annabel sought out her biological family in the hope they might be able to help.

Subsequent events had almost torn the whole family apart. Ronnie was found to be the perfect tissue match for her new-found niece Izzy but was ultimately too scared to donate. Annabel and Ronnie fell out. Ronnie fell out with Jacqui too, when Jacqui tried to persuade her to go ahead with the transplant and Ronnie interpreted Jacqui's actions as guilty favouritism towards the daughter she had given up.

It was Jack who brought everyone back together in the end. Jack and Granddad Bill, when they sparked a countywide police search by heading off in Granddad Bill's electric wheelchair to deliver Izzy a kidney bought in a supermarket. Jack didn't understand how transplants really worked and Bill was too out of it that day to put him straight. And they did make it as far as Annabel's house. When heavily pregnant Annabel brought Jack and Bill home and promptly gave birth in Ronnie's front room, it seemed silly for the sisters to continue their feud.

Jack's crazy mission had made Ronnie change her mind about becoming Izzy's kidney donor, but in the end, it made no difference. On Boxing Day, Izzy received a kidney from a stranger killed in a road accident.

It was a turbulent time. But half a year later, Izzy was doing well with her transplant and the Buchanans and the Bensons had a growing friendship. Though Annabel still called Sarah and Humfrey Cartwright her 'Mum and Dad' and would never use those names for Dave and Jacqui, she now saw the Bensons on a regular basis and referred to Ronnie and Chelsea as her sisters. Izzy's immediate connection with her cousin Sophie had helped. The two teenage girls were extremely close. They spoke every day on Skype and saw each other whenever they could.

On the night that Granddad Bill discovered he'd won the lottery, Sophie piped up in support of her cousin. 'It's only fair we include the Buchanans,' she said. 'Like Grandma says, they're family. Plus, Izzy did put the best part of a pound towards the cost of the ticket.'

'I put twenty pee,' Jack pointed out again.

'Can we let them know now?' Sophie asked.

So, Jacqui called Annabel while Ronnie called Chelsea to pass on the good news. Chelsea, as usual, didn't pick up the call so Ronnie had to leave a message.

When she heard, Annabel immediately insisted she and her family didn't need anything but it was agreed that the whole family should gather over lunch at Annabel's house the very next day to talk about the division of the spoils.

By the time that was arranged – Chelsea took an age to call back – it was almost midnight. There was nothing left to drink except the remaining half bottle of champagne that nobody liked except Jack (who had been given a thimbleful but would be allowed no more). So, Ronnie and Mark loaded their children back into the car and went back to their house. Dave helped Granddad Bill into bed. Jacqui tidied up the living room and kitchen, double wrapping the champagne bottle in two carrier bags before she put it in the bin, in case one of the neighbours dropped round unexpectedly and wanted to know what they'd been celebrating. The last thing they needed was for people to start asking for money before they'd decided what, if any, they could spare. Fifty grand wasn't much when it had to be shared between so many.

Jacqui and Dave finally got to bed around half one.

'I still can't believe it,' Jacqui whispered in the dark. 'Granddad Bill won the lottery.'

'He always said he would.'

'Oh Dave. This could change everything. Bill can have a new wheelchair. We could get a proper wheelchair-adapted car. It could go towards paying for the children to go to uni.'

'It could go towards tickets to see England play in the World Cup,' Dave mused.

'If there's anything left over,' said Jacqui. 'We've got to spend this money carefully. The whole family has to benefit. Oh, I'm so happy right now. Somebody up there is looking out for us.'

An hour later, Dave was sound asleep, but Jacqui lay straight as a board, with her eyes wide open. Beneath her were the biscuit tin and the winning lottery ticket. The responsibility weighed very heavy indeed.

Chapter Five

Chelsea

The next day, Chelsea drove up to Warwickshire from London with her boyfriend Adam and his daughter Lily. Though Adam and Lily weren't officially family as yet, it seemed unfair to exclude them from a big lunch, especially as they had been there for Granddad Bill's birthday.

Chelsea and Adam had been together for almost a year. They'd met on that fateful holiday in Lanzarote when Jacqui revealed the existence of Annabel. It was a trip for which Chelsea hadn't had high hopes.

The tacky all-inclusive Hotel Volcan in Playa Blanca wasn't the kind of place Chelsea would have chosen but it was the perfect location for the extended Benson family. It was inexpensive. There was wheelchair accessibility for Granddad Bill and an on-site kids' club for Jack. The kids' club was the main factor in Adam's decision to go to the same hotel. He had hoped that Lily, an only child, would make some new friends there. As it was, she made a new enemy instead. Lily and Jack had hated each other on sight. The children's subsequent battles had put Adam and Chelsea at loggerheads but eventually Chelsea decided Adam was rather nice – and handsome – and pretty damn sexy . . . He only got sexier when they were back in London, getting to know each other properly over a bottle of wine. Adam was everything Chelsea had wished for in a man. And goodness knows she'd done a lot of wishing.

Dating a father was very different from dating the average commitment-phobic single guy. Adam's responsibilities meant there was little scope for spontaneity. They also meant that Chelsea had to think seriously about where the relationship was going rather earlier than she might otherwise have done because it wasn't just Adam's life she was becoming involved with. Adam and Lily came as a pair, with a ghost.

Adam hadn't broken up with Lily's mother Claire; he had lost her to an aneurysm when Lily was just a baby. Plenty of Chelsea's friends had dated divorced dads and shared horror stories about ex-wives who made things difficult by constantly switching childcare arrangements. Suddenly dumping the children with the ex-husband on the new girlfriend's birthday was a classic move. Dating a widower brought different issues, however.

Though at first, Lily had been prickly around her father's new girlfriend, these days she and Chelsea were pretty close. Now whenever Chelsea was at Adam's house around bedtime, it was Chelsea Lily asked to read her a story and tuck her into bed. Chelsea enjoyed these little moments of intimacy with Lily, though she understood that her role was never going to be 'replacement mother'. She and Lily could have something different and just as satisfying. Chelsea didn't need to obliterate all memories of Claire. She was there to compliment them.

At least, that's what Chelsea told herself on a good day.

The first time Adam had accidentally called Chelsea by Claire's name, Chelsea had taken it very badly indeed. She had gone off the deep end, telling Adam he obviously wasn't ready to move on from the memory of his dead love. Adam, in a state of some shock at the violence of Chelsea's reaction to his genuine mistake, had concluded that she must be right and called time on their budding romance.

The split didn't last for long, thank goodness, and Chelsea had tried to be much more understanding since. Adam was certain he was ready to move on with his life. He'd attended counselling sessions for a year after Claire's sudden death and, as far as he was concerned, that was all he needed to do. However, there were moments when Adam did seem to be a million miles away and though when Chelsea asked him what he was thinking he always answered 'nothing', she was pretty sure he was in fact thinking of his lost wife, the woman he had vowed to love until 'death us do part'.

Chelsea herself was in counselling. Since her late teenage years, she had struggled with bulimia and still felt in danger of slipping back into its grip whenever she encountered stress in her outwardly glamorous London life as a fashion journalist. It was the love of her nephew Jack that had first persuaded her she needed to take her recovery seriously. He'd spotted that she was vomiting daily while they shared a room in Lanzarote and his innocent concern had made her feel ashamed and helpless. Of course, she didn't tell Jack that she was making *herself* ill but the fact that he had noticed shook her into seeking help. Since then, she'd been religious about attending her therapy sessions and she was evangelical about the ways in which therapy could help with all sorts of issues.

'I don't have an issue,' said Adam, when Chelsea dared to broach the subject. 'I have a dead wife. She was Lily's mother. Would you prefer that I never ever thought of her?'

'Of course not, but . . .'

Adam and Chelsea had been talking about Claire when Ronnie rang with the news about the lottery win. Adam jumped at the chance to cut the conversation short but Chelsea insisted on ignoring her sister's call so that they could continue to hash things out. That was why she hadn't found time to return Ronnie's call until midnight. Not that the conversation about Adam's past was exactly finished by then.

As they drove in Adam's car towards Annabel's house, Chelsea wondered what her next move should be. She wanted to spend the rest of her life with Adam, but was there actually enough space in his heart for a second Mrs Baxter?

Chapter Six

Annabel

Annabel had grown up in an entirely different world to her two younger sisters. While they were living in a terraced house in Coventry, she lived in a sprawling mansion. She'd studied English Literature at Oxford, which was where she had met her husband, Richard. 'Britain's Only Non-Bastard Banker,' as Mark liked to call his new friend and brother-in-law. Richard was very generous with his wine cellar. That was Mark's idea of the 'trickle-down effect' in action.

At first, the Bensons had found Annabel's grand house and her moneyed manners intimidating, but having known her for almost a year, and been through some serious drama with her during that time, the scale of Annabel's luxurious life no longer overawed Ronnie, Chelsea and Jacqui. Ronnie in particular no longer waited to be shown where she should sit, worrying that she might accidentally choose a priceless antique. She threw herself down onto Annabel's cream-coloured sofa, just as she would have done were she at home or at Chelsea's.

Annabel, taking advantage of Ronnie's relaxed manner, handed her Baby Humfrey and asked her to change his nappy. Annabel had a feeling it was going to be a particularly mucky one. Yep. They were proper sisters now.

* * *

That day, after the lottery win, Annabel cooked lamb for lunch. She wasn't a great cook but since meeting the Bensons, she'd thrown herself into the joys of mass catering. She even let Jacqui into the kitchen now, no longer upset by the way Jacqui liked to insert herself into proceedings just as any mother would. The only mother Annabel had known until the previous year – Sarah Cartwright – had also come to welcome Jacqui into her life. They were quite good friends these days, sharing photographs of their 'joint' grandchildren, Izzy and Humfrey, on Facebook.

Annabel thought it might be a good idea for everyone to eat before they started talking about Granddad Bill's lottery win but there was no chance of that. Everyone was so excited. Jacqui reprised the telephone conversation she'd had with the lovely people at the Lottery administration for the benefit of Annabel, Richard and Izzy. Jack told everyone what he was going to buy.

'A real Sonic Screwdriver!' he explained to Izzy. 'Not a plastic one, a real one, that really works. It will probably cost a hundred million pounds.' Jack had a loose understanding of maths.

Sophie kept her dreams a little closer to her heart. There was loads of stuff she wanted to spend the money on, but she guessed she wasn't going to be handed a sum with which to go nuts in New Look. There were more important things to save up for. Sophie secretly dreamed of a place at university. Her cousin Izzy considered a place at uni her birthright but Sophie was daunted by the cost of tuition fees.

By the time everyone arrived at Annabel's, Jacqui and Ronnie had already done some maths.

Jacqui smoothed the piece of paper out on the coffee table in Annabel's family room.

'So, this is what we've come up with so far. We've done the calculations based on the four great-grandchildren getting the largest share, then the three grandchildren, then me and Dave, then Granddad Bill. He says he doesn't want much except a season ticket and a new wheelchair.'

'Well, I can tell you right now that we don't need anything.' Annabel reiterated what she'd already said on the phone.

'You're not wrong,' said Ronnie. 'But you know what, Mark and me have got everything we need too, Mum. We've got a roof over our heads. We've got a car. We're getting a new kitchen.'

Mark worked as a kitchen fitter and his boss had given him a ninety per cent discount on the country-style cabinets of Ronnie's dreams.

'We don't need anything else,' said Ronnie firmly.

Mark opened his mouth to protest.

'So, you can take me and Mark out too.'

'If Annabel and Ronnie don't need anything, it seems to make most sense for the great-grandchildren to have the cash,' said Chelsea magnanimously, though she actually could have used something, having just had some bad news that she wasn't about to share.

'Well your dad and I won't be having any if you're not,' said Jacqui.

'Maybe we should just say that the children will have the money between them,' said Ronnie. 'Sophie, Jack, Izzy and Humfrey should have a quarter each. The children did buy the ticket, after all.'

'Izzy and Humfrey don't need a quarter,' said Annabel.

'They'll want money for their university fees.'

'That's taken care of,' Annabel assured her.

Richard put his hand on Annabel's arm. He had a much better understanding of where Ronnie was going with this. Annabel's insistence on pointing out that her two children were already well provided for financially was causing an atmosphere. Ronnie wanted to think they were equal. If they could just get a rough deal worked out now, then Annabel and Richard could always get the money back to Jacqui later.

More to the point, if the discussion went on for much longer, lunch would be spoiled.

So it was decided over the smoked salmon blinis Annabel had prepared as a starter that the bulk of the money was to be split four ways between Bill's great grandchildren. They would get eight thousand pounds each. A further four thousand would be spent on an electric wheelchair and an upgrade to Dave and Jacqui's car to make ferrying Granddad Bill around easier. But Granddad Bill said it was important that everybody got a piece of the action, thus the remaining fourteen thousand pounds would be spent on something that *everybody* could share in. A proper family treat.

'How about a caravan?' suggested Jacqui. 'We can take it in turns to use it.'

Sophie and Izzy shared their mutual distaste in a glance. Ronnie and Chelsea too had unpleasant memories of wet summers in Granddad Bill's old static van in Littlehampton.

'A hot air balloon ride?' suggested Richard.

'You're not getting me in one of those,' Jacqui said. 'They fall out the sky all the time.'

'And I'm scared of heights,' said Ronnie. 'What about a trip on the Orient Express?'

'Tiny carriages and shared bathrooms,' said Annabel. She and Richard had taken the Orient Express to celebrate their tenth wedding anniversary.

'A racehorse,' said Dave.

'For fourteen grand?' said Mark. 'It'd be a donkey.'

'Let's get a donkey!' said Jack. 'It can live here at Auntie Annabel's.'

'We're not getting a donkey,' said Ronnie, spotting Annabel's distress at that idea.

'This is like being Aladdin with his three wishes,' commented Chelsea. 'So many possibilities.'

'I would wish for ten *more* wishes,' said Lily cleverly. 'And a donkey.'

'Yes! Donkey! Donkey! Donkey!' chanted Jack. 'That's what we want!'

'It'd keep the grass down,' said Richard.

'You could call it Princess,' said Lily.

'We're not getting a *girl* donkey,' Jack protested.

'We're not getting any bloody donkey,' said Ronnie.

'Don't say b—'

Chelsea gently clamped her hand over Jack's mouth before he could say the 'b' word himself.

The discussion raged over lunch and continued over coffee in Annabel's garden. Tiring of the debate, Sophie and Izzy took Leander the Labrador for a walk. Jack and Lily tagged along. Sophie and Izzy were only too pleased to have the younger children there, since Jack and Lily still thought it was fun to use the pooper-scooper.

'Imagine how much poo a donkey makes,' mused Jack.

Later, Chelsea followed Annabel down to the kitchen garden to pick some strawberries. Richard took Mark down into his cellar to look at some new wine. Adam asked Dave if he wanted to join him for a walk to look at the war memorial by the village church.

By the time Chelsea and Annabel had finished preparing the strawberries, Jacqui and Ronnie had decided on the sort of proper family treat that would suit everyone.

'Another holiday,' said Jacqui. 'That seems like the best idea.'

Chelsea winced as she remembered the Hotel Volcan with its scratchy loo roll and Turin Shroud-style sheets. She couldn't imagine Annabel there.

'And because Granddad Bill isn't that mobile,' Jacqui continued, 'we've decided on a cruise.'

'Gosh,' said Annabel. 'How lovely.'

Chapter Seven

Chelsea and Adam

A cruise.

Chelsea listened to her mother with a growing sense of horror. In the time it had taken Chelsea and Annabel to pick strawberries, Jacqui and Ronnie had got it all mapped out. They'd even found the perfect Mediterranean itinerary, sailing in and out of Southampton. The lottery money wouldn't cover everything but it would mean that the cash Ronnie and Mark were planning to spend on a week in Cornwall, for example, could now take them all the way to the Med.

'You're to ask Adam and Lily to come along too,' Jacqui told Chelsea. 'It will be good for Jack to have some company his own age and they do seem to get along well these days. We're going in the school holidays, of course, so you don't have to worry about that. We've found an amazing ship. It's called the *European Countess*. There's so much to do: three swimming pools, entertainment for the kids, shows every evening, and the largest floating pastry shop in the world.'

'What?'

'That's what it says on the website. I wonder if they make the world's largest pastries?' Jacqui mused.

Ronnie showed Chelsea and Annabel the cruise line's website on her iPhone.

'How long is this cruise?' Chelsea asked cautiously.

'It's a fortnight,' said Jacqui. 'We could go for less time if we went from somewhere other than Southampton but that would mean getting on a plane and I don't think your Granddad Bill is up to flying.'

A fortnight. Fourteen days.

Chelsea exhaled audibly. She shared a look with Annabel. She knew that Annabel had the same misgivings. A fortnight was a very long time to spend with your family, however much you loved them.

'Where does it go?' Chelsea asked.

'All sorts of places! It goes to Barcelona, to Ajaccio – I've got no idea where that is but it looks nice.'

'It's in Corsica,' Annabel chipped in.

'Thank you, dear. Then it goes to Florence, to Rome, to Marseille . . . Gibraltar . . . Oh, Chelsea, it will be so glamorous. You'll have to help me shop for something to wear before we go.'

Thanks to her job on a fashion magazine, Chelsea had a reputation as the family fashion guru.

'And your dad and Granddad Bill are going to need dinner jackets.' Jacqui was getting really excited now. 'I still can't believe it. I never thought we'd get to go on a cruise. To go on a cruise with the whole family, it's a dream come true.'

It wouldn't be quite the whole family. Annabel, her husband Richard, daughter Izzy and baby Humfrey quickly established that they would not be joining the trip. It was still only six months since Izzy had her kidney transplant and the Buchanans were nervous about travelling too far from the hospital that had taken such good care of them. Everyone was sad about that, especially Sophie, who regarded her cousin Izzy as one of her best friends. It seemed a sensible decision however. The last thing they needed was for Izzy to be taken ill at sea, even though the *European Countess* boasted world-class medical facilities.

Chelsea had no excuses. She knew she would have to go along. But would Adam want to? It was one thing to holiday with your girlfriend's extended family in a resort. It was quite another to holiday with them on a ship, on the ocean. Where there was no possibility of jumping in a hire car and heading off for some much needed me time. Chelsea had just about survived seven days in Lanzarote without going berserk. Could she survive fourteen days at sea?

Chelsea had a bad feeling about the whole enterprise so she was astonished when Adam said, as they drove back to London with Lily sleeping in the back of the car, 'It sounds like a laugh, and Lily will love it. We can go up to the front of the boat—'

'The bow of the ship.'

'The bow of the ship, sorry. And pretend we're in *Titanic*.'

'Please do not mention the *Titanic* in conjunction with any ship I have to get on,' said Chelsea. 'You know I've never been able to watch that film.'

Chelsea had been traumatised by childhood viewings of *The Poseidon Adventure*, which seemed to be shown on television every Christmas when she was growing up. She'd never understood why it was such a festive staple.

'Ships are much safer these days,' said Adam. 'It could be really romantic. Plus, I've always secretly wanted to go on a cruise. And now I can tell everyone you made me do it. It's a win-win situation.'

'Can you get the time off?'

'Shouldn't be a problem. How about you?'

'Actually,' said Chelsea. 'I know I can. There's something I've been meaning to tell you.'

'What?'

'I'm being made redundant.'

'Oh, Chelsea. No.'

'The whole magazine is folding. They told us on Friday morning. *Society*'s figures have been falling for years and with the phoenix-like return of *Tatler*, they've suddenly got even worse. We're going to finish the issue we're working on and that's that. My last day is the first Friday of August.'

'What will you do?' Adam asked.

'Write about cruising?' Chelsea half-joked.

'No, seriously. What will you do?'

'I've got a fair few contacts. I can go freelance while I look for something full-time. I may even just decide to stay freelance. At least I won't have to go into an office any more that way. I can't say I'll miss the politics.'

'Have they told you what sort of settlement you'll be getting?'

'It isn't fantastic but it will keep me going for a while. My biggest expense is my rent.'

'Well, I could help you with that,' said Adam.

Chelsea shook her head. 'I'm not asking for money. I'll be fine for at least six months.'

'No,' said Adam. 'I mean, you wouldn't have to pay rent at all if you moved in with Lily and me.'

'Are you serious?' Chelsea asked.

'Why not?' said Adam. 'You spend most of your time round at our place anyway.'

'That's true,' said Chelsea. It was easier that way, since to do anything else would mean sorting out a babysitter for Lily or uprooting the little girl from her life. Chelsea understood that it was important for Lily to have a routine.

'How much notice do you need to give on your flat?' Adam asked.

'Not sure. Two months, I think.'

'Then that would mean you could move in with us at the beginning of September. After the cruise.'

'Do you mean *depending on* the cruise?' Chelsea asked, with a smile. 'Are two weeks at sea going to be the final test?'

'I'm sure they will be testing,' said Adam. 'But I'm also sure that nothing makes me happier right now than the thought of coming home to you every night.'

'Do you mean it?' Chelsea asked.

'Of course I do.'

'If you weren't driving, I would kiss you to bits.'

She leaned across the gearstick and kissed the side of his face.

'Honestly, it's like having a puppy,' said Adam, ostentatiously wiping his cheek. 'Hmmm, maybe we could get a puppy when you move in. Lily has been asking for one for ages. I've resisted because it's not fair, leaving a dog on its own all day while I go to work and Lily goes to school. But if you were there . . .'

'I'd love to have a dog,' said Chelsea. She'd always wanted to get one but an adult life of flat-shares and pokey studio apartments, not to mention a job that often involved staying late at the office, hadn't exactly been conducive to pet ownership. 'What breed would we get? How about a cockerpoo?'

'I'm not having anything with "poo" in its name,' said Adam. 'Besides, they look like floor mops. I want a Staffie.'

'But they've got such ugly faces.'

'You're kidding. They have lovely smiles.'

'Right before they bite you,' said Chelsea.

'They're not vicious if you don't train them that way. Same as any dog.'

'If we're not having a cockerpoo, we're having a lurcher.'

'They're so sad-looking and you can see all their bones.'

'They're lovely! And they don't need much exercise. That's what we're having.'

'Is this our first domestic argument?' asked Adam.

Chelsea touched the end of Adam's nose with her finger. 'I think it might be. Good job I won.'

Chelsea went back to her flat in Stockwell that night quite happily. Now she knew she wouldn't be there for too much longer, it didn't seem so bad. Once again she was able to see the features that had first attracted her to the place – the high ceilings and the big bay window, where she had imagined herself sitting with a book. Never mind that it looked straight out onto a busy main road. She wouldn't have to see that view ever again. She wouldn't have to dodge the drunks and the drug-dealers on her way to the Tube.

Likewise, the fact that she would be unemployed in little over a month no longer seemed as disastrous as it might have done. Adam had been so quick to come up with a solution. It would indeed take an enormous amount of pressure off, financially. But he wouldn't have come up with that particular plan so quickly if he hadn't been thinking about it for a while anyway, right? As she made herself a cup of tea in the crappy kitchen she would soon be bidding goodbye, Chelsea allowed herself a delicious little fantasy, in which she had a home office in Adam's spare bedroom, looking out onto the garden, where Lily played with the new lurcher pup.

Chapter Eight

Ronnie

Chelsea called Ronnie to let her know what was going on.

'I've got good news and bad news.'

'Bad news first,' said Ronnie, as was her wont.

Chelsea told her about the redundancy.

'You never really liked that job anyway,' Ronnie concluded.

'That's true. It's a good chance for me to do something different.'

'And the good news?'

Chelsea dropped her voice to a whisper. 'You'll never guess.'

'You're right. I won't. Just tell me.'

'Adam has asked me to move in with him.'

'OMG!' Ronnie gasped. 'I never expected that. What have you said?'

'I've said yes, of course. I'm going to hand in my notice on my flat tomorrow and move in with Adam and Lily after the cruise.'

'Will you survive it?'

'The cruise? I hope so. Are you definitely going? Can Mark get the time off? Can you?'

'Of course we're going. Mark's already told his boss. I'll tell mine tomorrow. If he won't let me have the time, I'll quit. Not many people are queuing up to work with dead bodies.'

Ronnie worked part-time as office manager for an undertaker.

'Plus, that ship has the largest floating pastry shop on earth on its top deck! Just try and keep us off it. It's going to be brilliant. Even more so now I know that you and Adam are getting properly committed!'

'I can't believe it,' Chelsea admitted.

'He's a lovely bloke, Chels. We all really like him, and Lily too. Jack thinks she's great. Most days.'

'Oh Ronnie, I feel like everything is working out for me at last.'

'You deserve it, sweetheart. You really do.'

While Chelsea floated around her flat like she'd won more than the lottery, Ronnie relayed her sister's news to Mark. He didn't share Ronnie's excitement.

'So, she's moving in with him,' said Mark. 'I don't see what the fuss is about. He's probably after free childcare.'

'Mark Benson-Edwards, don't be so bloody cynical. It's more than that. You know today, while you were in the wine cellar with Richard, Adam asked Dad to walk down to the War Memorial.'

'Did he?'

'Yes. He did. And what do you think they talked about?'

'I don't know.'

'When a man asks his girlfriend's father to take a private walk . . . There's only one conversation he wants to have. He's asked Dad for her hand in marriage. I bet you anything.'

Mark snorted. 'Don't be daft. Your dad and me had loads of private conversations before I told him I wanted to marry you. We had private conversations for years.'

'Yes. But Adam doesn't have the same kind of relationship you have with Dad, does he? They don't live near each other. They don't go down the pub together all the time. He asked to speak to him for a specific reason, I'm certain of it.' Ronnie paused as a thought struck her. 'I bet he'll propose on the cruise!'

Mark rolled his eyes. 'Why would he do that when Chelsea's already moving in with him? No need to buy the cow if you're getting the milk for free.'

'Don't say such horrible things. Adam's a decent man. He's a romantic. He's going to ask my sister to marry him.'

'For goodness sake don't go saying that to her,' said Mark.

Ronnie pursed her lips.

'I mean it, Ronnie,' Mark continued. 'Do not repeat a word of this crap to your sister. And don't go saying anything to your mother either.'

'It isn't crap,' said Ronnie. 'I've got a feeling in my stomach about this.'

'That'll be indigestion,' said Mark.

Chapter Nine

Jane

It was Jane's mother's idea that Jane and Greg should go on a cruise for their honeymoon. She'd been on one herself many years before and thought it the perfect way to see the world. Especially if you didn't much enjoy flying, which Jane definitely didn't.

'You can see three or four different countries in a week without having to go anywhere near an airport,' said Maggie.

'I'm sold,' said Jane.

But Greg wrinkled his nose when she first put the idea to him.

'A cruise? Are you having a laugh? That's what old people do,' he said.

'Not any more,' said Jane, tugging him down to sit on the sofa beside her so that he could see the Countess Cruises website on her tablet. 'Look at this. The ships are really amazing. It's like being in a five-star resort. Look at this one. It's got everything anyone could ever want.'

While Greg looked at the pictures, Jane ran through the advantages. 'It's just like a luxury hotel on the water. It's got a gym, a tennis court, three swimming pools, loads of restaurants, and an outdoor cinema. It's even got a proper theatre with shows like you get in the West End and you don't have to pay extra to see them. And it means we can get to see all sorts of places without having to pack and unpack all the time. You just dock and jump off – see Barcelona or Malaga or Lisbon or wherever and you're back in time for dinner. There's no fuss. And no flying.'

Greg knew how much Jane hated flying, though he also knew she would get on a plane if she had to. But if she didn't have to . . . Remembering how white-faced Jane had been for the whole of a recent flight to Dublin and how what was supposed to be a relaxing mini-break was ruined by Jane's anxiety at having to do the whole thing again to get home, Greg looked at the prices on the Countess website. He sucked his teeth.

'All meals are included,' said Jane. 'And it would be so romantic – a life on the ocean wave – sunset over the sea. Cocktails! Dancing! I've always wanted to be on a really big ship, ever since I was a little girl'

'OK,' Greg said at last, 'if it's what you want. Anything for my very own Countess.' He kissed her on the end of the nose. Jane snuggled in beside him.

'Oh, I love you so much,' she said.

'I love you more,' Greg told her. 'There are days when I wake up and I can't believe how lucky I am to have found a girl like you. What good things must I have done in a past life to deserve being this happy?'

Jane grinned. 'You just keep on being that good.'

Jane couldn't wait to be married to Greg. He proposed in Paris on Valentine's Day. Maybe it was a cliché but Jane wouldn't have had it any other way. Greg had arranged everything without being prompted. They took the Eurostar across from London. Jane thought that her Valentine's treat was going to be a night out in the British capital. She didn't know that Greg had colluded with her mum so that he had Jane's passport in his bag. When they got to King's Cross and he admitted that they weren't going to be staying in a hotel near there, Jane shrieked with joy. She'd always wanted to go to Paris.

They had seats in Standard Premier and the kind steward was only too happy to open the champagne Greg had brought in his rucksack when Greg let him in on the secret reason for their journey. In Paris, Greg had chosen a hotel near the Sacré-Cœur and somehow wangled a room on the top floor that offered them a spectacular view over the whole city. When she stood at that window, Jane felt like she was Amélie – the girl with the bob. That film was one of her favourites.

What a wonderful weekend it was. They saw all the sights. They went to Notre Dame and the Louvre. They queued to see the Mona Lisa.

'Isn't it small?' Jane complained.

Greg had even gone so far as to bring a special love-lock to leave on the Pont des Arts. He'd had the bloke with the stall by the railway station back home engrave the lock with their names and the date of their engagement. He actually popped the question on the bridge, getting down on one knee right in the middle.

'What if I'd taken my time in giving you an answer?' Jane teased later.

'Ha!' said Greg. 'You practically bit my hand off. I knew you weren't going to need to sleep on it.'

They attached the lock to the railings and took a selfie with the Île de la Cité in the background. The Pont des Arts was thronged with couples making similar pledges. Love was truly in the air.

When they got back to Kent and went straight to Jane's mother's house to tell her the news, they found the sitting room full of friends and relations keen to celebrate. Jane's mother had made an engagement cake. Kirsty, Jane's best friend, had brought enough helium-filled 'Congratulations' balloons to film a sequel to *Up*.

It was such a wonderful time. Everyone was pleased for them. Everyone who knew them was sure that Greg and Jane would be very happy together for the rest of their lives. The wedding date was set for the following February 14th, though they would have to wait until the summer to honeymoon. It was going to be a big affair with a hundred and fifty guests, maybe as many as two hundred. People were going to travel from all over to see Greg and Jane pledge their love for one another. Kirsty started referring to the upcoming nuptials as 'the wedding of the century'.

But of course they didn't make it that far.

When the police knocked on the door late on Christmas Eve, Jane didn't have to be told it was bad news. The female officer's face said it all. Jane sank to the floor, as though her legs had suddenly melted. The policewoman helped her up and half-carried her back into the living room. The Christmas tree lights were still on. The presents Jane had chosen so carefully were beneath the tree. They would be put away, two days later, unopened.

When Jane arrived at the hospital that wet, wintry night, Greg was on a ventilator. He didn't look so bad. She had expected worse. It was partly because he didn't look so bad that she simply couldn't believe the doctor who told her the man she loved was effectively dead. Only the machines were keeping him alive.

Greg's mother clung on to her husband and Jane while the three of them listened to the awful prognosis. It was a terrible moment. Jane could barely hold herself upright as the news sank in. She kept steady only for Greg's mum. The list of injuries Greg had suffered might as well have been delivered in Latin.

'Transplant . . .'

Just that one word broke through.

At eight o'clock in the evening on Christmas Day, Jane and Greg's parents agreed that they had to do what Greg would have wanted. He had been on the donor register for years and he'd made sure all his loved ones knew about it. Holding hands, the three of them stood in front of the doctor and confirmed that they agreed with Greg's decision. His parents signed some forms. Though they included her in everything, Jane still wasn't quite Greg's next of kin. Jane placed one more gentle kiss on her beloved's lips, then the transplant teams moved in.

Greg had always been Jane's hero. He could still save someone's life.

Jane didn't know anything much about the people who had received Greg's organs. The doctors had told her only their ages and sexes. So she knew that Greg's eyes were looking out from the face of a forty-five-year-old man. His strong heart beat in the chest of a thirty-seven-year-old woman. His kidneys were now shared between a forty-two-year-old man and a seventeen-year-old girl. All of them, she was assured, were incredibly grateful for the chance to go on and live longer, healthier lives.

There were moments when Jane wondered if she wanted to know more about those people. Sometimes it freaked her out to think that she might be walking down the street and lock eyes with the man who'd received Greg's retinae and not know it. Had receiving part of Greg's body given them part of Greg's personality too? Did his heart still carry memories of her?

But the transplant counsellor had warned her that the relationship between donor recipients and the families of those who had given their organs was a tricky one. What if she didn't like them? Perhaps it was better that they remained anonymous. That way she could imagine they were all good people who had deserved Greg's sacrifice. To think otherwise would be too awful.

After Greg's organs had been transferred to their recipients, Jane saw him one more time. The transplant team had done their best to tidy him up for her and Jane was hugely relieved to see that her beloved was still recognisable. As she gazed on his face again, she could almost believe he was sleeping. But when she pressed her cheek to his, it was cold and strangely waxen. It didn't smell of him any more. She pulled away as if in surprise. Greg was gone.

They had the funeral in the middle of January. It took a while to get everything sorted. People came from all over the place. Some of them had exchanged the tickets they'd bought to come to the wedding. Jane had known that Greg was loved by many people but by just how many she'd had no idea. The tiny church near to Greg's parents' house was packed out. Standing room only. Jane heard the verger even turned some people away on health and safety grounds. They raised the roof as they sang all Greg's favourite hymns, ending on 'Jerusalem', which had always made Jane cry at the best of times, even when it was being sung at a wedding. She had hoped it would be sung when she married Greg. He was carried out of the church that day to 'You'll Never Walk Alone'.

After the service in the church, Greg was cremated, which was what he had wanted. Fortunately, the party that went from the church to the crematorium was small: just Greg's parents, his siblings, Jane, Jane's parents and

Kirsty. Greg was a big fan of Jane's best friend. Jane was relieved to have a last moment of calm in which to say goodbye properly. The wake afterwards was as packed as the church service had been. People actually complained there weren't enough sandwiches to go round. Jane wished she could just tell them to fuck off.

She didn't care about sandwiches. She'd lost the love of her life.

Greg's mother said that Jane should have his ashes.

'You'll know what to do with them,' she said. 'You know all the places he loved. Take him to one of those.'

Jane and Greg had never talked about where to sprinkle their ashes. Except in jest. Greg had once said he would like to have his ashes spread at Nando's, after they'd eaten there three times in a fortnight.

As for the places he loved? Jane was pretty sure she wouldn't be allowed to throw him off the top of the Eiffel Tower and she couldn't face going back to many of the places that had real significance to them. She didn't want to look at their favourite views, without being able to rest her head on his shoulder. The thought that she now had to go forward in life and make memories without him made her feel sick and dizzy and angry at the whole bloody world.

So, for the time being, Jane kept Greg's ashes in her bedroom, on the bedside table, so that he was the last thing she saw when she went to sleep and the first thing when she woke up. How long would it take before she didn't roll over and expect to see him on the empty side of the bed?

The doctor gave Jane some tablets that were designed to help her sleep. She tried to resist them but eventually she gave in and since then she had been popping one every night. Now the problem was getting up.

Her boss called a few times a week. 'Whenever you're ready,' he said. 'If you want to come in for half a day, just to see how you feel.'

Almost six months later, Jane would get dressed most days but never made it as far as the car.

Chapter Ten

Kirsty

Jane spent her Sundays very quietly now. When Greg was alive and at home, he always made Sunday breakfast, making a huge mess of the kitchen as he prepared a fry-up, singing along to the radio as he worked. Jane didn't like to have the radio on any more. Somehow, music had more power than anything else to make her cry. She couldn't risk turning it on and hearing a song that had meant something to them both. She was sure she would never recover if she accidentally heard a snatch of 'You'll Never Walk Alone'.

That particular Sunday, Jane had spent half the day in absolute silence. She had no one to say 'hello' to. About a month after Greg's death, the cat they once shared had gone and got itself run over. It was barely out of kittenhood. Jane half wondered if it was deliberate, a feline suicide. She'd felt like doing the same. But there were so many people who were not going to let her do that. That Sunday afternoon, six months after Greg's death, was no exception. Jane was just staring into the fridge, wondering whether she could be bothered to warm up a carton of soup or whether lunch would be tea without milk again, when the doorbell rang.

'Bloody hell,' said her best mate Kirsty. 'It's a beautiful day out there. Why have you got the curtains closed? It's like a morgue in this place.'

Jane winced.

'Sorry! Didn't mean to say that. You can have the curtains shut if you want to. Probably a good idea. Keep it shady. It's actually a bit too hot.'

Kirsty fanned herself extravagantly.

'Anyway, are you all right today, love?'

Kirsty didn't wait for an answer.

'You don't mind if I come in, do you? Quick cup of tea? Then I'll be on my way home. I won't keep you long.'

She was already halfway down the hall, dumping her handbag and car keys on the console table, heading straight for the kitchen where she made a beeline for the kettle. Jane was still standing by the front door, feeling faintly bewildered.

Kirsty was one of those people who lived at high volume. Everything about her was big and bright and loud. She was five-foot-ten and blessed with 36FFs. That afternoon she was dressed in a sundress of bright teal with a rainbow-coloured scarf tossed round her neck. She wore enough beads to sink a battleship. As she walked, she rattled. Her hair was big too. Her naturally mousey curls were dyed a violent red and they stood out around her head like a sunburst. It suited her.

While the kettle boiled, Kirsty emptied out the carrier bag she had brought with her. It was full of goodies designed to tempt anyone back into eating. There was a crisp baguette, still slightly warm from the supermarket oven. The smell tickled even Jane's deadened taste buds. Then there was a big piece of pungent oozing Brie, some grapes, a few slices of ham, and a box containing four individual pots of chocolate mousse by Gü.

'And some chicken soup. You don't mind if I warm this up right away, do you? I skipped breakfast this morning,' Kirsty lied. 'So I can't wait until I get back to my house to eat. Do you want to share it?'

Jane shrugged.

'I'm not that hungry,' she said.

'You can have the small half.'

Kirsty got two bowls out. Jane knew that her zaftig friend never missed breakfast. Kirsty could be murderous if her blood sugar got low. She also suspected that Kirsty was claiming not to have eaten deliberately, making it impossible for Jane to just take the groceries and put them into the fridge, where they would be forgotten like the bundle Kirsty had delivered the previous week.

Kirsty poured hot water onto tea bags in two mugs, then she opened the carton of soup into a pan. While that warmed through, she sliced the baguette into pieces and topped one with the gooey Brie.

'You've got a much better sense of smell than me. Tell me if you think this is good or not,' she instructed her friend, knowing that as soon as Jane sniffed the cheese, her body would override her unhappy emotions and she would be bound to take a bite.

'It's great,' Jane admitted through a mouthful.

Kirsty smiled and nodded. Success. At least Jane would get one proper meal that day.

As they ate the soup, Kirsty filled Jane in on the gossip from her office. Kirsty worked as office admin for a very ordinary firm of accountants, but the way Kirsty talked about them made it sound as though her workplace was every bit the hotbed of sin and seduction you would expect to find in the City or on Wall Street.

The gossip kept Kirsty sane. She hated her job. When she and Jane first met, back when they were just starting secondary school, Kirsty filled every spare moment of her life with dance, singing and drama classes. She did ballet and modern and tap. She was always first in line for auditions for the school performance. She wanted to be an actress or a singer. Her heroine was Denise Van Outen.

Kirsty never got to fulfil her dream of going to drama school. When Kirsty was twelve, her father left her mother for another woman, remarried and had another daughter – Kirsty's half-sister India. When Kirsty was sixteen, her mother was diagnosed with breast cancer. Right after her GCSEs, Kirsty left school to become a full-time carer.

Even back then, when she was just a teen, Kirsty was good at caring for people. She never made you feel as though you owed her anything. She was just kind. She had a way of nudging you to keep going even when you didn't want to. Jane didn't know what she would have done without her. Kirsty even reminded her to pay the bills. That Sunday afternoon, she put her mind to Jane's finances again.

'Did you sort out getting the money back for the honeymoon?' Kirsty asked.

Jane shook her head. 'We weren't insured. Greg was going to look online for the best deal. He never got round to it.'

'Oh.' Kirsty pulled a sympathetic face. 'And they really won't give you a refund anyway? Not even if you tell them what happened?'

'I don't want to tell them what happened. I'm fed up of talking about it.'

'You don't have to go into specifics,' said Kirsty.

'I think I would,' said Jane.

'So you'd rather just lose the money . . .'

Jane stared down into her soup bowl.

There was a moment of silence, which Kirsty broke

with a random observation about an argument in the supermarket car park: two people going for the same space, neither of them willing to back off so that the rest of the people in the car park eventually became gridlocked, unable to get to the exit because of the two bull-headed people in their way.

Jane didn't add much to the conversation. She finished her soup and put her bowl in the sink.

'Thanks for bringing the soup,' she told her friend. 'But you really don't have to look after me like this, you know.'

'Who said anything about looking after you? I just wanted some company over lunch,' Kirsty fibbed. She placed her empty bowl next to Jane's. Then she put her arm round Jane's shoulders and said, 'You know, about the cruise . . .'

'What about it?'

'It's a lot of money, isn't it? Just to say goodbye to? You could put it towards a new car. I mean, I'm happy to call the travel agent up and tell them what happened and see if I can get it back for you.'

'They won't give me a refund. Why should they?'

'Well if you really don't think they'll refund you, then perhaps you should just take the trip?'

'Are you kidding?'

'No. Why not?'

Jane shut her eyes and shook her head.

'I can't go on my own.'

'You don't have to go on your own. I could come with you. I'd pay for my share.'

'You what?'

'I'll pay half. I've been thinking about it. Greg would want you to go. You know he would. Think about that year you were supposed to be going to Cornwall together but he couldn't get back from Afghanistan. He was happy for you to take me instead of him then.'

'But that was different. He was just stuck. He wasn't *dead*.'

Kirsty blundered on. 'But we're talking about a Mediterranean cruise this time. I still think he would want you to see all those places.'

'Without him?'

'Yes.'

'I can't. I can't face seeing them if he's not there too.'

Jane covered her eyes. She hoped that was the end of it but Kirsty was not about to let it lie.

'What are you going to do, Jane? Refuse to go anywhere you might have gone with Greg for the rest of your life?'

Jane's mouth dropped open in horror.

'I think you'd better go,' she told her friend.

'Look, that came out wrong,' said Kirsty. 'I just don't think it's doing you any good, keeping on moping—'

'Moping?' Jane's voice rose in outrage. 'Is that what you think I'm doing? *Moping*?'

Kirsty shook her head. 'I chose the wrong word.'

'Too bloody right.'

'I'm sorry. It just slipped out.'

'But it wouldn't have slipped out if you weren't thinking it.'

'I wasn't thinking it. I mean, not in the way you imagine.'

'I don't care. Look, I didn't ask you to come round today. You don't have to treat me like I'm a charity case. I can manage quite well on my own.'

'You don't look like you're managing, Jane.'

'Don't I? I think you've said enough. You should go. I want to be on my own.'

Kirsty left. Jane sank back down onto the sofa with her head in her hands.

'Oh Greg,' she cried. 'Why did you have to bloody do this to me?'

Two hours later, Jane felt like she couldn't cry anymore. She stared up at the ceiling as though she might find the answer there.

She'd known Kirsty for almost nineteen years, since they were both eleven. In all that time, Kirsty had always had her back. She'd always stuck up for Jane, and had never expected much in return. Not even when she herself was going through the worst of times with her mother. Kirsty knew what grief was like. She kept listening to Jane when so many of their other pals had tired of hearing about her pain. She was a true friend. Greg always said Kirsty was his favourite of the girls Jane called her mates. Kirsty would never deliberately hurt her feelings. That stuff about the cruise must have come from a good place.

That's what Greg would have said.

'Kirsty's a diamond.' Jane could almost hear Greg tell her.

She picked up the phone and dialled her best friend.

Kirsty started talking the moment she answered. 'I was so insensitive, babe. I can't believe I said those things to you. I understand if you never forgive me. Sometimes I just open my mouth and before you know it—'

'Kirsty,' said Jane. 'Would you shut up for just a minute? I was ringing to tell you I think you're right.'

'What?'

'You're right. Greg *would* want me to go on that cruise . . . and he would want me to ask you to go with me.'

'Are you sure?'

Jane took a deep breath. 'Yes. But are you really up for it? You promise you won't mind me bursting into tears every time we dock somewhere new and I think about how I'm not seeing it with Greg?'

'I don't mind,' said Kirsty. 'You can cry the whole way if you want to. But I don't think you will. Oh, Jane. This could be really good for you. You're going to love it. We're going to have a fabulous time.'

Chapter Eleven

Sophie

So, the cruise was booked. Each of the adults blocked out the requisite days in their diaries. Jack and Lily would both be on school holidays, as would Sophie, awaiting the results of her GCSE exams.

Actually, Sophie would not be going on the cruise after all. Prior to Granddad Bill's lottery win, Sophie had applied for several holiday jobs and the day after the cruise was mooted, she had an interview for the one she was keenest to bag. It was a paid internship at *County Class*, a local magazine; one of those glossy brochures that gets stuffed through the letterbox every month, containing two articles and an awful lot of estate agents' listings. It wasn't *Tatler*, but it was a start.

Sophie could not believe her luck. Neither her good luck – in getting the internship in the first place – nor her bad luck in getting the dream summer job that she would have to dump for two weeks on the *European Countess*. As soon as she heard about the dilemma, Ronnie announced that there was no way Sophie would be staying home alone while the rest of them were in the Med. She was only just sixteen – old enough to do a lot of things, legally, but certainly not old enough to look after herself properly. Sophie hadn't helped her own case. Earlier that month, she had almost burned the house down by putting some cheese on toast under the grill before going upstairs to Skype Izzy, forgetting all about the bubbling Cheddar. It would be a long time before Ronnie and Mark forgot about it, however. The smell of burnt cheese hangs around for ages.

But at the same time, Ronnie knew this was no ordinary summer job stacking shelves or picking strawberries. Sophie was keen to follow her aunt into magazine journalism and this offer of an internship confirmed she had the talent. It was her big chance. It would look great on future work and university applications. Sophie pleaded to be allowed to stay behind and take advantage of this huge opportunity. She promised she would never cook cheese on toast. In fact, she would eat only cold food the whole time her parents were away. She certainly wouldn't do anything so dangerous as use the iron.

'You do the ironing?' Ronnie snorted. 'I'd be more worried about you leaving all the windows open and letting in a flying pig.'

Ronnie didn't know what to do.

'Don't you want to come on holiday with us?' she asked her daughter.

'Of course I do,' Sophie responded unconvincingly. 'But . . . This is my future we're talking about, Mum. Two weeks at sea would be great but I won't be able to put that on my CV.'

In the end, it was Annabel who helped Ronnie make the final decision. Annabel and Richard were very keen on internships. If she remained well enough, Izzy would be doing one herself that summer, in the offices of a local law firm. Izzy had expressed an interest in studying law at university, just as her father had done. Ronnie should be proud that Sophie was taking her future so seriously, Annabel said. There were plenty of teenagers who didn't.

'Sophie is very mature,' Annabel assured her.

'But she's still not old enough to stay home on her own in Coventry,' said Ronnie.

'Then she can come and stay with us.'

'Really?'

'Of course. We've got plenty of space and Izzy would be delighted. We'll make sure she stays out of trouble.'

Sophie was jubilant when she heard the news. If anything, she was more excited than she had been the night Bill's lottery numbers came up. She would get to do the internship at *County Class and* stay at the Great House. Two weeks with her favourite cousin and *without* her little brother. She was going to have the time of her life.

Chapter Twelve

Ronnie and Annabel

A couple of days later, Ronnie drove Sophie and Jack over to Annabel's house to talk about arrangements for Sophie's stay.

When they arrived, Jack headed out into the garden with Leander and spent a happy hour throwing the dog's favourite toy then fetching it himself, while Leander watched lazily from a warm spot in one of the flower beds. Jack loved to play with Izzy's cuddly Labrador. He also had a passing interest in explaining the ins and outs of *Doctor Who* to his six-month-old cousin Humfrey, who mostly responded by blowing raspberries. Meanwhile, Sophie and Izzy went straight up to Izzy's room.

Annabel and Ronnie took their coffees into the conservatory. Though it was a bright day, there was a breeze and it wasn't quite hot enough to sit outside. The conservatory was made for days like this. The sisters sat side by side on a sofa with Humfrey propped up against the cushions between them. Anyone looking in on them would have assumed they were old, old friends. Ronnie and Annabel's relationship had certainly gone from strength to strength since Annabel accidentally gave birth in Ronnie's front room, ruining her carpet (Annabel had replaced the carpet just as soon as she was able). They had come to realise that they were very similar people. They were both feisty and strong-willed and fairly quick to anger – which is why they'd had so many clashes when they first met. But they were also both kind and generous. It was odd, considering they had grown up apart, that they had come to be so alike. They were devoted mothers and they had a lot of respect for one another. That's how Ronnie knew Sophie would be safe with her Auntie Annabel while the rest of the family was away.

After they'd discussed what Sophie would need for two weeks at the Great House – 'Nothing but herself' – Ronnie showed Annabel the brochure for the cruise the family would be taking.

'It looks amazing,' said Annabel. 'You must be very excited.'

'I am,' said Ronnie. 'Except I'm worried about what to take, for the formal nights.'

Though most of the time the restaurants on the *European Countess* had no Cunard-style dress code, each cruise had a couple of 'formal nights' on which guests were supposed to make an effort.

Annabel pointed out in return that the formal nights were not compulsory but she was sure Ronnie would enjoy them.

'It's one of those once-in-a-lifetime experiences, isn't it, dressing up for dinner on a cruise liner? You'll regret it if you don't go along.'

'But I don't have anything to wear,' said Ronnie. 'You've got to wear something long, haven't you? I haven't got a single long dress in my wardrobe except for the maxi dress I wore while I was pregnant with Jack and that's got a great big stain down the front.'

'Beetroot?' asked Annabel.

Ronnie had told her sister how she craved beetroot

throughout both her pregnancies. Annabel had the same craving while she was carrying Izzy and Humfrey.

'Yeah, beetroot,' said Ronnie now.

'I don't think it has to be a long dress,' said Annabel.

'I haven't exactly got any decent short dresses either.'

'Maybe I've got something you could borrow,' said Annabel.

'What? We're nowhere near the same size.'

'I don't think we're far off,' said Annabel. 'Why don't you come and have a look through my wardrobe?'

Picking up Humfrey and balancing him on her hip, Annabel led the way upstairs.

This was the first time Annabel had invited Ronnie into her bedroom. Ronnie had seen most of the house even before she knew Annabel was her sister – she'd visited it during a village open day – but she had never been into the master bedroom. She'd imagined it though. Ronnie was convinced that Annabel and Richard would have a four-poster. They didn't, but theirs was still the sort of room Ronnie dreamed of. There were two enormous wardrobes – one his and one hers – and one of those sleigh beds in mahogany. It was piled high with expensive-looking cushions.

In front of the window was an elegant dressing table and there was a free-standing full-length mirror off to one side. A cheval mirror was what they were called in John Lewis. Ronnie couldn't help feeling a pang of envy when she thought of her own cramped bedroom back in Coventry. The curtains were still drooping where Fishy the cat had fled up them to escape Leander one Sunday afternoon, months and months before. Mark spent so much time fixing up other people's houses, he could never be bothered to do anything at home.

Annabel opened her wardrobe. Ronnie was surprised that it wasn't completely stuffed. It was like the wardrobe in a picture from an interiors magazine. All matching hangers and hatboxes.

'You haven't got much stuff,' said Ronnie. But what Annabel did have was lovely. Ronnie recognised a pair of Louboutins on the wardrobe floor. Ronnie knew all about Louboutins, having borrowed a pair from Chelsea to wear on her wedding day.

'I think this could be the perfect thing for you.'

Annabel plucked a dress from her collection.

It was a beautiful dress – floor-length red chiffon with fluttering sleeves.

'It won't suit me,' said Ronnie.

'How can you tell until you've tried it on?'

'It won't go with my colouring.'

'If it goes with *my* colouring, it will go with yours. We're exactly the same.'

'I don't know.'

'Just put it on. I'll wait outside. You can call me when you're ready.'

Annabel insisted. She stepped outside with Humfrey. Ronnie carefully put on the dress, fearing for the seams. But her sister was right. They were the same size. Ronnie felt a little thrill at the thought. She called Annabel back in.

'There you are, you'll be the belle of the ball!'

Ronnie gamely gave a twirl in front of Annabel's cheval mirror.

'It looks all right,' she admitted.

'All right? You look amazing. Definitely fit for the captain's table. What do you think, Humfrey?'

Humfrey gurgled a happy sort of reply.

While Annabel set Humfrey down on a changing mat

on the bedroom floor, Ronnie sat down at Annabel's dressing table. She was starting to tear up.

'What's wrong?' Annabel asked. 'What are you sad about?'

'It's just . . .' Ronnie sniffed. 'It's just . . . These aren't sad tears. Well, they are, sort of. You're so good to us, Annabel. Offering to take Sophie while we go on the cruise, and now lending me your dress. I'm crying because this is how it should have been all the time – you and me, sisters sharing clothes. This is what we would have done if you'd grown up with me and Chelsea in Coventry. If Mum hadn't given you away.'

Annabel took Ronnie's hand and rubbed it.

'Jacqui did what she had to. We've got each other now,' she said. 'And I'm sure if we'd grown up together, we'd have spent much more time fighting than swapping clothes and make-up tips. You're a decade younger than me. You wouldn't have wanted to wear my things. You should have seen some of the clothes I had. All classic eighties stuff – big shoulders, batwing sleeves. Tartan. Velvet hairbands . . .'

Ronnie picked up the wedding photograph of Annabel and Richard that adorned the dressing table. The puffed sleeves of Annabel's wedding gown were bigger than her head.

'That dress was very fashionable at the time,' Annabel laughed.

'I wish you were coming on the cruise,' said Ronnie.

'Me too,' said Annabel. 'But the timing isn't right. I don't want to take Izzy too far from her medical team and Humfrey is still so tiny. It would be far more worrying than relaxing at the moment. Besides, this way Sophie gets to do her summer job.'

Ronnie sniffed again and nodded. 'We will go on

holiday together one day though, won't we? It'd be a laugh. The girls would love it.'

'Yes,' said Annabel. 'We'll definitely do something.'

Ronnie put Annabel's wedding photo back on the dressing table.

'I shouldn't be saying this,' she said. 'But I think our little sister is going to be getting married soon.'

'Oh,' said Annabel. 'Spill the beans.'

Ronnie reprised her theory about Adam and Dave's walk to the War Memorial. Annabel agreed that Ronnie's notion was plausible.

'He's bound to propose on the cruise!'

Chapter Thirteen

Sophie and Izzy

While their mothers were bonding over clothes for the cruise, Sophie and Izzy were in Izzy's room, sitting side by side at her desk, trawling for treasure on the Internet. They'd watched several Vine videos of cats doing stupid things, and then several Vine videos of boys doing stupid things. Now they logged onto the cruise line's website and looked at what was in store for Sophie's parents and her brother.

'I am so glad I'm staying here,' Sophie said.

'It's going to be amazing to have you here,' Izzy agreed. 'Just a pity we've got to go to work in the daytimes.'

'I've got to get something on my CV for when I fail my exams.'

'You won't have failed them.'

'I dunno. I'm pretty sure I passed them all but whether I actually got good grades, I can't tell. In English, probably. And German. The German exam seemed really easy. Maths was hard. And I nearly cried in Chemistry.'

'You'll have done OK in them all.'

'I wish I didn't have to wait until the end of August to find out.'

'You should have more faith in yourself. I'll have to work on you while you're here. Maybe Dad will give you one of the speeches he's always giving me. That might help.' Izzy impersonated her father's voice. 'We are a family of winners, Isobel Buchanan. Winners are always optimistic.'

Sophie laughed.

'Even when it seems like there's F-all to be optimistic about . . . I've got a hospital appointment next week,' said Izzy, abruptly changing the subject.

'Is everything all right?'

'It's just a check-up. And then I'm going to see a psychologist too.'

'Why do you need to see a psychologist?'

'Mum's idea. Apparently, I need to talk about a few things.'

'Like what?'

'Like . . . I can't stop thinking about the bloke who gave me his kidney.'

'How do you mean?'

'I feel so guilty. Every day I wonder how his family is getting on. I mean, since I got the transplant, everything has been loads better for me. It almost feels like life is back to normal. But for his family, everything must be so much worse. They must be grieving him so badly, Soph. I hope he didn't have any children. The patient advocate said he didn't but what if she just said that to make it easier for me?'

'She wouldn't have lied to you about that.'

'I wish I could be sure. It's freaking me out.'

'Can you really not find out who it was? I'm sure I read something in a paper about a girl who had a transplant saying thank you in person to her donor's family and how it made them all feel better. Why don't you just ask to meet yours?'

'They don't encourage it,' said Izzy. 'We wrote that thank you letter for the advocate to pass on – me and Mum and Dad. But beyond that it's sort of like with adoption in the old days. The idea is you don't know so you don't have to deal with the expectations of the donor's family. Or the donor's family might not want to meet me because they're angry I'm alive and their loved one isn't. Or they might disapprove of the way I live my life and think I'm disrespecting the donation.'

'The way you live?'

'There are probably people out there who'd think that a kidney is wasted on me, given I fucked mine up taking drugs.'

'It's not as if you're the first person ever to take ecstasy. You were unlucky.'

'You can say that again. But it's still a fact that *I* made the decision to do those pills. I could still be perfectly healthy. There are people out there who were born with kidney disease. They didn't have a choice. I got myself into my mess.'

'Everyone deserves a second chance. Is there anyone in the world who hasn't done something stupid? The only difference between them and you is that they got away with it.'

'Thanks,' said Izzy. 'But I think I'm going to beat myself up about this for the rest of my life, regardless.'

'Maybe it is a good idea for you to see a psychologist in that case. You're being way too hard on yourself.'

'Like you when anyone asks you about your exams.'

'Fair point,' said Sophie. 'Though I think it's much more likely that I've failed Physics than your donor's family wouldn't like you.'

Izzy smiled a little sadly.

'Seriously. Cut yourself some slack, Izzy.'

'I just keep going back to this time last year when I'd finished my exams and I was really looking forward to the summer. If I'd just stayed at home instead of going to that festival.'

'Don't think like that. You'll drive yourself nuts.'

'I can't help it. Every day I look at the date and think this time last year I was healthy. This time last year the person who gave me their kidney was alive. What must it be like for their family?'

Sophie moved to sit beside Izzy on the edge of her bed and gave her a hug. Sophie could appreciate some of Izzy's anguish. She often thought about the time she got so drunk, while the family was on holiday in Lanzarote, she fell off a pier and almost drowned. But Adam had dragged her out of the sea and now he was in love with her Auntie Chelsea. There was a silver lining. However, Sophie decided against pointing out to Izzy that had she not taken the pills, had she not fallen ill, Annabel would not have searched for the Bensons. Sophie and Izzy would not have become friends. Sophie knew that would probably never seem like a good deal.

'Think about this time next year,' she said instead. 'Anything could happen in the next twelve months.'

Izzy nodded and wiped a tear away.

'You're right. I'm going to write another letter to them, whatever – the donor's family. Mum pretty much wrote the last one. I want them to know how grateful I am in my own words. I might not tell them why I needed the kidney – I haven't decided yet – but I want them to know I'm going to take care of it. I will never take chances with my body again.'

'Are you never going to have a drink?' Sophie asked.

'Never.'

'I'm not going to put any money on it. You know what? I would bet that if the family of the bloke who gave you his kidney met you, they'd think you were really great.'

'Thanks, cuz. That means a lot.'

Ronnie called up the stairs.

'Sophie, we've got to go.'

Izzy gave Sophie a hug. 'I'll see you in three days for our super-mega two-week sleepover!'

The girls bobbed up and down with glee.

Chapter Fourteen

Jack

Downstairs, Jack reluctantly said farewell to Leander, then gave his baby cousin a dutiful goodbye kiss on the forehead. As he was doing so, Humfrey, who really was quite large for his age, accidentally gave Jack a thump on the nose. Fortunately, Jack took it in the spirit in which it was intended and allowed his Auntie Annabel to kiss his nose better. He didn't even try to take advantage of the situation by pretending the biff hurt more than it did.

'Are you sure you can't come on the cruise?' Jack asked his aunt.

'I'm sorry, Jack. It would be very difficult. We don't want to be too far away from a hospital because of Izzy, and Humfrey is really much too small to enjoy it. He might get seasick and he wouldn't be able to tell us. Besides, we're looking after Sophie now.'

'Awwww,' Jack complained. 'It won't be the same if everyone isn't there.'

'You'll still have a lovely time. I'll tell you what . . .'

Annabel peeped into Humfrey's pram, which was an enormous modern version of the old Silver Cross.

'*We* might not be able to join you on the cruise but I know someone who can.'

'Leander!' Jack jumped with joy.

'No. Not Leander. He's definitely not a sea dog. How about Ted?'

'Ted?'

Jack knew all about Ted. Ted was the ragged old bear that had belonged to Annabel since she was a baby. Jack's grandma, Jacqui, had bought Annabel the bear to keep her safe while they had to be apart for all those years. Annabel had subsequently given the bear to Izzy and now Izzy had given it to Humfrey.

'Take Ted on the cruise. She'll love it.'

Jack frowned. He was slightly disconcerted by Annabel's insistence that Ted was a 'she'. Surely Ted was a boy's name?

'Will he like it? Going on a cruise?'

'I know *she* will. And to make it even better, you can take pictures of Ted enjoying herself in all the places you visit and when you come back, we can make a book that Humfrey will be able to look at when he's a bit older. That's what my dad did for me when I was a little girl. He took Ted with him when he had to go to America for work and I couldn't go with him. Ted had a fantastic time. I've still got the little book somewhere. I'll show you next time you come.'

Jack was persuaded that it was a brilliant idea. Annabel took Ted out of Humfrey's pram and handed the bear over to Jack. Jack took Ted with due reverence.

'I'll look after Ted,' he said. 'I'll do it properly.'

'I know you will,' said Annabel.

The thought of his mission, to look after Ted on the cruise and report back to Humfrey, put Jack in a good mood. But there was more. He had a secret to share.

In the car on the way back to their house, Jack confided in Sophie that he was going to get a dog.

'In your dreams,' said Sophie.

'I am. When Leander has puppies. When I asked Mum

at lunchtime, she said I could have a dog if Leander had puppies.'

Sophie sighed. 'Oh dear. In that case, you're going to be waiting a very long time.'

'I'm not,' Jack insisted. 'Cathy Next Door's dog had puppies and she was only four. Leander will be four this year. That's twenty-eight in dog years.'

The concept of dog years was one of the latest things to capture Jack's imagination. He calculated everything in dog years now. From his own age and his sister's age to the amount of time he had to spend in the supermarket while Ronnie did the weekly shop. 'Three whole days! For a dog!'

'Yes, but Jack,' said Sophie now. 'Cathy Next Door's dog is a *she*.'

'I know that,' said Jack. 'But . . .' He pulled his sister closer to him by tugging on her collar. 'Listen to this. I've got to tell you something. You have to have a girl dog *and* a boy dog to make puppies. And they have to do *it*.'

'It?'

'It,' Jack confirmed. 'Lukas at school told me. So Leander can do it with a girl dog and then I can have a puppy.'

Jack settled back on his booster seat, looking terribly pleased with himself. Sophie burst out laughing.

'It's true!' Jack insisted.

'What are you laughing about in the back?' Ronnie asked.

'Mum, since you're the one who told Jack he could have a puppy from Leander, you can be the one to explain what it means when a dog's been castrated.'

Chapter Fifteen

Lily

Little Lily wanted Chelsea to help her pack for the trip. She was incredibly excited, though the only cultural reference point she had for big ships was the *Titanic* (she'd been reading Michael Morpurgo's *Kaspar: Prince of Cats*). Disney had yet to make a princess out of a cruise line hostess.

Lily laid out all her dresses on the bed and explained to Chelsea that she would need one for each evening they were to be away. Likewise Lily's favourite doll, Melinda, would need her own layette and a change of shoes for each night.

'We might not be able to take all of it,' Chelsea warned, as she regarded the frilly frock mountain.

Lily pouted.

'Well, we'll try to take as much as we can. Perhaps we should take this opportunity to design a capsule wardrobe for Melinda.'

'What's that?'

'It's what fashionable ladies do to put together their outfits. I've written about it in the magazine.'

Lily was deeply impressed by anything to do with Chelsea's job, which she imagined to be like spending the whole day in an enormous dressing-up box.

'How do we do a capsule outfit?' Lily asked.

'Wardrobe,' said Chelsea. 'Well, basically, it's about

thinking about things that match. So, for example, Melinda won't need to take all her shoes. She'll just need to take one pair that goes with all sorts of things. Perhaps these silver ones.'

Lily listened to Chelsea as though she were the oracle. Chelsea was very glad to have these moments with Lily, talking about dresses and shoes. She wondered if Claire, Adam's wife, would have done the same. Was she a girls' girl? Adam hadn't said so and she didn't like to ask.

'Melinda has to take this dress,' said Lily, holding up a pink extravaganza.

'It's a bit bridesmaidy,' said Chelsea.

'I've never been a bridesmaid,' said Lily with a pout.

'Oh,' said Chelsea. 'That's a shame. I was never a bridesmaid either. Even though I wanted to be. Nobody ever asked, until Jack's mum Ronnie did last year but by then I was much too old. I never got to wear a frilly dress.'

'But I will. I'm having a frilly dress because I'm going to be your bridesmaid,' said Lily. 'Aren't I?'

'Are you?' Chelsea put her head to one side.

'Yes. When you get married to Daddy.'

'Ah, well,' said Chelsea. 'The thing is, Lily, he hasn't asked me if I want to get married yet.'

'But when he does, I'll be your bridesmaid then,' said Lily quite matter-of-factly.

'Well, of course,' said Chelsea. 'If it happens then you would be my first choice.'

'I'm going to have a dress like Elsa from *Frozen*.'

Lily was all about *Frozen*. Chelsea had watched the film with her at least twice a week for the past six months. Now that Lily had mentioned the dreaded film again, Chelsea had to battle hard to prevent a case of 'Let It Go' earworm. She prayed that Lily wouldn't burst into song and make the earworm inevitable.

'Perhaps I might fall in love on the cruise,' said Lily dreamily. 'Then I could get married too.'

'Perhaps.' Chelsea smiled. 'You've got an awful lot of adventures to have before you settle down though.'

Disney had a great deal to answer for.

But Lily wasn't the only one who was hoping for the traditional happy ending to her personal fairy tale. Back at her flat in Stockwell, Chelsea took just as much care over her own packing. Of course, she'd been out and bought a few new things for the trip. Unlike her sister, she was especially looking forward to the formal nights on board ship. Chelsea loved a chance to dress up. Since Adam had asked her to move in, this cruise should be extra romantic.

And now here was Lily, announcing her candidacy for bridesmaid. Had Adam said something to her? Had he been sounding out Lily's opinion on the possibility of officially bringing Chelsea into their family? Most likely he hadn't. He'd probably just talked to her about Chelsea moving in. Lily was simply the sort of little girl who liked to think about weddings and romance, and at her age it still seemed inevitable that becoming boyfriend and girlfriend was a precursor to marriage. It didn't mean Lily had thought about it, except in the same way she thought about marrying Melinda to the ancient Ken doll that had once belonged to Claire, her mother.

Still, Chelsea allowed herself a little romantic daydream. All the monthly magazines were in the library at the *Society* office. Chelsea usually gave the wedding mags a body swerve unless she had been tasked to write something about that year's fashionable flowers or some such guff. Now she surreptitiously flicked through a copy of *Bride* while she was waiting for the kettle to boil in the staff kitchen.

Her last day at *Society* magazine was drawing close. She was about to go on a fourteen-day cruise with her entire family. Had she been facing both those things just twelve months earlier, Chelsea would have been desperate to the point of outright despair but, right then, she had never been happier.

Chapter Sixteen

Kirsty and Jane

Kirsty was very much looking forward to her holiday. On payday, at the end of July, she went straight to the shops. Some of the summer sales had already started and Kirsty was determined to buy a whole new wardrobe for the cruise. If only Jane would come shopping with her. It was no fun to shop alone.

'I don't feel up to it,' said Jane when Kirsty called to see if she wanted to hit Bicester Village. 'It's always chaos there with the busloads of tourists.'

'But don't you need some new clothes too?'

'What for?' Jane asked, genuinely clueless.

'For the . . . the cruise?' Kirsty said.

'Oh,' said Jane. 'Yeah. Of course.'

Jane's refusal to join the shopping trip put the dampers on Kirsty's enjoyment of the whole experience. It made her wonder again whether she was wrong to be pushing her friend to go on the trip at all. Was Kirsty being selfish because she needed a holiday herself?

No. She was doing this for Jane's good as well. Of course Jane was still mourning. She would grieve for Greg for the rest of her life. But Jane needed to get out into the world again and see that the future wasn't entirely hopeless.

* * *

What Kirsty didn't know was that Jane had already been on a shopping spree for the cruise. Almost a year before, when she and Greg were still planning their wedding and honeymoon, Jane had spent a small fortune while on a day trip to London, thinking it was a good idea to stock up in the sales for the busy year ahead.

While Greg watched TV in a pub, Jane went through the last of the summer sale at Harrods, compiling a 'trousseau'. She didn't let Greg see any of it, promising him he would enjoy the big reveal on their honeymoon all the more. If only she had known he would never see the bra and knickers by Myla that cost a fortune even at seventy-five per cent off. She wished she'd worn them the day she bought them. There were so many things she wished she'd said or done.

With just a couple of days to go before the cruise, Jane packed her case. Why was so much memory attached to everything? Even the clothes that Greg had never actually seen reminded Jane of the excitement she had felt that one day he might give her a wolf-whistle as she stepped out in that new bikini or wore that great dress to a restaurant by the sea.

For the past three years, everything she'd bought to wear had been chosen with Greg in mind. Would he like it? Would he tell her if he didn't? She folded a pink dress she knew he would have adored. Or at least pretended to adore.

Having packed her clothes, Jane chose the jewellery she would take with her. She didn't have much but almost everything she did have and really liked had been a present from Greg, like the gold hoops he'd given her on the anniversary of their first date or the solid gold bangle he gave her for their second Christmas. She still wore her engagement ring.

Greg had chosen it himself. It was a large sapphire, surrounded by a collar of smaller diamonds. It was not unlike the engagement ring that the Duchess of Cambridge inherited from Princess Diana. That was why Greg had chosen it. The first summer he and Jane were together was the summer of Kate and Wills' wedding. Jane commented on how much she liked the engagement ring. Greg had not forgotten.

From the moment Greg put the ring on her finger, Jane had not taken it off. He'd got the size right by enlisting her mother's help. Maggie had been only too delighted to help Greg with his mission.

The ring didn't feel quite the right size any more. While once it had been snug and secure – even slightly too tight on a warm day – now the ring twisted easily round Jane's finger. She'd lost a lot of weight. Her engagement ring revealed that just as much as the notches on her belt. Jane would have to get it resized soon or perhaps start wearing it on a necklace until she put the weight back on – if she ever put the weight back on.

With her case packed, Jane sat down on top of it, twirling her ring and looking at her reflection in the mirrored door of the wardrobe.

'Should I be going on this cruise at all?' she asked out loud. 'Give me a sign will you, Greg?'

No sign was forthcoming. Jane didn't count the fact that Kirsty texted right that second.

'Don't forget your cozzie,' Kirsty said.

Chapter Seventeen

Granddad Bill

No matter how grey and gloomy the morning, Granddad Bill could usually be relied upon to greet the day with a smile. Jacqui or Dave generally helped the old man to get up at around eight o'clock. Jacqui would take a cup of tea in to him and while he was drinking that, she would pick out the clothes Bill needed for the day. That was getting easier now Bill pretty much refused to wear anything other than a Coventry City FC shirt and jogging trousers accessorised with those infamous velvet slippers.

But when Jacqui pulled back the curtains that morning, Bill just groaned. He'd not been too well for the past few days – for just over a week, if Jacqui was honest. He'd picked up a summer cold, which Jack brought home from school, but Jacqui had hoped that was on its way out by now, in time for the cruise. It clearly wasn't.

'Morning to you too,' she joked with him. 'Sun too bright?'

Outside the sky was gunmetal grey and heavy with rain. Another perfect English summer day. Hail was forecast for the afternoon. But it seemed it really was too bright for Bill. He groaned again. The groan turned into a splutter.

'Are you all right, Bill?' Jacqui went over to him. She

laid her hand on his forehead, as though he were one of her long since grown-up children. 'You feel a bit hot.'

'I feel terrible,' Bill confirmed.

'What did we have to eat last night?' Jacqui asked herself out loud. Her first resort was always to consider food poisoning. She wasn't the best of cooks. But as far as she could remember, they'd had nothing that should have caused a problem.

'Can you sit up?' she asked her father-in-law.

With Jacqui's assistance, Bill dragged himself into a sitting position, which immediately set off a horrible coughing fit.

Jacqui took a closer look at him. 'Oh dear,' she said. 'You don't look well at all.'

Trying to persuade the woman at the doctor's surgery that Bill's case was serious enough to warrant a home visit was a Herculean task. But as luck would have it, it was a slow day and the doctor was there in just *four* hours. She examined Bill from head to toe, taking his temperature and listening to his heart and lungs.

'I'm afraid your father-in-law has a chest infection,' said the doctor. 'He's going to need antibiotics, rest, plenty of liquids. As much food as he can manage. He probably won't be out of bed for a while.'

'But we're supposed to be going on a cruise on Saturday,' said Jacqui.

'Your father-in-law shouldn't be going anywhere.'

Jacqui gasped in anguish. 'But we can't leave him here.'

'Do you have any relatives who might look after him?'

'No,' said Jacqui. 'All of us are going on the cruise together.'

Jacqui filled the doctor in on the whole tale, from the

moment when Jack presented his great-grandfather with the lottery ticket.

'We never thought it would win. Our family never wins anything.'

The doctor was sympathetic but there was nothing she could do to change the situation. Jacqui could try calling the council and see if they were able to arrange emergency respite care but the doctor warned her that a Mediterranean cruise probably wouldn't count as an emergency. Wasn't it just Sod's Law?

Jacqui did her best not to seem upset when she took a cup of tea in to Bill as soon as the doctor left.

'Thank you, love,' he said. 'I'll be right as rain after this.'

'I'm afraid you won't, Bill. Not with a chest infection like you've got. You need antibiotics. The doctor says you've got to take it easy for a while. She doesn't think you should go on holiday.'

'What? Not take my holiday?'

Bill seemed confused.

'You can't, Bill. Even if you felt better in yourself, the cruise company wouldn't want to take the risk of having you on board and our travel insurance probably wouldn't be valid. Oh,' Jacqui sighed, 'this is just typical of our luck.'

Chapter Eighteen

Annabel

Jacqui resigned herself to the fact that she and Dave would not be going on the cruise. They would not be waking up in Rome the following Friday morning. They would never get to see Ajaccio, wherever Annabel had said that was. The lovely new dress Jacqui had bought in the clearance sale at John Lewis in Solihull would not be getting its first outing at the captain's table.

The day after Granddad Bill's diagnosis, Jacqui telephoned her eldest daughter. Jacqui still didn't speak to Annabel quite as often as she spoke to Ronnie and Chelsea but they had definitely reached a stage in their relationship where Jacqui didn't feel awkward about ringing up to chew the fat. She no longer needed to have any concrete reason to make the call.

She told Annabel about the latest disaster.

'Jacqui,' said Annabel. 'You've been looking forward to this cruise for weeks. Can't the council organise anything? Or there are private agencies, surely. Have you tried them?'

'I just don't think it would be right, sweetheart. Your granddad isn't well and then there's his dementia. I couldn't leave him with someone he doesn't know. Besides, did you see that report on the news the other night, about agency workers? They had some poor bloke tied to his bed!'

'That's a one-off, I would hope,' said Annabel.

'No. It's best if Dave and me stay home with him. That way your sisters can still go on the cruise and enjoy themselves. Dave and me will go another time.'

Alone in her kitchen after Jacqui's call, Annabel stuck a pod in the Nespresso machine and gazed out onto the wet garden. For the past month, Humfrey had been sleeping well. Izzy had been on good form. Life had settled into a nice, easy rhythm. They were already going to be having Sophie to stay while Mark and Ronnie were away. Sophie would be no trouble but if Izzy *and* Sophie helped out with Humfrey just a little then perhaps they could take one more house-guest. Annabel gave chest infections a quick Googling. She didn't want to expose Izzy to anything dangerous, of course. Her transplant made her vulnerable. But if Bill was on antibiotics, that meant it wasn't viral, didn't it?

Having talked to Izzy's doctor for reassurance and offered Izzy herself a substantial raise to her allowance in return for light babysitting duties, Annabel called Jacqui.

'Jacqui,' she said, without preamble. 'If you think he would be happy with the arrangement, Richard and I would like to have Granddad Bill here.'

'You're nuts,' said Richard when he heard the news, which was presented to him as a fait accompli that evening. 'Absolutely barking. We can't have your grand-father here.'

'Izzy and Sophie have agreed to help out.'

'Granddad Bill needs watching round the clock!'

'So does Humfrey. We still have to get up from time

to time. I don't see how it will make all that much difference.'

'When Humfrey's playing up, I can pick him up and tuck him under my arm,' said Richard. 'Granddad Bill is six foot tall, he used to be an amateur boxer and occasionally thinks he's a sixteen-year-old.'

'His new medication has been working really well,' said Annabel. 'You saw him on his birthday and when we had that lottery lunch. Completely lucid.'

'But what if he decides to have a bad patch while Jacqui's not around?'

'Richard, I've already told her we're taking him.'

'Why?'

The truth was, Annabel had surprised herself by offering to take her grandfather on. Annabel had been extremely reluctant to meet her birth family and the early days of her renewed relationship with Jacqui, Dave and her new-found sisters had not been easy. But the Bensons had rallied around the Buchanans when Izzy was sick and Annabel firmly believed that had Izzy not received a kidney from an anonymous donor, Ronnie or Chelsea would have stepped up in time.

Annabel had heard the stories of how Granddad Bill was, back in the eighties, when Chelsea and Ronnie were small. She was envious of the close relationship they'd had with him. Bill was her grandfather as much as theirs.

'And he's just given Izzy and Humfrey sixteen thousand pounds,' said Annabel.

Though the Buchanans had insisted their children didn't need a share of the lottery winnings, when it came down to it, they were grateful. Richard's bank was having a bad year. There were rumours that redundancies were ahead and though Richard would get an excellent payout if he did get the chop, he was getting to that age where it wouldn't be so easy to walk into a new position.

'If the Bensons think we're family enough to have that money then we're family enough to take our share of the responsibilities too.'

Richard shook his head. 'Well,' he said. 'It sounds as though it's already a done deal. Just so long as you don't expect me to do anything.'

'The only thing I'll ask you to do is share the odd bottle of Spitfire with him.'

'All right.' Richard smiled. 'I think I can do that.' He kissed his wife on the forehead. 'You're getting soft in your old age.'

Jacqui and Dave were over the moon at Annabel's kind offer. Jacqui repacked Bill's suitcase, and her own and Dave's, and they drove Bill over to Annabel's the very next morning, just as Mark and Ronnie were dropping Sophie off. The idea was that Bill would have a trial night at Annabel's before they had to leave to catch the cruise. If that first night was a disaster, Jacqui and Dave would stay home after all.

But Bill seemed to be on good form. He recognised his eldest granddaughter and her husband and blew kisses to Izzy, who kept a little distance as a precaution. Humfrey gurgled happily when he saw the old man. Leander, of course, was pleased to see anyone who habitually carried Trebor mints in his pocket. He almost wagged his tail off.

While Jacqui and Dave settled Granddad Bill, Ronnie and Mark bid a surprisingly emotional 'goodbye' to their Sophie. Jack gave her a farewell kiss without being prompted and Sophie didn't act as though Jack had given her impetigo in the process.

'Be good and work hard,' Ronnie told Sophie.

'Be good and don't be hard work,' Dave told Granddad Bill.

Then the Bensons were gone, leaving Sophie and Bill with the Buchanans. Sophie and Izzy disappeared into Izzy's bedroom right away, just as Humfrey started crying and Bill started asking 'What's for tea?'

'What was that you said about the girls helping out?' Richard asked Annabel.

'We'll manage,' said Annabel. 'This is going to be an adventure.'

Chapter Nineteen

The Bensons

Saturday morning arrived at last. The *European Countess* would be setting sail at six that afternoon but boarding began much earlier and the Bensons wanted to be on the ship as soon as they possibly could.

Ronnie had arranged for a minibus to take them to Southampton's swanky Ocean Terminal. The first pick-up was at Ronnie's, so the bus was already piled high with luggage when it arrived at Dave and Jacqui's house. Luggage allowances for a cruise ship were not as strict as for an aeroplane and Ronnie in particular was taking advantage of that fact. She was bringing everything but the kitchen sink.

'Ronnie,' said Mark. 'We're going to be stopping at six different ports. If you've forgotten anything, we're bound to be able to find it in France, Spain or Italy. They're certainly going to have toilet paper on board.'

Ronnie was unconvinced there would be enough. She had packed two emergency rolls.

Jack was also taking lots of things that he thought might be in short supply on the Continent. His little Dalek wheelie case – a gift from Annabel and Richard for his birthday – was full of such important items as his Sonic Screwdriver and small figurines of all the Doctor Whos Jack had watched. There were important things related to Ted too. Jack had packed the plastic dish and spoon he'd used as a baby for Ted's on-board dinners. And, because he had recently watched *Paddington*, Jack had made Ted a special label, should they become parted on their big adventure.

It said, 'Please look after this bear.' Just like Paddington's. On the back was Jack's name and address.

Chelsea, Adam and Lily were coming to Southampton in a taxi from London.

When they met at the port, Jack and Lily greeted one another joyfully, holding hands and spinning round and round faster and faster until one of them screamed – probably Lily, though it was hard to tell while Jack's voice was still so high-pitched. Anyway, they were full of excitement about the days ahead, though it soon became clear they had slightly different agendas when it came to how they thought they might spend their time at sea.

'There are dancing lessons,' said Lily. 'Jack, you can be my partner.'

'I'm not dancing,' he said. 'I'm doing bowling.'

Lily laughed as though she thought he was joking.

'There's a Wendy house in the children's club.'

'I'm not going in a Wendy house,' said Jack. 'I'm doing crazy golf.'

'I'm sure there will be plenty of time to do dancing and bowling and crazy golf and going in the Wendy house,' said Jacqui diplomatically. 'We're going to be at sea for several days.'

'The sea! The sea!'

The children danced around each other again.

'And I've got Ted,' said Jack, showing Lily the raggy old bear. 'Auntie Annabel asked me to bring Ted with us.'

Chelsea, who saw the exchange, held her breath as she waited for Lily's reaction. Ted wasn't quite the lovely toy Lily was used to.

'Oh,' said Lily. 'She's all sad.'

She gently took the bear from Jack and gave her a big cuddle.

'We'll look after you, Ted,' said Lily. 'You can wear some of my dolls' dresses.'

'Actually,' said Jack. 'I think Ted's really a boy.'

Lily just laughed at that.

The *European Countess* dominated the port of Southampton that day. Her sleek white hull gleamed in the summer sunshine. When Jacqui saw the ship that would be the family's home for the next fortnight, she suddenly became tearful.

'I didn't expect it to be so beautiful,' she said.

'Her,' said Dave. 'Ships are always female.'

Certainly, the *European Countess* seemed right then to be a living creature. Perhaps a gigantic mythical seabird, resting her wings before heading to a warmer climate. Elegant and mysterious but friendly too, the *European Countess* would take care of them.

'She's humungous,' said Jack.

'She'll never float,' said Lily, looking suddenly worried.

'She will,' said Chelsea, taking Lily's hand. 'She already is.'

'We need a picture,' said Ronnie. She took the first snap of the cruise.

As the Benson party boarded, they had to pass the ship's photographer, who was waiting to take the first of many official photographs. The whole gang duly lined up in front of a backdrop that was painted with a picture of the ship. Raised as they were on selfies, both Jack and Lily pulled out their stock poses. Lily turned three-quarters on and pouted. Jack did something weird with his hands that was supposed to be a gang sign. What kind of gang, no one knew.

'I feel bad, leaving Sophie behind,' Ronnie told Chelsea as they joined the queue of people waiting to be told how to find their cabins.

'Oh come on,' said Chelsea. 'She's going to have a great time. Remember when you were sixteen? Did you want to go on holiday with Mum and Dad? I know I would have given *anything* to be left behind.'

'Me too,' Ronnie agreed.

'Are you ready for this?' Dave popped his head between his grown-up daughters. 'Last chance to get off without needing a lifeboat.'

'Ready as I'll ever be,' said Ronnie.

Chelsea glanced at Adam, who was squatting down to be introduced to Ted by Jack. He was pretending Ted was whispering in his ear. Chelsea's heart squeezed. 'I'm ready too.'

Chapter Twenty

Jane and Kirsty

Jane and Kirsty arrived at Southampton's Ocean Terminal for check-in half an hour after the Bensons. Of course, the terminal had security x-ray machines, just like an airport. Jane and Kirsty loaded their bags onto the conveyor belt and Jane held her breath as her handbag went through. She watched the face of the woman scanning the security screen closely. There wasn't a flicker of concern or surprise as Jane's bag drifted past.

Kirsty, as usual, was carrying about four times as much luggage as the average traveller and caused a small amount of chaos as the straps from one of her bags got tangled up in the side of the conveyor. Luckily, a sharp-eyed attendant plucked the strap free before everything ground to a halt. Kirsty batted her eyelashes at him. He just handed her the bag so that she could put it through again, more carefully this time.

'Thank God for that,' said Kirsty. 'I hate going through those things. I always think I'm going to be pulled to one side and body-searched and they're going to find something they shouldn't.'

'But you're not carrying anything you shouldn't be, are you?' Jane asked.

'Only an enormous vibrator,' said Kirsty.

'Noooo,' said Jane. 'That's gross.'

'I'm joking, you silly moo,' said Kirsty. 'There's nothing I shouldn't have in my bag except a few vodka miniatures. But I put them in with my toiletries and disguised them as shampoo. They'll never guess.'

'Cunning,' said Jane.

There were strict limits to the amount of alcohol one could take onto the ship: one bottle per person before you had to start paying corkage. Kirsty had used her allowance, of course. And Jane's too. Jane hadn't had a drink – an alcoholic drink, that is – in six months. Not since she got the visit from the police telling her about Greg's accident. They'd had beer and wine at his wake, because that's what he would have wanted, but Jane had not touched a drop. She was afraid that if she allowed herself even a sip, the floodgates would open. She still felt as though she was only able to hold herself together if she remained absolutely sober and balanced at all times. Fortunately, though Kirsty was as wild as she had ever been, she was sensitive enough to know that she should not push Jane on the issue.

'So come on then,' said Kirsty. 'Why did you look so nervous going through security? Don't tell me there's a Rampant Rabbit hidden in your Radley!' She whooped at the thought.

'No,' said Jane quietly. 'But Greg is.'

'What?'

Kirsty came to a sudden halt at the top of the escalator.

'Kirsty,' said Jane. 'You can't stop there. You'll cause a pile-up.'

Kirsty duly stepped out of the way. She dumped her bags in a heap and pulled Jane towards her by the sleeve. 'What did you just say?'

'Look, I'll tell you in the cabin.'

'Tell me now.'

'There are loads of people around. Come on. Let's keep going.'

They didn't get far before they were stopped by an official photographer.

'Boarding photograph?' the photographer asked.

The friends paused in front of the backdrop and the photographer fired off a couple of shots. In the one that would make it to the photo stand that evening, Kirsty looked as though she was about to fire lasers from her eyes.

Kirsty and Jane got to their stateroom, as the cabins were officially called, after several false starts. The ship was enormous and every accommodation deck looked exactly like every other once you were out of the lift and in the corridor, as the friends discovered when they accidentally got off on 'Orca' rather than 'Turtle'. They were very glad they had brought wheelie bags.

Their stateroom, when they found it, was actually a suite. Greg had said he and Jane should push the boat out, seeing as how it was their honeymoon. Now that Kirsty was taking Greg's place, the enormous double bed had been made up as two queens fit for a very plush convent. Kirsty bagged the one nearest the bathroom by throwing her handbag onto the pillow.

Once inside, Jane made straight for the balcony doors. Kirsty followed her. The balcony was impressive but the excitement of having such a sumptuous cabin with a huge (by liner standards) balcony was lost on both girls right then.

'What did you say when we were going up the escalator in the terminal?' Kirsty pushed. 'Because if my ears didn't deceive me, I thought you said you had Greg in your bag. Greg, your fiancé.'

Jane nodded.

'Metaphorically or actually?' asked Kirsty.

'Actually,' Jane admitted.

'Oh. My. Days.' Kirsty put her hand to her forehead.

'Look, he always wanted to go to Rome,' Jane said, as she brought Greg's modest urn out of her case. A distribution urn, was what the undertaker had called it. It was biodegradable cardboard. And it was small. It surprised Kirsty how someone so big in life now took up so little space. 'And Marseille. And Barcelona,' Jane continued. 'He wanted to see those too. So I thought I would bring him with me.'

Kirsty gulped. But she put on a smile as she turned to her friend.

'Well, that's fine. I understand,' she said. 'It's probably for the best you didn't tell me before we got on board. What would you have said if a security officer had asked you what you were carrying?'

'I would have told the truth,' said Jane. Her eyes were glittering with tears. She sniffed hard and did her best to hide the fact she was about to cry from Kirsty by looking out onto the Solent.

'Come here,' Kirsty wrapped her arms round Jane and hugged her close. 'I'm glad you've brought him along. Really I am. It's only right that he should get to see all the places he dreamed of. Only you're not going to try and take him on and off the ship every time we dock, are you? I don't think my nerves could stand that.'

'No,' said Jane. 'I'll just show him the view from the balcony.'

'Bloody hell,' said Kirsty, taking the urn from Jane

and giving it an affectionate pat. 'Greg always said he would come back to haunt me.'

There was a knock at the door.

'Housekeeping!'

Kirsty stuffed Greg's urn up her jumper just as the on-board butler let herself in.

'If only Greg had known where he'd end up,' said Jane.

Chapter Twenty One

Jacqui

Once everybody was on board, before the ship could set sail, all the passengers and the crew had to practise the safety drill. Jacqui started worrying about it the moment she heard what they had to do. The first thing she did upon getting into their stateroom on Turtle Deck was check the sign on the back of the door for the position of their muster station. Dave had other priorities. He went straight to the fruit bowl on the well-polished coffee table and helped himself to a banana.

'It's good here,' he said.

They'd booked their cabin thinking they were going to be sharing with Granddad Bill and need wheelchair access, so it was one of the bigger suites with its own sitting room. Jacqui and Dave had never stayed in such a luxurious room in their entire lives. While Dave unpeeled a second banana, Jacqui panicked.

'We might have to pay for that,' she said. 'They're probably ten pounds each.'

'They're free,' said Dave. 'They're to welcome us on board.'

'How do you know?'

Dave passed his wife the little card that explained everything.

'Oh. Well, in that case.' Jacqui picked off a couple

of grapes and ate them while she inspected the rest of their accommodation for the fortnight.

'This is amazing,' she said, almost in tears again. 'I never thought we'd ever get to stay somewhere like this. But I feel so bad because your dad isn't here. He'd have loved this. And Sophie. It doesn't seem right to be doing all this without them.'

'They'll be having the time of their lives at Buchanan Manor,' said Dave. 'And I'm especially glad Dad's not here if it means we've got this lovely cabin all to ourselves.'

He grabbed Jacqui and gave her a cuddle.

'Not now. We've got to be at our muster stations at four o'clock.'

'That's nearly an hour away.'

'We don't know how long it will take us to get there. It took us ages to find our cabin.' Jacqui wriggled free of her husband's embrace.

'Crikey, Dave! Have you seen the bathroom?' she called a minute later. 'There's a whirlpool bath! Can you put bubbles in them? I'm not sure. Do you remember that programme we saw on TV where he put bubble bath in the Jacuzzi and flooded the whole house?'

Dave was already out on the balcony, taking in the sea air. He leaned out and saw that the people in the suite next door were taking the air too.

'All right?' he said, by way of greeting.

'All right,' responded two female voices.

Dave ambled back into the cabin.

'We've only been on board ten minutes and you're already chatting up the women next door.'

'And very lovely they are too,' said Dave, earning himself a swat with Jacqui's new 'nautical-themed' scarf. 'But you know I've only got eyes for you, my love.'

'That better be the truth,' said Jacqui.

She unwound her scarf. Dave took it as a hint and pitched her onto the bed.

'I told you! Not until we've done the muster!'

Jacqui got back up and this time she actually put her life preserver on.

'I'm wearing this all fortnight.'

Meanwhile, Ronnie and Chelsea and their entourage were in cabins on the deck below their parents – Orca Deck. When Jacqui booked the cruise, she'd assumed that Jack would be sharing with his parents, but somehow Jack had negotiated the same arrangement as in Lanzarote. He would be sharing with Auntie Chelsea again. That suited Chelsea, since she and Adam had decided it would be best for Adam and Lily to have a room of their own on this trip. They were still fairly careful when it came to sleeping arrangements back home and the last thing Chelsea wanted was to upset Lily on this cruise.

Besides, Chelsea didn't mind sharing with Jack. He was very sweet and easy-going and he had promised on his Sonic Screwdriver that he would not wake his aunt before seven. Especially not by shining said Sonic Screwdriver in her eyes. And while their stateroom wasn't huge, it was bigger than the room they had shared in Lanzarote and considerably nicer too. It was in a different league. There were no splatted mosquitoes on the walls for a start. The twin beds looked clean and comfortable and there were no rules about not putting toilet paper in the loo. It was all remarkably civilised and very tastefully decorated. There was a huge photographic print of Aix-en-Provence on the wall over the beds. Chelsea approved. She was especially looking forward to visiting Provence when the ship docked in Marseille.

Almost as soon as they were inside the cabin, Jack had spotted the bright orange life jackets stacked on the top shelf of the wardrobe. He insisted that his Auntie Chelsea fetch them down for him so he could take a closer look. Unfortunately for everybody, Jack's class had, like Lily's, been reading Michael Morpugo's *Kaspar* that term and thus Jack was full of facts and figures about the sinking of the *Titanic* that nobody really wanted to hear.

Chelsea helped Jack put one of the life jackets on. It was so big and square on his skinny little body that it made him look like SpongeBob Squarepants. As far as Jack was concerned, that was a big plus. He asked if he could wear it all the time.

'I'm sure you won't want to,' said Chelsea.

'I do,' said Jack, ricocheting through the cabin like a drunken banker in a sumo suit at a corporate shindig. He kept the jacket on while he unpacked his Dalek case.

Ted was soon installed on the pillow on Jack's bed. The *Doctor Who* figurines were arrayed in decreasing order of height along Jack's side of the table that separated his bed from Chelsea's. Meanwhile, Chelsea unpacked Jack's clothes. His little jeans with their impossibly tiny elasticated waist made her smile and she imagined for a moment what it might be like to be caring for clothes belonging to her own child. A child she might one day have with Adam. Chelsea's world was suddenly soft-focus.

'What's the matter?' Jack asked.

'What do you mean?'

'Your face has gone all funny, Auntie Chelsea.'

Chelsea quickly composed herself. 'Well,' she said. 'Your face looks funny all the time!' She went to tickle him. Jack squealed and bumped his way back towards his bed. If he was going to keep that jacket on, thought Chelsea, there was going to be some damage.

Chapter Twenty Two

Jane

After the dedicated butler who would be looking after Jane and Kirsty's suite for the fortnight was out of the way, Greg's ashes were safely installed in the safe. Jane felt odd about shutting him in there but Kirsty persuaded her it was the best, if not the only, place for him. They had no idea how rough the sea would be. If Jane put him on the table between the twin beds, which was what she wanted to do, a big wave might cause him to pitch off onto the floor. What if they weren't in the room at the time? What if the lid came off? Housekeeping might hoover him up, or throw the whole thing away. Greg's plain cardboard urn looked like nothing so much as an old-fashioned talcum powder tub to Kirsty.

Kirsty was possibly a little more brutal than she needed to be in her attempt to persuade Jane to put Greg out of sight but much as she had been fond of her best friend's fiancé when he was alive and taking the mickey out of her, she really wasn't keen on having to look at his mortal remains every time she woke up.

'The safe is just the right size. Tucked in there, he simply can't fall over. He'll be safe. Ha ha! You can take him out and look at him when you want,' she added.

Jane reluctantly put Greg into the little metal box. She chose the combination for the lock. It was Greg's birthday. September the eighteenth. One. Eight. Zero. Nine.

For the next hour the girls spent their time getting used to their cabin. Jane asked Kirsty to have the bed nearest the sliding doors to the balcony so she could be closer to the cupboard which contained the safe and Greg's ashes. Kirsty was fine with that. Then they divided up the wardrobe. That was slightly less equitable, since Kirsty seemed to have brought along every piece of clothing she owned, no matter whether it was suitable for the time of year or not.

'Do you think you'll need a Puffa jacket?' Jane asked.

'Can't be sure. Apparently, it can get quite cold at night when you're actually at sea.' Kirsty had also brought along an incredible number of pairs of shoes. She was one of those women who believed in having a different pair for every outfit. The concept of the capsule wardrobe was completely lost on her.

Jane had not brought much. She hadn't brought a single pair of heels. Kirsty's brow wrinkled as she looked at her friend's meagre luggage. There was nothing in there that suggested Jane was going to throw herself into the spirit of cruising and take the opportunity to dress up and let rip. In the end, Jane had left her carefully chosen trousseau behind – she just couldn't stand thinking back to how happy she'd felt as she bought it – and packed as though she was taking the train from Birmingham to Leeds, not for a Mediterranean cruise that would be taking in some of the most glamorous spots in the world.

'You know you're welcome to borrow anything of mine,' Kirsty said. Though Jane had lost so much weight since Greg died, anything she borrowed from Kirsty would hang off her like a rag. It would always have been too big, in fact. Kirsty was a good three stone heavier than her friend.

'Thanks,' said Jane.

There was a complimentary bottle of prosecco in the minibar. Kirsty fished it out, along with a couple of glasses.

'So,' she said. 'We made it on board. We've unpacked our cases, and Greg. How about we have a little drink to toast our first day at sea?'

'I might have some later,' said Jane. 'Still feels a bit early.'

Kirsty put the bottle back. 'I suppose you're right. And we've got to do that drill thing at four. Water?'

Jane accepted a glass of sparkling and they went out onto the balcony. They said 'hello' to the chap on the next balcony along. Kirsty raised her glass to him. The girls' cabin had a great view of the water traffic on the Solent. An enormous container ship was coming in on the other side. The sight of it was rather awe-inspiring. The bustle in the channel did make it feel as though an adventure was about to begin.

'Well, this is nice,' said Kirsty, hoping that it would be sometime soon.

Chapter Twenty Three

Everyone

At four o'clock precisely, the ship's horn gave the three short blasts that told the passengers and crew it was time to go to the muster stations. In their cabin, Jacqui and Dave had been ready to go for the past quarter of an hour. Jacqui had insisted upon it, telling Dave that he could have only one glass of complimentary prosecco before they did the drill. In the run-up to the big moment, there had been several announcements explaining that the safety drill was absolutely compulsory and that passengers would be counted in by means of the swipe cards they used to get into their cabins and pay for things on board.

Jacqui had always been the conscientious type, from when she was a little girl. She wasn't about to change. Dave grumbled but he knew there was no getting round it. Before the first blast of the horn sounded, Jacqui was in the corridor and heading for the muster station with the surety of a salmon heading home to spawn.

Next door, things were not going quite so smoothly. Kirsty may not have persuaded Jane to have any prosecco but she'd almost finished the half bottle herself. Whenever the muster announcements came on, Kirsty was more interested in the sound of the captain's voice than what he was actually saying.

'Do you think they have special classes at captain school where they learn to speak like that?'

When the horn blasts finally came, neither Jane nor Kirsty was sure what they actually had to do.

'Where do we have to go?' Jane asked.

It took them a moment to remember that the location was marked on the plan on the back of the door. And then they had some trouble getting the life jackets down from the high shelf in the wardrobe. And then Kirsty wanted to retouch her make-up. And then Jane headed for the safe. She plugged in the code.

'What are you doing? Kirsty asked.

'I've got to take him with me,' said Jane.

'No way,' said Kirsty. 'This isn't a real emergency. This is a drill. You are not taking that thing . . . I mean, Greg with you on a drill. Come on. We're supposed to be there already.'

Reluctantly, Jane picked up her life jacket and followed Kirsty out into the corridor. It was fortunate for her that Kirsty had worked out where they had to go. Jane was continually surprised by how 'out of it' she could be on a day-to-day basis. She would think she was doing all right and then she would find herself standing in the aisle at Tesco, with no memory of having driven there or collected a trolley or picked out the things with which she had filled it. She was having one of those moments now.

Maybe coming on the cruise was not such a good idea after all. She wasn't ready. She would never be ready. The thought of Greg, shut into the safe back in their cabin, suddenly had Jane feeling as though she couldn't breathe. She might as well have been shut in that safe too.

Kirsty soon noticed that her friend was lagging behind. She stopped to let her catch up. Jane leaned against the wall.

'I can't do this. I don't know what I'm doing here,' Jane said. 'Is it too late for me to get off?'

Kirsty came back to her. Jane was starting to cry.

'If you want to get off,' said Kirsty, 'we'll get off.'

Jane sank to the floor in the corridor with her chunky life jacket beside her.

'We can get off this ship whenever we like. Whenever we dock, we can walk off and fly straight back to the UK. And if you really want to get off now, we can just repack our bags, tell them we're going and have someone call a taxi to the train station. You don't have to do this. It's up to you.'

Kirsty sat down beside her friend. She took Jane's left hand, which still sported her loose engagement ring, between both of hers and rubbed as though she was trying to warm the hands of a small child just come in from the cold.

'You've been through an awful lot, my darling. And I know there's still much more to go. Things will never be the same. But you've been getting through it day by day and that's the way to keep on. We're only ever going to be at sea for a maximum of three days at a time. Every other day you'll have a chance to get off again. So you only ever have to get through seventy-two hours at the most.'

Jane nodded.

'That said, if you want to get off right now, then that is what we'll do. Otherwise, it's only three days before we're in Barcelona and we can get off there instead. There'll be loads of flights back to the UK from Barcelona. Or we can take a train. But that's up to you. If you really want off now, we're going. Just say the word. I'll sort everything out.'

Jane squeezed Kirsty's hand.

'I can do three days,' she said.

'Are you sure?' Kirsty asked.

'I am.'

Kirsty beamed. 'That's great. Then that's how we're going to do it. Day by day. You can let me know how you're feeling in every port.'

Jane got to her feet.

Another announcement was made, asking the passengers to hurry to their muster points.

'Come on,' said Kirsty. 'This is our best chance to scope out the talent.'

She took Jane's hand and they headed towards the stern.

Chapter Twenty Four

The Bensons

The muster for the stern section of Orca and Turtle Decks took place in one of the ship's nightclubs. Jack was all ears for the safety demonstration, just as he had listened with great interest to the safety talk on the plane to and from Lanzarote a year before. Ronnie was impressed that her son took such things seriously. She was less impressed when he 'sshhed' her for talking to Mark while the lady on stage was running through the way to wear a life jacket.

Jack, because he was small, would not be wearing the same kind of jacket as the adults. He was very disappointed that the huge orange device Auntie Chelsea had carried for him was officially too big.

Having shown the passengers how to put the life jackets on and make sure they wouldn't come off too easily, the crew members leading the muster practice gave instructions on leaving the ship if you weren't able to leave it on a lifeboat. All the first-timers were a little surprised by the advice that if they had to launch themselves off the side of the ship, they shouldn't jump but hold their noses and *step*.

'Step, don't jump? I ask you! If it comes to it, I'm bloody jumping,' said Ronnie.

'Don't say bloody,' said Jack.

'I'll swear all the way down.'

Jack practised holding his nose and stepping off an imaginary precipice. Lily did the same. Then the two children made Ted practise jumping – or rather *stepping* – off the back of a chair.

The demonstration continued. When the young woman in charge mentioned that the life jackets were equipped with a light and a whistle for 'attracting passing sailors' – a comment that made all the adults laugh – Jack caught sight of another young woman with red hair giving him a wink.

'That lady with horrible hair just winked at me,' Jack told his father in outrage.

'I hope you winked back,' said Mark.

'I can't take you anywhere,' Ronnie complained to her husband.

'I wasn't saying *I* would have winked back at her,' said Mark.

Ronnie folded her arms over the enormous orange vest.

'You look like Les Dawson in drag when you do that,' said Mark.

'Bad move, Mark,' said Chelsea.

'I don't think we're going to make it to our first wedding anniversary,' said Ronnie. 'I should never have married you. I had my freedom before. I could have left whenever I wanted. All I had to do was pack a bag. Now I have to get a divorce!'

'Mum!' Jack squealed. 'Don't say that!'

Having waited most of his life for his parents to get married, Jack was desperately sensitive to the idea that it might not stick.

'You can't get a divorce!'

'We're not getting a divorce,' said Ronnie, ruffling Jack's hair.

'If you ask me,' said Mark, 'it wouldn't be such a bad thing. Children of divorces get two lots of Christmas presents.'

'Do they?' Jack perked up.

'No they bloody don't,' said Ronnie. 'Don't encourage him.'

'Don't say bl—,' Jack managed before Lily held Ted up to his mouth.

While Mark and Ronnie were having one of their famously dramatic but good-natured spats, Adam found himself looking for the young woman who had been the catalyst for this latest outburst. The redhead was accompanied by a small blonde, as thin and delicate as a sparrow. Though it was a warm day, the blonde was wearing a thick woollen cardigan as if she were feeling the cold. Adam watched her as she watched the closest crew member running through evacuation proceedings. She tucked a strand of hair behind her ear in a gesture that seemed familiar, though Adam couldn't put a name to the person she reminded him of.

'Adam? Adam?' Chelsea broke into his thoughts.

'Sorry,' he said. 'I sort of zoned out. The demo was going on a bit . . .'

It was finished now.

'I hope you got the important parts,' said Chelsea.

'Step, don't jump,' said Lily.

'Good advice for every part of life,' said Adam.

The crew members checked everybody out of the muster stations. Life jackets had to be returned to cabins. After that, there was just time to get to one of the open decks to bid Southampton goodbye. The *European*

Countess would sail at six o'clock on the dot. Already, the gigantic chains that held her steady were being reeled in, groaning as they came.

'This is it!' said Jack. 'We're off.'

Chapter Twenty Five

Chelsea

Chelsea had not expected to feel such a wave of emotion as she did when the ship finally weighed anchor and set sail. As was traditional for a Countess Cruise ship, the *European Countess* did not bid goodbye to shore with a single blast of its horn but with a little tune: a jaunty hornpipe.

The guests were delighted. Some were also half-deafened.

'Note to self,' said Mark. 'Do not stand anywhere near the bloody horn.'

'Don't say bloody,' said Jack, delighted that he managed to get the whole word out this time before anybody could stop him.

Standing at the rail on the top deck, looking back over the dock, Adam slipped his arm round Chelsea's shoulder. He held Lily's hand. Lily reached for Jack's hand. Jack danced out of the way, right round the back of his aunt, and slotted his sticky little paw into Chelsea's free hand instead. Jack held Ted up to the rail so that she could see over.

'Say goodbye to England, Ted.'

Another blast of the horn.

'We're going!' Lily yelled. 'Goodbye! Goodbye! Goodbye!'

Jack joined his little friend in waving at the not

inconsiderable crowd that had gathered down below to see the *European Countess* off: friends, relations and ship-spotters.

Chelsea felt a lump rise to her throat as she imagined the many hundreds of thousands of people who must have sailed out of Southampton dock before her, some of them never to return. It was much more emotional than taking off in a plane, where everything happens so quickly and if you're not sitting in the window seat you've got no chance of seeing anything anyway. As the *European Countess* moved into the Solent, at a sedate speed of ten nautical miles an hour, it really did feel as though they were slowly tearing themselves away from their homeland. Smaller boats sounded their horns to wish her well.

'Oh, this is so poignant,' said Chelsea. 'Why do I feel sad?'

'We'll only be gone a fortnight,' said Adam.

'I know. But there's something about it, isn't there? This slow saying goodbye to England. It's like we're going for ever. I feel as if whatever happens, we're definitely going to come back changed. Is that nuts?'

'No. I think I know what you mean,' said Adam. He turned to kiss her on the cheek. Chelsea beamed at him.

Within minutes, Jack and Lily were bored of waving. Up on the top deck there was so much to do. The deck was home to the ship's gym and an impressive array of equipment for outdoor circuit work, should anyone be able to tear themselves away from the ship's even more impressive array of restaurants. While Adam and Chelsea watched the Isle of Wight come into view, Jack was busy amusing Lily with his pull-ups, as she held on to Ted.

Mark saw what his son was up to and waded in to give the boy a hand by lifting him from the waist.

'No, Dad!' Jack protested. 'I can do it myself.'

And he did. He managed two. Lily was slightly too small to reach the bars, so she let Mark lift her up. Her tiny arms quivered and gave in without her being able to raise her body an inch.

'Now it's your turn,' said Ronnie to her husband. 'Show us what you're made of, He-Man.'

Mark pretended to spit on his hands to give them better grip, and then he launched into a pull-up of his own. Lily, Jack and Ronnie watched in something approaching awe as Mark managed five, then ten, then fifteen pull-ups.

'It says here you're supposed to aim for fifty,' said Ronnie, pretending to read the instructions.

Mark carried on. All those years of lugging around kitchen appliances meant that he was surprisingly strong, though he had never deliberately seen the inside of a gym.

Then he let go and crumpled to the ground, clutching at his heart.

'Dad!' Jack squealed.

Jacqui's head whipped round from the view to see what had happened now. She and Dave rushed to their son-in-law's aid.

'Mark!' Ronnie fell to her knees at his side. 'Mark! Mark! What's happening?'

'I need the kiss of life,' Mark choked out. Ronnie, bewildered, pushed her hair out of the way and leaned over him.

'I don't know how to do this,' she said, in a panic.

At which point, Mark wrapped his arms round her neck and pulled her so that she landed on top of him.

Then he planted a smacker on her lips. Jack and Lily saw the joke at once.

'Oh no.' Lily rolled her eyes.

'You can stop kissing her now, Dad,' said Jack, after an excruciating (to him) twenty seconds.

'Kissing's disgusting,' Lily agreed.

It was a good job Lily had her back to Chelsea and Adam, who were at that very moment in a clinch of their own.

Chelsea and Adam remained at the rail, with their arms round each other, until the Isle of Wight was out of view. They were setting sail on a voyage of the heart.

Chapter Twenty Six

The Bensons

Jack and Lily broke into the romantic moment.

'We're hungry!'

But no one need ever be hungry on a Countess Cruise.

With the formalities of the muster and the ceremony of setting sail out of the way, it was time for the Bensons to get to know the *European Countess* properly. And there was so much to explore. The show-stopping atrium at the centre of the ship, with its grand, gold-accented spiral staircase and all that marble, was just the beginning. Six decks of accommodation were topped with seven more decks dedicated to eating, shopping and entertainment, including a five hundred-seater theatre and the spectacular Sky Walk, a glass-floored gallery jutting out from the fourteenth deck, which gave a vertigo-inducing view of the decks and ocean below.

'You won't catch me on that,' said Ronnie. 'Makes me ill just thinking about it.'

'Same for me,' said Jacqui.

By contrast, Jack and Lily couldn't wait to make the trip across the glass. Especially since Mark had likened it to walking the plank without having to get wet at the end. It was the very first thing they wanted to see.

After crossing the Sky Walk, Adam and Chelsea took the two children down another deck to look at the main swimming pool, with its fountains and shallow pools perfect for lounging with a cocktail. Blankets were being laid out on the sunbeds ahead of that evening's open-air cinema performance. That night, the outdoor screen would be showing *Jurassic Park*.

'At least they're not showing *Titanic*,' said Chelsea.

'When will they show *Frozen*?' Lily asked.

'I'm not sure,' said Adam. 'But I'm sure we can get it in our cabin,' he said, to avoid a pout. Lily soon forgot about her favourite film anyway. She'd seen a notice about ice cream and Jack had spotted the pizza bar.

'Can we get some?' he asked.

'I don't know, Jack,' said Chelsea. 'We ought to ask your mum. It's nearly dinnertime.'

'But I'm staaarving,' said Jack, letting his eyes roll back in his head and his knees buckle as though he really had been deprived of food for a month. He could do drama when he had to.

'A tiny piece won't hurt,' Adam suggested. Chelsea guessed that Adam didn't want to have to tell Lily 'no' right then.

'Just a tiny piece,' Chelsea echoed.

But there were no tiny portions here.

Chelsea's idea of an all-inclusive holiday was largely informed by the family's trip to Lanzarote the previous year. It brought to mind dubious-looking buffets, where you suspected the food had been out all week, and food poisoning. This was something else: freshly cooked pizza straight from the oven. And the moment they sat down to eat it – insisting on some semblance of manners to make up for the fact that they were eating between meals – a waitress appeared to take their drinks order. Lily and Jack had both ordered Cokes before Adam and Chelsea could stop them.

'I'm not sure you're allowed Coke,' Chelsea told Jack.

'It's not for me,' he said. 'It's for Ted. And she wants another piece of pizza too.'

While the children did the Sky Walk and ate pizza, Jacqui and Dave went back to their stateroom. Jacqui wanted to try out the whirlpool bath. Dave merely wanted a snooze on the bed covered in fat white pillows. They would both make the most of the five-star luxury that was to be theirs for two whole weeks.

Ronnie and Mark did not go straight back to their cabin. They'd decided to investigate the Anchor Bar at the bow of the ship but were waylaid on their way through the Sea View Court twenty-four-hour dining room. Mark's nose picked up the smell of Mexican food and he persuaded Ronnie that they should have just a few tortilla chips and guacamole to go with the margaritas they planned to order.

A few tortilla chips and some guacamole quickly turned into a full-blown 'pre-dinner' for Mark. How could he resist testing the boat's freshly made chilli?

'I love this ship already,' said Mark, as he held out his plate for a large spoonful.

'We're meeting the others for dinner in an hour.'

'It won't take me that long to eat this,' said Mark.

He was right. He chowed down as though he was in a competition.

'Do you think Chelsea's going to be all right sharing with Jack?' Ronnie mused as Mark sat back in his chair and groaned at the amount he'd just eaten.

'They love each other's company,' said Mark. 'Besides, Chelsea needs the childcare practice, doesn't she, if she's going to be moving in with Adam?'

'Has he said anything to you?'

'What?'

'Has Adam said anything to you about Chelsea moving in or getting married? Or has he asked you anything about our family? About what it's like to be part of it?'

'No,' said Mark.

'You will tell me if he does, won't you? I want to know everything.'

'I still think you're reading too much into things. So Adam went for a walk with Dad when we were round Annabel's. He's not going to propose. He's asked her to move in with him, that's all. If a proposal was on the cards, he would have done it then if he was going to.'

'Not necessarily. Perhaps he was sounding her out. He didn't want to ask the big question and get rejected so he's started with moving in. Baby steps.'

'Rubbish. What bloke ever gets rejected if he asks a woman to marry him? It's all you lot can talk about as soon as you're old enough to speak. It's all weddings, weddings, and weddings. Doesn't matter who the groom is. You'd have married Genghis Khan if he asked you before I did.'

'What? How can you say that?'

'Only joking, my love.'

'You're horrible, you are. I'm your wife.'

'Well, it's only a bit of paper, isn't it? We men see it differently from you women. And the way you women see it is downright scary. So don't go getting your sister's hopes up, is all I'm saying. Adam probably thinks he's already done all the committing he needs to for now, asking her to move in. If she starts banging on about getting married too, he just might change his mind.'

'I can't believe you think it's only a bit of paper. Why did you ask me if that's what you really think? Don't you feel any different being married than when we were just living together?'

Mark looked dangerously close to telling Ronnie 'no'. Being married did not feel any different from living in sin. It was true that they hadn't changed much, if anything, about their daily routine. Mark still left his socks on the floor next to the laundry basket instead of putting them in it. Ronnie still wore a fifteen-year-old Snoopy T-shirt to bed.

'Honestly?'

'Yes, honestly,' said Ronnie. 'This is your chance to save the whole holiday.'

'OK. If I'm being honest, I feel safer,' said Mark. 'You can't run away from me so easily now.'

Ronnie was pleased with that. 'Why would I ever run away from a man like you?'

Mark belched.

'Oh yeah,' said Ronnie. 'I forgot . . .'

Chapter Twenty Seven

Granddad Bill and Annabel

Back in Warwickshire, Bill and Sophie seemed to be settling in well at the Buchanans'. Sophie was delighted to be there, of course, and having spent so much time with her cousin, she already knew her way around the old house as though she'd lived there for years.

On the day that the *European Countess* set sail, Annabel helped Bill find the perfect spot in the conservatory, where he could enjoy the summer sunshine without being in any sort of draught. Leander was beside himself to have the elderly visitor in the house. For some reason – which everyone assumed to be the Trebor Mints – Leander had always adored Granddad Bill. At lunchtime, however, the dog didn't know quite where to put himself. Humfrey or Bill? Bill or Humfrey? Which of the two was more likely to drop food first? Neither was terribly good with solids.

After lunch, however, there was no contest. Whenever he could, Humfrey was always lunging at Leander, making a grab for his ears or tail. Leander took it well. He was very good with small children, patient and gentle, as was typical of his breed. But there was no doubt that Leander preferred the quiet life. So while Humfrey languished in his bouncer by the kitchen door, Leander followed Bill into the conservatory and settled down by the front wheels of Bill's chair, as if to stop the old man from rolling away. Leander didn't stir from the spot until his super-sensitive nose and ears picked up the smells and sounds of dinner being prepared in the kitchen that evening.

Annabel was relieved that everything seemed to be going so well so far. When she'd told Izzy that Granddad Bill was coming to stay, Izzy wasn't exactly thrilled with the idea but she had come round to it and was actually being extremely helpful; as was Sophie. Sophie was very good with Humfrey, having had plenty of practice with babies when Jack was small. The girls were taking it in turns to change nappies and do feeds.

And Granddad Bill was on good form. Fortunately, the antibiotics seemed to be kicking in. He was in much less discomfort than he had been when Jacqui called the doctor and though he asked several times where Jacqui and Dave had gone, he didn't seem unduly worried that they had left him behind. Perhaps having Sophie around reassured him, though he did keep mixing her up with Ronnie.

At dinnertime, Granddad Bill was seated at the head of the table (it was the easiest spot to get to with the wheelchair) with Leander at his side. Now that he was feeling better, he ate everything Annabel had prepared for him and asked for seconds. Annabel was enormously flattered whenever anyone asked for seconds.

And as the plates were cleared away, the inevitable happened.

'I'd like to show my appreciation to the chef,' Bill began, 'with a song.'

Izzy and Sophie shared a wide-eyed look.

'Oh, that's OK, Bill,' said Annabel. 'I'm sure you're

tired after a long day. I was thinking you might like to go straight to bed.'

'No, you've got to be properly appreciated,' Bill insisted. 'And so, I dedicate this song to you.'

Leander looked at Bill expectantly.

'I'm going to sing "Stand By Me".'

Izzy, Richard, Sophie and Annabel knew exactly how he would sing it: There was no point trying to stop him. Granddad Bill would never be stopped mid-song. He burped his way through the first two verses. Sensing defeat, everyone else joined in – with the singing, if not the burping – and they finished with a round of applause.

'No one who isn't related to us must ever know what kind of shit goes on in our family,' said Sophie to Izzy. The girls made a pinkie promise.

'Secret to the grave,' said Izzy. 'But I am going to ask him to teach me how to play the spoons.'

Jacqui had told Annabel all about Bill's evening routine. Thankfully, he didn't usually need too much physical assistance. It was more a matter of reminding him of what he needed to do than actually doing it. The en-suite bathroom was extremely useful.

Eventually, Bill was in bed, resting on the thick white pillows.

'Have you put the cat out?' he asked.

'We haven't got a cat,' said Annabel, fearing that this was a sign that Bill was getting confused again.

'I know,' said Bill. 'It's just something we used to say to each other, me and Jennifer. We never did have a cat either. It was just something we said. It was our joke.'

Bill's eyes looked far away and Annabel suddenly felt very sad indeed that she had never known her paternal grandmother.

Annabel leaned over the bed to give Bill a goodnight kiss.

'You look just like her,' he said.

It was a strange thing to be told you look like people you'll never know. Annabel had seen photographs of her grandparents on both sides and hadn't noticed much resemblance between herself and her paternal grandmother, but perhaps the resemblance was in gesture rather than actual physical appearance. Richard had remarked early on in their getting to know the Bensons that she and Ronnie had several similar tics. The way they laughed. The way they frowned. The way they both subconsciously rubbed an earlobe when being told something they didn't want to hear. They'd developed those ways of moving without ever having met each other until Annabel was forty-three and Ronnie in her thirties.

Meeting her birth family had been a bittersweet experience for Annabel. In the first instance, she had not wanted to go there at all. Then, when Izzy's need for a kidney donor forced her hand, she had still resisted the idea that she might grow to like the people who had, from her point of view, abandoned her, even though she needed so much from them.

She felt differently now. In the end, the Bensons had not been the key to Izzy's recovery, but they had definitely added to Annabel's life and that of the whole Buchanan family. Izzy had become incredibly close to Sophie and she had no other cousins but Sophie and Jack, the cousins who were related to her through the family Annabel had wanted to forget.

It was important for Izzy to know where she came from. For Annabel, there had always been a piece of the jigsaw missing. When she was growing up, she knew she could always rely on her adoptive parents Sarah and Humfrey to guide her in the wider world. They taught her manners and morals and gave her the education and polish she needed to succeed. But there were some questions to which they couldn't give her the answer. When was she going to hit puberty? Were her boobs really going to keep on growing? What can you do with lank straight hair?

The questions continued into adulthood. Every time Annabel went for a medical check-up and the doctor asked the family history questions. Every time she read an article that said the best way of finding out what your menopause will be like is to ask your mother.

Annabel wanted Izzy to know about her history and Bill was a big part of that history. Annabel was going to make the most of this opportunity to get to know him properly at last.

As she got into bed herself, Annabel texted Jacqui, though she wasn't sure whether Jacqui would be able to pick texts up until the *European Countess* was next in port.

'Granddad Bill safely tucked in. Sophie and Izzy still up chatting. Hope you're having a wonderful time on the high seas!'

Meanwhile, Cathy Next Door texted Ronnie to confirm that Fishy was very happily settled in on her front room sofa. Like Sophie, Fishy was rather glad to have a little break from Jack.

All was right in the world.

Chapter Twenty Eight

The Bensons

'Never a dull moment on a Countess Cruise'. That was the company's motto and it certainly seemed to be true so far. On the first night, returning to their staterooms – which nobody seemed to be able to stop calling 'cabins' –, all the passengers found a copy of the next day's itinerary tucked into the special letter holder to the side of the door. There were activities scheduled from dawn until dusk (and beyond), starting with a variety of exercise classes in the fitness centre and on the top deck at seven a.m.

'It's making me feel tired just thinking about it,' said Dave, when Jacqui told him there was a choice between Pilates, yoga and circuit training before breakfast if he fancied it.

Dave didn't fancy it. He lay down on the bed – he was very pleased with the bed – and let Jacqui continue to read aloud.

At eight o'clock, the action continued.

'You can do Zumba on the tennis court,' Jacqui told him.

'Or I could stay in bed.'

'At eleven o'clock, there's line-dancing!' Jacqui exclaimed. 'Oh, we've got to do that, Dave.'

'I can't dance.'

'It's because you never try. Oh! There's a chocolate tasting in the atrium at three.'

'Now that,' said Dave, 'might just be worth getting up for.'

Jack was much more enthusiastic about the possibilities on board. When he and Chelsea got back to their cabin, he snatched up the itinerary and went through it with a complimentary *European Countess* pencil, ticking the things he wanted to do. There were dozens of kids' activities: sport, art, cooking, acting.

While Jack planned his day, Chelsea remembered their last trip together. The days she'd spent with him at the Kidz Klub in Lanzarote had turned out to be surprisingly rewarding but, all the same, Chelsea was determined she would not be busting a lung in any kids' club races on board this ship.

'Adults can't go in the kids' club here,' said Chelsea. She had no idea if that was true but she and Adam and Ronnie and Mark had agreed that if Jack and Lily were happy to be at the club together, they would be very happy to let them get on with it. They'd been assured that the club was extremely well run. All the TripAdvisor reviews Chelsea and Ronnie had seen raved about the programme of activities for the under-twelves. It was very safe and secure. Children had to be signed in and out. Allergies and intolerances were catered for. The staff was highly trained and professional.

'They haven't lost a single child overboard this year,' said Mark.

'But what will you do while me and Lily are doing the activities?' Jack was worried for his auntie. 'Won't you be bored?'

Chelsea could imagine nothing better than the possibility to get very bored indeed. Now that she'd finished at *Society* magazine, the email traffic on her iPhone had dwindled from hundreds a day to around fifteen from people she actually liked. She'd brought dozens of books to read. And the prospect of spending a little time alone with Adam was bliss.

'If I get bored, I can always go and play bingo,' said Chelsea to Jack. There were four bingo sessions a day.

So Jack was persuaded that he need not worry about his aunt and as soon as the kids' club was open the following morning, he and Lily were in there, with Ted in tow, staking out the place and getting the measure of the other children. As Lily glared at a girl who was wearing the same *Frozen* T-shirt, Jack was very glad that Lily was officially his friend and it was unlikely they'd ever have a T-shirt clash.

Sitting by the pool in The Retreat, a part of the ship that was designated adults-only and tricked out like a fancy spa, Chelsea began to think she could get used to this cruising lark. Away from the main pool and the enormous cinema screen that ran pop videos when it wasn't showing films, The Retreat offered a very different experience, as grown-up and sophisticated as any expensive spa resort. There was butler service; sushi for lunch; smoothies made to order. A range of treatments that made Chelsea feel blissed out just thinking about them.

The first full sea day of the cruise the weather was beautiful and the sailing was smooth. Chelsea turned her face to the sun. With Adam beside her and two whole weeks of holiday time in front of her, she felt very happy indeed.

Chelsea found her niche in The Retreat. But the cruise really could be all things to all people. Every taste was catered for in the wide range of restaurants, the activities and the evening entertainments that ranged from hula hooping demonstrations to opera recitals. And far from feeling claustrophobic, the ship was so large that you could spend all fortnight on board and not see the same people twice. You definitely had to be quite specific when making arrangements to meet up with the people you *did* know.

Meanwhile, the stateroom balconies were well designed so as to be surprisingly private. Add to that the luxury of having a dedicated housekeeper who was always just a phone call away. There was free room service. Jacqui and Dave tried it out for lunch and confirmed that it worked.

At the end of their first full day at sea, everyone had something exciting to report and yet everyone had had a thoroughly different experience. Though they had all been on the same ship and travelled the exact same distance in nautical miles, it was as though they had been in different hotels in different resorts. Jack was full of praise for the kids' club table tennis facilities. For at least half an hour after Chelsea picked the children up, Jack talked of becoming a world table tennis champion. Meanwhile, Lily had spent the whole day in the club's princess-style Wendy house with its impressive array of dressing-up clothes.

'They had a proper bride's dress,' she said.

Jacqui and Dave had watched an old movie by the pool. Mark and Ronnie had tried out the Italian restaurant, the deli café and the ice cream parlour and found the closest sunbeds to the Anchor Bar where there was waiter service and an impressive array of bar snacks.

As far as the Bensons were concerned, the cruise was already a success.

Chapter Twenty Nine

Sophie

Back in the United Kingdom, Sophie was not missing her family at all. It was such a treat to be able to stay with Izzy and the Buchanans, even if Granddad Bill had crashed the party. Because Bill had the official best guest room, Sophie was staying in the attic room next door to Izzy's on the top floor. That was actually better, as far as the girls were concerned. Up there, away from the adults, the girls felt as though they were already sharing a flat, which was what they planned to do when they were both out of school and earning money. They were going to move to London as soon as they were able.

On Monday morning, Izzy and Sophie both had to start their internships. Because Granddad Bill was in the house and couldn't be left alone, the girls had to make their own way into Coventry on the bus. Annabel had to stay with Bill and Richard was in London for a couple of days. The girls felt terribly mature as they bid each other goodbye at the bus station and went to their respective offices.

Sophie was especially excited about her month at *County Class* magazine. She already knew a little bit about how magazines worked from having talked to Chelsea. She knew that they were produced months ahead of release and so she wasn't surprised to find that the *County Class* staff were already working on their

November issue. On her first day, while Izzy was sent to make tea for everyone at the solicitors' office, Sophie joined the magazine's planning meeting, sitting between the editor and his deputy. She was nervous and also thrilled to be included. She had not really expected to be allowed to do anything more exciting than count paperclips – definitely not on her first day.

As the meeting got under way, the seasoned staff members suggested themes for the fashion and features pages. Sophie was disappointed that their ideas were far from original: autumn colours on the fashion pages; bonfire night recipes; jacket potatoes and toasted marshmallows; a feature on a local author.

'What about you, Sophie?' asked Adrian the editor. 'Any ideas?'

Sophie sat up a little straighter. If she was surprised to be able to attend the meeting, she was flabbergasted to be asked her opinion. She took a deep breath to give herself time to marshal her thoughts.

'Well . . . this November is the seventy-fifth anniversary of the Coventry Blitz,' she said when she was ready. She knew this because they'd been talking about it over breakfast at the Buchanans'. The village church was going to be holding a special memorial service. Annabel was organising a lunch at the Great House for afterwards.

The rest of the staff looked slightly embarrassed that they hadn't thought of it first.

'Of course,' said Adrian. 'Why didn't we think of that?'

It was the night that had defined their city: 14th November, 1940. After months of small raids aimed at damaging the city's important factories, the air raid the Luftwaffe so romantically named 'Operation Moonlight Sonata' destroyed more than four thousand homes and the medieval cathedral. 568 people were killed, not counting those who died of their injuries later. More than a thousand were injured. Sophie had learned all about it both at school and at home. Granddad Bill's childhood home was among those flattened.

'It's a bit heavy, isn't it?' asked Zara, the deputy editor. 'We're more of a lifestyle magazine. History isn't our thing.'

'I don't know,' said Adrian. 'We're a Coventry mag. If everyone else is going to be covering it, then it will look a bit remiss if we don't. It doesn't have to be feel-bad. If we had a personal angle . . . from a survivor.'

'I can talk to my great-granddad,' Sophie said. 'He was about twelve when it happened.'

'And he's still alive? That's good going,' said Adrian. 'Would he be happy to be interviewed?'

'I think so. He never stops going on about the war,' said Sophie.

'Got any photos?'

'Loads,' said Sophie. Though she wasn't sure that was true. She would worry about that later. For now she was taking her Auntie Chelsea's advice and going in with as much confidence as she could fake. It seemed she was faking it pretty well.

'Excellent,' said Adrian. 'Would you like to do the interview, Sophie?'

Sophie's mouth dropped open.

'Zara will help you work out what to ask. And then perhaps you could have a stab at writing it up.'

'I . . .' Sophie began to say that she wasn't sure she was up to it but Adrian was already moving on.

'So, Sophie and Zara will be covering the Coventry Blitz. What restaurant reviews do we have for the month?'

Sophie wrote 'talk to Granddad Bill about Blitz' on her notepad. Zara the deputy editor gave her the thumbs up.

Sophie and Izzy met at the bus station for the journey home.

'How was your first day?' Izzy asked. 'Mine was so boring. I did loads of filing, made a hundred million cups of tea and I already know I don't want to be a lawyer.'

'Mine was interesting,' said Sophie. 'And guess what? I'm going to help write a feature for the November issue. Fifteen hundred words.'

'Ugh. That's like having to write an essay!'

'I don't mind,' said Sophie.

The only hard part would be getting Granddad Bill to make sense for long enough to get fifteen hundred words' worth of copy.

Chapter Thirty

Ronnie and Chelsea

Every day of the week there were religious services for all in the *European Countess*'s multi-denomination chapel, which was where you could also get married at sea.

'Perhaps we should go and have a look?' Ronnie suggested to Chelsea. 'Check it out.'

'Why? Are you and Mark thinking of renewing your vows?' Chelsea asked.

'Fat chance,' said Ronnie. 'Though if it's possible to get divorced at sea . . . No, I was thinking of you.'

'Me? Why would I need to look at the chapel?'

'Uh? Duh!' Ronnie pulled a face to suggest it should be obvious. 'You and Adam?'

'Don't be daft,' said Chelsea.

'Am I being daft though?' Ronnie asked. She raised her eyebrows suggestively.

'Probably,' said Chelsea. 'You're certainly being weird. Don't pull that face while you're standing on deck, will you? The wind might change.'

The sisters did not go to the chapel. They went instead to the spa to check out the available treatments.

'You know how I forgot your birthday?' Ronnie said as they stood at the counter, listening to the calming sound of Tibetan bells played over the loudspeakers.

'Yes,' said Chelsea, warily. She had not made a fuss about it, though truthfully she had been a little disappointed. Chelsea had never once forgotten Ronnie's birthday. Even when they weren't, in theory, on speaking terms, she had always made sure to send a card.

'Well, I'd like to make up for it now.'

'Oh. Thank you.'

'Let me get you a treatment.'

'Really?'

'Yes. It's my treat.'

Chelsea picked up the brochure.

'A manicure. You should have a manicure,' said Ronnie.

'But I had my nails done before we came away,' said Chelsea. She flickered them in front of her sister.

'It's quite a wintry colour that, isn't it?'

'It's the latest thing.'

'And it's chipped,' said Ronnie, leaping to point out the imperfection on Chelsea's right thumb.

'OK,' Chelsea gave in as it struck her that a manicure was the cheapest treatment on offer. Perhaps that's what Ronnie was really driving at.

'Excellent.'

Ronnie booked to have her nails done at the same time and within ten minutes they were ushered into a treatment room and seated side by side in enormous plush cream leather chairs that could give you a massage while a therapist attended to your hands.

'So,' said Ronnie. 'How do you think Adam is finding it so far, being on holiday with the whole lot of us?'

'I think he's having a good time,' said Chelsea.

'Jack certainly appreciates having Lily around. I've always thought it was a shame he doesn't have a cousin his own age. Sophie's got Izzy now. I know there's

Humfrey but he's so much younger. Lily, though, is Jack's contemporary. It'd be nice if they could grow up together and be friends when they're adults.'

'That's a long way off,' said Chelsea.

'Comes faster than you think,' Ronnie observed. 'Seems like just a few weeks ago that Jack was Humfrey's age. Anyway, all I'm saying is that we'd be very happy to welcome Adam and Lily to the family properly.'

'Thank you. That means a lot to me.'

'I mean officially. *Legally*.'

'Ronnie,' said Chelsea. 'What is this all about? Do you know something I don't?'

Ronnie shrugged.

'Ronnie . . .'

'Oh, I don't know. Mark says I'm being daft.'

'About what?'

'About you moving in with Adam and how I don't think that him asking you to move in is going to be the end of it.'

Chelsea turned to look at her sister, causing the therapist who was doing her nails to tut as the nail file slipped.

'Sorry,' said Chelsea, straightening up. This time she moved only her head to stare at Ronnie. 'What do you mean? Tell me what's going on.'

'Oh, I shouldn't say. Mark said I should keep my mouth shut.'

'You've already opened it. Better finish the sentence.'

'I shouldn't.'

'Ronnie, don't make me pinch you until you do.'

When the sisters were small, they'd often had fights that ended with Chelsea pinching Ronnie hard. Ronnie, as big sister, was not to fight back.

'OK. But you promise you won't tell Mark I told you.'

'I promise.'

Ronnie looked pleased with herself as she began.

'That afternoon we were at Annabel's, the day after the lottery numbers came up. Didn't you think it was strange that Adam went for a walk with Dad? A private walk?'

'I didn't think anything of it.'

'Come on. Our dad's great but I can't imagine him and Adam having that much to talk about. Unless . . .'

'Unless what?' Chelsea was getting really annoyed now.

'Unless he had something he wanted to ask for.'

'You're being way too cryptic for me, sis. What on earth would Adam want to ask Dad for?'

'Your *hand*,' Ronnie told her. 'In marriage.'

'Don't be silly,' said Chelsea.

'What's silly about that? He's asked you to move in with him and he asked to speak to Dad alone. What else did he want? Dad's advice on investments?'

'Maybe Adam really just wanted to see the war memorial.'

'Wouldn't he have been better off asking Richard to show him, in that case?'

'Dad knows a fair bit about local history,' Chelsea reminded her sister. 'That'll be all it was.'

'I don't know why you're so determined to think the worst,' said Ronnie.

'Think the worst? I'm thinking logically.'

'Well, I'm being optimistic. Which is why you don't want to have nasty bitten nails.'

'I don't bite my nails,' said Chelsea.

'Whatever. You want your hands to look beautiful for the ring pictures.'

'There will be no ring pictures!' Chelsea sighed.

'Have you chosen your colour?'

Chelsea had picked out a sort of grey-green that was all the rage since Chanel had put a version of the colour in their spring collection.

Ronnie pulled a face.

'That'll make you look like you've got some kind of fungus. I think you should go for something more neutral. That way, it won't matter what kind of ring he's bought.'

'Adam hasn't bought a ring,' said Chelsea firmly.

Truth was, Chelsea suddenly worried that getting a manicure would actually jinx her chances of receiving a proposal. Crazy!

'What do you have to do to get married at sea?' Ronnie asked the manicurist who was working on her own nails.

'I'm not sure,' said the young woman, whose badge announced that her name was Elena and she could speak five languages.

'Is it like Gretna Green? Do you have to be on board for a certain amount of time before you can do it? The captain is allowed to do the ceremony, isn't he?'

'Yes,' said Elena. 'We have lots of brides come here to get ready for their wedding day. My colleague, she was married on a ship. I could ask her.'

'Please don't,' said Chelsea.

'You could be married before you get back to Southampton!' said Ronnie.

'Ronnie,' said Chelsea. 'Shut *up*. I love you but sometimes you're a pain in the arse. Please don't go saying any of this nonsense in front of Adam. Or Dad. Or Mum. Especially not in front of Mum. I don't want her to get her hopes up.'

'Maybe her hopes are already up,' said Ronnie.

'What has she said?' Chelsea asked.

Ronnie mimed pulling a zip across her mouth.

'This isn't fair,' said Chelsea.

Chelsea refused to say another word on the subject until her nails were finished.

'There,' said Ronnie. 'Now you're ready for all eventualities.'

When they left the spa, Ronnie and Chelsea went to find the men and the children in the pizza bar for lunch.

'Can I see?' said Lily, when she heard about Chelsea's nails. 'Oh, I like that colour! It's like a princess would have.'

'Thank you,' said Chelsea.

'Let's have a look at those princess fingers,' said Adam.

Chelsea held her hands in his direction. Adam caught Chelsea's left hand. He turned it this way and that so that the nail polish gleamed in the light.

'You have such beautiful hands,' he said, seeming to linger as he ran his thumb along each of her fingers in turn. Chelsea had such a strong sort of premonition of Adam taking her hand in earnest that she had to look away to compose herself. She couldn't help wishing that Ronnie's daft predictions might be right.

Chapter Thirty One

Ronnie

It just so happened that the Bensons' third night on board the *European Countess* was a 'formal night' when guests were invited to don their finest clothes for dinner. It wasn't compulsory. You could stay in your jeans and eat in the Sea View Court. But if you wanted to go to one of the smarter restaurants on board that evening, you had to dress up.

'I'm dreading this,' said Mark.

Ronnie had hired him a penguin suit from the cruise line's recommended outfitter. It had been delivered to the cabin and was hanging in the wardrobe when Mark and Ronnie arrived. Mark pulled it out of the polythene.

'I don't even know what this is,' he said, examining the cummerbund.

While Mark struggled to get his trousers on, Ronnie got the dress that Annabel had lent her out of the wardrobe and placed it reverently on the bed. She had not actually looked at it properly since she tried it on in the bedroom at Annabel's house. Once it was decided that Ronnie would take the dress, Annabel had wrapped it in tissue paper (she had a whole ream of tissue paper for just that purpose in the bottom of her wardrobe) and put it inside a garment bag to keep it from creasing. Ronnie had transferred it to her suitcase and thence to the cabin wardrobe without taking it out. Now that she did, the dress seemed impossibly tiny, though it had fitted her perfectly just a short week ago, and she'd been attempting to do the 5:2 since (not easy on a cruise ship). Now Ronnie could only think she'd made a terrible mistake. She would never get into it.

'Is that what you're wearing?' Mark asked.

'No,' said Ronnie, picking it back up. She'd have to wear the black midi-dress that she always wore whenever they had to go somewhere special. It wasn't special in itself but it was inconspicuous and that was suddenly what she wanted to be.

'Why not?' asked Mark.

'Because I don't think I can get into it.'

'Then why did you bring it?'

'I don't know.'

'I haven't seen it before, have I? When did you get it?'

'I didn't buy it, if that's what you're worried about. It's Annabel's.'

'Well, you should be able to get into it then. She's bigger than you are.'

Ronnie looked at Mark in disbelief.

'Is she?'

'Yeah. Not up top but definitely round the bottom.'

'Why were you looking?'

'I couldn't help it. She was blocking out the sun.'

Ronnie hesitated to laugh. 'Don't be so rude. She's my sister.' But she was secretly pleased.

'Just put the dress on,' said Mark. 'We're keeping everybody waiting. And I need you to help me with my tie.'

Mark did not need help to put on his bow tie. It was elasticated.

Ronnie took the dress into the tiny bathroom, not

wanting Mark to see whether or not the dress fitted before she had decided for herself. It was tough, getting changed in that small bathroom. At one point, Ronnie backed herself into the shower curtain and got a wet arm. But eventually she was in the frock.

'You look amazing,' said Mark, as he heard the bathroom door opening.

'I haven't even come out of the bathroom yet,' said Ronnie. 'Don't tease me. You're to be honest if you think I look like a sausage coming out of its skin.'

When Ronnie did finally venture out of the tiny cubicle, Mark didn't need to say anything at all. The expression on his face did all the talking for him. His mouth dropped open in delighted surprise.

'Do you like it?' Ronnie asked as she turned one way and then the other.

Mark just nodded, still open-mouthed.

'You don't think it's a bit much?'

'Don't talk yourself out of it,' said Mark. 'My love, you look like a goddess. That dress was made for you. I don't think I've ever seen so much . . .' he indicated an hourglass with his hands, '. . . va-va-voom.'

Ronnie's face relaxed at once.

'It bothers me, you know, that I can't just give you the money to go out and buy dresses like that one whenever you feel like it. You deserve to have things like that.'

'Mark Benson-Edwards,' said Ronnie, cupping her husband's face in her hands. 'You give me everything I need.'

The door to the cabin was ajar and Jack let himself in.

'Nooooo!' He shrieked with horror. 'They're kissing again.'

Jack held Ted in front of his face for protection.

'Your mother is a very beautiful woman,' Mark told his son.

Jack looked at his father as though he had just said, 'Your mother is a shape-shifting witch.'

Chapter Thirty Two

The Bensons

Everyone made a real effort that evening. Chelsea wore a little black number that was straight out of *Breakfast at Tiffany's*. Jacqui was resplendent in pale green Jacques Vert. Dave and Mark looked remarkably dapper in their suits. Adam was no stranger to wearing a jacket – he often wore one when meeting clients at the architectural practice where he worked – and he put his on as happily as if he were slipping on a T-shirt and jeans. Likewise, despite his tender age, Jack was already a big fan of formal wear. He was delighted to wear a bow tie because it reminded him of one of his heroes: Matt Smith, a former incarnation of Doctor Who.

Lily had chosen to put on her full *Frozen* regalia. She'd been given the Elsa costume for her birthday by one of her godmothers and it was the first piece of clothing she put into her luggage. Chelsea's explanation of the wonders of a capsule wardrobe had captivated Lily but in the end she built her particular capsule wardrobe around a pair of sequined ballet shoes from Monsoon.

Chelsea's challenge that evening had been to do Lily's hair to match. The *Frozen* 'fish plait', as Lily called it, was fiendishly complicated and Lily's hair was so baby-soft and fine that it wouldn't stay put. Chelsea resorted to using enough hairspray to cut Lily her very own hole in the ozone layer.

'How do I look?' Lily asked Jack when they met in the queue for the restaurant.

There was very nearly an incident when Jack replied, 'You look like the toilet roll holder at Grandma's.'

Thankfully, the Bensons were shown to their table before Lily could properly absorb Jack's unfortunate and almost certainly unintended insult.

Everyone liked the restaurant, which was modelled on a glamorous fifties brasserie, full of mirrors and low-hanging lights. And there was something very relaxing about being in a restaurant where everything except the premium alcohol was already covered.

The children were extremely well catered for. The special junior menu was full of things to please even the fussiest child. Ronnie was relieved that Jack was on his very best behaviour, charming the American waitress – Michele from Florida, speaker of four languages including Mandarin – who was assigned to their table.

'Your accent is so cute,' she told him.

'I haven't got an accent,' said Jack. 'You've got an accent.'

Ronnie widened her eyes at him, to warn him not to elaborate.

'Oh, you're so funny,' said the waitress.

'She said I had an accent,' said Jack, once the waitress was out of earshot.

'Well, you have,' said Chelsea. 'To her.'

'I haven't got an accent,' Lily said firmly. 'Because I go to a school where accents are not allowed.'

All the adults looked at her curiously. Adam closed his eyes in horror.

'That's not quite true, Lily,' he said. 'But they do try to make sure the children speak clearly,' he continued for the benefit of the adults. 'And stamp on all that business of saying "like" and "innit".'

Chelsea feared that Ronnie would take it as some sort of dig. Lily was at a private school. Jack was at the local state primary. So Chelsea was relieved when Ronnie leaned across the table towards Adam and said in a ridiculously plummy voice, 'Oh, I know. Every day I'm like, "Jack, you've got to like speak proper, innit".'

The adults laughed but everyone was grateful when the waitress returned with the bread rolls.

'No throwing them,' said Ronnie to the children. 'Remember we are being posh tonight. Our manners must match the occasion.'

'My manners are always good,' said Lily.

'I'm not sure it's good manners to point that out,' said Adam.

'Pointing definitely isn't good manners,' said Jack. 'If you see someone who looks really weird at the bus stop, you must never point and laugh. You must cover your mouth and whisper so they don't know that you're talking about them.'

'I don't know where you got that from, Jack Benson-Edwards,' said Ronnie.

'I got it from you,' said Jack.

'And you mustn't burp at the table,' said Lily, warming to the theme. 'But Dad said it's OK when Granddad Bill does it because he's old and people used to burp all the time in the olden days because they only had cabbage to eat.'

'Children say the funniest things,' said Adam. 'I don't think you heard that from me, Lily Baxter.'

'I did. And it's true because it's in Roald Dahl.'

'*Charlie and the Chocolate Factory*!' said Jack. 'They all had cabbage all the time. It makes you fart as well. Like this.'

Jack's expression was full of concentration as he strained to break wind to order.

'Jack!' said Ronnie. 'We're supposed to be having a sophisticated evening.'

Inspired by Jack, Lily took a big gulp of her Coke and transformed it into an enormous belch.

'Lily!' Adam cried.

'It's a good job we're not on the captain's table,' said Jacqui. 'He'd have you both walking the plank.'

'Is there an actual plank on this ship?' Jack asked his father.

'I expect so,' said Mark. 'So you'd better be on your best behaviour.'

Jack and Lily shared a look of horror.

'He's joking,' said Ronnie. 'But there is definitely a police cell. I'm going to ask if you can both be taken there right now.'

'Nooooo!' the children wailed. 'We'll be good again. We promise!'

Chelsea pinched the bridge of her nose to prevent herself from bursting out laughing. Thank goodness the waitress was back with the starters.

'I've forgotten how to eat soup,' said Mark. 'I know there's a way to do it proper but I can't remember. How does Annabel do it?'

'With a spoon, you donut,' said Ronnie.

After dinner, the whole family made their way to the ship's theatre to see that evening's entertainment. The show was called *Mysterioso* and there was a touch of the Cirque du Soleil to it. Jacqui gushed that they couldn't have seen anything better in the West End. Even Chelsea, who sometimes acted as though she had seen it all while living in London, was quietly impressed.

Jack and Lily were enthralled. When the show ended, they danced out of the auditorium, pausing only to attempt unsuccessful cartwheels in imitation of the show's stars. Alas, neither Jack nor Lily was especially good at gymnastics so they settled in the end for whirling each other round and round down the long corridor decorated with photographs of the destinations the Countess fleet visited: Athens, Venice, Florence, Rome.

Adam pointed out a shot of Barcelona's exotic Park Güell.

'Tomorrow,' he said, 'we'll actually be there.'

Chapter Thirty Three

Kirsty and Jane

Kirsty and Jane did not join the other passengers for the formal night. Though Kirsty had packed at least four knockout dresses she would have appreciated the opportunity to wear, she was unsurprised that Jane was not so keen on getting scrubbed up. Jane's meltdown on the way to the muster on the first day had set the tone for the cruise so far. She had been very subdued. Kirsty got Jane to take a turn round the top deck for some air after breakfast each day but most of the time, Jane just wanted to be on their stateroom's private balcony. And the blasted room service was making it all too easy for her to get her way. Kirsty was beginning to wonder whether she shouldn't have just helped Jane off the ship while they were still in Southampton.

'Are you sure you don't mind not going up to join the party?' Jane asked. 'I know you were looking forward to getting dressed up.'

'There will be plenty of opportunities to get dressed up on this trip,' said Kirsty. 'Besides, this is none too shabby, is it? We're sitting on our own private balcony. We've got room service. And an amazing view.'

They'd seen a school of porpoises a little earlier. Jane seemed to lighten up just a little when she saw the sleek black mammals skipping through the waves. Their dancing and dashing would have brought a smile to the saddest of faces. Then Kirsty commented that the porpoises reminded her of the way her dad could make stones skip across the sea. And that reminded Jane that Greg could also do that thing with pebbles and the gloom descended again as she reminisced about an afternoon on the beach soon after she and Greg first got together. He'd taken her for a surprise picnic. It seemed there was nothing – no topic of conversation – that Jane could not bring back round to Greg.

'You won't let me stop you from making the most of things though, will you?' Jane said. 'If you want to go and do something, promise me you will?'

'Sure,' said Kirsty.

'I saw they do karaoke every night.'

'Do they?' Kirsty feigned disinterest.

'Come on,' said Jane. 'You love karaoke.'

'When I'm out with a gang of mates,' Kirsty qualified.

'Karaoke nights at the Welsh Harp,' Jane said suddenly. 'Always the same people every week. Remember that bloke who thought he was the next Michael Bublé? The one with the comb-over?'

'How could I forget him?' said Kirsty. 'He asked me to duet with him. Said we should audition for *Britain's Got Talent* together.'

'What a come-on.'

'He had a good voice but I couldn't take my eyes off the flap of hair on his head that always came unstuck halfway through the night and ended up blowing in the wrong direction.'

Jane laughed.

'What happened to him? He just suddenly stopped coming.'

Kirsty shrugged. 'Dunno.' Though she'd heard the

bloke had a heart attack and died. That was the last thing she wanted to tell Jane.

Jane's face had already settled back into the plain old mask she had been wearing since Greg's death.

'You should go and do the karaoke,' she said to Kirsty.

'Some other night,' said Kirsty. 'I'm very happy to stay here and watch the sun go down from the balcony.'

They ordered food – enormous club sandwiches, on a bed of potato chips, garnished with two bits of lettuce as a nod to healthy eating – and Kirsty opened the first of the two bottles of wine they had brought on board. Jane turned down a glass in favour of sparkling water. Kirsty knew better than to try to press it upon her. She understood that Jane was afraid that drinking alcohol might let the genie out of the bottle.

The food was delicious. Jane didn't touch much but Kirsty helped her out with that. The portions were huge. It was going to be tough to get home from this cruise without having put on a stone. Maybe she would get up for a Zumba class the next day. Maybe not.

'We had some great nights at the Harp, didn't we?' Kirsty said.

'Yeah,' said Jane.

Jane had met Greg there. She was with Kirsty, of course. They always went to the Harp at the weekends and often on a Wednesday for karaoke. That night, Kirsty did her usual song – 'It's Raining Men'. She belted it out with such *joie de vivre* that everybody always joined in by the end. Later that evening, she tried her hand at 'Back To Black', but Amy Winehouse's anthem was slightly wrong for Kirsty's range and she ended up with her chin on her chest as she tried to hit the lowest notes. She didn't try anything by Winehouse again.

The girls had never seen Greg in the Welsh Harp before that night. They clocked him as soon as he walked in. At that time, both Jane and Kirsty were single and looking so they were well attuned to the arrival of any fresh meat.

'Not bad,' said Kirsty. 'Bit short for me.'

But for Jane, who was three inches shorter than Kirsty, he was perfect. And, it turned out, not just in the way he looked.

That night, Greg persuaded Jane to duet with him. They sang 'Summer Loving', which is actually a terrible song for someone who can't really sing, as was the case with Greg. But though he hit about one note in three, Greg had the audience in the palm of his hand with his jokey delivery and his impromptu dance-routine in the middle. He also sang the high-pitched girls' chorus in response to Jane's impression of Olivia Newton-John. Kirsty, in the front row of the audience, was doubled over with laughter. And so was Jane by the time she and Greg left the stage.

Yes, it was clear from the very beginning that they would be a fantastic double act.

Only Jane's mother sounded a note of caution when she heard about her daughter's new flame.

'He's a soldier, love. Soldiers spend a lot of time away from their families. It's a dangerous job. Do you want to spend all your time worrying? And what if you had children? And something happened to him?'

While Greg was in Afghanistan, Jane felt as though she was in a state of suspended animation. When work finished, she would immediately log on to the BBC news website via her iPhone and literally hold her breath until she'd checked the headlines. Reassured that there had been no casualties since she last looked, she would go into the supermarket and get herself something for tea. Then she'd call Kirsty and they'd arrange to go out. There were advantages to the fact that Kirsty was still single (though she was always looking). Jane never had to stay in on her own if she didn't want to.

Jane had wondered what it would be like when Greg was home all the time. It sounded like a dream, having him come back to her every evening. He was going to work as a plumber. But would he find it boring, going from the high-adrenalin environment of the front line to normal civilian life? Jane heard horror stories about retired soldiers who just couldn't settle back into the mainstream. They needed that adrenalin rush and they'd find a way to get it.

Jane sometimes wondered whether it was that need for adrenalin that led to Greg's unexpected death. Not in the face of enemy fire but in a horribly ordinary traffic accident. The other driver, who died at the scene, was definitely drunk. Greg wasn't around to tell his side of the story but was he entirely blameless? Was he driving too fast? Had he squeaked through on a red light, as he sometimes did when Jane was in the car beside him, gripping the side of her seat and shrieking at him to slow down? Jane hated herself for even thinking that might be the truth.

'Earth calling Jane,' said Kirsty. 'Do you want to come to the atrium to get an ice cream?'

Jane did not. From thinking about the first time she met Greg, her thoughts had travelled all the way to the very last time she saw his face. It would not be easy to eat ice cream when her mind's eye was still seeing Greg in his hospital bed.

'OK. I might just go down to the atrium to stretch my legs,' said Kirsty.

'Sure.'

Jane waved her off.

Chapter Thirty Four

Kirsty

At nine o'clock in the evening, the deck where Jane and Kirsty's stateroom was situated was eerily silent. Everybody was elsewhere enjoying the ship's entertainment. Kirsty felt a little nervous in the long narrow corridors on the accommodation decks, which brought to mind the scene in *The Shining* where the kid rides his tricycle through the empty hotel. She raced to the lift, wanting to be with other people as quickly as possible.

Stepping out of the lift onto the seventh deck was like stepping into a different world. This was the deck where everything happened: restaurants, bars and shops. It was so busy. It reminded Kirsty of the scenes of Las Vegas she'd seen on television. Vegas was somewhere Kirsty had always wanted to go. Walking through the atrium towards the bow, she peered down into the casino on the deck below. There everyone was playing his or her part in the movie in Kirsty's mind to the max. A small man in a smart suit was splashing the cash, putting chips on everybody's lucky numbers. He had a woman draped over each shoulder, competing to show the most cleavage. Kirsty wondered how much he would have to win before one of them accompanied him back to his cabin.

In the centre of the atrium, which became a stage by night, the ship's very own hula hooping marvel was giving her nightly display. Kirsty paused to take a look. The girl started out with just a couple of hoops but within moments she'd added several more. Six, eight, ten, twenty! Kirsty held her breath as the girl disappeared in a blur of colour, transforming herself into a human slinky, as the hoops whirled and undulated around her. The effect was tremendous. Kirsty wouldn't have been surprised if, when the hoops finally dropped to the ground, the girl was gone. The hoops dropped. The girl took a bow. Kirsty applauded enthusiastically.

Passing by the ship's luxury gift shop, Kirsty spotted a crowd gathered around a young man with a tray. Perhaps she smelled the chocolate before she saw it. Kirsty joined the queue and helped herself to a couple of truffles – one for herself and one for Jane. Unfortunately, the one Kirsty tasted first was so delicious – a sort of passion fruit parfait – that Jane never got to taste hers. Kirsty told herself it would have melted before she could get back to their room anyway. She'd buy Jane a whole box later on.

On the other side of the atrium, in the ship's most glamorous bar – Songbirds – the resident crooner was just beginning his act. Dressed in a tuxedo, he was straight out of the Rat Pack. Kirsty leaned against a wall to listen for a while. He was very good. He soon lifted the energy, which was already high, with his rendition of 'Luck Be A Lady.'

Kirsty loved those old Sinatra songs. 'Fly Me to the Moon'; 'The Lady is a Tramp'; 'Strangers in the Night' . . . She sometimes thought she had been born in the wrong era. Her tastes were out of time. Even her figure was out of time. She looked much better in fifties' style wiggle dresses than the modern uniform of skinny jeans. Glamour was definitely her thing.

Feeling a little too self-conscious to buy herself a cocktail and stay there on her own, Kirsty slipped out of the bar and followed the stream of people towards mid-ship. Here a pop-up photographic studio had been set up so that the passengers could pose in their formal night finery. The backdrop was of a starry sky. Kirsty smiled as she watched a couple who must have been in their sixties transformed into love-struck teenagers again when the photographer asked them to recreate their first kiss for the camera. The wife blushed when her husband said, 'She's just as lovely as she was back then.' The wife revealed that they were celebrating forty years of marriage. Her confession drew a round of applause from everyone within earshot. The photographer took another photo of the couple as they hugged in delight at the reaction of their fellow passengers. That would turn out to be the best shot.

Kirsty could see how this might have made the perfect honeymoon for Jane and Greg.

Moving on, Kirsty happened upon the karaoke, which was being held in the ship's television studio. Yes, the ship was so big it even had its own television studio, where news and chat shows were recorded for the ship's own TV channel every day. The auditorium-style layout of the studio meant Kirsty didn't feel so self-conscious as she might have done. It wasn't immediately obvious that she was there on her own when she slipped in to join the excited audience. A blast of feedback announced that the mike was on and the first contestant took the stage.

Kirsty was her very own panel of *X Factor* judges as she watched her fellow passengers take their turns at the mike. It was the usual mix of awful and amazing. Since

Susan Boyle, everyone expected the less conventionally attractive people to have the best voices. Unfortunately, SuBo's gift was rare indeed. Likewise, good looks didn't guarantee a good performance. There were plenty of people who looked the part and had all the actions but who couldn't sing a note. Kirsty winced her way through a performance of 'My Heart Will Go On' by a woman who'd clearly had a little too much Dutch courage before she went on. Still, she gave it her all and her mates gave her a standing ovation.

Likewise, the bloke who sang 'New York, New York' did not compare well to the professional crooner in Songbirds. He murdered every note. Not that his family cared. They whooped their appreciation and were so enthusiastic that Kirsty couldn't help whooping too.

A young girl went next. She was about fifteen, Kirsty guessed.

'And what would you like to sing?' the compère asked.

'I'm going to sing "Let It Go",' she said.

That drew a mixture of groans and sighs from the crowd. You either loved it or hated it. Kirsty secretly loved it. She had a DVD of *Frozen* back home. A gift bought for her half-sister India but never given after India announced one Sunday lunch that *Frozen* was 'lame' . Lame or not, that film had Kirsty crying buckets within the first ten minutes every time. She knew all the words to its anthem.

Fortunately, it was possible to adjust the soundtrack so that it wasn't immediately obvious that the girl's voice was too small for such a big song. In any case, just watching her movements was entertainment enough. She had obviously watched plenty of *X Factor* auditions in her short life. She closed her eyes and waved her arms around. If you closed your ears, she was the perfect diva in waiting. Kirsty clapped hard when the song came to an end.

Kirsty had not intended to sing that evening. She generally needed a drink or two first and though she had probably had half a bottle in the cabin, the downbeat atmosphere that followed Jane around had a strangely sobering effect. So, Kirsty surprised herself when she got up next and told the compère she'd like to sing Adele's 'Someone Like You'.

It wasn't exactly upbeat but then Kirsty didn't quite have the energy she needed to sing 'It's Raining Men'. 'Someone Like You' was a better match to how she was feeling. She wanted to sing but she couldn't imagine belting anything out. Someone cued the song and Kirsty took the mike.

The audience stilled as Kirsty sang. 'Someone Like You' wasn't one of those songs that encouraged singing along to the chorus. Kirsty began to wonder if she had chosen the wrong song. Here were all these people, on their holidays, all dressed up and ready for a good time and she was singing about lost love. She should have gone for 'It's Raining Men' after all. When Kirsty finished singing, the audience remained silent for just long enough for her to panic before they rewarded her with a very healthy round of applause and a fine selection of whoops.

'Thank you,' she said, offering them a little bow.

'There's a proper competition later in the cruise,' one of the other passengers told her when she got back to her seat. 'You should have a go. The prizes are really good. And you've got a great voice. You could be a professional.'

'Thanks,' said Kirsty. 'You're very kind.'

* * *

But she nearly *had* been a professional. As she walked the long walk back to the stateroom she shared with Jane, Kirsty's thoughts drifted to her mum. Kirsty's mum Nicole had a great voice. That was where she got it. Nicole had encouraged her daughter to have all those singing and dancing lessons when she was small, perhaps hoping that Kirsty would fulfil the dreams Nicole herself had abandoned when she met Kirsty's dad and got pregnant so soon after.

When Kirsty was about seven, Nicole took her for her first professional audition. It was to play the daughter in an ad for an energy company. Though officially she had 'given up on all that', Nicole still read *The Stage* in the local library.

The audition was a secret. Kirsty was not to tell her dad. Kirsty's dad, Stu, would not have approved. He was OK with Kirsty having ballet lessons and doing singing and things like that. That's what little girls did, while boys played football. But the idea that Kirsty would take the singing and dancing beyond a hobby bothered him.

So, Nicole pretended she was taking Kirsty to stay with her gran. Luckily it was half-term, so she didn't have to miss any school. The auditions were held in the offices of an advertising agency in London. When they arrived, the waiting room was full of girls who looked perkier and prettier but Kirsty got the part. She'd aced her time in front of the producers, singing 'Over The Rainbow' – her mother's favourite song – as though her heart was breaking. The producers were so impressed they told Kirsty she was their girl before she left the room.

Kirsty had never felt so loved as she did right then. Her mother picked her up and danced her around, singing the theme from *Fame*. Nicole had introduced her daughter to the television series early on.

'Fame costs . . .' Nicole prompted.

'And right here's where you start paying,' Kirsty completed the line.

More than twenty years later, Kirsty could still remember how wonderful it had felt to please her mother so much. The memory of Nicole's glittering eyes and the feel of her hugs and kisses was as fresh as if the whole thing happened yesterday. Her mother had assured her, 'This is it, baby. This is just the beginning.'

But it wasn't to be. Nicole told her husband the news over dinner. Stu did not dissolve into laughter and joy and fatherly pride, as Kirsty had hoped he would. Instead, he said, 'You must have danced and sung very well,' to Kirsty. Then he asked her to leave the table while he and her mother had a 'chat'.

It was a very loud chat that Kirsty could hear from the top of the stairs, which was where she hid, with her face pressing through a gap in the bannisters. She knew that her fate was being discussed.

'I'm not having her on the telly, Nicole. It will change everything and not for the better. She won't be able to walk down the street. She'll get picked on at school. At the very best, she'll start thinking she's worth more than the others. It'll spoil her for real life.'

'She wants to do it.'

'She doesn't know what she wants. She's a seven-year-old. She has no idea what the fall-out could be like. Look, I'm all for her carrying on with the dancing classes as a hobby but you're not to take her to any more professional auditions. Call whoever you need to call first thing tomorrow and tell them she's not doing it.'

'I can't. She'll be devastated.'

'She'll have forgotten all about it in a week.'

'I won't do it, Stu. I won't.'

'If you don't, I will. You're not thinking straight. You've got to put our daughter first and if that means disappointing her, that's what will have to happen. This is not about you, Nicole. It's not always about you. You've got to let Kirsty have her own dreams. She doesn't want yours second-hand.'

'This *is* my own dream!' Kirsty wanted to shout. But she was too frightened. After all, she wasn't supposed to be listening.

It was the first time Kirsty had heard her parents argue but it wasn't to be the last. Three years later, when they separated, Kirsty couldn't help wondering if it was partly her fault for acing that long-ago audition.

Alone in the corridor of Turtle Deck, Kirsty felt that horrible prickling sensation in the back of her throat that told her she was going to cry. With her larger-than-life image, her bright clothes, her big hair and her loud voice, Kirsty epitomised the life and soul of the party. Perhaps that was why people never expected her to be unhappy. Kirsty knew she had constructed a sort of wall around herself too. After her mother's death, she tried to get her life back to normal as quickly as possible. She squashed her sadness under layer after layer of bad jokes and big nights out and partying until dawn.

And right now, she couldn't afford to indulge her sad memories. She was on this cruise to take care of Jane. Jane who had so recently lost the love of her life. Jane didn't want to see Kirsty crying. She had enough problems of her own.

Kirsty took a deep breath and plastered on a happy face. That was an acting technique that had come in incredibly handy her whole life. It didn't take first time though. Kirsty shook out her shoulders and rolled her head from side to side. Another breath. This time the smile took and stayed.

All the same, Kirsty was very glad indeed to discover, when she got into the suite, that Jane was already fast asleep.

Chapter Thirty Five

Everyone

On Wednesday morning, the ship docked in Barcelona. Almost everyone on board was woken before seven by the sound of the enormous chains, which would hold the ship to the dock, being unwound. It was a terrible noise. Jack sat bolt upright in bed and took a while to be persuaded that the sounds were quite usual and there was no need to worry. The ship was not about to capsize. There was no need to put on a life jacket, much as he wanted to.

Chelsea took him out on the balcony to reassure him.

'Look,' she said. 'Dry land! This is Spain, Jack! We're going to Barcelona.'

Chelsea said it in the traditional way, lisping on the C.

'Why are you talking funny?' Jack asked her.

'I'm not talking funny. That is the way people say Barcelona here. They are Catalan.'

'Bath-er-lona.' Jack tried it out.

'Not bad. And you can say *hola* and *gracias* as well. Like in Lanzarote last year.'

'Grassy-*arse*!' Jack was delighted to reprise his language skills.

'Yep,' said Chelsea. 'Grassy-*arse*. Granddad Bill would be very proud of you. Now we need to go and have breakfast so we're ready for our day trip.'

'I'll bring my Sonic Screwdriver,' said Jack.

'Good idea.'

'And Ted! I can't believe I nearly forgot Ted.'

'That would have been terrible,' Chelsea agreed.

'We've got to take photographs of her everywhere.'

'Everywhere except the balcony,' said Chelsea, reminding Jack of the previous evening when he'd tried to perch Ted on the rail for the sunset. Thank goodness the breeze blew her back into the cabin rather than straight out to sea. When the ship was sailing at top speed, the force of the wind was quite something. If you didn't remember to shut the stateroom's balcony doors before you tried to open the door onto the corridor, it was like being sucked into a wind tunnel – if the door wasn't snatched out of your hand and slammed shut first. No wonder there were notices everywhere reminding passengers not to throw anything overboard.

Chelsea helped Jack choose his outfit for the day and they loaded his little Dalek backpack with everything he would need: sunscreen, snacks and Ted. Jack arranged the stuffed bear with her head poking out of the top of the pack so that she could see where they were going. Then, at the last minute, he tucked in three of the *Doctor Who* miniatures.

'They've never been to Spain,' he explained.

Jane had never been to Spain either and, like everyone else, she was woken in plenty of time for the excursions by the commotion that accompanied the ship docking. But she pretended she was still asleep. She heard Kirsty get up and even ask if she was awake but she kept her eyes tight shut. The previous evening, she had suggested to Kirsty that she might – only might – be up for going ashore, but now that they were in dock, she no longer felt able to go for it.

Greg had been to Barcelona on a stag do. He'd spent just a weekend there and had hardly seen the city in daylight but he'd loved it so much that he told Jane he could see himself (and her, of course) retiring there. When they booked the cruise, he was especially excited about taking Jane to see the sights.

He told her about the Gaudí architecture. The modern Gothic marvel that was La Sagrada Família – the cathedral that looked as though it had been made by a giant child, dropping wet sand to create a melting tower. Even a walk along the seafront was magical when Greg described it. He promised they'd eat tapas in a beachfront café.

'Then we can go up Las Ramblas.'

Jane was booked onto the excursion for that day but she couldn't face it. She really couldn't. What she really wanted to do was get off the boat and head to the airport and fly straight back to England.

Kirsty crept around the cabin, trying to get ready without making too much noise. When she came out of the bathroom, Jane was sitting up in bed. 'I overslept!' Jane said. 'I'm going to make you late!' As if she still intended to get off the boat.

'It's all right,' said Kirsty. 'Really. You don't have to come along. You know me. I'll find a friend on the coach. I can talk to anyone.'

'If you're sure?'

'I'm sure.'

Kirsty kissed Jane on the forehead like a mother kissing a poorly child, then she headed off for her little day trip.

Waiting to disembark, Kirsty caught sight of the little kid she'd winked at during the muster. She smiled at him and he immediately hid behind the legs of the woman Kirsty assumed was his mother.

'I've still got it,' Kirsty joked to herself.

When Adam saw Kirsty on her own in the queue, he recognised her as the woman who had winked at Jack during muster practice and immediately looked for her friend. Though he had seen her only briefly, the fragile blonde had made quite an impression on Adam. Somehow, her face was sticking in his head. He wasn't sure why. She wasn't especially pretty and he'd never have said that blondes were his type. But there was something about her that seemed to have touched something deep inside him. Thinking about it again now, prompted by seeing Kirsty, Adam shook his head at the daftness of the thought. How could he feel as if he knew someone to whom he had never even spoken?

'Daddy! Daddy!' Lily broke the spell. 'Come on. We've got to get on the bus. I want the front seat.'

Kirsty ended up sitting towards the back of the bus, next to a seventy-something with flat batteries in his hearing aid, as she discovered when she tried to make small talk.

Chapter Thirty Six

Everyone

That day's excursion would take in the very best of Barcelona at a whistle-stop pace. They had just four short hours to do everything. The tour began at the Parc Güell, one of Gaudí's most famous creations, high above the city. This was no ordinary park. Indeed, when Gaudí began work on Parc Güell, it wasn't intended to be a public space at all. It was conceived as a sort of gated estate for the wealthy, but Gaudí's crazy designs were ahead of their time and no one wanted to live there. A century later, Jack and Lily were entranced by the fairy-tale buildings, the enormous colourful mosaic lizards and the curious colonnades and crooked gatehouses that might have been made out of gingerbread.

'Who needs rides? It's better than Disneyland,' commented Mark, as the children ran helter-skelter and climbed on walls they should probably not have climbed upon.

The park was the perfect place for the children to play hide and seek, while the adults enjoyed the shade. Even at ten in the morning, it was already thirty degrees. Chelsea was grateful for her floppy sun hat. She thought it made her look like Ali McGraw in her prime.

'Can you actually see where you're going in that?' Adam asked her, recalling an incident in Lanzarote where, blinded by a sun hat, Chelsea had walked into a post.

Fortunately, there were no unfortunate hat-related incidents at Parc Güell. It was a shame they had so little time there. After just an hour it was back on the bus.

The next stop was La Sagrada Família, Gaudí's most famous work and Barcelona's most famous landmark. An unfinished cathedral, which had been under construction for the best part of a century, La Sagrada Família was every bit as weird and wonderful as one might have expected it to be.

'It's like a wedding cake,' said Lily, looking up at the intricate Nativity Façade.

'It's like pointy shells,' said Jack.

They were both right.

'What an imagination to have come up with this. How sad that Gaudí wasn't able to see it finished,' said Chelsea.

Adam agreed. When Chelsea moved on to see what Jack and Lily were up to, Adam remained for a little while, looking up at the extraordinarily complicated towers and the Venetian mosaics. It was terribly sad that Gaudí had not lived to see his vision fully realised. In fact, it wouldn't be complete until 2026. There was something so poignant about that. Just as there had been something especially awful about the half-sewn summer dress that lay on the sewing table in the spare room on the day that Claire died.

The thought popped into Adam's head unbidden and it was certainly unwelcome. Why was he thinking about it now? Claire had been making the little frock for Lily – then a baby – to wear to a family wedding.

She was smocking the bodice – something she assured Adam took a great deal of skill. She'd got about two-thirds of it done. Three months after she died, Adam bundled the unfinished dress into Claire's sewing box and stuffed the whole lot in the loft where it couldn't torment him. There were an awful lot of things hidden in the loft at his house. That was something Adam would need to sort out before Chelsea moved in. She had plenty of stuff of her own.

Adam exhaled deeply. He needed to bring his mind back to where his body was in that moment. His mind was in the spare room in south London on a winter's day. His body was in the bright sunshine in Barcelona. He was at La Sagrada Família with the two people he loved most in the world. Lily. And Chelsea.

'Can we get an ice cream?' Lily asked, appearing by her father's side.

'You've had so much ice cream already this trip,' said Chelsea.

'Please,' said Lily.

'It's nearly lunchtime,' said Adam.

'I've been good all day,' Lily persisted.

'So you have,' said Chelsea.

'So?' Lily gave Chelsea her most winning smile. 'You can get me an ice cream to make sure I don't play up all afternoon.'

Chelsea laughed and scooped Lily into a hug. 'You little monster. That makes it a bribe!'

The sight of Chelsea and Lily together never failed to touch Adam's heart. The unfinished dress faded back into his memory.

'I can see how it's going to be when you move in,' said Adam to Chelsea as Lily was tucking in to a vanilla cone. 'Ice cream for breakfast, lunch and dinner.'

'No,' said Chelsea. 'But it is hot today and she has been very good. It can't be much fun for her and Jack being stuck on the coach while we grown-ups all gaze in awe at the Gaudí. Plus, when I do move into your place, of course we will have to have rules and of course I will do whatever it takes to support you as a parent.'

Adam smiled. 'You're very special to Lily, you know.' He lifted Chelsea's left hand and kissed it. Chelsea pressed a kiss to Adam's cheek.

'Auntie Chelsea!' Jack called. 'Stop kissing! It's disgusting.'

'That told us,' said Chelsea to Adam.

'We need to take a picture of Ted by the cathedral,' said Jack. 'And we need you to help us.'

Jack and Lily had decided Ted should appear in most of the photographs alone, as though it really was her adventure and they were just documenting it. They'd already got some good shots on board ship with the help of the staff in the kids' club. Now was the first opportunity to get a shot of Ted on shore. Chelsea and Lily helped Jack to find the perfect spot. They agreed that Ted should perch on some railings with La Sagrada Família in the background. Shooting upwards, they could get most of the incredible towers in shot.

'Can she be holding my ice cream?' Lily asked.

'I think she'd have trouble with her paws,' said Chelsea. However, they did decide that Ted needed to be accessorised. She was soon sporting Lily's hat and Jack's sunglasses. Both were much too big and as a result, you could only see Ted's back legs. Like a good stylist, Chelsea suggested that they shoot Ted without her hat and sunnies too.

'Poor old Ted,' said Chelsea. 'We've brought her all the way to Barcelona and she doesn't look happy at all.'

Ted really was the most melancholy-looking toy animal you ever saw. At some point in her long, stuffed life, she had lost an eye. It had been glued back into place and through the years the glue had aged and blackened to give the impression that she had a shiner. Then there was the way her mouth was sewn. It turned down at the edges instead of up. She couldn't have smiled if she wanted to.

'She's just got bitchy resting face,' said Mark. 'Like your sister.'

'What's he saying about me?' Ronnie asked.

'I was joking about Annabel,' Mark lied.

From the Sagrada Família, the coach tour took in some more iconic Barcelona sites. Everyone was grateful for the air-con on the bus as they were driven to see a number of the houses Gaudí had built. After that there was another brief stop on Las Ramblas, for lunch and a taste of the town's social life. Barcelona's most famous street was busy with locals and tourists. The children were enchanted by the mimes who performed – if you can call standing on a box performing – in the shade of the trees. Lily was especially delighted by the mime dressed as Ella from *Frozen*. She made the whole family stand and watch the silent, still figure for what seemed like ages.

'When I'm queen of the world,' whispered Chelsea to Ronnie, 'mimes are going to be banned.'

Chelsea was more interested in the newly refurbished Gran Teatre del Liceu and in finding the Miró mosaic that most people walked right by. She captured the attention of the children for just a couple of moments by offering fifty euro cents to the first person to find the tile signed by the artist. Neither child spotted it before they were distracted by another human statue, dressed as a spectacular winged demon, setting up just a few feet away.

After marvelling at the wonderful food on offer in Barcelona's famous market, La Boqueria, the Bensons ate tapas – well, chips really – at a restaurant with a photographic menu. Though Mark and Dave had talked the talk about wanting to try real Spanish food, when it came down to it, they plumped for pseudo-English food and Spanish beer.

Adam, however, thrilled the children by ordering boquerones and eating the little fish head-first as though he were a performing seal.

After lunch, Jack and Lily begged their parents for a little money to buy souvenirs. Though they were in the wrong part of Spain for such things, Jack bought a pair of castanets (made in China).

'For Granddad Bill,' he explained to his family. 'So he doesn't have to use his teeth.'

Chelsea was reminded of the first night of the family's holiday in Lanzarote when Bill took his dentures out to perform an impromptu flamenco.

Meanwhile Lily bought a plastic doll (also from China) dressed in a red flamenco dress. She then spent ten minutes begging Adam for a flamenco dress that she herself could wear. Chelsea fingered the fabric of the one Lily had set her heart on. The feel of the nylon set Chelsea's teeth on edge.

'I'll make you one much nicer when we get back to London,' she said.

Lily pouted.

'We could make a flamenco Elsa dress,' Chelsea continued. 'Wouldn't you rather have a blue and silver one?'

Thank goodness, Lily agreed that she would. She settled for another, small, ice cream.

Adam tried not to think about the half-made dress in the attic again.

The day in Barcelona was soon over but there was so much left to see. As the Bensons climbed back on board the *European Countess*, they all vowed they would be back to visit the city properly one day soon. Kirsty, who had been on the same trip, felt the same way. She had liked what little she'd seen. She felt very envious of the people who didn't have to get on a bus to the port right then. She could imagine herself enjoying an aperitif in one of the bars they passed. Eating tapas. Dancing until dawn. Kirsty definitely had the impression that the city was only just waking up as her day trip to see it was ending.

'Did you see the museum?' Kirsty's elderly seat-mate asked as they were getting off the bus at the waterside.

She turned to him with a big smile. 'The Picasso museum?' she replied.

'The erotic museum on Las Ramblas,' her seat-mate clarified with a grin.

'No,' said Kirsty sharply. 'I'm not really interested in ancient artefacts.'

'What was it like?' Jane asked when Kirsty got back to their stateroom.

'Lovely. You would have liked it. There was an amazing view of the city from the park we went to first. I wish I could remember its name.'

Jane remembered it. 'Park Güell?' Greg had talked about it.

'That's the one. What did you do?'

'Oh, I had lunch in the pizza restaurant and went for a bit of a swim on the main deck,' Jane lied. Kirsty didn't push her on it.

'Where do you fancy eating tonight?' Kirsty asked. 'I've heard good things about the Italian restaurant on deck eight. I could ring and see if they've got room for us.'

'Actually,' said Jane. 'I had quite a lot for lunch. I don't think I need to eat again. Except perhaps a sandwich?'

'Room service?' Kirsty suggested.

Jane jumped at the chance.

It was their fourth night on the ship and the fourth time Jane had refused to move from their cabin.

Chapter Thirty Seven

Everyone

Ajaccio was the next stop on the cruise itinerary, on the French island of Corsica, beautiful birthplace of Napoleon. The ship docked there in the early hours of Thursday morning.

None of the Bensons had been to Corsica before and they were all very excited to have the chance to visit.

'Now Jack,' said Chelsea. 'There's no point saying *grassy-arse* here. The people on Corsica speak French. Do you remember any French words?'

'*Bonjour*!' said Jack. '*Sond-veech*, please.'

Jack's teacher had done her best to teach her class some French by getting them to order their school lunch in the language. None of them had got much further than pronouncing 'sandwich' with a slight accent.

'You're a linguist,' said Chelsea admiringly.

The water off Corsica was a perfect blue. It was tempting to dive straight off the ship and swim to shore. Except that diving off a ship so large into the sea would be like diving off a tower block onto concrete. However, the Benson party had opted for an excursion that would give them a chance to get into that blue water. They were boarding a coach bound for *A Cupulatta*, a tortoise reserve, home to some three thousand turtles and tortoises.

'Why am I doing this? I hate tortoises,' muttered Ronnie to her sister as they climbed on to the bus. 'Those horrible necks . . . Give me the shudders.'

'It does make one think about getting a better anti-ageing cream,' Chelsea agreed.

Jack and Lily were much more excited about seeing the animals.

'What is the difference between a turtle and a tortoise?' Jack asked.

None of the adults in his party had any idea. Fortunately, the staff at the sanctuary was more helpful.

The difference between a tortoise and a turtle is that tortoises dwell on land, of course, while turtles spend most of their time in the water.

'You'd think that would make the turtles even wrinklier than the tortoises,' Ronnie observed.

Naturally Ted went along for the ride. The previous evening, Lily had discovered that Ted was the same size as her doll, Melinda, and thus Ted was allowed to wear some of Melinda's clothes. Until then, Ted had been wearing a rather shapeless shift dress in Liberty print (sewn by Annabel's adoptive mother, Sarah, some twenty years before). For her trip to Ajaccio, Ted took a huge departure from her usual style. Lily dressed her in Melinda the Doll's *Frozen*-inspired party dress, with its silver-threaded bodice and skirts of tulle.

Jack wasn't sure about it at all. Somewhere inside, Jack still clung to the hope that Ted would turn out to be a boy. Eddie Izzard-style shift dresses he could cope with. The tulle was a bit too much.

'She'll be too hot,' he said.

'This is what she wants to wear,' Lily insisted.

Ted did look a little overdressed for the tortoise

sanctuary and certainly for the Corsican beach they visited next.

This stop in Porticcio, a resort close to the capital Ajaccio, was the part of the day trip that the adults were looking forward to most: the chance to chill out and enjoy the sun, the sea and the sand. When they arrived at the beach, Mark and Adam were off the coach in a flash, tasked with getting six sunbeds and some umbrellas in the very best position.

The horseshoe-shaped beach at Porticcio was perfect for families. The sand was as white as icing sugar. The sea was calm and warm as bathwater. A row of smooth rocks formed a natural climbing gym for the adventurous. The mountains inland provided shelter from the wind.

While Adam and the children splashed in the cerulean blue, Chelsea posed Ted on a sunlounger, with a copy of *Le Monde* and a croissant bought from a beach café for authenticity. Jack was pleased with the way the photos came out. Even with the dress.

With Ted's photo-shoot over, Chelsea took a walk alone around the edge of the water, enjoying a moment's solitude and the feel of the damp sand between her toes. She found a cluster of tiny, curly shells, pink as one of Lily's little fingernails, and gathered up a handful, thinking she would display them in a jar when they got back to London. That way she could always be reminded of this moment. She pictured them on the shelf in the bathroom at Adam's house, soon to be her home.

It was a perfect day. The sound of children's laughter and the susurration of the gentle waves caressed her ears. The bright light of the Mediterranean sun warmed her face. The smell of the pine trees and the local myrtle tickled her nose. The hot sand and cool water teased her feet. This was the stuff that great memories were made of, thought Chelsea. She looked back along the beach to the little cluster of parasols where Ronnie was wrapping Jack in a towel and Lily was making Ted dance along a sunbed, while Adam tried to persuade her to put on some sun cream. Chelsea's mother was reading a book. Mark and Dave were deep in discussion, probably about the upcoming football season. So many people Chelsea loved in one place. She smiled as she watched them from a distance and tried to fasten the image in her mind for all time.

Later, while the children splashed in the surf with Adam again, the other adults found a beach bar. Dave and Jacqui liked the food. Mark liked the beer. Ronnie liked watching the comings and going on the private yachts moored out in the bay. She was convinced she'd seen Beyoncé as they drove through pretty little Ajaccio itself. A glance at her gossip mag confirmed that Beyoncé had indeed been spotted holidaying on the Med that summer. It was perfectly possible that she had popped to Corsica on her way to the Costa Smeralda.

'See?' said Ronnie to Mark. 'We're holidaying with the stars.'

She texted Cathy Next Door to tell her about it.

Now that she had a signal, Jacqui also sent an SMS. She texted Annabel to find out how Sophie and Granddad Bill were getting on. She held her breath while she waited for Annabel to respond, which she did satisfyingly quickly. It was good news. Jacqui could relax again.

'Say hello to Corsica for me,' Annabel wrote. 'Richard says don't forget to try the rosé.'

Mark and Dave needed no encouragement.

The children joined the adults for a couple of bottles of pop. Chelsea watched with pride as Adam regaled her family with some funny story. She caught Ronnie's eye. Ronnie nodded as if to say 'he fits'.

'Let's have a family photo,' said Jacqui, just as they were thinking they should head back to the coach. She handed her camera to a helpful waiter so that they might all be in the frame.

Jack and Lily both scrambled to be on Chelsea's lap.

'She's mine,' said Lily firmly.

'She's *my* auntie,' said Jack.

'But she might be going to be *my* step-mummy,' Lily told him in a whisper that everyone heard.

Chelsea looked at Adam. Adam looked straight at the camera but he was smiling. Properly. Chelsea noticed that. As though he was in on the joke.

When Adam took Lily back to the cabin at her bedtime, Chelsea took Jack back too. He was very keen to upload that day's photographs of Ted to Chelsea's laptop. They were keeping a little diary as well, so that they would know how to caption the photographs when they got back to the UK and prepared the book for printing.

'And what did Ted think of Ajaccio?' Chelsea asked. 'Did she like the food we had at lunchtime?'

'Everything except for the salmon ham,' said Jack, referring to the finely sliced local *jambon* that had given him and Lily conniptions with its unfamiliar texture.

'She also didn't like her outfit,' Jack confided. 'She says she wants me to choose what she wears tomorrow. She doesn't like Lily's doll clothes.'

'Fair enough,' said Chelsea. 'I don't think we'll put that in the diary, though. Lily was only trying to make

Ted look extra pretty. If only we could make her look less sad.'

'She isn't sad. Look,' said Jack. 'You can actually tell when Ted is happy. She's happy now. Her eyes are shining.'

Indeed they were, with the reflected light from the laptop.

'OK.' Chelsea started again. 'What was her absolute favourite bit of the trip? Did she like the beach? Did she like seeing the fishermen bringing the catch in? Did she like the tortoises or the turtles?"

Jack snuggled a little closer. 'Her favourite bit was being with you.'

'Oh Jack.' Chelsea always found it hard not to tear up when Jack was being so sweet. She kissed the top of his head.

'It's time to go to sleep. Which of us is sharing with Ted? I don't think I want her,' said Chelsea. 'She snores.'

Jack laughed as though Chelsea had told a joke worthy of the Perrier Prize. Seven-year-olds made a very forgiving audience.

When Jack was asleep, Chelsea went out onto the balcony and whistled for Adam. Lily was asleep too, so Adam came out onto his own balcony and they held hands for a moment round the dividing screen.

'I love you,' they both said at once.

Chapter Thirty Eight

Sophie

Back in the UK, Sophie was very much enjoying her time with Izzy and her internship at the magazine. So much so that she felt quite bad for Izzy, who wasn't having half so much fun at the offices of Stern and Co Solicitors.

'All I get to do is lick envelopes and make tea. Make tea and lick envelopes. I'm sure I'm going to get envelope glue-poisoning after this.'

The editorial staff at *County Class* were taking much better care of Sophie. They were keen that she should have a proper experience of their working life. Of course, she made the odd cup of tea. But so did the editor and his deputy. There was a sense that everyone mucked in. No one was too grand to stuff an envelope. No one was too lowly that their ideas didn't count at the editorial meeting.

Sophie still couldn't quite believe that she would be helping to write the lead article for the November issue. She'd started her research, spending hours on the Internet reading accounts of that terrible night of the full moon in November 1940 when Coventry faced the Luftwaffe. Richard and Annabel had been able to point her in the direction of some reliable sources but the thing that would make the article really special was Granddad Bill's first-hand account. Sophie had heard it many times, of course. As far back as she could remember, like clockwork, Bill would start talking about the Blitz every autumn. When the leaves started to change colour and fall to the ground, Bill would say that the smell of the decaying vegetation took him right back to that awful night all those years before.

Yes, Sophie knew the story. She knew how Bill and his mother had gone to the shelter in their neighbours' garden just as they had on so many other nights that year. The first raids had happened in the late summer. August. In the early days, the people of Coventry bore their misfortune with humour, even managing to laugh at the fact that the new Rex Cinema was blown up the day before it was due to screen *Gone with the Wind*. The cinema's doors were found in Gas Street. By the autumn, everyone was used to the drill. They knew where they had to go when the sirens began to wail. On the night of 14th November, however, Bill's father and his older brother were not in the shelter with them. They were on fire watch, ready to race to the scene with extinguishers if the bombs scored a hit.

Young Bill found the air raids more exciting than frightening but somehow they all sensed that night would be different. Or did they? Had Bill really noticed that there were no birds in the garden that day or was that a romantic detail he'd added afterwards? Sophie's grandfather Dave had once said that the story was a little different every time Bill told it. The one thing that didn't change was the ending.

Bill's older brother Eddie died in the direct hit on Owen & Owen, once the city's most glamorous department store.

Getting back from work on Thursday evening, Sophie found her great-grandfather in the conservatory, with

Leander at his feet. Leander thumped his tail on the carpet in greeting.

'All right, our Ronnie,' said Bill.

'It's Sophie,' said Sophie. 'Your great-granddaughter. Ronnie's eldest.'

Sophie was used to having to explain her place in Bill's family.

'Oh aye,' he said. 'Sophie.'

'Can I talk to you for a bit, Granddad Bill?'

'What about, my sweetheart?'

'About the war,' said Sophie.

'What war?' asked Bill.

'The Second World War.'

Sophie held her breath as she watched her great-grandfather's face change from neutral to concerned.

'What are you talking about?' he asked.

'The war.'

'Is there a war on?'

'Not now, Granddad Bill. No. Not here at any rate. It was seventy years ago, remember? You were a kid when it started but by the end you were on the front line. You went to France.'

Bill tipped his head to one side. He narrowed his eyes as if some of what Sophie was saying was beginning to make sense.

'I've been asked to write about the Coventry Blitz for the November issue of the magazine I'm working at. They want me to get a personal angle. I told them I'd ask you.'

'Ask me what?'

'About the Coventry Blitz.' Sophie tried not to sigh in exasperation.

'I don't know what you're talking about.'

Sophie decided she would help to jog his memory. She

needed to get this interview done. She needed some colourful details. That's what Zara had told her to look out for.

'You were there, Granddad Bill. You were twelve. When the sirens went off just after dinner, you and your mum went into the Anderson shelter in your next-door neighbour's garden. You said your neighbour's grandma wouldn't go in it without her dog.'

'The dog!' said Bill.

'That's right.' Sophie was relieved. 'She had a dog. It was a pug, I think. And you said the old lady used to fart all the time and blame it on her pet. You said that if the Nazis' gas didn't get you, the little old lady would.'

Bill's mouth twitched up at the corners in amusement. Was he remembering now? Sophie pushed on.

'But none of you minded her pretending the dog was farting because it gave you all something to laugh about. You said it was like a party in the shelter, sometimes. Everybody would bring something to eat and you'd share it round. You got spoiled because you were the only kid down there after the family from up the road were evacuated to the country. And your neighbour could get hold of sausages and butter when no one else could and he sometimes slipped some to your mum because he fancied her. Isn't that right, Granddad Bill? And your dad said the neighbour could have her if he'd only get you a joint of beef for Christmas.'

Bill nodded, though he seemed unsure.

'Good,' said Sophie. 'I'm definitely going to write about the dog and the sausages, but the night I really wanted to talk about was 14th November. When the cathedral was destroyed. When your dad and brother

Eddie were on duty as firemen and Eddie didn't come home.'

'Why didn't he come home?' Bill asked.

Sophie hesitated. 'Because . . . because he got killed by a bomb.'

'What bomb?'

Bill sat up a little straighter, agitated.

'The German bomb. On the night they hit the cathedral, your brother Eddie was in town. He was in Owen & Owen with the people who were stuck there when it got that direct hit. The Nazis got him, Granddad Bill.'

'They got Eddie?'

'Yes.' Sophie's voice was suddenly small.

'Eddie, my brother?'

'Yes, Granddad Bill.'

'Why didn't anybody tell me? Where is he? Where is he now? He can't be dead! Why didn't anybody say?'

'It was seventy years ago.'

'I saw him this morning. You're having me on. You're telling me lies, you are. My brother isn't dead. I saw him this morning. I saw him.'

'Granddad Bill,' said Sophie. 'Eddie's been dead since 1940.'

'I'm not having it. It can't be right. You don't know what you're talking about.'

Bill tried to get to his feet. Leander stood with him as though he might be able to help if Bill looked in danger of toppling over. Thinking quickly, Sophie put her hands on Bill's arms and pushed him back down into his chair.

'It's all right,' she said. 'Sit down, Granddad Bill. Don't worry. You're right. I don't know what I was saying. Eddie isn't dead. I must have been mixing him up with someone else. I'm sorry.'

Bill sank back into the cushions.

'I knew you hadn't got that right,' he said. 'I saw Eddie this morning. I saw him just this morning. He isn't dead. Stop talking rubbish. He isn't dead.'

Sophie crept away, shaken. She joined Annabel and Izzy in the kitchen. Izzy was giving Humfrey a bottle. Annabel was preparing supper.

'Granddad Bill mistook me for Mum again,' Sophie told her aunt. 'And when I tried to talk to him about the Blitz, he told me his brother's not dead. I think I upset him.'

Annabel stopped what she was doing to wrap her niece in a hug.

'He's never going to get any better, is he?' Sophie asked.

'No,' said Annabel. 'No. I'm afraid he isn't.'

Sophie couldn't stop her tears.

'It's hard,' said Annabel. 'When people get old and they can't remember exactly where they are or who they're with, any more. It breaks your heart because you know they won't get better. It isn't like when a child makes a mistake. Then you can laugh because you know that in just a little while they'll know more. But with the elderly . . .'

Annabel felt tears springing to her eyes too.

'The most important thing is that Granddad Bill feels loved. It doesn't matter if he thinks you're Ronnie and I'm Jennifer and Richard is the postman who delivered the mail back in the 1950s. He knows that we all love him and he still loves you too.'

'I just want him to be like he used to be,' said Sophie. 'I wish I'd listened to him more carefully then.'

'Then you must do him proud in your story for the magazine.'

'I'm going to.' Sophie extricated herself from Annabel's hug and wiped her eyes.

Chapter Thirty Nine

Kirsty and Jane

'What was Ajaccio like?' Jane asked.

Kirsty hadn't fancied the tortoise sanctuary. She'd opted instead for a tour around the old town, with its pretty pink and sand coloured buildings and its romantic town square, where locals lingered in the shade. It was the quintessential French town with its patisseries and bars selling pastis. Brightly painted fishing boats bobbed in the harbour. Kirsty had freshly caught fish for lunch. She had loved it but she felt the need to play it down, just a little.

'It was all right,' said Kirsty. 'I think I saw Beyoncé.'

'Seriously?'

'Looked like her. And today's *Sun* had a picture of her in the South of France so it's not inconceivable that she came over on someone's yacht. There's serious money in this place. Some of the boats parked just off the island are out of this world. Nearly as big as this one only shared between ten oligarchs instead of three thousand people like us.'

'Sounds fun. I'm sorry I'm being so rubbish,' said Jane. 'I will get off board at some point, I promise.'

'I told you that you could do exactly what you want on this trip and I meant it,' said Kirsty. 'I don't want you to do anything that makes you feel uncomfortable. If you're happy on the balcony, then that's fine by me.'

'But *you* can't be happy, sitting on the balcony night after night when there's so much going on.'

'Oh, I'm tired after my day in Corsica,' Kirsty said. 'Pass the room service menu.'

She could tell Jane was relieved.

After eating, the two friends lazed on their beds and watched a film on the enormous flat screen television. They chose an oldie – *Roman Holiday*.

'To get us in the mood for our next stop,' said Kirsty.

It was the perfect choice, possibly the ultimate chick flick, apart from *Breakfast at Tiffany's*. And it was not something that had any association with Greg whatsoever. It definitely wasn't the sort of film he would have wanted to see when there were at least three films from the *Fast and Furious* franchise on offer. Kirsty and Jane, however, drooled over Gregory Peck and over Audrey Hepburn's enviable holiday wardrobe.

It wasn't the first time they'd watched the film. Kirsty almost knew it off by heart. Her mother had been a big fan of Audrey Hepburn. Jane too knew the movie well. Back when she and Greg were planning the cruise, Jane had been very specific about wanting to see Rome because of Hepburn and Peck.

'Well, we're in Italy tomorrow,' said Kirsty. '*La Dolce Vita* and all that. I bet it's going to be just like *Roman Holiday*.'

Jane seemed enthusiastic.

'Are you going to come ashore?' asked Kirsty.

Jane nodded and said, 'Of course.'

Chapter Forty

Everyone

Of all the ports that the *European Countess* would visit on that cruise, the one everyone looked forward to most was Civitavecchia, the port closest to Rome. Who could resist the chance to visit the Eternal City?

Jack was well prepared. He'd been reading *Horrible Histories* and was full of how the Romans dealt with their poo. Lily too, was very excited. Her class had been studying the Romans and she fancied herself as a grand Roman lady with a couple of slaves. Jack, of course, wanted to be a gladiator. The Colosseum was high on his list of must-sees.

'Will there be lions?' he asked his mother over breakfast.

'Probably,' said Ronnie. 'So you'd better not play up or we'll leave you behind to be lion food.'

Jack was thrilled at the idea.

'I'll throw Ted at them,' he said. Then he immediately apologised to the stuffed animal, in case he had caused offence. 'I wouldn't really do that,' he whispered. 'Though you'd be OK anyway, because you're a bear. Bears always beat lions. Fact. Everybody knows that.'

'It depends on the kind of bear,' said Lily, between mouthfuls of toasted bagel. 'A lion would beat a panda.'

'Ted isn't a panda,' said Jack.

'She's got a black eye,' Lily pointed out.

'Yeah,' said Jack. 'But that's because she's been in a fight. She would beat up a lion. No trouble.'

'Girls don't fight,' said Lily.

'Ted isn't really a girl anyway,' Jack whispered.

'She's wearing a dress,' Lily countered.

'No,' said Jack. 'This isn't a dress. This is a gladiator's tunic.'

The night before the ship docked in Rome, Jacqui had told Ronnie that she and Dave would be taking the children for the day.

'It's our treat to you,' Jacqui explained to Ronnie. 'Rome is such a romantic city. You should have a chance to enjoy a bit of that.'

'But what about you and Dad?' Ronnie asked.

'Oh, we're past romance. I've been washing his underpants for more than thirty years. Besides, we don't get enough time with our grandchildren. That's what will make the best memories for us.'

'But Lily too? She can be a handful, Mum.'

'Not for me, Ronnie. I brought *you* up, remember. I can handle Lily Baxter. Besides, Adam asked if I might help him find a way to be alone with Chelsea for a while on one of the excursions.'

'I knew it!' Ronnie exclaimed and clapped her hands in delight.

'Knew what?'

'Mum! Don't tease me. What has he said?'

'He just said he'd like for them to have some time together.'

'Mum, stop pretending you don't know why.'

'I don't know what you're talking about.'

'They've been together a year. They're planning to move in together. He went off to have a private conversation with Dad when we were all at Annabel's house. Mum! Of course you know.'

Ronnie was fizzing with excitement.

'Admit it, Mum! Tell me.'

'I am saying nothing. It's not my place.'

Jacqui's mouth twitched as she tried and failed to suppress a grin.

'Then you definitely know. Oh, I can't believe it! This is brilliant.'

'I'm not saying anything,' said Jacqui, though as far as Ronnie was concerned, Jacqui's smile said it all. 'Now, do you want me to have Jack tomorrow or not?'

Of course Ronnie wanted her parents to look after Jack, and Adam was touchingly grateful when Jacqui confirmed that the offer was open to Lily too.

Chelsea was over the moon at the thought of a day alone with Adam. She had never been to Rome, though it had been top of her wish list for years. When she was going out with Colin Webster, her previous boyfriend, she'd hoped he would take her there for a romantic weekend. As it was, he took the girl he dumped her for there, just a week after Chelsea was off the scene. She knew because she had phoned him eight times in a row, getting desperate when she heard the foreign dialling tone, and he had texted 'Can't talk now. In Rome' in response. She knew he didn't have any business there. It had to be romantic.

Well, now Chelsea was going to get her own *Roman Holiday* moment. Not so much a holiday as a day trip, but at least she would see the Trevi Fountain for the first time in the company of the man she really loved. She was so happy she thought she might burst.

* * *

Chelsea channelled Audrey Hepburn when dressing for her day in the Italian capital. She chose a blue gingham blouse and white broderie anglaise dirndl. She was very pleased with the final effect. Jack pronounced it 'OK'.

'Is that what you're wearing?' Adam asked, when they met him and Lily in the corridor.

'Er, yes,' said Chelsea. 'Why?'

'No reason.'

'No, come on. You asked me if this is what I'm wearing as though there might be a reason why I should change.'

'No,' said Adam. 'That's not what I meant. I like it. It's very pretty. I just want you to be comfortable, that's all. We're going to be doing a lot of walking.'

Chelsea smoothed out her skirt, suddenly not feeling much like Audrey Hepburn at all. But her annoyance at Adam's comment was soon forgotten as the tour bus chugged into the Eternal City.

It was going to be another beautiful day.

Chapter Forty One

Adam and Chelsea

The excursion to Rome included time to explore without a guide. Adam and Chelsea stayed with the group from the ship as far as the Forum that had formed the heart of the city in Roman times, and then they nipped off. They had just four hours to themselves. Four hours wasn't long to see such an ancient and wonderful city. Especially not if you intended to have a bloody good lunch.

Chelsea loved Rome from the moment she stepped off the coach near the Colosseum. It was a crazy place. She loved the juxtaposition of the ancient and the brand new. The Colosseum itself was awe-inspiring. It was far bigger and more complete than Chelsea had expected. It was easy to imagine it as it had once been, when the citizens of Rome streamed through its many arches to watch a spot of murder and mayhem. Their modern equivalents preferred their mayhem on the roads. Vespas nipped in and out of the traffic, carrying handsome young men and beautiful young women who wore diaphanous little skirts that flipped up and showed their slim brown legs as they zipped along. They seemed undaunted by the cars and vans around them, though there seemed to be no highway code to speak of and Chelsea felt nervous just watching from the pavement.

'Do you want to see inside the Colosseum?' Adam asked. 'We can join a tour, if you like.'

'I'd rather just, you know, wander,' said Chelsea.

'I was hoping you would say that,' said Adam, grasping her hand. 'Let's go this way.'

'But I've got to see the Trevi Fountain because we need to throw some coins in it so we get to come back.'

'Agreed,' said Adam. 'Let's do that first. That's over here.'

He whirled her round so that they were heading in the opposite direction. Chelsea felt giddy with love.

The Trevi Fountain was heaving with people all desperate to secure their chance of coming back to the wonderful city. As fast as the visitors threw in their coins, a couple of dodgy-looking blokes were fishing them out with magnets and nets, keeping the higher denominations and throwing back the pennies as though they were chucking back sprats.

'That's terrible,' said Chelsea.

'That's Rome,' said Adam. 'Here.' He handed her three euros. 'These are your wishes. You have to do it backwards. Over your shoulder.'

'I've seen the film,' said Chelsea. 'But what if I hit someone?'

'That's probably extra good luck.'

Getting close to the edge of the fountain, Chelsea shook the coins in her hand to give them extra power. She closed her eyes and pitched them over her shoulder.

'Not bad,' said Adam. 'You got two in the water and the other coin took someone's eye out.'

'What?' Chelsea looked about her in panic.

'They all went in,' Adam reassured her.

'And now they're all coming straight out,' said

Chelsea, observing that one of the men with nets had moved to sift through the coins close to where Chelsea had cast her euro-shaped wishes. 'Do you think they still count if they get fished out within a minute?'

'I don't know. What did you wish for?'

'I can't tell you that,' said Chelsea. 'You'll have to guess.' Then she planted a comically passionate smacker on Adam's lips that made the people around them laugh.

From the Trevi Fountain, they walked to the Pantheon and gazed in awe at the enormous concrete dome, built by Emperor Augustus long before anyone had invented a cement mixer. They ambled up the Via del Corso and posed on the Spanish Steps, which were crowded with groups of teenagers from every nation, all doing their best to look cool. Chelsea pointed out the house where Keats and Shelley had stayed for a while. It was a museum now but the lovers didn't visit it. There was enough to discover just by strolling any street you cared to take.

'Via Margutta,' said Chelsea, as they turned into a road towards the Piazza del Popolo. 'This is where Gregory Peck's character lived in *Roman Holiday*.'

'Hence your Audrey Hepburn skirt,' said Adam.

'You don't like it, do you?' said Chelsea.

'Look!' said Adam, changing the subject. 'A Bugatti!'

The smart car was parked outside the Hotel De Russie, one of the city's smartest hotels. Chelsea and Adam walked into the hotel's secluded courtyard garden and admired the terrace laid out for lunch.

'Good spot for a romantic weekend,' Adam mused. 'We'll have to come back.' He squeezed Chelsea's hand. She felt her heart soar. 'Come on. We've still got so much to see.'

Around every corner, they found something to marvel

at. Chelsea knew that Rome had a long and illustrious history but she had not expected to see so much evidence of the city's glorious time as the hub of the Roman Empire so nonchalantly jumbled in with more modern buildings. Trajan's Column was so enormous and still in such wonderful condition that Chelsea was sure it must be a replica. It certainly looked in better shape than the full-sized plaster model in the cast courts at the Victoria and Albert museum.

'It's amazing, isn't it? I can't imagine that anything being built here today will last so long.'

The Romans certainly had ambition.

Adam had investigated the possibilities for lunch and they found themselves in a little place in the Jewish part of town, south of the Campo de' Fiori and near the smaller amphitheatre, the Teatro Marcello, with beautiful frescoed ceilings. It was off the beaten track and the other clientele were clearly locals, dressed in immaculate suits despite the summer heat. The dark interior of the restaurant was a welcome retreat from the hottest part of the day. The food was delicious. Adam wanted everything on the menu. He chose a dish of homemade pasta with *pomodori a mezzo*. Chelsea couldn't resist the stuffed zucchini flowers. They both ate the fish of the day. It was nice to eat something simple after the excesses available on the ship. That said, afterwards, they had to find somewhere to buy gelato. Unfortunately, the price for two ice creams was far more memorable than the ice creams themselves.

'Twenty euros for two scoops! Two scoops!' Adam exclaimed. 'It's a good job Lily isn't with us. She'd have bankrupted me with a single knickerbocker glory.'

Talk of Lily brought their attention to the time.

'I suppose we should be heading back to the pick-up point,' said Chelsea.

'There's just one thing near here that we have to do first.' Adam looked at the map. 'It's this way.'

Chapter Forty Two

Adam and Chelsea

Adam took Chelsea to see the Bocca della Verità – the mouth of truth. Chelsea knew of the scary-looking stone sculpture, a huge round face with a gaping maw, which was used as an early lie detector in Roman times. Rumour had it that if a liar put his or her hand in the stone mouth, the monster would suddenly come to life and bite his or her fingers off. It is thought to have been part of an ancient fountain and it was made famous in *Roman Holiday*. The scene in which Gregory Peck pretends that it has eaten his hand was one of Chelsea's favourites. Just the thought of it made her smile. Audrey Hepburn's shocked little face. Apparently Hepburn had no idea that Peck had hidden his hand up his sleeve and she was genuinely horrified when he appeared to have lost it. The laughter afterwards was very real. How ironic it is that both characters really are lying to each other at that point in the story.

When they got to the monument, there was a small queue of people waiting to take their turn and pose with their fingers in the stone face's mouth.

'Does it bite your hand off if you're an untruthful person in general or just if you actually tell a lie while you've got your fingers in there?' Chelsea asked.

'I don't know,' said Adam. 'We'll have to see. I'll have to ask you a difficult question when we get our turn.'

'A difficult question?'

'Very difficult.'

Chelsea's stomach did a little flip. She could certainly think of the question she wanted him to ask. She wouldn't find it difficult to answer, though.

When they got within three people of the statue, Chelsea was embarrassed to find she was feeling slightly nervous. She could see it on the faces of the people ahead of them too. Though rationally, everyone understood that the thing about getting your fingers bitten off if you lied was just a fairy tale, no one exactly rushed to put their hands into the grim stone mouth. Instead, keeping their feet firmly on the right side of the red rope that was supposed to keep people from touching the statue at all, they gently placed their hands on the stone lip and stood tense, hardly wanting to look away from the mouth to the camera they were supposed to be facing in case the teeth came out while they weren't watching.

'Look at that guy sweating,' said Adam. 'He's definitely got something to hide.'

At last it was Adam and Chelsea's turn.

'You go first,' said Chelsea. 'I've just had a manicure.'

'Ah yes. Don't want to hurt the princess nails!'

Adam stepped up to the sculpture full of bravado but, like everyone else, he rested his fingers quite gingerly on the edge of the mouth.

'Ask me a question then?'

'I can't think of anything,' said Chelsea.

'You must be able to think of something. Come on. This is your chance. Ask me anything you like. I can't risk telling a lie.'

Chelsea thought hard. She could think of plenty of

questions she wanted to ask but questions she *should* ask? In front of a queue of tourists, eager to wait their turn? Eventually, she plumped for, 'Do you really like my skirt?'

Adam suddenly gasped and collapsed towards the sculpture. And though she had seen *Roman Holiday* a hundred times, for a moment Chelsea was utterly convinced that Adam would withdraw his wrist from the creature's mouth to reveal a bloody stump.

'You horrible man!' She swatted him with her tourist map. 'How could you do that to me? Anyway, you didn't actually answer the question.'

'Do I need to?' Adam asked. He brought her close and kissed the top of her head. 'I like everything you wear because you're wearing it. And I'm not just saying that now that I don't have to worry about getting my fingers bitten off. I promise. OK. Your turn.'

They swapped places. Chelsea rested the fingers of her right hand lightly in the horrific maw and tried not to think irrationally. All the same, her heart did start to race. And it got faster still when Adam spoke.

'Now, I want you to think very seriously before you answer this question.'

He looked grave. The outcome of this question was going to be far more important than whether or not Chelsea thought he should wear green with his complexion (he shouldn't).

'Chelsea Benson,' Adam began. 'Will you . . .'

He hesitated and the world seemed to go very still.

'I mean, do you . . . do you love me?'

Chelsea stared at him. Her mind was still following those first two words – will you – down the traditional phrase. It took her a second to realise that *wasn't* what he'd asked.

'Well?' he said.

'Do I love you?' Chelsea echoed. 'Of course I do. My heart says yes.'

'And your fingers?' Adam asked.

Chelsea withdrew her hand from the Bocca della Verità and gamely waggled her fingers at him.

'They say yes too.'

They'd say 'yes' to another question, Chelsea said to herself. Ask me. Ask me now.

It wasn't to be.

'Thank goodness for that,' said Adam. 'Quick. I didn't actually get a photo of you with your hand in the mouth.'

Chelsea gamely pulled a pose.

Later, when she looked at the photo, it seemed obvious that she was disappointed.

Chapter Forty Three

Everyone

Adam and Chelsea caught up with the rest of the family back on the ship.

'Daddy! Daddy! We saw a real gladiator!' said Lily.

The children were full of their visit to the Colosseum. They'd both acquired gladiator helmets in a gift shop. Jack had a small plastic sword. Lily had a trident, like one of the *retiari*, who traditionally fought with a net and three-pronged spear.

'They used to fill the whole thing with water and have sea battles,' said Jack.

'And there were lions and elephants,' said Lily.

'And Christians!'

'They ate sparrows' noses!' Lily squealed.

'Do sparrows have noses?' Adam asked.

'They do in *Life of Brian*,' said Mark.

'I don't think that's a factual representation of Roman life, dear,' said Chelsea.

'We took pictures of Ted in a cage where they used to keep real bears,' said Jack.

'She didn't like it,' said Lily.

'She did,' Jack insisted. 'She wasn't afraid.'

'She was worried she would get her dress dirty.'

'It's a gladiator's tunic!' said Jack again.

'Time to get washed before supper,' said Adam, pre-empting a fight.

Both Jack and Lily insisted on dressing as gladiators for dinner. Ted wore Melinda's *Swan Lake* outfit.

Jacqui tucked her arm through her youngest daughter's as they entered the Sea View restaurant. It was 'British Curry Night'. What constitutes a British curry? Chelsea wondered out loud. Did it have to come from Marks and Spencer?

'Did you have a lovely day in Rome?' Jacqui asked her youngest daughter.

'Yes,' said Chelsea. 'We did.'

'It's a very romantic city, isn't it?' Jacqui said.

'Yes,' said Chelsea. 'I suppose it is.'

Ronnie caught up with them. She was less subtle. 'Anything to report?' she asked. 'Anybody ask someone an important question?'

'Oh, for goodness' sake,' said Chelsea. 'Mum, Ronnie, will you please both leave it out. Adam did not want to get me on my own so he could propose. He just wanted a breather from Lily, that's all.'

When Chelsea sat down at their table, Ronnie and Jacqui shared a look over the top of Chelsea's head. Jacqui bit her lip and subtly shook her head to warn Ronnie not to push it.

Chapter Forty Four

Kirsty and Jane

Kirsty had joined the tour of Rome but Jane had stayed on the ship. Again.

In the end, she just couldn't face the idea of Rome without Greg. It was one of the places that had excited him most when they first looked at the cruise itinerary. He was a keen history buff and the city was stuffed with sights he wanted to see. Jane didn't want to see them without him.

While Kirsty was on shore, getting some retail therapy on the Via del Corso, Jane remained in their stateroom. She got Greg's ashes out of the safe and placed them on the table next to her on the balcony. He would come to no harm there while the ship was docked and steady.

Jane spoke out loud to him.

'I wish you were here for real,' she said. 'This doesn't feel right without you. This should be the best holiday in the world, but everything I do, I wish I could be doing it with you. This was supposed to be our special cruise.'

Jane looked at the ring on her finger. The Mediterranean light made the stones shine especially brightly. She twisted it anxiously, as if hoping to screw it on.

She fell silent and listened hard, as though she might hear Greg's voice on the sea breeze. What would he say to her? What would his advice have been in such a situation? What would he have done had everything happened the other way round, so that Jane was the one whose organs were walking around inside strangers and he was the one left behind?

In the letter that he'd written when he was about to go to Afghanistan – the letter that Jane was only supposed to read if he was killed in action – Greg had said, 'Be happy for me. Go on and live a joyful life. Make sure you have lots of adventures.'

Why was it so hard to believe that's what he really wanted?

When Kirsty came back at about six o'clock, she looked quite hot and bothered. It was a very warm day to be traipsing around the Eternal City. She tossed three shopping bags onto her bed.

'I didn't get as far as the Vatican,' she said, rifling through one. 'But I found this on a souvenir stall.'

She presented Jane with a calendar. On each page, a black-and-white photograph of a different young priest.

'They can't be real priests,' said Jane.

'It says they are,' said Kirsty. 'Maybe I should take holy orders after all, if this is what they're like.'

'I'm not sure nuns and priests get to mix,' said Jane.

'No harm trying.'

Because Jane felt so bad, she decided that she must make an effort to be more sociable that evening. She could see the surprise on Kirsty's face when she said that she would dine with her in the ship's Italian restaurant rather than order room service.

'Are you sure?'

'I'm fed up of club sandwiches.'

Jane put on the one presentable dress she'd brought along. It had not seen the light of day since she and

Greg went on that weekend to Dublin. It was a little tight back then. Now it fitted her perfectly.

'That's lovely,' Kirsty said.

Jane even put on some make-up. She hadn't dared wear mascara for months.

'How do I look?'

'You look like you're ready to have a good time,' said Kirsty.

'I was thinking about the letter Greg left for me this afternoon.'

'Oh yes?' said Kirsty.

'He said I should try to have fun,' Jane said.

Kirsty visibly relaxed.

'Come on then,' said Jane. 'Lead the way.'

Chapter Forty Five

Adam and Kirsty

Adam caught a glimpse of her walking through the atrium. The blonde girl he'd seen on the very first day. She was dressed for dinner. She had make-up on. But the mascara and lipstick went no way to disguising the blonde's vulnerability – the dark shadows beneath her eyes, the hollow look to her cheeks. Adam wondered how old she was. Her fragility made her seem very young but her eyes looked as though they'd seen an awful lot of life. She looked as if she understood a few things. He wished he could ask.

Adam suddenly realised that he was staring at the blonde and her friend had noticed. He quickly looked down at his feet.

'They're showing *Grease* on the big cinema screen on the top deck tonight,' said Chelsea. 'Ronnie and Mark say that Jack's allowed to watch a bit of it. How about Lily?'

Adam nodded. 'Cool,' he said. 'Of course.' He knew he was blushing, though the blonde and her friend had already moved on. 'It's hot tonight, isn't it?'

'I was just thinking that they have the air conditioning on way too high in here,' said Chelsea.

Kirsty saw the man watching her friend. Jane was oblivious. Back in the day, before Greg, Kirsty would have drawn Jane's attention to her admirer right away but it didn't feel right now. She didn't want Jane to feel any guilt, especially not because the man was obviously with his wife and their two children. The sleazeball. Kirsty kept quiet about what she'd seen.

'Do you mind if I go to bed now?' said Jane. 'After all, we've got Florence to see tomorrow.'

'Yeah,' said Kirsty, though she didn't believe for one moment that Jane would get off the ship.

Chapter Forty Six

Adam and Chelsea

Overnight, the *European Countess* sailed north up the Italian coast and on Saturday morning, she docked in Livorno. The excursions available to the passengers from here were to two more fabulous Italian cities: Pisa, home of the famous leaning tower, and Florence, home to the Renaissance and so many historical treasures, from Michelangelo's *David* to the magnificent Duomo, and the Gucci Museum.

Chelsea needed no time to make her choice. She'd always wanted to go to Florence. She'd heard fantastic things about the city from her colleagues at *Society* and had always hoped the magazine would send her on a trip there to review a spa or a five-star hotel. Alas, it never happened. But as soon as she heard there was an excursion to the city on the day the ship docked in Livorno, she knew she would be on it. Pisa didn't stand a chance.

'But Jack and Lily will want to see the Leaning Tower,' said Jacqui. 'We'll take them there while you go on the other tour.'

'But you had the children in Rome, Mum. You need a rest.'

'Just go to Florence and enjoy yourselves. I won't offer twice.'

Chelsea checked with Adam. Adam said he was more

than happy to leave Lily in Jacqui and Dave's care again. Lily was very fond of Jacqui and Dave and she'd be far happier spending the day with them and Jack than traipsing round the Uffizi. Plus, the drive to Pisa was far shorter than the drive to Florence – half an hour, as opposed to an hour and a half. The children would prefer that. It was starting to feel as though they were spending as much time on air-conditioned coaches as at the places they were supposed to be visiting.

'Are you sure you don't want to see the Leaning Tower?' Chelsea asked Adam.

'Seen it,' he said.

'Oh,' said Chelsea. 'What's it like?'

'Wonky,' said Adam. 'But to be honest, there's not much else to see in Pisa, as far as I'm concerned. Florence is much better.'

'I didn't know you'd been there before,' said Chelsea.

Adam hesitated. 'I came to Florence with Claire. We had a couple of weeks in Tuscany the year before Lily was born.'

'You didn't say.' Chelsea's face fell.

'I didn't think I should.'

'Why not?'

'Well, Chelsea, you know . . . I didn't think you would want to hear about it, that's all.'

'What makes you say that?'

'It doesn't matter. You know now. It was just a holiday. It was a long time ago now.'

Chelsea nodded. 'I don't mind,' she said. 'I'd prefer to hear about it than find out like this, that's all. If there's anywhere else on the itinerary that you've already done with Claire – or anyone else – please let me know.'

'OK,' said Adam. 'I will.'

'Promise?' Chelsea asked.

'Promise.'

They weren't going to have much time in Florence so it turned out to be a good thing that Adam had been to the city before. Once they split from the rest of the tour group on arrival, he was quickly able to guide Chelsea away from the worst of the crowds. The queues for the Uffizi were ridiculously long, it being the very height of the holiday season, so Chelsea was glad when Adam suggested that they skip the museum for a start.

'It's all Madonnas,' he said.

'Is it very wrong to keep skipping the cultural bits?' Chelsea asked.

Adam assured her that it wasn't.

'Good.'

They settled for a selfie in the Piazza della Signoria in front of the replica of Michelangelo's *David* that towered over the bewildered tourists trying to work out which of the many guides holding aloft broadly identical umbrellas was the guide they were actually supposed to be following. They avoided the expensive bars that flanked the square and headed away from the crush.

It was astonishing how quiet it was away from the main drag. Just a couple of streets behind the Uffizi it was as if the town was deserted, and Chelsea could more easily imagine what it might have been like centuries before when the Guelphs and the Ghibellines fought for supremacy over Tuscany. Adam took Chelsea by the hand and, without looking at the guidebook, led her through what seemed like a series of shrinking streets until he brought her safely to Santa Croce, the beautiful Franciscan church.

'I'm impressed by your memory,' said Chelsea. 'Finding your way back here.'

'Oh,' he said. 'I haven't actually been to this church before.'

Chelsea was secretly pleased. She wanted Adam to have memories of Florence that didn't feature Claire.

'But I heard there is something very special around the back of it and I thought it would be the perfect spot.'

'For what?'

'For you.'

Chelsea felt a bubble of excitement rise inside her again. Since the disappointment at the Bocca della Verità in Rome, she had been trying not to think about her sister's ridiculous theories but . . .

'So, you've been researching the best places in Florence to bring your girlfriend?' she asked.

'I have.'

Chelsea couldn't keep her imagination down. Was this where it was going to happen? Maybe Rome *was* too obvious a place for a proposal. Chelsea could already hear herself saying, 'We got engaged in Florence.' Then the little voice inside her head warned her to get a grip on herself. Ronnie's 'feeling' over that walk Adam had taken with their dad didn't really amount to anything. Did it? Likewise, her mother's insistence on babysitting meant nothing. Jacqui was just kind like that. All the same, Chelsea decided it was best to be prepared and took a surreptitious look at her reflection in the screen of her phone while Adam consulted a map.

'It's just around here.'

Adam led Chelsea off the street into a little garden at the back of Santa Croce. It was very pretty and quiet, away from the hustle of the street. Someone had taken care to keep the flowers watered through the heat of the summer.

'This was known as a place of kindness,' said Adam. 'People who couldn't look after their children would bring them here . . .'

Chelsea was spinning her own story. If Adam asked her to be his wife, she would become a stepmother too. Was that the significance of bringing her to a place where people gave up their children to the care of the church?

'Here it is,' said Adam.

They ducked through a door in the wall.

It was a very pretty courtyard but it wasn't as romantic as the garden on the other side.

'What is this place?' Chelsea asked.

'*La Scuola del Cuoio*,' Adam said in his best Italian accent.

'What?'

'*Scuola del Cuoio*. It means the school of leather. The orphans entrusted to Santa Croce needed to be taught a craft so they could eventually make their way in the real world. The Franciscan monks decided to create their very own school of leatherwork. It's still open today, though it's not staffed by orphans any more.'

'Oh,' said Chelsea.

Adam was clearly excited to have found the place. 'I read that it's the best place in the whole of Florence to buy leather goods. Apparently, the stuff you get on those stalls in the piazzas is all made in China from dog skin.'

'Ugh.'

'Well, maybe not dog skin. Anyway, here, it's the real deal. Made on the premises. Italian leather. Top quality. I thought you might like to have a look.'

Chelsea had never knowingly passed up the opportunity

to look for a new handbag but all the same she couldn't help but feel a little deflated. Nothing meaningful was going to happen in a leather shop. However, Adam had gone to the effort of researching the place for her. That was a very sweet and thoughtful thing to have done.

'Better hide your credit card,' said Chelsea, leading him into the workshop.

And Adam was right. The Scuola del Cuoio was exactly the sort of place Chelsea enjoyed discovering and it was an interesting place to spend half an hour. As it was the weekend, the factory itself wasn't in operation but a single workman offered to stamp monograms on anything bought that day. There were hundreds of handbags to choose from. If Chelsea hadn't been hoping for an altogether more important souvenir of Florence, she would have been delighted.

Adam brought Chelsea a lovely red purse and, as was the tradition, he put a penny in it – well, a euro cent – to bring her luck, before he handed it over.

She kissed him.

'Thank you.'

By then it was time for lunch and a couple of snaps of the Duomo – the beautiful terracotta domed cathedral that was Florence's most famous landmark – before they headed back to the coach.

'We'll come back here some day,' said Adam. 'I think Lily would like this place. Maybe in a couple of years when she's old enough to appreciate some of the history.'

'Yes,' said Chelsea. The day was the hottest of the holiday so far and she was feeling tired and, if she was honest, more than a little disgruntled. She told herself to count her blessings. Adam had asked her to move in. He was talking about a future. What did it matter if there wasn't a ring in it? Before Ronnie started spouting her nonsense, Chelsea had been perfectly happy with the thought of moving into Adam's house. She'd seen it as a sign of real commitment. It had been enough. Bloody Ronnie.

As they walked back along the bank of the sludgy brown Arno, Chelsea and Adam saw a wedding party having photographs taken with the Ponte Vecchio in the background. For one shot, the bride and her bridesmaids all threw their bouquets in the air. The bride's bouquet was about to go sailing right into the river when Adam reached out and caught it with the skill of a professional cricketer. He handed it back to the bride, saying '*Auguri*' as he did so – Italian for congratulations or best wishes.

'Good catch,' said Chelsea.

'Does that mean I'll be married within the year?' Adam asked Chelsea.

Before she could answer him, he had spotted their coach and, grabbing her hand, set off at a run to get on it.

Chapter Forty Seven

Everyone

Lily and Jack had very much enjoyed their day in Pisa. They showed Adam and Chelsea the photographs they had taken in front of the Leaning Tower. They'd spent half an hour trying to get one of those comedy shots in which the subject appears to be holding the tower up. Naturally, there were plenty of pictures of Ted too, in front of the tower and propped up against a pepper pot in the pizza restaurant the children had chosen for lunch, looking as miserable as ever.

'It's because she hates that dress,' Jack complained. Ted was wearing one of Melinda the Doll's frou-frou ball-gowns again.

'She looks very elegant,' Lily insisted.

'She looks like Grandma's toilet roll holder,' Jack muttered. 'Like you did in the restaurant in your *Frozen* dress.'

Lily just narrowed her eyes.

'And how about you?' Jacqui asked Chelsea. 'What did you get up to? Anything you want to tell us?'

'We pottered around,' said Chelsea. 'There was a huge queue for the Uffizi so we decided to skip it and explore instead. Adam took me to—'

'Yes?' Jacqui's eyes lit up.

'The school of leather.'

'Leather?' echoed Jacqui.

'Make you buy her a nice whip so she can keep you in line when she moves in, did she?' Mark asked Adam.

Ronnie gave him a vicious nudge.

'Not that kind of leather,' said Chelsea. 'They make the best handbags in Italy. Adam did his research.'

'Oh,' said Ronnie. 'Why didn't I know about that? I'd have gone into Florence if I'd heard about that. Apart from the first sight you get of the Tower, Pisa's really dull. It's full of people pestering you to buy crappy sunglasses and plastic towers. What did you get?'

Chelsea showed off the pretty little purse with her initials on it.

'That's nice,' said Ronnie.

'You didn't get anything else?' Jacqui asked.

'There wasn't time, Mum. We had lunch and then we had to go back to the coach.'

'Aw. Well, there's always Genoa, eh Adam?' said Jacqui.

'What is going on?' Ronnie asked her mother when they were alone.

'I don't know, love,' said Jacqui. 'Perhaps we read too much into it, Adam asking if we could help them have some time together without Lily again today.'

'How could we have misunderstood?' said Ronnie. 'What exactly did he say, Mum? When he went for that walk after lunch at Annabel's? Did he ask Dad for her hand in marriage or not?'

'I don't know. I'm all confused. Perhaps your dad got it wrong.'

'How could he get it wrong? Adam either asked if he could marry Chelsea or he didn't. I'm going to ask him.'

'Adam?'

'No. Dad.'

'Don't, love. It'll upset him if he thinks he's caused any upset. Thinking back on it, the conversation wasn't exactly straightforward.'

Ronnie frowned.

'Oooh look,' said Jacqui, changing the subject. 'I've just got a text from Annabel, letting me know how Granddad Bill's getting on.'

Chapter Forty Eight

Annabel and Bill

That day, Annabel had taken Granddad Bill into town. They dropped Sophie and Izzy off at their respective offices first, then parked up by the cathedral. Now that he was feeling completely better after his chest infection, Bill had been talking about wanting to get his hair cut, so Annabel found a suitable barber and took him to get a short back and sides. After that, they went to have tea in a café, with Humfrey next to them in his pushchair. Richard was at work. Only Leander had been left at home. He was probably pining for the man with the mints.

Annabel was determined to take advantage of having Granddad Bill to herself. She wanted to hear as much of her birth family history as he was able to tell her. Fortunately, Granddad Bill was having another good day and when Annabel asked about her grandmother, he knew exactly who she was talking about and was able to give Annabel an amusing account of how he and Jennifer had met.

'It was at a dance,' he said, 'at the Massey Ferguson social club. I was there because my mate was working at Massey and he took me along as his guest. He said they had the most beautiful women in Warwickshire in his factory and he was right. My head was turned the minute I walked in the door. I'd never seen anything like her. She was a goddess. She was wearing a green dress. She had blonde hair, piled up on her head like Carmen Miranda's fruit. She had great ankles, a tiny waist. I remember saying that to John. And he said to me, she's too good for you, Bill Benson. She's too good for the likes of any of us. Well, I told him I wasn't having that. Cupid got me right through the heart with his arrow and I was determined to make her mine.'

'So how did you persuade her?' Annabel asked.

'I got my comb out and slicked back my hair. I asked John to check my tie was on straight and there was no dandruff on my shoulders. Then I took a deep breath and walked straight across that dance floor to ask her if I could have the next waltz.'

'And what did she say?'

'She never even noticed me. Just as I was getting close, some other bloke stepped in and whisked her off from under my nose.'

'Oh no.'

'I didn't want to look like an idiot so I pretended I wasn't ever going to ask her to dance anyway. I offered my arm to her friend. Luckily for me, she said she'd be delighted. And that's how I met your grandmother.'

'She was the friend?'

'Aye. Fortune was smiling on me that day. I definitely got the right girl despite her thick ankles.'

Annabel had to laugh. She'd never liked her ankles and now she knew from whom she'd inherited them.

'Isn't life strange?' said Annabel. 'So many of the most important things in our lives come about by chance. If that other bloke hadn't beaten you to asking the goddess to dance, you might have married her instead. Dave, Ronnie, me and Chelsea, we might never have existed.'

'Yes,' said Bill. 'It's a funny old life.'

'We try so hard to make plans but it's the things that are out of our control that end up defining us. I wish I had met my grandmother.'

'She was a wonderful woman.'

Annabel reached across and rested her hand on her grandfather's. As she did so, she noticed his expression change. The cocksure smile with which he had relayed the story of his first meeting with Jennifer was replaced with a look of confusion and distress.

'I keep forgetting she's not here any more,' he said. 'Why do I keep forgetting?'

After that, Granddad Bill seemed to take a turn towards the melancholy and Annabel decided it was probably best not to ask any more questions for a while. Instead, they went back to the big house.

'Why are we here?' Bill asked. 'What are we doing here? This isn't my house. Take me home.'

'You're staying with us, Bill.' Annabel braced herself for a meltdown. 'You and Sophie. Dave and Jacqui are on the cruise. You weren't well enough to go so you came to stay here.'

'I don't know this house.'

'But you know us,' Annabel tried. 'I'm your granddaughter Annabel. And look, here's Leander.'

Leander greeted Bill as though he had been away for a month. To Annabel's great relief, Leander's appearance seemed to break the spell. Bill gave the dog a scratch between the ears and forgot all about where he was supposed to be for a moment.

'That dog is completely in love with you,' Annabel laughed. 'He doesn't even bother saying hello to the rest of us any more.'

'He's a good dog, is Barney,' said Bill.

Annabel didn't correct him, though she knew that Barney was the name of the dog Dave had as a child.

'Let's get you settled in your chair, Bill,' she suggested.

'Come on, Barney,' said Bill.

Leander led the way.

The sudden change in Granddad Bill, from lucid to confused, had rattled Annabel. After she had settled him in the conservatory, she went into the kitchen and poured herself a glass of wine from the bottle Richard had opened the night before.

How heartbreaking to forget that you'd lost your wife, only to remember again and experience the grief anew. Better to forget altogether. Perhaps it didn't actually help that Izzy looked a lot like Jennifer – as did Sophie. It was funny the way that a family face could turn up generations later.

That moment in the dance hall, Annabel smiled to think of it.

There were so many sliding door moments in everyone's lives. What if Annabel hadn't met Richard? What if Izzy hadn't taken that fake ecstasy tablet at the festival? What if that poor chap hadn't been killed in an accident on Christmas Eve?

Thinking about all the ways in which her life had changed direction in a heartbeat, as though it was a pinball buffeted by flippers, made Annabel feel quite dizzy. Truth was, she was worried. Izzy had been very introspective lately. Even with Sophie around, she'd not been her old self. Right after the transplant, she had been almost euphoric. It was really as though a life sentence had been lifted. No more dialysis. The prospect of a normal life – going back to school; going to university. Now Izzy had quietened back down. She was too quiet.

Annabel hadn't pushed Izzy for details of her appointment with the psychologist. She and Richard had discussed it and decided that Izzy was old enough to have some privacy. However, Annabel knew that Izzy was preoccupied with thoughts of her donor. She knew that Izzy had talked to Sophie about it. She hoped Sophie was helping Izzy to see that good could come of bad. Like Granddad Bill failing to dance with the woman he wanted. Like Jacqui giving Annabel up so she was able to grow up as a Cartwright, with all the happiness and privilege that brought. Like Sophie getting drunk and falling into the sea in Lanzarote so that Adam rescued her and became a hero in Chelsea's eyes. Izzy wasn't responsible for her donor's death but she was, in some way, enabling him to keep on making a difference through her.

Optimism was exhausting. Annabel found herself wishing for the way things had been. Not just before Izzy's drug disaster. Sometimes she wished for the way it had been when she was a teenager and had no one to care about but herself. Just so that she could sleep easy and feel free again. Just for a moment or two. Sometimes love could be a very heavy burden indeed.

Chapter Forty Nine

Adam and Chelsea

On Sunday, the ship docked in Genoa, home to Christopher Columbus, the explorer who discovered America. Genoa was the port where a million adventures had begun. That day, the *European Countess* was offering excursions to Genoa itself or further afield to Portofino and the Cinque Terre, the nearby resort towns. Adam and Chelsea chose Portofino. Once again, Jacqui leapt in to offer babysitting.

'I think the children would like to stay on board today,' Jacqui said. 'Chill out in the kids' club rather than get on another coach.'

Adam accepted her generous offer at once.

'Jacqui,' he said. 'You're a marvel. It'll be great for me and Chelsea to have the chance to explore again.'

'Yeah. Thanks, Mum,' said Chelsea.

Chelsea had given up wondering if Adam had an ulterior motive.

So Adam and Chelsea joined the excursion to Portofino. It may once have been a simple fishing village, but the picturesque town became a playground for the rich and famous in the 1950s and had stayed that way ever since, with the brightly painted shops along the waterfront selling designer goods that would not have been out of place in Knightsbridge or on Bond Street. Hermès,

Ferragamo and Gucci all had shops there. Not much tourist tat to be had.

The *European Countess* tour group were first driven from Genoa to Santa Margherita, where they took a small boat along the coast to reach their destination. Once there, they were free to explore.

Adam and Chelsea wandered the cobbled streets of Portofino hand in hand. They found a lovely restaurant on the Piazetta where the pasta was only the price of a three-course dinner back home. It was insanely expensive but the restaurant terrace was the perfect place to people watch. The tourists in Portofino could not have been more different from the crowd at the Hotel Volcan in Lanzarote. Chelsea spotted all the designer brands. Why buy espadrilles for seven euros when you could have a pair by Chanel? There were more Birkins than beach bags. Certainly, no one was wearing a sarong that had come free with the August issue of a women's mag, such as the one Chelsea had in her own beach tote that day.

After lunch, over which they lingered in an attempt to get their money's worth, Adam and Chelsea walked up the hill opposite the town to Castillo Brown, a magnificent folly that was now often used for glamorous weddings. *Society* magazine had featured one just the previous year: a couple of chinless wonders marrying in haste. The bride wore three dresses over the course of the day. Chelsea had written up the story, fighting the urge to gag.

Though Castillo Brown was beautiful with the most spectacular vista, Chelsea would not want to marry in such a place. She had always treasured the idea of marrying in the Chelsea Register Office on the King's Road: a small, modest private ceremony, with a big party afterwards, perhaps. Maybe not even on the same day.

Chelsea had seen the photographs from Adam's wedding to Claire, of course. There were several around his house. The largest one was in the sitting room, where it had a prominent position on the mantelpiece, alongside school and nursery photographs of Lily. Chelsea had examined the pictures closely when Adam was out of the room. She was impressed by Claire's choice of dress, which was restrained and elegant with a hint of the 1920s to the styling. Chelsea also liked the way Claire had done her hair, which was as fine and straight as Lily's.

Adam had told Chelsea about the wedding too. He'd seemed a little reluctant but Chelsea had pushed him, assuring him that it was good to talk about it. Adam explained that they had married in Claire's hometown and her parents had hosted the reception in their garden. They were the kind of people who had a garden big enough for a marquee! How different Claire's upbringing must have been from Chelsea's. There was no chance the Bensons could fit a marquee in their back garden. These days even a two-man tent would be pushing it with all the wheelie bins that the council's new recycling regime required.

Chelsea often wondered about Claire's parents. Of course, they were still a part of Adam's life. They took a keen and active interest in their only granddaughter, Lily. And Lily did look so much like her mother. They hadn't asked to meet Chelsea yet but they would have to, wouldn't they? Now that she was moving in. Perhaps it should happen even before Chelsea left her Stockwell flat. That way they could feel as though they'd been consulted, though Chelsea hoped their opinion wouldn't ultimately hold any sway.

'Penny for your thoughts?' said Adam.

'Oh, I wasn't thinking about anything much,' Chelsea lied. 'I was just looking at the sea. Isn't it the most amazing colour today?'

It was the blue of a child's painting of the ocean.

'Let me take a picture,' said Adam. 'Beautiful backdrop for the most beautiful girl in the world.'

While Adam was firing off a few shots, Chelsea mentioned the *Society* magazine photo-shoot that had taken place on the hill.

'This would be a great place to get married,' said Adam. 'I mean, if your intended was at all undecided, they'd be rather stuck. Unless they decided to go for it and jump right off the cliff.'

Adam leaned over to look at the sea.

'I wonder how many reluctant grooms have gone over those rocks?'

'Don't be horrible,' said Chelsea.

'Come here,' he said, taking her hand and pulling her close. 'I want to ask you something.'

Now? The blood rushed to Chelsea's cheeks. Was this going to be the place? It was certainly picturesque but there were quite a few people about. Shouldn't they be somewhere more private?

'What do you want to ask?' Chelsea stuttered.

'Will you hold my camera bag while I take a leak?'

Adam grinned.

'Oh, I should throw you off the cliff right now,' Chelsea complained.

They wandered back down to the harbour arm in arm and had another drink at a bar there. Portofino was definitely somewhere Chelsea would have liked to linger. As they waited for the tender to take them back to Santa Margherita where they would get back on the coach to

Genoa, Adam and Chelsea watched a taxi boat arrive from the next village along the coast. It was carrying a bride and groom and a handsome wedding party. The groom leapt out to help his bride ashore. She was an extremely stylish bride. Her dress was a glittering sheath. Her hair hung loose about her shoulders. There seemed to be wedding parties all over Italy.

Adam saw Chelsea looking at the beautiful newly-weds. He kissed her on the nose.

'What's that for?' Chelsea asked.

'Nothing,' said Adam. 'I just felt compelled to kiss you.'

It seemed significant.

That night, when Jack was finally asleep, Chelsea looked at the selfie she and Adam had taken high on the hill over Portofino. She was looking at the camera. He was looking at her. The love in his eyes made Chelsea feel warm all over. So, he hadn't proposed to her. So what? She could tell how much she meant to him. Would a ring really make any difference?

She went out onto the balcony. She could sense that Adam was on the other side of the partition before she leaned round and saw him leaning out to see her.

'Is Lily asleep?' Chelsea asked.

'Yes. And Jack?'

'Out for the count.'

They kissed their fingertips and pressed them together.

'You look especially beautiful right now,' said Adam.

'I feel so lucky to have you,' Chelsea told him.

'I'm the lucky one,' said Adam.

Chapter Fifty

Jane and Kirsty

Kirsty had spent the day touring the Cinque Terre – a string of picturesque villages, which cling to the Ligurian coast like brightly coloured limpets. She ate lunch in a seaside café where she flirted with the two waiters who were, between them, fifteen years too young and fifty years too old. Never mind. They were gratifyingly attentive and brought Kirsty a small glass of limoncello and a tightly furled rose with her bill. She tucked the flower behind her ear and imagined, as she wandered through the narrow streets, that she was the red-headed Sophia Loren. She put some wiggle in her walk and enjoyed the admiring glances.

Jane, meanwhile, spent another day on board. She tried to read but couldn't concentrate and, from time to time, she looked towards the Ligurian hills a little wistfully and wished she'd gone with Kirsty after all.

When Kirsty came back on board they ate dinner on the balcony again. After that, they watched another film.

'I'm sorry I haven't been able to go ashore,' said Jane. 'I know it can't be much fun for you. You might as well be taking this cruise on your own, for all the company I've been. You've been doing the tours on your own. Going to dinner on your own. I thought I would feel better than this. I thought that once we got going, I'd be able to stop thinking about Greg so much and enjoy all the places the cruise took us.'

'We can still get off the ship early. We're in Marseille tomorrow. I'm sure we can fly home from there. Or take a train to Paris and catch the Eurostar. I'm sure it wouldn't take much to sort it out.'

'No,' said Jane. 'We're over halfway now. I can make it.'

'Are you sure?'

'I want to.'

The two friends stretched out their arms and held hands over the gap between their beds.

Tired from the combination of a busy day on shore and half a bottle of rosé, Kirsty was soon asleep but Jane's mind was buzzing. She went out onto the balcony. It was cool, out on the ocean. She could feel that the ship was moving fast. Sometimes it felt as though the ship was a living being. She imagined it now like some huge celestial sea-creature. A cross between a dolphin and a mystical sea-horse, cutting through the waves at a gallop.

Standing outside, Jane felt the prickle of salt-water on her face. She embraced it. It felt gentle and life-affirming. Almost like a kiss. Though the cruise had been difficult at times, she had enjoyed the feeling of being at sea. She liked the gentle rocking that began as soon as the ship loosed its moorings. She liked the sound of the wind rushing by. She even liked the tinkling of the coat-hangers in the wardrobe. It reminded her of the clanging of the rigging on the fishing boats in Cornwall, where she'd holidayed so often as a child. The coat-hangers were not so tuneful to Kirsty, who had got up on three occasions and taken all the empty hangers out of the wardrobe so they couldn't clash. The housekeeper always put them back. The hangers were quiet now.

Jane glanced back into the room. Kirsty was sleeping soundly with her mouth open.

After a while watching the lights of distant fishing boats on the horizon, Jane leaned over the balcony bar and looked down below. There was someone sitting there. Someone she knew. Jane's heart stuttered when she saw him.

'Greg,' she whispered.

The shape of his head – the way his hair curled around it. Though Jane had never actually seen her fiancé from this angle, she would have known him anywhere. For a moment, she didn't even dare blink, so desperate was she to keep Greg in her sight, alive and waiting for her downstairs.

'Darling.' This time the word came out as a croak. A soft one, but just loud enough to attract the attention of the man below, who looked up to see who was calling him.

Jane stepped back into the shadows as he turned his face up to her. It wasn't Greg. Of course it wasn't – just another cruel trick of the mind. It was the young father she and Kirsty had seen around that week, the one with the little girl who was always dressed as a princess, and the girlfriend or wife who dressed like she was straight from the pages of a magazine. Not a ghost, just an ordinary man. Someone, like Jane, who couldn't sleep.

Someone who had looked at her as though he was hoping to see someone different too.

Chapter Fifty One

The Bensons

On Monday morning, the ship reached France and docked in the famous port at Marseille. There was an opportunity to visit Marseille itself but the Benson party had already decided that they wanted to go further afield and so they joined the coach trip going to Aix-en-Provence. Jacqui had been re-reading *A Year in Provence* after finding a copy in the ship's extensive library and she was keen to see if the region matched her expectations. The children were drawn in by the promise of a visit to a flea market. A *marché aux puces*.

'I'm going to buy a whole circus of fleas,' said Jack.

Nobody had the heart to tell him that the fleas wouldn't officially be on sale. It was much too interesting listening to the tricks he planned to teach them. 'I'll teach them to go through a ring of fire. I can make that out of half a toilet roll.' And the flea facts: 'A flea can jump over fifty times its own height. If I could do that, I could jump over the top of the cathedral back home!'

'That would be a very useful trick,' said Mark. 'For when your mum's after you for not having tidied your bedroom.'

'I always keep my bedroom tidy,' said Lily.

Aix-en-Provence is a very beautiful town with its elegant eighteenth-century boulevards and pretty pavement cafés in the shade of enormous plane trees. When the *European Countess* tour visited, it was not officially market day but a series of stalls lined the main street, catering to the tourists with their bright painted Provençal pottery, delicate lace and lavender-scented soap. Jacqui stocked up on muslin bags of dried lavender.

'Our house will smell like an old people's home!' said Dave.

'Well, that'd be just about right,' said Jacqui. 'Since you and your dad are already in it.'

'I'm six months younger than you are,' Dave reminded her.

Once again, Jacqui insisted that Adam and Chelsea went off to explore on their own, while she and Dave looked after the children. Ronnie had already jumped at the chance of more babysitting, though she and Mark didn't want to do much more than find a nice French bar.

'We can stay around here,' Jacqui told Chelsea. They had found themselves beside the city's famous fountain of the Three Graces. Jack and Lily were busy splashing each other. 'I don't want to do too much walking around. It's hot and it's all too much uphill.'

'And we've got to find the fleas,' said Jack. 'Ted wants some too.'

'If Ted gets fleas,' said Ronnie, 'Auntie Annabel will not be amused.'

Adam and Chelsea joined hands as soon as they were out of sight of the rest of the gang.

'This really is a whistle-stop tour of Europe,' said Chelsea.

'Yep. It's Monday so it must be Provence,' said Adam.

'It's very pretty here,' said Chelsea. 'I can see why people retire to this part of the world.'

'Sit around all day, smelling of lavender, with nothing to do but play boules and drink cassis.'

'Oooh, cassis,' said Chelsea. 'We've got to find some of that. What shall we do? Walk first then lunch or the other way round?'

'Walk first,' said Adam. 'I feel like my legs are getting out of practice.'

'I know what you mean. I wonder how long it will take for the rocking sensation to finally go when we get back to Southampton. It's like I'm perpetually drunk.'

They weaved up the Cours Mirabeau, the tree-lined main street that featured in all the picture postcards, then ducked into a narrow alleyway that looked as though it led somewhere good. They were heading for the oldest part of Aix, which dated back to the twelfth century. They soon found the Cathedral of Saint Sauveur and cooled down for a while in its beautiful cloisters. After that, they strolled towards the Quartier Mazarin. Chelsea was keen to see some art at the Musée Granet. She'd checked the collection online.

There was a church next to the museum: the church of Saint-Jean-de-Malte.

'Can we go in there?' Chelsea asked. 'I'd like to light a candle for Granddad Bill. To say thank you for his getting over that chest infection.'

When the ship had docked in Marseille and she got a phone signal, Jacqui had shown Chelsea Annabel's text confirming that Bill was much better.

'Haven't we done enough ecclesiastical sights for today? I'd rather go and get lunch,' said Adam.

'It won't take a moment. It's just that I've got a good feeling about this one. It looks so pretty in there.'

Chelsea dragged Adam closer.

'It won't take long. Come on.'

'I'm fine out here,' said Adam.

'You were just complaining about being too hot. It'll be cool in there. Why don't you want to come in?'

Adam's face grew grave and Chelsea knew the answer before she finished asking the question.

'You came here with Claire, didn't you?'

Adam confirmed Chelsea was right.

'OK,' said Chelsea. 'I get it. I wish you'd said.' She paused before asking, 'When?'

'It was the year after we were married. We drove down and rented a house near Orange. We did a day trip here.'

'And you found this church?'

'Look, we came here just after she found out she was pregnant with Lily. We were wandering round. We weren't looking for anywhere in particular but we came across this place and Claire insisted we go inside to light a candle to ask for a safe pregnancy. She'd had a couple of false starts and she was getting really bad morning sickness. She was frightened she was going to have another miscarriage. You can go in there if you like but I think . . . I think it would make me sad.'

'I understand,' said Chelsea. She turned away from the church door.

'No, seriously, you should go in. I remember there's a really beautiful painting in there. You should see it. And you should light a candle for Bill. If you want.'

Adam practically pushed Chelsea back towards the door. He seemed so determined that she should go inside and light a bloody candle, she didn't bother to protest. Besides, she suddenly felt a strong urge to be away from him before she said something she would regret later on.

'All right,' she said. 'I'll see you in a minute.'

'I'll wait over there,' Adam pointed to a bench.

Chelsea walked into the church. It was empty but for an old woman on the front row of pews who was bent over in prayer, her shopping bags arrayed around her feet like pets. Chelsea was very glad she was the only tourist. She picked up a votive from the stand at the back of the nave and put three euros in the box to pay for it. It was three times more than requested but Chelsea felt she needed to make her prayers three times as strong.

Most of the candles were burning on a rack beneath the portrait of the Madonna and Child. Chelsea deliberately chose the lonely looking saint on the opposite side of the aisle. But when she was praying, she forgot all about giving thanks for Granddad Bill.

'Please let me work out how to get through this,' she said. 'Please let me be strong enough to work out what to say next. Please let me get through the next hour without fucking this up completely.'

Chelsea couldn't help it, her face crumpled. She didn't even quite know for whom she was crying. For Claire? For the expectant mother who would have the safe pregnancy she prayed for but still not get to see her daughter grow up? Or for herself? Chelsea was definitely feeling very sorry for herself. She was feeling upset and guilty and ashamed to boot. How could she possibly feel jealous of Claire because she'd been there with Adam before? How could she be jealous of someone who no longer even lived to love Chelsea's beloved back?

It wasn't in the least bit rational but it was very, very real.

Chapter Fifty Two

Adam and Chelsea

Though she had said she wouldn't be long, Chelsea had to stay in the church for almost fifteen minutes in order to stop crying and hide the evidence. The woman, who had been praying, frowned to see Chelsea touching up her make-up in the back row of the pews.

'*Desolée*,' Chelsea mouthed.

She straightened herself up and stepped back out into the sunshine. She longed to be away from this town and the thought of Claire and her futile gesture of hope, but there were another three hours before the bloody coach came back. Three hours of walking in the shadow of Adam's marriage.

Adam had been sitting on a stone bench opposite the church door. He stood up. He looked anxious.

'Let's go and find something to eat,' Chelsea said.

Adam nodded and they set off at a trot. He was as keen to be away from that church as Chelsea was.

Lunch was not the jolly occasion either of them had hoped for.

Adam felt guilty. Though Chelsea did not say so, he knew he had upset her deeply. He hadn't wanted to ruin Chelsea's day but he simply could not have gone into that church. He couldn't stand it. What reason could he have given other than the truth? If he'd been thinking straight, he would have made sure that they never even went anywhere near the place. Why hadn't he thought about it? It was as though some subconscious urge had drawn him in that direction, dragging Chelsea along with him. He could have steered her to the other side of the old town. She could have lit her candle in some church he'd never seen before and right now they would be laughing and joking and having a wonderful time while they sank a delicious bottle of the local rosé.

Well, they'd bought that delicious bottle of rosé and the waiter had poured out two glasses but neither of them had taken much more than a sip. Adam knew this meant that Chelsea still felt herself on the verge of tears. She had told him in the past that she'd learned to avoid drinking when she was unhappy. It only made things worse. And despite her best efforts with the concealer, of course he knew that she had been crying in the fifteen minutes while she was inside the church and he sat outside trying to pluck up the courage to walk in there and join her, proving to her and to himself that the present was more important than the past.

Could the day get any worse?

Chelsea was not the only one who felt like crying right then. Adam was astonished to be so upset by the memories that seeing that church had unpacked. When Chelsea first told him about the cruise itinerary and said that there was a possibility of an excursion to Aix-en-Provence, he had tried hard not to show any reaction whatsoever to the name of the city he remembered only too well. And he had convinced himself that it would be fine to visit the place again. It was eight years since he had last been there. How fresh and potentially dangerous could the memories possibly be?

As it turned out, the memories were very fresh and

the thought of Claire lighting the candle in the church was just the beginning of it. Even when he was staring at the menu, trying to read the choices written upon it, he could see Claire's face as she turned towards him with a big beaming smile, convinced she had just bought their future child's safe passage into the world with a couple of tea-lights.

And then he remembered how it had been afterwards. They'd walked – it must have been in the same direction he'd just taken with Chelsea – and talked about baby names. Lily wasn't the first name they came up with. First they went through the boys'. Claire was convinced she was having a boy. Her mother had told her she was carrying 'high' and apparently that was a sign. Claire liked Harry for a boy's name, followed by Lukas. Adam lobbied hard for James, which was his grandfather's name and his own middle name. Wouldn't it be nice to honour the baby's forebears like that?

'Well, we could call him after my grandfather,' said Claire. Her grandfather had been called Hilary, which was a very fine name but Adam could imagine how it would go down at primary school.

'Let's not set the poor little thing up from the start,' said Adam.

'OK, then maybe Hilary as a second name. He wouldn't have to tell anyone.'

They were agreed. James Hilary Baxter. They were satisfied that the initials were suitably innocuous. Nothing rude to be made from those.

'What do you think?' Claire asked her bump. 'Oh, I'm sure the baby moved in approval,' she claimed, though of course at just twelve weeks, the foetus was much too small to have made itself felt.

When it came to girls' names, Adam didn't have a

clue what he liked. Claire was only dead set against Saskia, which had overtaken Chloe and Sophie as the most popular girls' name in the smart part of London where they'd just bought their first home together.

'I don't want to shout our child's name in the playground and have six little girls and three dogs look up.'

Adam agreed. Though ironically, their actual choice would be far from unique. There were three Lilys in Lily's primary school class. Right then, however, Adam and Claire thought they'd hit upon something different.

'Lily was my great-grandmother's name,' said Adam.

'Then it's perfect!' said Claire. 'Perhaps she'll be the reincarnation of your great-gran. Was she nice?'

'I hear she was feisty,' said Adam.

The memory of that conversation was so fresh in Adam's mind that he could still hear Claire laugh. And he wanted to tell her that she was right. Lily had turned out to have all the attributes of Adam's great-grandmother, who lived to be one hundred and three and was terrorising waitresses, hairdressers and shop assistants until the very end.

But Claire wasn't there with him. Chelsea was.

And then Adam realised that in the fog of misery that followed the revelation in the church, he had somehow brought Chelsea to the exact same restaurant where he and Claire had plumped for James Hilary for a boy and Lily for a girl. How had he failed to recognise it? Now that he looked again, he saw that even the waiters were the same guys who had been so friendly when Claire told them her good news. They had brought him a drink on the house that day to celebrate his impending fatherhood.

'What are you having?' Chelsea asked.

A nervous breakdown, thought Adam.

'I can't see anything I want here,' said Adam. 'Maybe we should just pay for the wine and find somewhere else.'

'Everywhere else was jammed,' said Chelsea. 'Besides, I'm tired and I'm hungry. I'm going to have a *croque madame*.'

'I'll have one too.'

'It's got a fried egg on it. I thought you didn't like fried eggs?'

'Just pick something for me then,' said Adam.

'Is that what Claire would have done?'

Chelsea bit down on the thought just too late.

'I just hoped you'd do it for me because you're fluent in French,' said Adam.

Chapter Fifty Three

The Bensons

While Adam and Chelsea were sitting outside the restaurant, Jacqui, Ronnie and the others came walking by. It was Jack who spotted them.

'Auntie Chelsea!'

He waved Ted above the flower boxes that marked out the restaurant's terrace. And of course Lily wanted to stop and say 'hello' to her dad.

'Are you having a nice day?' Chelsea asked her nephew.

'We are. Except we couldn't find any fleas at the market at all. Grandma said they must have sold out.'

'I think that's probably a good thing,' said Chelsea. 'The last thing the captain wants is an infestation on the *European Countess*.'

'I think that would be funny,' said Jack. 'Everybody itching!'

'Can we stay with you, Daddy?' Lily asked. 'It's too hot and I'm tired of walking around.'

'Of course.'

A waiter quickly pulled across another table to accommodate the new arrivals. More drinks were ordered. Jack and Lily wanted *frites*.

'That's French for chips,' Jack explained to his aunt.

'Chelsea knows that,' said Lily, with a proprietorial air. 'She lived in France when she was a little girl.'

'Well, I wasn't so little,' said Chelsea, remembering the year she'd spent in France as part of her language degree.

Chelsea was grateful for the arrival of the rest of the gang. It made the fact that she and Adam were struggling to find anything to say to one another much less obvious. There was never a moment's silence when Jack and Lily were around. They talked at each other and over each other, eager to be the one who told the story about the mime dressed as Napoleon who had scared the wits out of both of them when he suddenly moved as the children were posing for a picture in front of his pedestal. Lily spoke wistfully about a doll's house she had seen in the window of a shop.

'But it's too big to go on the boat.'

'The ship,' everyone else chorused.

'Melinda could have lived in it. And my new Spanish doll. And Ted.'

'You'll have to put a doll's house on your Christmas list,' suggested Jacqui.

'Or get one for my birthday,' said Lily. 'Chelsea, you can help me to decorate. Daddy said we're going to decorate when you move in.'

Chelsea looked at Adam. He was looking at something on his phone.

'Let's take a picture of Ted in this restaurant,' said Jack. They arranged the sad old toy on the table, propped up against another pepper pot with a glass of wine by her right paw.

'Ted needs a glass of wine,' said Lily. 'She's worn out. Ladies have wine when they're worn out. That's what my grandma says.'

'Ted is not a lady,' Jack said under his breath.

* * *

Adam watched his daughter organising Ted's photo-shoot. He was struck, as happened more and more often, by how much she was like her mother. She had Claire's confidence. She wasn't afraid to state a preference or tell someone she thought they were wrong.

Adam was very glad indeed that Lily was inheriting so many of her mother's personality traits as well as her heart-shaped face and heartbreaking eyes. He only wished that Claire might have been there to see her Mini-Me coming into her own. He wondered whether they would have butted heads, as Adam's sister had done with their mother. Would they have been too alike?

What made Adam saddest of all that afternoon was that he couldn't tell Lily that this was the place where she had first become real to him, where he and her mother had chosen her name.

Adam was torn between the past and the woman he had hoped was his future. Chelsea.

'Ted is happy with that photo,' said Lily, choosing the perfect picture on the screen of Chelsea's iPhone with the confidence of a fashion magazine editor. 'But she needs to wear a different outfit tomorrow,' she told Jack.

Normally, a remark like that would have made Chelsea laugh. She didn't.

'Oh! It's nearly five o'clock,' said Jacqui. 'We better be getting back to the coach. We don't want to miss it. I overheard a woman on the way here this morning saying that someone was left behind in Genoa yesterday and they were going to have to get a taxi all the way to Marseille and get back on again there. Can you imagine how expensive that would be? I dread to think.'

'Cheaper to fly back home,' said Ronnie.

'Yes. But they'll have left all their clothes and things on board. Come on, Jack and Lily. Don't forget Ted.'

Adam and Chelsea walked back to the meeting point in silence, trailing behind the rest of the gang. She tucked her hand through his arm, as a gesture of reconciliation. Adam smiled, but it didn't quite reach his eyes. The smile Chelsea gave him in return was exactly the same. They both knew that something had changed.

Chapter Fifty Four

Kirsty and Jane

It was in Marseille that Kirsty had persuaded Jane to leave the ship at last.

Having not set foot on dry land since the *European Countess* left Southampton, Jane found her first few moments on solid ground to be quite a shock. Far from feeling firm beneath her feet, the land felt as though it was roiling like waves in a gale. The ship had been steady by comparison.

'I feel a bit sick,' she said, having managed not to get seasick on board the ship at all.

'You get used to it,' said Kirsty, helping Jane onto the coach. Kirsty was very relieved to have Jane with her that day when she spotted her elderly seat-mate from the trip to Barcelona.

The friends were taking the excursion to Avignon. Kirsty couldn't help singing the song they'd learned in French lessons at school. But she wasn't really interested in seeing the famous bridge or '*pont*'. No, Kirsty had something else in mind.

'What do you want to do?' asked Jane once the coach had dropped them off near the centre of town.

'Well, we're not going to spend the day traipsing around museums, that's for sure. We can do that anywhere. What we need is a unique French experience. I think it's this way.'

Jane followed Kirsty.

Kirsty found the place she was looking for. 'I've been doing some research. Apparently, this is the best restaurant in town. If not in Provence.'

The restaurant was called Restaurant Christian Etienne and it was set in the walls of the Palais des Papes in the heart of the old city.

'Wow,' said Jane. 'Are you sure? This place is pretty fancy.'

They walked into the frescoed dining room. Kirsty told the maître d' her name and they were shown through to the beautiful shady terrace, which was the only place to be in the summer. A waiter showed them to their seats with a flourish.

'Aperitif?' he asked.

'Oh definitely,' said Kirsty. She attempted to order a couple of glasses of champagne in her best French. The waiter replied in his best English. 'Ah well,' she said. 'At least I made the effort.'

'I haven't had a drink since Greg, you know,' said Jane. 'I'm not sure I can handle it.'

'You don't have to "handle it". I know you haven't had a drink in a while but just have a sip. Indulge me. It's my birthday after all.'

Jane gasped and covered her face with her hands. It was indeed Kirsty's birthday and, for the first time since they met at secondary school, Jane had forgotten.

'Kirsty, I'm so sorry! I can't believe I didn't remember.'

'No need to be sorry,' said Kirsty, catching the eye of a waiter. 'You've had other stuff on your mind.'

'I should have organised something.'

'No need. I did. We're in France. We're in a fancy restaurant. And as far as I'm concerned, that's the best start to a birthday ever.'

But it wasn't just any birthday. It was Kirsty's thirtieth. Twelve months ago, they had celebrated Kirsty's twenty-ninth with a meal in a gastropub back home. That day they'd been full of plans for the big 'three-O'. They were going to have a girls' weekend in London – or a spa day – or a full-on party.

'I feel like such an idiot,' said Jane. 'How could I forget such a big day? Why didn't you remind me at the beginning of the trip? Or at least tell me this morning?'

'I sort of thought you might just be pretending to have forgotten or it would come back to you as the day went on. Maybe you'd have a reminder on your phone or something. It doesn't matter.'

The waiter returned with their aperitifs, accompanied by a basket of bread and a bowl full of fat green olives.

Kirsty snatched up her champagne. Jane followed suit. They chinked glasses.

'*Bon anniversaire*,' said Jane, remembering her own schoolgirl French.

'*Merci*. Well, I had hoped to be making my first visit to Provence with George Clooney but now he's taken I'm very glad to be here with you. Thank you for coming ashore.'

The champagne was delicious and it did slip down very easily. When Kirsty ordered a second round, Jane didn't protest.

Kirsty was in her element. Though she really didn't know a word of French beyond '*s'il vous plait*', she managed to strike up a flirtation with the two old gentlemen on the next table after they complimented her wild red hair. This was the perfect way to spend a thirtieth birthday.

'Do you remember my eighteenth?' Kirsty mused.

'How could I forget it?' Jane asked. 'I was the one who had to go with you to the accident unit.'

'Yeah. But it was great up until that moment, wasn't it?'

'True.'

Kirsty had an amazing eighteenth birthday party but it all went awry when she jumped onto a table, intending to dance while her guests sang 'Happy Birthday' to her. She'd slipped on a stray maraschino cherry (she'd insisted on proper cocktails for her big night), fell off the table and landed badly, spraining her wrist. Jane had gone with her for the long wait at A and E. The night had ended with the medical staff downing tools to sing 'Happy Birthday' instead. Kirsty could start a party anywhere.

'Well, I'm not going to dance on any tables this afternoon, you'll be relieved to hear. I'm not sure the good people of Avignon could stand it.'

'I'm sure they've seen worse.'

'You're right,' said Kirsty. '*Sur le pont*.'

For dessert, the waiter, who had overheard Jane wishing Kirsty 'bon anniversaire' several times throughout the meal, brought out a small chocolate cake topped with a candle. He led the whole restaurant – staff and patrons – in singing. They had another glass of champagne then, courtesy of Kirsty's admirers. And Kirsty did get up and dance with one of the waiters. It was a wonderful afternoon.

When lunch was over, there was just a little time left for shopping before they had to be back on the bus for Marseille. Jane insisted on buying Kirsty a glass pendant from a gift shop. It was clear and shaped like a heart with a swirl of red in the middle. Kirsty loved it.

'I will treasure this for ever.'

'I'm so sorry I forgot your birthday,' Jane said, her words slurring ever so slightly. From not having touched a drop of alcohol in six months, she'd tucked away three glasses.

'You're my best friend. You *never* have to say you're sorry to me.'

'But I am sorry. Today is the proof of how wrapped up in myself I've been. It's your birthday. Your thirtieth birthday! I should have had something planned. We should have done something really special.'

'We did,' said Kirsty. 'We had lunch in Avignon. And you've been there for every other birthday I've had since I turned twelve. I will never forget how, when we were fifteen, you actually queued up from five in the morning outside HMV to get Lee Latchford-Evans's autograph on a copy of *Steptacular* just for me.'

'That was a serious sacrifice,' said Jane. 'Anyone might have seen me. Steps!' Jane pulled a face. 'I'd never have lived it down.'

'Steps were great,' Kirsty insisted. 'And what about my nineteenth birthday, when I'd just been dumped by that idiot Jamie and you got a bunch of people together at the Welsh Harp for a surprise party to cheer me up? And then there was my twenty-first. You persuaded everyone to chip in to buy me that gorgeous silver bracelet from Tiffany. And you didn't give me grief when I lost it down the loo in The Cuckoo Club the night of my twenty-fifth.'

'That was a big night,' Jane remembered.

'My head ached for a month,' said Kirsty. 'Didn't I vomit over your handbag?'

'You did,' Jane confirmed. 'It was suede. Cream suede.'

'But you didn't complain! So, you see, you've always been the very best *best* friend a girl could hope for and that's why today has been perfect. Because I got to share it with you. I hope we get to share our fortieths, our fiftieths and our sixtieths in exactly the same way.'

'Me too,' said Jane.

The two girls linked arms and headed back to the pick-up point.

Kirsty's birthday lunch in Avignon had gone so well that she dared to suggest to Jane that they continue the celebrations on board ship. They ate in the Italian restaurant, moving from champagne to prosecco. After that, they took a turn round the atrium, to see what sort of entertainment had been laid on for the evening. That night, an acrobatic troop was performing. Three guys dressed as mobsters. They were very impressive: back-flipping and climbing on each other's shoulders as though they had springs in their heels.

'Shall we poke our heads in at the karaoke?' Kirsty asked when the acrobats finished.

Jane agreed. But they had hardly been in the room for two minutes when events took a turn for the worse. Jane recognised the song from the very first note. It was their song: Robbie William's 'Angels' – one of Greg's favourites, which had become hers too as the soundtrack of their early dates and their falling in love. Jane had avoided this song as much as she could, swiftly turning off the car radio, the kitchen radio or the television whenever it came on. She would run out of shops rather than hear the chorus. She had to do the same now.

'I've got to go,' she told Kirsty. She didn't have to

explain. Then she raced for the door. By the time she was in the corridor, the tears had overtaken her.

Adam, Chelsea and the children were walking back from the ice cream parlour to the lifts when the woman ran past them. When she got to the bank of lifts, she ran into the first open carriage and, rather than hold it for the passengers coming behind her, she punched at the buttons to make the doors close.

'Hey!' Jack and Lily exclaimed in outrage. You didn't have to be on board ship long to work out that the lifts were very, very slow. That's why people held the doors for others coming along behind them. If you missed one, you could be waiting ages (hours, in dog years, as Jack pointed out) for the next one.

'She didn't wait!' said Lily.

But she had mouthed 'sorry'. Adam had seen it. They'd locked eyes. And, once again, he felt a curious sense of recognition. It was an oddly comforting moment in what had been a terrible day.

Chapter Fifty Five

Chelsea and Jack

Jack and Chelsea were back in their cabin after having supper and watching another show in the ship's theatre. Chelsea had persuaded Jack to put on his pyjamas and clean his teeth with the promise of another chapter from *Kaspar*. It turned into three chapters and still he wasn't feeling sleepy. He wanted to talk.

'Were you a bit sad this afternoon, Auntie Chelsea? When we were in France?'

Jack was so perceptive.

'I was fine,' she lied. 'I wasn't unhappy.'

'Your eyes were all red when we saw you in the restaurant.'

'I got some suntan lotion in them.'

'That stings,' Jack agreed. 'Mummy got some in my eyes once. She said it was my fault because I moved.'

'Oh dear,' said Chelsea. Typical of Ronnie, she thought.

'Anyway, I'm glad you weren't really sad,' said Jack.

'Thank you, Jack.'

'Because I was a bit sad today.'

'Really?'

'Yes. When Lily told me again that her mummy isn't alive any more.'

'That's right.'

'It's very sad. She says she can remember her mummy

a little bit but not very much. I asked if she's a ghost now. Lily told me not to be silly because ghosts don't exist. But they do exist, don't they? Granddad Bill said he saw one.'

'Granddad Bill was pulling your leg,' said Chelsea.

'No,' said Jack. 'He was serious. He said it was the ghost of someone who died in the Blitz. They didn't get into the shelter in time, like Granddad Bill's brother. He said it was a lady, walking up and down the street looking for her hat. She had it blown off by the bombs, he said.'

'Well,' said Chelsea. 'Perhaps that's what Granddad Bill thought he saw. It wasn't real. Our imaginations can do strange things. Especially when we're getting old and we've got a lot of fuzzy memories to choose from. You know what Granddad Bill's like. Sometimes he thinks he's back in the olden days with his own mum and dad.'

'That's because he's not very well. They'd be hundreds of years old by now. A hundred and seventy in dog years.'

'Exactly. Granddad Bill's mind plays tricks on him and sometimes he sees people who aren't really there but they're not ghosts, Jack. They're figments of his imagination.'

'I don't want to see any ghosts,' said Jack. 'Or *fig-men*. But if I do see one, I'm going to get it with my Sonic Screwdriver!'

'That's a very good idea. Fortunately, you'll never have to use it.'

'Because ghosts don't exist, do they? Not really.'

'You got it.'

At last, Chelsea persuaded Jack it was time to go to sleep.

Ghosts do exist though, thought Chelsea. Perhaps not in the old-fashioned sense, wearing sheets and jangling chains and saying 'Boo' to scare you. But Claire was definitely haunting her.

Chelsea wondered how she would feel in the spirit of Claire's position. Would she want Adam to find love again? There were loads of novels in which dying women prepared the men in their lives for a future without them and then hung around to make sure the men were coping. Those fictional women were always admirably open-hearted, wanting the men they had to leave behind to find love again, sometimes even engineering a meeting with their own successor. Wasn't it far more likely that you would want the person you left behind to mourn you eternally and never ever find someone to match you in their heart? Chelsea had to admit that was the kind of ghost she herself would be: possessive and jealous and vengeful. Maybe that was how Claire felt too.

Chelsea thought of the woman in the wedding photographs. There was one picture in which Claire was throwing her bouquet. She looked triumphant as she hurled the flowers high over the heads of the single women she had left behind. She had the expression of someone who was never going to let her man go. Not even death could part them.

Chapter Fifty Six

Bill and Annabel

The Great House was rumoured to have a ghost. It was the spectre of one of the house's previous owners, Mary Cavanagh: the lady of the manor back when the ancient manor was new. Mary Cavanagh was a pioneering woman, highly educated at a time when most women were barely schooled. She'd written books and fought for the welfare of the poor. She died of old age, well respected and well loved by everybody who knew her. She had no reason to haunt anybody, unless she was regretful that she hadn't done more during her lifetime and wanted Annabel to take up her cause. None of the Buchanans had ever seen her, though Annabel believed she'd felt something when she walked through the library. It wasn't an uncomfortable feeling. Mary Cavanagh was a benevolent sort of person in life so she'd be the same in death, Annabel thought.

But something had definitely gone bump in the night. Annabel opened her eyes and sat up, listening intently for another sound. She heard another heavy thump.

'Richard.' She shook him awake. 'Richard! Did you hear that?'

'Nnnngh,' said Richard.

'I heard something. I think there's somebody downstairs.'

'I didn't hear anything,' said Richard, though he

already knew that his chances of being allowed to roll over and go back to sleep were very low indeed. Sighing, he swung his legs out of bed and got up.

'What if it's a burglar?' Annabel asked.

'Leander didn't bark,' said Richard. 'It's not a burglar. He'd have gone berserk.'

'Unless it's a burglar carrying Trebor Mints,' said Annabel. 'I'm coming with you.'

It wasn't a burglar. It was Granddad Bill. Somehow, he had found his way from the ground floor guest room to the kitchen in the dark. He had not turned on any lights, which explained in part why he was making such a racket. He was standing in Annabel's pantry, grabbing things off the shelves – bags of flour, tins of soup – and stuffing them into a pillowcase that he must have taken off the bed. Leander was right behind him, wagging his tail, obviously hoping that something edible might be dropped in the kerfuffle. Illuminated in a circle of light from Richard's torch, Bill turned towards them with a look of terror on his pale old face.

If Bill was surprised, Richard and Annabel were equally freaked out. Jacqui had warned them about the possibility of nocturnal wanderings but, during the day, Bill could barely get from his chair to the bathroom. They guessed that he was having one of his episodes when he went back in time, but they were astonished that he seemed to have gone back in time physically too. When he turned, it was the fastest they had ever seen him move.

'I'm not going!' he said. 'I can't.'

Annabel stepped forward and touched Bill lightly on the arm, hoping it would be enough to bring him back to the present. It didn't work.

'I can't go,' he said.

'Go where?' Annabel asked.

'To the front. I can't go. I can't do it. I've got to hide. You've got to help me, Mother. I'm too young to die.'

Annabel tensed as Bill called her 'Mother'.

'It's Annabel, Bill. I'm your granddaughter. Dave and Jacqui's eldest.'

Richard turned the kitchen lights on. Bill blinked but remained locked somewhere else.

'Bill,' said Richard. 'Sit down. Come here.'

Richard brought a chair towards the pantry.

'Give me the pillowcase.'

Bill held the pillowcase more firmly.

'I need this,' he told Annabel beseechingly. 'I'm going to the woods. You won't tell them, will you? You promise you won't. I can't go, Mother. Don't make me. I don't want to die.'

'What should we do?' Annabel asked her husband.

'Perhaps we should try humouring him,' Richard suggested. 'Just until we can get him back into bed. Come on, Bill. We'll hide you. Come on. Follow me. We'll keep you safe.'

Bill gripped Richard's arm tightly and Richard manoeuvred him back to the guest room. Annabel and Leander followed. Izzy and Sophie had been woken by the palaver and were standing on the first floor landing.

'What's happening?' asked Sophie.

'Can we help?' Izzy asked.

'I don't think so,' said Annabel.

'Who are they?' asked Bill. 'They've seen me. They're going to tell!'

'It's OK, Bill,' said Richard. 'They're friends. They're not going to say anything.'

'I'm just a kid,' said Bill. 'I'm just a kid. I can't go to war. They can't make me.'

Frightened by the change in Bill, Izzy ran upstairs. Sophie remained frozen on the landing.

'I can hear the bombs,' Bill said. 'The Germans are coming!'

Sophie cried out. 'This is my fault,' she said. 'I shouldn't have asked him about the Blitz.'

'Sophie,' said Annabel. 'Go back to bed. It's the middle of the night and you've got work in the morning.'

'No. I've got to help you.'

Sophie helped Richard and Annabel get Bill back into the guest room.

'What's she doing here?' Bill pointed at Sophie. 'Tell her to get in the shelter.'

'Go to the shelter, Sophie,' said Annabel. 'We're going to be right behind you.'

'This is my fault,' said Sophie. 'This is my fault. I shouldn't have pressed him.'

Annabel didn't know who to comfort first.

'Go back upstairs,' she told her niece. 'We've got this under control.'

Just at that moment, Bill shook both Richard and Annabel off with incredible force. 'Eddie!' he yelled. 'Where's my brother?'

It took a long time to get Bill back to bed that night. In the end, they could only persuade him by promising him that the Germans had surrendered and there was no need to go to the front after all. As he asked, they let him keep the pillowcase full of provisions next to him. Annabel smoothed his brow. It seemed to soothe him.

Once all seemed calm, Sophie finally went back upstairs and Richard went back to bed too. Only

Annabel sat with her grandfather until it started to get light outside. She was thinking about Bill's flashback. He really had been back in the Second World War.

Annabel's adoptive grandfathers, on both sides, had exemplary war records but Bill's experience must have been very different. They were senior servicemen. They spent most of their war sitting in cosy offices. Bill was very young in 1944, which was when he signed up. Just sixteen. And he was a grunt. He would have seen the real action. How was it possible to go through something like that and leave it all behind? Of course it came back to haunt him. It seemed so cruel. Now that Bill's mind was going, he could no longer keep the worst of it down.

Annabel decided not to let Jacqui and Dave know what had happened. They were into the last leg of the cruise now. They'd be home soon enough. What was the point in spoiling their holiday? There was nothing they could do.

At around six, Bill began to stir. Annabel went to make him a cup of tea to wake up to. By the time she got back to the bedroom, he was sitting up, regarding the groceries in the pillowcase in some confusion. Leander had his head on the mattress, watching Bill carefully. The dog took the business of looking after the elderly family guest very seriously.

'Hello, Bill,' said Annabel. 'I brought you some tea. You had a busy night,' she added.

'I was a coward, Jennifer. A coward.'

Annabel knew this was not the moment to tell him she was not his wife.

'What do you mean, Bill?' she said.

'In France. I let everyone think I was a hero but I spent the whole time shaking like a dog.'

'Oh Bill. I'm not surprised.'

'It was like walking into Hell – half of us dead before we even got ashore. The minute I hit the sand, I ran as fast as I bloody could and hid as soon as I could find somewhere to hide. I hid for hours and hours. I was next to a dead body. I didn't know who he was. I can't even remember if he was one of us or a Nazi. I didn't want to go. I wouldn't have been there at all if Dad hadn't found me in the woods and marched me to the barracks. I only signed up for him, because of my brother and the Blitz. Dad lost his son. Eddie was always his favourite. We all lost our home. I wanted revenge. I didn't get any. I just hid in a pile of bloody lobster pots. You shouldn't be calling me a hero, Jennifer, because I'm no hero.'

'You are,' said Annabel. 'You're a hero to have been there at all. You weren't much older than Sophie.'

'Who's Sophie?'

'Never mind.'

'I should have died that day. I should have stood up like a man and gone down fighting. I never even fired my gun. I didn't get a single shot in for my brother. I didn't get vengeance for Eddie. I was a bloody disgrace.'

'What difference would it have made if you had shot someone?' said Annabel. 'Eddie was already gone.'

'I should have avenged him. An eye for an eye.'

'And we all end up blind,' said Annabel, remembering what one of her adoptive grandfathers had told her about the reality of war, quoting Gandhi to illustrate the futility. 'And you were so young. You shouldn't have been there in the first place. You did what you could. You lived to tell us how bad it really was. That's important too.'

Bill nodded but his eyes were far away. And when

he looked back at Annabel, she knew he was not seeing her.

'I was just a kid,' he said. 'Just a kid.'

Annabel turned to see Sophie standing in the doorway. She'd been listening to the exchange. Now she stepped into the room and took her great-grandfather's hand between both of hers.

'You'll always be my hero, Granddad Bill.'

Chapter Fifty Seven

Everyone

Tuesday was a sea day for the *European Countess*. After all the day trips and the racing around, most of the passengers looked forward to the chance to stay put and enjoy the best of what their floating home had to offer.

The Benson party met for breakfast, then went their separate ways. Jack and Lily went gleefully to the kids' club. Mark and Ronnie opted for a lazy day between balcony and bars. Jacqui and Dave drifted between the top deck pool and the bingo, where Jacqui seemed to be on a roll. Now that she knew it really was possible to win the lottery, Jacqui had been trying her luck at the bingo and on the slot machines too. She was at least a fiver up overall. Meanwhile, Adam had booked Chelsea in for a massage at the Retreat's secluded spa.

The massage was supposed to be a treat but Chelsea couldn't help thinking Adam wanted her out of the way. Since they'd been back on board ship, they had tried to pretend that nothing had happened in Aix-en-Provence – they certainly hadn't spoken about it – but the masseuse told Chelsea, 'Your shoulders feel like they're made of rock. Are you holding any tension?'

Chelsea didn't know whether to laugh or cry. In the end, she cried. The incredibly professional masseuse handed her a tissue and a chance to pretend it wasn't really happening, saying, 'Sometimes deep tissue work affects people this way. It's a good sign that you're letting all the toxins out.'

The image of releasing toxins made Chelsea think of all the vomiting she had done over her life. It was only being under the scrutiny of her family that was keeping her from binging and purging now. She was miserable. She couldn't even phone her counsellor because the ruinous cost of calling from sea would make her feel even worse.

'Do you want to talk about it?' the masseuse asked.

Chelsea shook her head but she allowed the masseuse to finish her 'deep tissue work' and, honestly, the combination of that and the woman's concerned kindness did make her feel just a little better.

'There's nothing you can't work out if you have faith in people's good intentions,' the masseuse said at the end, guessing that Chelsea's problem must be of an emotional nature rather than a muscle knot born of bad posture.

That gave Chelsea hope.

However, when she rejoined him on their sunbeds, Adam seemed more absorbed in reading *Flash Boys* than previously and Chelsea couldn't help but interpret that as a means of avoiding any conversation, especially a difficult one. Over lunch, which was sushi brought to their poolside cabana by one of the excellent, elegant butlers, they talked about anything but the previous day's excursion. Or Chelsea's moving in. Was that suddenly off the table? Chelsea didn't dare ask.

'This book is really great,' said Adam, acting as though he couldn't bear to put it down. As soon as the food was finished, he was straight back into it. Adam did a lot of reading that afternoon. Chelsea tried to, but she found it impossible to concentrate. Though the cruise so far had whizzed by – too quickly for most of the people on board – the hours between lunch and five o'clock, when they would be picking up Jack and Lily from the kids' club, crept by for Chelsea that day. The muscles the masseuse had loosened so vigorously were soon tense again, while the words of the novel Chelsea held in front of her face seemed to undulate with the waves.

At last it was five o'clock. Chelsea went to sign Jack and Lily out of the kids' club and took them straight to the pizza bar, where they would be meeting Adam just as soon as he had finished the last chapter of the book that had so absorbed him.

Jack and Lily had been taking part in an art project that afternoon, creating a representation of their homes and families in whatever medium most appealed. Jack had recreated his home in Coventry using collage. He was especially proud of the cotton wool balls he had used to represent both Fishy the cat and his mother Ronnie's hair. Chelsea wasn't sure that Ronnie would be entirely thrilled to be represented as a cotton-top but she told Jack he'd captured his mother perfectly.

Lily had decided to use felt-tips to draw her home in London. She got the red brick house quite well. The people in her life were more difficult to capture. Adam was completely cross-eyed. Lily herself was only recognisable by the colour of her *Frozen* dress.

Chelsea was sure that the third figure could only be one person. Her hair was blonde. She was wearing red. Chelsea never wore red and she was a brunette. Lily had, of course, drawn her mother.

'What do you think?' Lily asked.

'I like it,' said Chelsea, forcing herself to sound

happy and light. 'You've made your daddy look very handsome.'

'Thank you,' said Lily. 'I did him in his work outfit.'

'But that doesn't look anything like Auntie Chelsea,' said Jack. 'Her hair isn't that colour.'

Chelsea waited for Lily to state the obvious – the figure didn't look like Chelsea because it wasn't Chelsea – but instead she said, 'I told you, Jack. They didn't have any brown pens.'

'Is that *me*?' Chelsea asked.

'Yes. And that's your Christmas dress. It's my favourite.'

Of course. There was just one dress in Chelsea's wardrobe that was red. It was a velvet number that was far too festive for anything but the brief period between 23rd December and Boxing Day. Lily had been very impressed by it when Chelsea dragged it out the previous year.

'Look, Daddy!'

Adam had joined them at last.

'I've drawn you and Chelsea outside our house.'

'Very good likenesses,' he said.

That Lily had included her in a family portrait should have lifted Chelsea's heart, but instead it made her feel faintly ill. She and Adam really had to talk about whether it was possible for them to have a future together. It wasn't fair on Lily to mess around if they weren't going to go the distance. They had to talk about what had happened in Aix.

Chapter Fifty Eight

Jacqui

On Wednesday, the ship reached its final port of call before Southampton: Gibraltar. Dave was particularly interested in stopping off here, since an uncle of his had been stationed in the British military base there. Dave had seen photographs and he wanted to try to recreate them so that he could show his aunt back home how much had or hadn't changed since her husband was garrisoned on this edge of Europe.

Jack and Lily were more interested in the monkeys they would see at the Apes' Den. They had been warned, on the coach to the cable car that would take them up the Rock, that the Gibraltar macaques, the tailless Barbary apes, were far from cuddly and that they should absolutely not be fed. In fact, feeding the monkeys was an offence punishable by law with considerable fines for those found guilty. Women were warned to keep their handbags close.

'The last thing you want is for a monkey to make off down the mountain with your Prada,' the guide joked.

It was no joke to Jacqui. She was terrified. She wasn't a big fan of animals at the best of times. She got on OK with Fishy, Ronnie's ancient cat, but she was nervous of Leander, Annabel's boisterous Labrador, and his effusive way of greeting anyone who came to the house. Leander wouldn't frighten a burglar but he could take anyone out with an overenthusiastic wag of his tail. As for monkeys! Awful! Jacqui shuddered at the thought of a pair of wizened paws in her hair.

The coach pulled up in the car park for the Rock and the passengers started to file off. It was a clear day and you could see all the way to Africa quite easily.

'I might just stay here,' said Jacqui, not moving from her seat.

'Don't be silly. You can't see anything from the coach,' said Dave.

'I know, dear, but it's lovely and cool with the air conditioning on. It's hot out there and I'm finding it hard to handle today. I should have stayed on the boat.'

'Ship,' said Dave.

'Mum, are you afraid of the monkeys?' Ronnie asked bluntly. 'They're the only wild monkeys in the whole of Europe. You've got to come and have a look.'

'As far as I'm concerned, they could be the only wild monkeys in the whole bloody world. I don't want to be anywhere near them.'

'Oh come on, Mum. They won't hurt you. They're far more scared of you than you are of them.'

'I'm not sure that's true.'

'Whatever. I want a photo of you with the monkeys in the background. Come on. We'll miss the cable car.'

Jack too wanted some pictures. This was the last stop before Southampton so Ted needed to make the most of the photo opportunity. That day, she was back in her old shift dress since Lily claimed that Melinda was fed up of sharing her clothes. Jack was glad. He hated those frilly dresses. Ted looked much more like herself in her faded old frock. She almost looked like the boy Jack still hoped she really was.

* * *

After much cajoling, Ronnie persuaded Jacqui to get off the bus but she was not happy about it. That was clear. She clutched her handbag to her so tightly that her knuckles were white. While the rest of the tour group followed their guide to the cable car, Jacqui lurked in the shadow of the coach.

'It's no good staying there, Mum,' said Ronnie. 'The monkeys head straight for the coaches, to check through the litter that gets chucked off them. I've heard stories about them getting in and hiding under the seats.'

When she heard that, Jacqui scuttled across the tarmac to join her daughter. Safety in numbers.

'I'll protect you, Grandma,' said Jack, showing her the Sonic Screwdriver.

'You're not to get anywhere near those monkeys,' Jacqui told her grandson. 'Even if they're trying to steal my glasses. I don't want you touching them. Not even with your Sonic Screwdriver. They might have rabies or anything.'

'What's rabies?' Jack asked Ronnie.

Ronnie frowned at Jacqui. 'Mum . . .'

It was a constant battle, keeping Jack from having nightmares about the things he heard from the grown-ups.

'Rabies is like a really nasty cold,' Ronnie told him.

'Oh, I don't mind having a cold,' said Jack. 'Then I can stay home from school.'

'It's the holidays,' said Ronnie. 'You'd have to miss holidays instead.'

'That's not fair!' Jack exclaimed as though he'd already caught it.

The tour guide paused in a picturesque spot to explain the history of the region. The monkeys were an integral part of the Rock's mythology. It was said that so long as they lived there, the Rock would remain British territory. The myth was taken so seriously that the British Army appointed officers whose main duty was to ensure the animals' safety. During the Second World War, the monkey colony dwindled until there were just seven animals and Churchill was so worried he had someone despatched to North Africa to bring back simian reinforcements.

There was no concern that monkey numbers were dwindling now. Far from it; the Rock was now home to three distinct troops numbering nearly three hundred individuals and one of the troops had become such a nuisance to the local people that several of the more disruptive animals had been culled.

'They don't look very sweet, do they?' said Ronnie. 'I thought they'd be all nice and fluffy but they look kind of hard and flea-bitten. Like they've got animal ASBOs. Stand a bit closer to me, would you, Jack? Lily, don't wave your doll about at them. They might think she's something to eat.'

Lily stood close to Mark. Her father and Chelsea had remained on the ship but Lily had been persuaded ashore by the thought of the monkeys. However, she didn't look quite so sure they were the treat she had imagined now that she was within six feet of the furry things.

'I knew I shouldn't have come on this trip,' said Jacqui. 'I feel like they're all looking at me and the minute I take my eye off them, they're going to jump on my back and start pulling my hair.'

'Do *not* feed the animals,' the guide was reiterating. 'It is an offence to feed them. A criminal offence! You could be fined a thousand pounds.'

'You couldn't get me to go anywhere near them if you

gave me a thousand pounds,' said Ronnie. 'Ugh, look at that one. He's picking his bum.'

'Which one's picking his bum?' Jack piped up.

'You don't want to see that.'

'I do, I do!'

'You're your father's son, you are.'

'Look at that one!' said Lily, drawing Jack's attention to a young monkey engaged in more wholesome activities. 'He just did a backflip.'

Indeed the young monkey did seem to be practising his backflips. His mother patiently chewed on an old crisp packet while the youngster used her back as a springboard. He would climb up to her shoulders then 'flip' and land on his feet every time.

'Look, Ted.' Jack held Ted up so the battered old toy could get a better view. 'Look at that funny monkey. Look!'

Chapter Fifty Nine

Ted

It happened in the blink of an eye. The young monkey that had been entertaining the visitors with its acrobatic antics had taken a fancy to Ted. Before Jack even knew what had happened, Ted was gone, snatched from his hand and whisked away down the hill to be a monkey's bride. Or breakfast.

'Noooo! Teddddd!' the wail went up.

Mark and Dave did their best to retrieve the sorry stuffed bear but the monkey was too far out of reach. It sat on a rock, holding Ted by the ear, and stared back at Jack as if to taunt him.

'I'll swap you Ted for this . . .' Dave tried to tempt the monkey with a half-eaten cereal bar. The monkey looked unimpressed.

'Don't feed the monkeys!' the guide shrieked.

'I wasn't going to feed it. I was going to do a bait and switch,' Dave explained.

The monkey moved a little further off, with Ted still dangling from its wizened-looking claw.

'Is there nothing you can do?' Ronnie asked the guide. 'Don't they have nets or something? Cattle prods? This can't be the first time this has happened. Look, my son's distraught.'

'You're not to interfere with the monkeys,' said the

guide. 'I'm sorry, Madam. It's the law. You'll just have to hope he gets bored and drops it.'

The monkey did not get bored. The tour group was given forty-five minutes to explore the Rock at their leisure and to take photographs. The Benson group did not explore. They remained in place, as if by all staring at the monkey thief together, they might persuade it to change its mind.

'Please let us have Ted,' Jack pleaded.

His little voice was heartbreaking. No human who heard Jack's plea would have remained unmoved. Right then, Ronnie would have given Jack anything, just to see him smile again. Lily joined in the pleading.

'Please, Mr Monkey,' she said. 'That teddy isn't even ours. It belongs to Humfrey Buchanan. He's only a baby. He'll cry if we don't take Ted home. And we'll get into trouble.'

Jack spun round to his mother. 'Will we get into trouble?'

'You won't get into trouble,' Ronnie assured him.

'But Auntie Annabel told me to look after Ted.'

'And you did,' said Ronnie. 'The monkey was just too quick.'

'I should have held onto Ted harder.'

'Oh, sweetheart,' said Jacqui. She pulled Jack close for a hug. Lily wiggled into Jacqui's arms too for a group cuddle/cry.

The monkey remained untouched by the human display before him, though he was definitely a little intrigued. Transferring Ted's ear from his paw to his mouth, so that he could move more easily, the monkey actually hopped a little closer.

'That's it,' muttered Dave. 'That's it. Just keep coming. Come on, Monkey Face. Come to Daddy.'

The monkey sat down again and cradled Ted almost gently, perhaps mimicking the monkey mothers with their babies.

'Please.' Jack's little shoulders shook with emotion as he continued to make the bear's case. 'Ted is frightened. I can tell by her face.'

The monkey, perhaps fascinated by the noise Jack was making, took Ted by the ear again and hopped forward another foot.

'Come on,' whispered Dave. 'Just a little bit more.' He had taken off his T-shirt now, exposing his white belly and his trucker's tan.

'Dave,' Jacqui hissed. 'What are you doing? Why have you got your top off?'

'Just stay quiet, my love, and keep an eye on that guide. If she starts coming back in this direction, let me know.'

The monkey put Ted down for a second. Dave tensed, ready to take his chance. The monkey noticed the change in Dave's posture and picked Ted straight back up.

'Pleeeease!' Jack and Lily whined in chorus.

'We'll give you loads of bananas,' said Lily.

'We haven't got any bananas,' said Jack.

'The monkey doesn't know that,' said Lily, with characteristic pragmatism.

Jack cottoned on. He offered the monkey imaginary bananas too.

The monkey cocked his head to one side as though considering the offer. He took another leap towards the children. He was within six feet of them now. Dave was ready. This was his big chance. It was time to be a hero.

Dave flung his T-shirt in the direction of the young monkey, intending that it should cover the creature like a net or, at worst, scare the critter into dropping Ted and scampering off. Neither of those things happened. The T-shirt was caught by a gust of wind and drifted away, wide of its target. The monkey watched Dave's effort with an expression of amusement. Then, before Dave could retrieve his T-shirt for another go, the monkey bounded across, snatched the T-shirt up and disappeared for good with both the T-shirt *and* the bear.

'Why you bloody . . .!' Dave did his best to follow but the monkey was too fast. Soon he was completely out of sight.

'Granddad!' Jack cried. 'Don't say bloody!'

'It didn't work!' shouted Lily.

And now it was time to go back to the ship.

'We can't leave without Ted!' Jack wailed when the guide arrived to encourage them back onto the cable car down to the coach.

Soon, Lily was wailing too.

'We can't leave her!' Lily agreed. 'We've got to get her back.'

'The coach will be leaving for the ship in three minutes,' said the guide. 'If you don't get on board, we will have to leave you behind.'

'There's nothing we can do,' said Mark to Jack. 'We can't climb down the mountain to look for her.'

'If we don't go now,' said Ronnie, 'the ship will sail without us. I'm sure Ted will be very happy. She's with a new family now.'

'She's a *bear*,' said Lily, 'not a monkey. They won't understand how she talks. We've got to try to rescue her again.'

'I promise you that we will do everything we can to bring your teddy bear home,' said the guide, as she put a hand on Lily's shoulder and steered her towards the cable car. 'We'll ask everyone to keep an eye out for her.'

'She's got her label on,' Jack sniffed as Ronnie picked him up to carry him.

'Then whoever finds her will know exactly who she belongs to,' said the guide.

'This is so embarrassing,' said Jacqui as Dave walked down the aisle of the coach and their fellow travellers stared at his bare chest. The sort of people who took European cruises on the *European Countess* were not the kind to go around with their tops off, unless they were by the pool or on a beach. What's more, it was cold on that coach with the air conditioning turned up to full blast.

'That bloody monkey,' Dave muttered on and off all the way back to the ship.

Chapter Sixty

Jacqui

The loss of Dave's T-shirt would become the stuff of family legend but the loss of Ted had rattled Jacqui Benson. She had mixed feelings about that scruffy old bear. She found it hard to see the thing without remembering the day she bought it, forty-odd years before, in Mothercare, as a Christmas present for the daughter she had just given up for adoption.

'Aaah,' the shop assistant had said. 'Isn't this pretty?'

Back when she was new, Ted had been soft pink in colour with white paws and a white muzzle – the perfect gift for a little girl, back when people didn't worry so much about gender stereotyping.

'Are you buying a present for your niece or a godchild?' the assistant asked.

'Actually,' Jacqui had told her, 'it's for my daughter.'

The shop assistant's face briefly registered something unsettling. It was either disapproval or disbelief. Jacqui didn't look her age and even if she had, she was still young to be a mother. And she had no ring on her finger.

'Oh,' said the shop assistant. 'Right.'

The tone was very different after that. The assistant didn't offer to wrap the bear up, as she had offered to wrap up the purchases of the women ahead of Jacqui in the queue. She just put the bear into a plastic bag and gave Jacqui a tight smile with her change.

'I had a baby but I've given it away!' Jacqui felt like screaming. As it was, the moment she got outside Mothercare, she burst into tears.

Would anyone ever console her? The social worker and her parents had been so matter-of-fact about the whole thing, refusing to acknowledge that, while the adoption might be 'for the best', Jacqui was bereft. She was sure that everyone was judging her. How could she have been so careless, getting pregnant without a husband? How could she have been so heartless, giving her baby away?

Jacqui had to send the gifts she bought for Daisy's first Christmas through the social worker who had overseen the adoption. The social worker promised they would be passed on to Daisy's new family but there was no guarantee they would accept the baby clothes and the teddy that Jacqui had chosen so carefully.

When, forty years later, Jacqui found out that Annabel's new mother Sarah *had* passed the teddy on, and that Annabel had kept the bear close by her entire life, Jacqui had been thrilled. It felt as though the bear was a lucky charm.

Now Ted was gone. They would never get her back. The label round her neck was certainly already chewed to bits by a monkey who could have no idea of the significance of the greying, ancient toy. He was probably just disappointed to find out that Ted wasn't edible.

Jacqui wanted to cry along with Jack and Lily, who were inconsolable all the way back to the ship and its Italian ice cream parlour.

Ted was just a soft toy. She had done the job she was supposed to do. She had looked after Daisy/Annabel when Jacqui couldn't be with her. Now Jacqui and Annabel were reunited. They had a relationship. They talked to each other every few days. They hugged each other warmly when they met and when they parted. Annabel was even looking after Granddad Bill. All the same, it felt as though a thread to the past had been broken and Jacqui felt strangely untethered.

'Are you all right, Mum?' Ronnie asked, noticing that Jacqui was still quiet over dinner.

'Grandma, we need to text baby Humfrey and tell him what happened,' said Jack solemnly.

'Do you think the monkeys are looking after Ted?' Lily asked.

'Of course they are,' said Ronnie. 'They kidnapped her to be their queen.'

Lily was happy with that. 'I always thought she was a secret princess.'

For once, Jack didn't question Lily on Ted's gender.

'That's how she'll live out her days,' Ronnie continued, 'in the sunshine in Gibraltar. Ted Buchanan, Queen of the Monkeys. It was her destiny.'

'What's my destiny?' Jack asked.

'I don't know, Jack. You have to decide for yourself. But whatever it is, I know it will be exciting.'

Jack was happy with that.

'My destiny is to marry Prince George,' said Lily.

Chapter Sixty One

Chelsea and Adam

After Gibraltar, the ship was on the home straight. The *European Countess* had just two sea days left before she returned to Southampton. Her passengers were determined to make the most of what little time they had left on board. Suddenly everyone studied the ship's daily news sheets more diligently, trying to make sure they didn't miss anything good. Jacqui and Dave had an itinerary that would keep them busy from breakfast to bedtime as Jacqui insisted they pack in all the activities Dave had been putting off since the first day of the cruise. He'd made the mistake of promising Jacqui that he would join her on the ship's crazy golf course and for a line-dancing class 'at some point'. Now that 'point' had come.

'I can't believe I've got to spend the last two days of my holiday dancing to Dolly Parton,' he complained to Mark. But he put on his dancing shoes all the same and was secretly pleased when the line-dancing instructor informed him he was a natural.

Mark was altogether happier with the activities he and Ronnie had planned for their final forty-eight hours at sea. While Jack was safely in the kids' club, they were going to test the six remaining cocktails they had yet to try from the Anchor Bar's extensive menu. The Anchor Bar staff knew Ronnie and Mark by name by now. They had even come to have their own bar stools. As soon as they saw Mark and Ronnie coming, the bar staff put out an extra large bowl of tortilla chips for him and a dish of salted peanuts for her.

Meanwhile, Jack and Lily were very excited about their last two days in the ship's kids' club. There was going to be a party and they'd been promised extra-special surprise visitors.

'I think it will be Elsa from *Frozen*,' Lily speculated over breakfast.

'Doctor Who,' was Jack's only wish. 'But not one of the rubbish ones.'

Both the children were wrong but they weren't too disappointed by the substitutes: a magician who made balloon animals – he made a cat for Lily and a hippo for Jack – and the hula hoop expert, who brought along a batch of small hoops and shared some of her tricks. The captain also dropped in to see how his youngest charges had enjoyed their time on board the *European Countess*. Jack was completed awed to meet the man who had sailed them around the Mediterranean. Lily fell instantly and hopelessly in love. For a while, Prince George was forgotten.

Only Adam and Chelsea saw those last two sea days as something to get through rather than time to be savoured. They spent much of the day apart. Chelsea wandered disconsolately around the ship's mini shopping mall. She swiftly exited the jewellery store when a couple came in and asked to see engagement rings. The lucky woman was so happy she seemed high.

Adam stayed on the balcony of his stateroom, reading through some files he'd downloaded while the ship was docked in Gibraltar. He had to work. He claimed he would have to hit the ground running when he went back to the office two days after they all got home.

Adam and Chelsea were both glad when dinnertime came, the children were back from the kids' club and the fact that they had so little to say to one another wasn't so obvious. Lily and Jack would not allow a moment's silence. Lily outlined her plans for marrying the ship's captain. Jack demonstrated his hula hoop wiggle. They were full of news and questions.

'What do you think Ted is having for her dinner tonight?' being the most difficult, from Jack.

Chelsea conjured up a magnificent meal fit for a monkey princess: chips, followed by more chips, and ice cream. At the ship's gelato parlour, the children created huge sundaes in Ted's honour. Chelsea ordered an enormous sundae of her own and shovelled it down. She needed comfort food, though she knew that she would only want to throw up later on and, with Jack in the cabin, that was simply not an option.

Chapter Sixty Two

Jack and Chelsea

'Are you sure the monkeys won't make Ted eat vegetables?' Jack asked his aunt as they settled down in their stateroom for the night.

'They wouldn't dare,' said Chelsea.

'Good,' said Jack. 'If I was the King of the Monkeys, I would never eat a vegetable again.'

'An excellent idea.'

'Will you make Lily eat vegetables when you're her mummy?' asked Jack.

Chelsea was folding Jack's clothes. She paused and sat down heavily on her bed.

'I'm not going to be Lily's mummy, Jack.'

'She said you are. She said her daddy told her but she's supposed to keep it a secret. She's not very good at keeping secrets,' Jack mused.

'No,' said Chelsea, a little sadly, 'she isn't. But it doesn't matter.'

'I would like you to be Lily's mummy,' said Jack, 'because I don't want you to be lonely. If you were her mummy you could live with her and Uncle Adam for ever. Then I wouldn't have to worry about you any more.'

'You don't have to worry about me,' said Chelsea.

The conversation took her back to another conversation she and Jack had had before, by a paddling pool in Lanzarote, when he asked Chelsea who she lived with and flatly refused to believe that she could live alone. The idea was completely incomprehensible to Jack's six-year-old brain.

'The thing is, Jack, it's not as simple as Lily wanting me to be her mummy. It's between me and Uncle Adam. We have to decide that we want to be together for ever first. We have to decide if we want to get married.'

'Daddy says all ladies want to get married. He said Mummy bit his hand off.'

Chelsea managed a smile.

'I think your dad is a very lucky man.'

'Will I have to get married?' Jack asked then. 'When I'm a grown-up?'

'Only if you want to. It's not compulsory. You certainly shouldn't get married if you don't want to. It's a big step to take.'

'Lily said she wants to marry me. After Prince George and the captain. But I definitely don't want to marry her because she isn't nice all the time. She says Doctor Who is stupid. I would rather marry you, Auntie Chelsea. You're nice and you're kind and you're very, very pretty.'

'Oh Jack.'

'And you wouldn't make me eat sprouts.'

So, it was true. Lily's indiscretion to Jack had confirmed it. Adam had been intending to propose on the cruise. He'd put the idea that Chelsea would become her step-mother into her head. What was supposed to have happened? Did Adam deliberately raise her hopes in Rome and in Florence and again in Portofino because he knew that he was intending to pop the question later on and somehow knew she was expecting it too? She thought back to the way he had started to ask at the Bocca della Verità. The way he had asked, when he caught the bouquet in Florence, whether that meant he would be married within the year. The 'important question' in Portofino. He had been playing with her, teasing her, because he was planning something for later in the cruise.

But what was he thinking now? The atmosphere that had settled between them since Aix had surely put paid to any proposal plans. Was Lily still expecting something to happen? And how about Chelsea's parents? No wonder Adam had spent the day hiding in his cabin.

Chelsea wished she could go back to that moment in Aix and agree with Adam that they'd seen the inside of one too many churches. Then he wouldn't have had to tell her about Claire and the candle for Lily. They would have had a lovely lunch in the sunshine. They would be holding hands round the balcony divider now, whispering.

Once Jack had dozed off, Chelsea went out onto the balcony. Just as she stepped out, she heard the doors to Adam and Lily's room slide shut.

Chapter Sixty Three

Adam and Chelsea

With the children out of the way in their club, Chelsea and Adam might have done anything with their last day at sea. There were still plenty of parts to the ship that they hadn't explored. They'd never been in the Jacuzzi pool above the Anchor Bar, for example. They'd never visited the ship's art gallery. They'd never eaten in the on-board steakhouse. But Chelsea and Adam were spending their last day in their cabins. Separately.

If Chelsea had been OK with the fact that she and Adam had separate cabins next door to each other, she wasn't happy about it now. Previously, she had been impressed by how well insulated the cabins were. She could really only hear what was going on in the outside world when she had the doors to the balcony open. Now she was sure she could hear rustles and sighs from Adam's cabin as he went about his day without her. This was the real reason why people didn't go on cruises. If you weren't in dock, you were doomed. You couldn't get away from your fellow travellers unless you were prepared to nick a lifeboat.

Eventually, Chelsea couldn't stand it a moment longer. She washed her face and brushed her hair and tentatively knocked on the door to Adam's domain. Adam opened the door and smiled the sort of smile that was impossible to decipher. Was it happy or sad?

Was he pleased to see her or not? Chelsea's heart was in her mouth.

'Can I come in?' she asked.

'Of course. Quickly.' Adam still had the balcony doors open and because the ship was moving so fast, the door was in danger of slamming. With Chelsea inside and the door to the corridor shut, they went straight through to the balcony. Adam offered Chelsea one of the chairs.

'Do you want a drink?' he asked.

'What have you got?'

'Not much. Fizzy water. Or that bottle of champagne we brought from home.'

Chelsea had been quietly thrilled when she saw Adam put that bottle of champagne into his luggage back in London. Now she wasn't sure how she felt about it. For a while, after that day in the spa with Ronnie, Chelsea had hoped he'd brought the bubbles along because he was planning something special. Now that he was offering to open it while they were technically in the middle of a serious domestic, she wondered whether it was simply that it had been knocking about the house and he felt like using it up.

'OK,' she said.

Adam went back into the cabin and brought out the bottle from the mini-bar fridge.

'Afraid we haven't got any proper glasses,' he said.

'All tastes the same to me,' said Chelsea.

Chelsea opened the batting. 'Look, I know we've both been trying to avoid the subject but I'm sorry about what happened in Aix.'

'It's OK,' said Adam.

'It's not OK. I acted like a brat. I should have been more understanding.'

'I didn't exactly cover myself in glory. I could have made it easier on both of us. I handled it badly. You asked me to let you know if I'd been somewhere with Claire and I didn't. Though it's as if I'd forgotten myself. I was surprised how clear the memories were when we got to that church. I hadn't thought about it in years. Suddenly it was just like it all happened yesterday.'

'I'm sorry,' said Chelsea. 'If I'd known, I never would have tried to make you go in there. I'd have made sure we didn't go anywhere near the place.'

'But you didn't know because I didn't tell you. It's my fault.'

'No—' Chelsea began to protest.

'It is my fault. I was an idiot. I promised you I would be honest about where I'd been before but I still chose not to say anything about having been to Aix before because I thought it would be easier. I didn't want to have the conversation so we ended up like this instead. Ridiculous.'

'I was jealous,' said Chelsea. 'That's what's ridiculous. I was jealous of Claire for having been there with you before. I was jealous of her being pregnant with Lily. I was jealous of how much you still love her.' Chelsea choked her way through that last sentence. Her eyes welled up.

'Oh Chelsea, I want so much to make you happy,' said Adam. 'It tears me apart to see you cry.'

'I can't stand to see you unhappy either,' said Chelsea. 'The last couple of days have been terrible.'

'I know.'

Chelsea put her glass down and reached for Adam's hand. 'I've been in agony since we sailed from Marseille, wanting to talk to you but never seeming able to find the right moment. And then, when eventually I did feel like perhaps you were ready to talk about it, we'd have to go and fetch the children from the kids' club.'

'We're on our own now,' said Adam. 'We've got two hours before kids' club finishes.'

'So we can talk about it now.'

'Let's not,' said Adam. 'Let's make the most of the time we've got to ourselves. Let's make up properly instead.' He looked deep into her eyes.

'What do you mean?' asked Chelsea.

Adam answered her by taking her face in his hands and planting the gentlest of kisses on her mouth.

Making love was the perfect way to reconnect after all the heaviness of the past couple of days. Chelsea felt her body flood with relief as much as desire. When she and Adam were naked together, they were able to show each other how they really felt. Adam kissed her with a passion and she was certain this time that he was thinking only of her. He told her he loved her. She assured him she felt the same way.

'We'd better get up,' said Adam after an hour.

'If only we could have a whole day like this.'

'We'll have plenty of them, once you've moved in,' Adam said.

'I thought you were going to withdraw the offer.' Chelsea laughed nervously.

'Are you kidding? I want you to bring your stuff over the minute we get back to the UK. I don't want to be without you for a single night. I love you, Chelsea Benson.'

'I love you more.'

Everything was going to be all right.

Chapter Sixty Four

Jane

Jane was alone on the balcony of her cabin on Turtle Deck. Kirsty was up on the top deck by the ship's biggest pool. She was making the most of the last chance to top up her tan. They'd had a big lunch at the ship's Italian restaurant, which had become their favourite eating spot. Jane's head was still spinning from having had half a bottle of wine. Kirsty had ordered the bottle, saying that she would have more than her share, but Jane was pretty sure she'd held her own. She should have stopped after one glass. She shouldn't have started at all. Oh, it was too late now to berate herself for not staying on the sparkling water.

Jane sat down heavily on one of the loungers. She was having another of her silent conversations with Greg.

'I still wish you were here,' she said. 'It's been great and I love having Kirsty around but it's not the same. This was supposed to be our honeymoon. Why did you have to go drinking on Christmas Eve, you bloody idiot? Why didn't you stay home with me? You could be here right now.'

Jane blew her nose. She grew more maudlin as she continued to berate Greg in her head.

'I've gone to pieces. I'm nothing without you,' she told the spirit of her dead love. 'I feel like I might as well be dead as well. I'm not living. I'm just existing. Why did you have to go? My mother always told me you would break my heart. I don't know how I can go on living without you. How can I possibly be happy if you're not with me? You should be here, Greg. We should be looking at the horizon together. You should be here.'

She cocked her head as if listening for an answer. Suddenly she got up.

'OK. I'm going to do it right now.'

Jane got Greg's ashes out of the safe. Now, she had decided, was the moment. Greg should be cast into infinity right here because her love for him was infinite as the ocean. Now was the time.

Jane needed to make sure that she threw the ashes well clear. There were signs all over the ship reminding people that they must not, under any circumstances, throw anything off any of the decks. Not cigarettes. Not paper cups. Nothing. Jane was soon to discover why.

She unscrewed the lid of the plain cardboard tube that had been Greg's home since his cremation. Though she had lived with the urn for more than six months, she had never looked inside before. She didn't know quite what she had expected to find in there. She was relieved to discover that there was nothing especially human about it. In fact it was like the dust that gathers in the Dyson – that same sickly grey.

Tentatively, Jane shook some of Greg's ashes out into her palm. She half laughed, half choked at the ridiculousness of it. Her big brave man, who lit up every room he walked into, who had travelled the world as a soldier, who was going to love her for the rest of her life, had been reduced to Dyson dust.

'This isn't really you,' Jane said out loud. Then she flung out her arm so that the dust flew from her fingers.

The wind blew those ashes right back into her face.

'Ugh!' Jane batted the dust away and spat it out of her mouth.

She staggered back into the cabin and sat down heavily on her bed. She wiped her lips on a tissue. She had never experienced anything quite so awful in her life. But while she'd been having that silent conversation with Greg, she was sure she'd heard him tell her it was time to let go and she had to start with those bloody ashes. She had to do it now.

She went back out onto the balcony. She was determined. She would have to throw the whole thing at once. Jane was left-handed. She drew back her arm and threw the urn with all the force she could muster. Not realising, as the box flew from her hand and was whipped by the wind clear of the ship into the inky blue sea, that she was casting off something else at the same time.

Chapter Sixty Five

Adam and Chelsea

'Adam,' said Chelsea. 'What is this?'

Adam looked at her curiously.

Chelsea put a finger into her glass to fish something out.

'Oh,' she gasped, when she saw what it was. 'Oh! Oh, Adam! Oh! Oh, darling!'

'What is it?' Adam was confused.

Chelsea had it on her finger before she showed him.

'It fits! It's lovely. When did you get this?'

Adam could only gawp in astonishment and horror. Chelsea had on her finger something that appeared to be an engagement ring, in the style of the ring that Prince William had given to Kate Middleton – the ring that had once belonged to Diana – a big blue stone surrounded by small diamonds. It was not the sort of ring that Adam would have chosen for Chelsea. And indeed, this was not a ring that Adam had chosen for Chelsea, or even seen before. He had no idea whatsoever how it had come to be in Chelsea's glass.

Chelsea gazed in delight at the rock on her finger, even though, if she had ever dreamed of an engagement ring, she had dreamed of something quite different, something much more subtle. But already Chelsea was weaving a story in her head around this new piece of jewellery. Perhaps Adam had just bought it as a placeholder – a flashy ring for a flashy proposal. It probably wasn't real. A genuine untreated sapphire the size of the one she was now wearing would cost hundreds of thousands of pounds (Chelsea had compiled an article on engagement rings for the magazine when Wills and Kate got engaged, so she knew a little bit about the cost of these things). Yes, Adam had bought this fake ring but would without doubt invite Chelsea to choose something a little closer to her taste once they were back home in London.

Though now that she had it on, perhaps it was growing on her. Perhaps it wasn't too big after all. And it made a change to have a coloured stone instead of a boring old diamond solitaire.

While Chelsea moved her hand this way and that so the stones glittered, Adam was still trying to find a way to tell her that he didn't know what was going on or where the ring had come from. But then she threw her arms round his neck and started crying, and this time she was crying with joy.

'I love you so much,' she said through honking, snorting great tears. 'I can't tell you how happy you've made me. I am just over the moon. Of course I'll be your wife! I've been hoping and longing for you to ask me.'

Adam stiffened in Chelsea's embrace. She was wrapped around him like a hungry octopus, squeezing him tightly and snuffling at his neck. When she momentarily released him to cup his face in her hands and gaze at him lovingly, Adam took hold of her shoulders and held her at a distance so he could make sure that she heard him.

'Chelsea,' he said. 'Hold on for a minute. Sit down.' He gently pressed her into her chair.

'Take that thing off.'

'You want to ask me properly? I see.' She laughed.

'No,' said Adam. 'No. That's not my ring. Or your ring. I have no idea where it came from.'

'What?'

Chelsea's face switched from joyous to suspicious in a heartbeat. 'What do you mean?'

'I mean, I don't know what that ring was doing in your glass. I've never seen it before in my life.'

'You . . . didn't put it in there?'

'No,' said Adam. 'I didn't.'

'Then you aren't . . .?'

Adam didn't complete the sentence. He just shook his head. It was all Chelsea needed. She was no longer crying with joy, that was for sure.

'You don't want to . . .?'

Adam didn't shake his head this time. It probably seemed a bit risky. But Chelsea read everything into his failure to say anything at all.

'Oh God,' she choked.

Chelsea pulled the ring off as quickly as she could. Though it had gone on very easily, now it stuck on her knuckle as though to taunt her. In the end, she had to tug it with such force that it nearly flew straight off the balcony. Adam rescued it. He placed it carefully on the table between them.

'Then where did it bloody well come from?' Chelsea asked. The way she glared at Adam now suggested that she truly thought he had placed the ring in the glass then changed his mind about the proposal, and that was why he was suddenly trying to pretend he'd never seen it before.

'I don't know. It's just bizarre. I'm really sorry, Chelsea. You have to believe that I had nothing to do with it. It isn't some kind of prank. The only thing I can think is that the last person who had this cabin must have left it behind. Or maybe the housekeeper dropped it when she was cleaning this morning.'

'But it wasn't in the glass when you took it out of the mini-bar,' said Chelsea. Her voice was flat. She looked at the ring on the table as though she were looking at the carcass of a cockroach.

'Then maybe it was in the bottle of champagne?' Adam suggested hopelessly. 'Perhaps it's a competition prize, like a golden ticket in a chocolate bar.' He picked up the champagne bottle to check the label for clues.

'I don't care where it was,' said Chelsea.

'There's nothing about a competition on the bottle,' Adam confirmed.

'Of course there isn't. That's the most stupid explanation imaginable.'

'Well, wherever it came from, we've got to hand it in. It looks as though it's real diamonds. I don't know how the hell it got into that glass but someone must be looking for it.'

'You can sort that out,' said Chelsea. 'I'm going back to my cabin.'

She left, leaving Adam staring at the ring that had come out of nowhere and blown another hole in his relationship.

Chelsea was still red-eyed when Mark brought Jack back from the kids' club to the cabin he was sharing with his aunt. Seeing his sister-in-law's face, Mark said, 'I'll take him straight back to our cabin instead. See you later, Chels.'

'Why can't I go in there?' Jack wanted to know. 'Why,

Daddy? I want to tell her about what happened at kids' club.'

'I think Auntie Chelsea needs some rest,' Mark said.

Right then, Chelsea felt like throwing herself into the sea. How on earth had that ring ended up in her glass? As far as she was concerned, there really was no rational explanation other than that Adam had surreptitiously put the ring in the glass before they went inside to make love but changed his mind about proposing before they went back outside to finish drinking. The idea that the ring had been in there all along, dropped by a cleaner who wore a sapphire as big as a cashew nut to change beds and scrub toilets, made no sense at all.

It was the cruellest trick. Chelsea cringed as she thought about how joyfully she had reacted when she first saw the tacky bauble. How could Adam have watched that, seen her so happy, and then disappointed her?

And now Mark and Jack had seen her crying, it was a matter of time before they told Ronnie. What was she going to say when Ronnie inevitably wanted to know what had caused Chelsea's tears? Bloody Adam. Bloody men. Chelsea never had any luck with them. Why should Adam have turned out any different?

Indeed Ronnie texted just five minutes after Jack and Mark left.

'Sounds like you need to talk. Want to go to the Anchor Bar?'

Chelsea replied, 'Everything's fine. I'm going to have a nap.' But she knew that wouldn't hold Ronnie at bay for long.

Chapter Sixty Six

Adam

Adam wanted to be rid of that ring as soon as he could. He was relieved when Jack and Mark knocked to ask if Lily wanted to join them for a last game of crazy golf on the top deck. Lily leapt at the chance and Adam was glad he didn't have to explain the whole ring debacle to get the chance to take the blasted thing to lost property.

The owner of the ring was called Jane Thynne. She had reported it missing as soon as she realised it was gone, so Adam only had to fetch it out of his pocket to have the customer services director say, 'I know exactly who that ring belongs to.'

The customer services director immediately called Jane with the good news. Adam waited while they had a brief conversation, at the end of which the director said, 'Miss Thynne says she'd like to buy you a drink as a thank you.'

'Oh. OK,' said Adam. 'That would be nice.'

Why not? thought Adam. He needed a bloody big drink.

'The Anchor Bar in ten minutes?' was the suggestion.

While he waited for Jane Thynne to turn up, Adam wondered what she would be like. At this point, he still imagined that the ring had been thrown in anger to make a point to an errant fiancé. He began to feel concerned that Jane's insistence that he let her buy him a drink was calculated to upset the poor bloke. Perhaps he should have let customer services deal with it. There was no reason for Adam to meet the ring's owner except out of nosiness.

After waiting for ten minutes, Adam watched a tall brunette stalk up to the bar. She looked like the kind of woman who would toss a sapphire into the sea and expect a bigger one as a replacement. Adam braced himself for their meeting. But it wasn't her. The tall brunette was meeting an older guy who seemed to be very much in favour. Adam relaxed a little.

When Jane Thynne finally arrived, Adam didn't notice her at once. She was so small and huddled, even in the heat.

'Are you Adam?' she asked.

'Jane.'

It was the sparrow girl, the thin shy blonde from the muster practice. The one Adam had seen racing into the lift in tears. Adam felt his heart swell towards her.

'I can't believe you found it. I'm so relieved.'

Jane took the ring from Adam and cupped it in both hands, as though it were a small living creature – a chick or a baby mouse. She kissed it, then she slipped the ring onto her finger. It was much too big for the finger it had been bought for so she took it off again and put it over her forefinger instead.

'Don't want it to fall off again. I've lost a bit of weight,' she explained.

'That's quite a feat on this ship,' said Adam. 'The curse of twenty-four-hour dining; room service; all the ice cream.'

'I haven't felt much like eating,' said Jane. 'Not for a while.'

She looked at the ring as though she had just received it for the first time. 'Oh, I thought I had lost this for ever. I was so worried I almost threw up. It came off when I was shaking out my swimming costume over the edge of the balcony,' she lied. 'Where did you find it?'

Adam shook his head. 'It's so ridiculous, you won't believe it.'

He explained how the ring had landed in Chelsea's tumbler full of champagne.

'It must have bounced off the balcony rail! Thank goodness. My fiancé had a wicked sense of humour,' said Jane. 'He would have thought this was really funny. The ring ending up in your glass.'

'Yeah, well he didn't have to deal with my girlfriend when she realised I hadn't put the ring in her drink because I meant to propose.'

Jane nodded. 'I'm sorry. I bet that was awkward.'

'Just a little. In fact, I'm not sure she'll ever speak to me again.'

There was a moment of silence, while it occurred to Adam that Jane had referred to her fiancé in the past tense. Perhaps he was more attuned to it because of what had happened to him. He wanted to ask if he was right. He didn't have to.

'This was supposed to be our honeymoon,' said Jane, clearly surprising herself as she said it to this stranger. 'My fiancé . . . Greg was his name . . . he died last Christmas Eve. He was in a traffic accident on his way home from the pub.'

'That's terrible. I'm sorry,' said Adam.

'It's Sod's Law. He'd just decided to leave the army. I thought that at last I would be able to stop worrying about him getting himself killed . . . I don't know why I'm telling you this,' Jane said, giving herself a little shake as if to pull herself out of the coming funk. 'You don't need to know about my story. I'm just grateful you gave the ring back. And I really hope it doesn't cause too much trouble with your girlfriend. If you tell her what happened, I'm sure she'll understand. Thank you.'

Jane searched in her pockets for a tissue. Failing to find one, she pulled the paper napkin from beneath a discarded cocktail glass and used it to dab her eyes. 'Sorry. You don't need this. You thought you were coming here to have a nice, thank you drink, not watch some complete stranger blubbing. I've got to go. I'm sorry.'

'Wait,' said Adam, impulsively grabbing Jane's thin wrist as she turned to leave. 'Wait. If you'd like to talk about it, I'm really happy to listen.' Adam dropped his voice. 'I'm not a weirdo, I promise. I went through the same thing too. My wife . . .'

Jane turned back towards him.

'Getting on for six years ago now. Aneurysm. Our daughter was just a baby.'

'That's terrible.'

'Perhaps we can help each other. Talk about both of them? I think it might do us good.'

Jane nodded.

'OK,' she said. 'Let's go somewhere quiet.'

Chapter Sixty Seven

Adam and Jane

They left the Anchor Bar. It was getting close to sunset and the place was filling up with people who wanted to watch the sun go down with a drink in their hands. The atmosphere was all wrong for the conversation Adam and Jane wanted to have.

But where could they go? Adam knew he couldn't ask Jane to go back to his room. That would have been too strange. And Jane couldn't invite him to her suite for the same reason. Kirsty might come in at any moment. Adam had a while before he was due to meet Lily and the Bensons for dinner in the Sea View restaurant. The new friends chose to go down to one of the lower decks, where you could usually find a free sunlounger.

They lay back on two loungers, facing the sea.

'This is like therapy,' said Adam, as he settled back. They couldn't see each other's faces as they both gazed out at the waves. It was easier to talk that way.

'Tell me from the beginning,' said Adam.

'No,' said Jane. 'You go first.'

Adam found Jane very easy to talk to. It was a long time since he'd had a conversation about Claire and what it felt like to have lost her.

'I know it's been a long time,' he said. 'It's getting to the stage where she's been gone for almost as long as I actually knew her. But there are still days when I wake up and it's like I only lost her yesterday.'

Jane nodded. 'I know how that feels.'

'You're a lot closer to it,' said Adam. 'Six months is no time at all.'

'But I still get the sense that my friends and family think I should be starting to get over it by now. They were all really good at first, but now if I want to talk about it, I can see their eyes glaze over. My friend Kirsty is the only one who really listens any more.'

'The worst of it is when you want to talk about the happy times,' said Adam. 'It's as though you have to pretend they never existed. It's different when you're talking about someone who lived to a ripe old age. Then it seems like death is just the next verse in the song. Everybody loves to reminisce about someone who lived into their eighties. But a sudden death is somehow shameful.'

'Exactly,' said Jane.

'I've upset my girlfriend so many times on this trip because I didn't want to tell her I'd already seen Pisa and Florence with my dead wife. Then she found out anyway and it was even worse than if I had told her.'

'You shouldn't have to pretend it never happened to keep the peace.'

'I thought she understood. Chelsea, that is. I've been surprised by the way she's reacted.'

'I suppose she's a bit jealous – the same as she would be if you were talking about a living ex. And I can see how the ring thing would be terribly disappointing. Humiliating even.'

'The irony is, I *was* thinking about proposing to her on this trip.'

'You were?'

'Yes. The ring is in the safe in my cabin. I had all sorts of plans but . . .'

'What happened?'

'We had a row when we were in Aix-en-Provence. I was there before, years ago, with Claire. I wasn't going to mention it, but we were just wandering around, and then all of a sudden we came upon this church I remembered.'

Adam told Jane about Claire's wish for her unborn baby.

'How sad,' said Jane. 'For all of you. For Claire, for you and for Chelsea.'

'What would you have done?' Adam asked. 'If you were in Chelsea's position, would you have gone into the church anyway? Should I be in this relationship at all?'

Jane pinched the bridge of her nose.

'I can't tell you that. Look, I ought to go.'

'Don't,' said Adam. 'Not yet.'

He took her hand.

Chapter Sixty Eight

Ronnie

Six storeys above, Ronnie was finally taking the Sky Walk. Alone. It seemed like the best way to do it. The last thing she needed was any one of her travelling companions – more specifically Jack, Dave or Mark – playing silly beggars, jumping up and down as if to break the unbreakable glass. Ronnie hadn't even told them she was going to do the walk. She was far happier to inch her way along the edge of the glass-floored gallery with no one forcing her to stand on the clear panels.

Everyone else in Ronnie's party had done the Sky Walk at the beginning of the cruise. Jack and Lily had crossed the glass several times with various adults in tow. They were full of praise for the experience, but even the selfies Jack and Mark had taken made Ronnie feel a bit ill. To see her seven-year-old son seemingly suspended in mid-air, hundreds of feet above the ocean, triggered all Ronnie's maternal instincts to keep him safe.

'But you've got to do it,' everybody said. 'When will you next get the chance?'

It was the last day of the cruise. It was now or never. She was doing it.

And it was quite something. Ronnie felt a visceral lurch as she looked down through the floor panels for the first time. The sea looked very different from this angle and it was possible to see just how fast the ship was moving through it.

When she first read about the Sky Walk on the Countess Cruises' website, Ronnie thought that it would be right out over the waves. Actually, much of the glass was over the decks and the lifeboats. Ronnie felt a little easier, looking down on those. And after a short while, she thought she might actually be coming to enjoy it.

The people on the deck below were like Borrowers. At that time of the evening, most of the passengers were either in their rooms getting ready for dinner, or having an aperitif with a view of the sunset. The Sky Walk was on the wrong side of the ship for that tonight, but there were a still a few people down there, making the most of the peace. Ronnie guessed that some of them must be people who had inside cabins and no balcony where they could sit in private. There's no way she could have done this cruise in an interior room, though she had heard that some people actually preferred it.

Then she saw him.

It was Adam. Ronnie didn't immediately recognise him from the angle at which she saw him now. It's not often you get to see the top of your sister's boyfriend's head. But shortly after she spotted him, he tipped his head back as if in some sort of agony, and she saw his face. Though he'd looked up, she was pretty sure he hadn't seen her.

Adam wasn't on his own but he wasn't with Chelsea either. He was with a woman Ronnie didn't recognise at all. She was a small blonde. Very skinny, thought Ronnie enviously. She wasn't flaunting it, though, like some of the women on board. Mark's eyes had been out on sticks all week. This woman was wrapped up in all sorts of layers, like the way Sophie dressed when she was going through one of her 'everybody hates me and I hate everything' phases, which came around like clockwork once a month.

Who was Adam's companion? Ronnie completely forgot about her fear of heights as she tried to get a better look at her sister's boyfriend and the unknown woman. They were certainly talking intensely. Adam had started out lying down on the sunlounger, facing out to sea, but now he sat up and swung round so that he was looking at the woman. His hands were moving as he talked, as though he was describing something about which he was especially passionate. Then he put his hands in his hair, as though he wanted to tear it out in despair. The woman sat up too. She put a hand on Adam's arm as if to calm him down. Then she rested her hand on Adam's knee and left it there while she made an impassioned speech back at him.

What was going on? If Ronnie didn't know Adam and know that he was meant to be moving in with Chelsea and perhaps even ready to propose to her, she might have thought that he and the woman on the sunbed were together. Their body language was intimate. It was as if they knew each other very well. Perhaps they did. But wouldn't Adam have said if someone he knew was on the same cruise? Though there was no reason he would know. The ship carried three thousand passengers. Ronnie had been on board for almost two weeks and yet she still felt as though she saw new faces every night. Perhaps Adam had just bumped into the woman today. Maybe she was an old girlfriend. The woman made as if to leave. Adam took her hand.

Ronnie kept on watching. Adam and his friend were so deep in their conversation, Ronnie was tempted to lean over the rail and drop something between them.

Eventually, Ronnie saw them stand up and embrace. Her heart was in her mouth now, not because she was looking down a giddying six storeys but because she was watching Adam take a woman other than her sister into his arms and hold her there for far longer than seemed natural or reasonable, whether he had just met her or had known her for years.

Ronnie stopped watching and leaned back against the wall.

'Makes you feel real dizzy, don't it?' said an American matron who was also taking the walk alone.

'Yes,' said Ronnie. 'I feel quite sick.'

She went back to the cabin she shared with Mark.

Ronnie told her husband what she'd seen.

'I've got to tell Chelsea. Something's going on. When you went to take Jack to the cabin earlier on, she had been crying. Now this.'

'Don't go jumping to conclusions,' said Mark. 'It might not have been Adam. You were God knows how many storeys above him.'

'Oh, Mark. Of course it was Adam. It would be a bit of a coincidence, wouldn't it, if there was someone else who looked just like him on this boat.'

'Ship,' Mark corrected her automatically.

'Ship,' said Ronnie. 'Oh, I'm so upset about this. I thought he was going to ask Chelsea to marry him. Now he's messing about with another woman.'

'If it *was* Adam,' said Mark. 'So he gave another woman a hug. So what?'

'So, if I saw you hugging another woman like that, I would have changed the locks before you got home. I swear it looked as if he was about to kiss her. It's not right. I've got to say something.'

Mark groaned. 'Not tonight, Ronnie, please. It's our last night on board. What's going to happen if you confront him now? Chelsea will spend the night sobbing. Adam and Lily won't be able to join us all for dinner. Your mum and dad will be really upset. If you've got to say something, save it for when we're back in Southampton, please.'

Ronnie chewed her lip.

'He's messing my sister around.'

'You don't know what's going on,' said Mark. 'Just as you didn't know why Adam wanted to go for a private walk with Dave that afternoon at Annabel's. It's dangerous, spinning these theories like you do. I'll bet Chelsea was crying because you encouraged her to think she had a proposal coming and it hasn't happened. She was quite happy with just moving in. And maybe Adam bumped into an old friend, like you said, and he hugged her because she had some bad news. Adam would be a special kind of dickhead if he really has been having an affair on board this ship with all of us on here with him. I don't think he's that sort of man.'

'I didn't think he was either but . . .'

'Ronnie, I get that you want to protect your sister but I really think it's for the best that you say nothing right now. Let us all make the most of the rest of the cruise.'

'OK. You're probably right.'

Ronnie decided to sit on her discovery for the sake of keeping the peace and allowing everyone to enjoy their last night on the *European Countess*.

Chapter Sixty Nine

Chelsea

Dinner on the last night was another formal affair. This time, everyone knew what to expect and no one was as nervous as they had been that first formal evening. Lily insisted on wearing her *Frozen* dress again and Chelsea was pressed into service to do the 'fish plait'.

'Your little girl's hair looks lovely,' said an American matron as they walked into the dining room. 'I can see she gets her good looks from her mom.'

Chelsea was thrown off-balance by the comment. It was on the tip of her tongue to tell the woman everything. That Lily wasn't her daughter and she couldn't take any credit for her heart-shaped face and her heartbreaking blue eyes. And she had thought she might have the honour of becoming Lily's stepmother but that wasn't going to happen after all.

'Thank you,' she said eventually, by which time the American woman's expression had changed, as though she could read Chelsea's mind. Or just thought she was rude for taking so long to respond to the compliment.

'Quick!' said Lily. 'Everybody is already here. Chelsea, please sit next to me.'

Chelsea knew that her sister would be studying her closely. She hadn't told anyone about the events of that afternoon. Perhaps one day, many years from now, the story of the engagement ring that ended up in her champagne glass by accident would be an anecdote she could laugh about, but right now Chelsea was embarrassed and upset. She knew she wouldn't be able to tell the story without crying. She had asked Adam not to talk about it either. He'd agreed there was no need to tell anybody.

Adam told Chelsea that by the time he found the customer services desk and handed the ring over, its owner had already reported the loss.

'They said they would call her and ask her to come and collect it.'

As far as Chelsea was concerned, that was what had happened. Adam had left the ring at the customer services desk then gone to sit in the Retreat for a while, alone. Lily was playing crazy golf with Jack and Mark. Adam said he'd needed a little bit of time to himself. Chelsea didn't question it.

'Thanks for understanding,' Adam said when they met up again just before dinner. Then he gave Chelsea a hug that didn't quite feel like the hugs she was used to. He kissed her on the top of her head. Distractedly. Dismissively.

But it was their last night on board. Chelsea made a conscious decision to take Adam's hug and kiss as a rapprochement. She wasn't going to worry about it.

She was worrying about it, of course. How could she not? Chelsea just couldn't keep the afternoon's horrible denouement at bay. She kept thinking about how happy she had been and then how angry. Adam's face was so horrified when he saw the ring and realised Chelsea's mistake. If he had been intending to propose on the cruise, he could have turned the misunderstanding into an impromptu proposal. Instead he'd let her get so upset. And now he was drifting away from her.

Thankfully, once again, the children covered up any gaps in the conversation with excited chatter about their last day on board. The kids' club had run a series of competitions that day and both Jack and Lily had won prizes. Jack won for his drawing of Ted living with the monkeys of Gibraltar. Lily won for her drawing of a wedding party, in which she was the chief bridesmaid.

'And I drew Jack,' she said, 'being a pageboy.'

Lily showed Ronnie the drawing, which was folded into the *Frozen*-themed rucksack she was using as her evening bag. Ronnie gave her sister a look of pity that made Chelsea shrink inside. Worse was to come.

Adam got up from his seat. 'I'd like to propose a toast,' he said. 'Several toasts, actually.'

The rest of the table took up their glasses.

'The first toast is to Jack, who picked the numbers on Granddad Bill's winning lottery ticket.'

Jack stood up and took a small bow.

'Thank you, Jack, for getting nearly all of them right. The second toast must go to Granddad Bill, for sharing his birthday winnings so generously. If only he could have made it on board the *European Countess* with us.'

'He's been sorely missed,' said Dave.

'To Granddad Bill.'

Everyone raised their glasses to their absent benefactor.

'Finally,' Adam concluded. 'I'd like to raise a toast to all of the Bensons – and the Benson-Edwards,' he nodded towards Ronnie and Mark, 'for making Lily and me so welcome. We've really felt like family on this trip.'

'Oh Adam.' Jacqui couldn't help herself. 'We wish you really were part of our family, love!'

Unable to stand it a moment longer, Chelsea abruptly pushed back her chair and fled for the sanctuary of the ladies', leaving Adam standing there, still holding his glass aloft.

Chapter Seventy

Kirsty and Jane

The last night of the cruise was also the night of the karaoke competition. There was a sheet tacked to the noticeboard outside the on-board TV studio, where anyone who was interested in competing could leave his or her name. Kirsty had glanced at the sheet as she passed on her way to the ice cream parlour that afternoon. At four o'clock there were already a dozen or so names. The prize was significant – a five-night cruise from any port of your choice. Kirsty would have loved to win that. She was already addicted to the cruising life. It was very easy to get used to all that luxury.

'Are you doing the karaoke competition?' Jane asked as they were getting ready for their final dinner on board.

Kirsty pulled a face.

'You'd ace it.'

'I don't think so. There's some stiff competition here. Besides, I'm not dressed for it.'

'What are you talking about? You look perfect.'

'I don't know. This dress is a bit tight. It shows too much cleavage.'

'You? Show too much cleavage? Has my best friend been stolen away and replaced by a replicant?'

'I just don't know if I feel like it. Plus, it's too late now. It starts at nine o'clock and I haven't signed up. And anyway, we won't have finished our dinner by then.'

As it happened, the waiting staff was so efficient, Jane and Kirsty were onto their coffees by half eight. And they had to walk back past the TV studio on their way to the lifts that would take them to their deck. A steady stream of people was headed in the same direction. Those dozen people who had signed up earlier had all brought an entourage. Kirsty was ready to keep walking but the crew member who had overseen the karaoke earlier in the cruise, and remembered Kirsty's fabulous rendition of 'Someone Like You', spotted her trying to slip past.

'Are you singing for us tonight?' he asked.

'It's too late. I didn't sign up,' said Kirsty.

'You don't need to sign up,' said the crew member. 'That's just to give us an idea of how we need to structure the evening – how many rounds and all that. If you want to come and sing, we'd love to have you. You haven't got much competition,' he added in a stage whisper.

'Go on,' said Jane.

'Oh, I don't know. I'm not really prepared for it.'

'The only preparation you ever needed at the Welsh Harp was a large white wine,' Jane reminded her. 'I can get you one of those right now. Come on. You've spent the past fortnight doing what I want to do. I know you want to get up there.'

'I don't know what to sing,' Kirsty lied.

'You need two songs,' said the crew member. 'One for the first round and one for the final. We're trying to keep it as interesting as possible, so it'd be good if you could avoid the songs people have already chosen like "New York, New York".'

'Fortunately, I've never liked that song,' said Kirsty. It was the only Sinatra song she didn't love.

'Has "It's Raining Men" gone?' Jane asked.

'No! You can have that.'

'Jane,' Kirsty started but they already knew that she was going to get on that stage.

'What's your other song,' asked the crew member. 'For if – or should I say *when* – you get through to the final?'

Jane looked at Kirsty expectantly. She was pretty sure she knew what her old friend would choose.

Though the crew member running the contest that night said that he didn't think Kirsty had much competition, she soon felt otherwise. There were a couple of people who'd had a bit too much to drink and thought they were better than they were but there were also some genuine stars up there and they were taking it seriously too, checking sound levels and asking for certain lighting.

Kirsty, having entered the competition late, was last to go on.

The friendly atmosphere in the room was uplifting. She tried not to think about the fact that she wasn't just singing to the people in that room. Her performance was being transmitted live into every stateroom on the ship. If the people there cared to watch.

'I'm going to sing "It's Raining Men".'

The intro began. Kirsty gripped the microphone tightly and tried to open herself up to the music. As she growled her way through the first few words, Jane led the crowd in a cheer. That vote of confidence gave Kirsty the lift she needed to take her singing to the next level.

As the song progressed, Kirsty prowled the stage. She picked out an old chap – possibly in his eighties – sitting in the front row of the audience and gave him a suggestive wink. The crowd loved it. When the song ended, they clapped louder and harder than they had for any of the previous acts. Kirsty made her way back to her seat.

'You're definitely going through,' said Jane.

The audience cast their votes. While they were being counted, there was time for everyone to get another drink. Jane bought Kirsty a big glass of white wine.

Chapter Seventy One

Kirsty

Kirsty and Jane barely had time to finish their drinks before the second round of the contest was announced. As Jane had predicted, Kirsty was through. The field had been narrowed down to three but the other two contestants were not going to be pushovers. One of them was the man who had sung 'New York, New York'. The other one was the young girl who'd sung 'Let It Go' right back at the beginning of the cruise. She'd reprised that song tonight, thereby guaranteeing the vote of the younger female audience members.

The auditorium had filled up considerably during the interval, as other guests finished eating dinner and looked to be entertained. There were no seats left and people were squeezing into the aisles.

'Ladies and gents,' said the compère, 'if you're looking for a seat and don't find one, remember that the final is going to be beamed straight onto the screen on the top deck, so you can always watch from a sunbed.'

Kirsty joined the other two contestants in the small space behind a screen that was known as the 'Green Room'. The 'Let It Go' girl, Kayleigh, admitted that she was terrified.

'I've never sung in front of so many people before,' she said. 'I'm worried I'm going to make a fool of myself.'

'You'll be great,' Kirsty assured her. 'It's not that many more people than were here for the first round.'

'But we're going to be on the big screen.'

'You can't even see the people up on deck,' said Kirsty. 'Don't give them a second thought.'

The man, Roy, said that he'd once sung at the Cavern Club. Kirsty nodded in recognition. Kayleigh had never heard of the club where the Beatles had cut their teeth. But then she'd barely heard of the Beatles either. She thought Mick Jagger was their lead singer.

Kirsty did not reveal anything of her own stage experiences. There had been occasions when she'd sung in front of such a big crowd. When she was thirteen, after her father had left and no longer had any say in the matter, Kirsty had got a part in the chorus of a big pantomime. Her mother Nicole attended every single performance. Kirsty imagined her mother now, taking a place near the stage, getting ready to sing along, willing her to success.

Nicole would have loved to go on a cruise like this one. She had a friend from her West End days who worked on a cruise ship. Nicole had made that girl's life sound so glamorous. She was going to get Nicole and Kirsty a discount on a Mediterranean trip to celebrate Nicole's recovery from breast cancer. Alas, it wasn't to be.

Kirsty exhaled deeply to breathe that particular memory away.

Kayleigh sang first. For her second song, she chose Beyoncé's 'Crazy in Love'. It wasn't a wise choice. It was slightly beyond her vocal powers. Still, she gave it everything and once she got past the first verse, she really seemed to be enjoying herself. Her stage fright was completely forgotten as she strutted across the platform, giving Beyoncé a real run for her money on the choreography front.

In honour of his Cavern Club days, Roy switched from Sinatra to Lennon and did a pretty passable version of 'Imagine'. He certainly got the audience swaying along with him. Some of them were even crying. Kirsty knew that Roy was the one she'd have to beat.

Roy gave Kirsty and Kayleigh high fives as he walked back into the Green Room. Now it was Kirsty's turn.

Kirsty checked her make-up one last time. She popped a bit more powder on her chin and her forehead and slicked on a little more lipstick.

'You're on,' said the compère.

Kirsty stepped into the lights.

'This song is dedicated to my mother, who always encouraged me to sing.' Kirsty hadn't intended to make a speech before she started singing but right then, the words wanted to come out and she let them. 'My mum was the best mum in the world. She gave me confidence and self-esteem. She taught me that when life knocks you down, you've got to get back up and have another go. When I lost her, eleven years ago, I lost one of my best friends. There'll never be another woman quite like her. Anyway, Mum, this one is for you.'

The music was cued up and ready to go.

'I think most of you will know this song. It's called "Over The Rainbow".'

By the time Kirsty had finished the first chorus, the whole audience was on its feet. Jane couldn't help but feel sorry for the other two contenders who must surely have known, from the audience reaction, that they never stood a chance. Clapping until her hands were sore, Jane cheered loudest of all.

Kirsty made the most of her moment. When she finished singing, she took half a dozen bows and accepted a flower brought to the stage by a little girl.

The compère tried to keep people interested in the vote but it was fairly obvious that Kirsty was going to be the winner. She accepted the prize and a commemorative cup and her fellow finalists were graceful in defeat. After they'd taken a few obligatory photographs, Kirsty reprised her winning song. She got another standing ovation. If anything, she sang even more movingly than the first time round.

'That's my best friend,' Jane told the glamorous older woman sitting beside her. 'She can sing anything.'

'Will you introduce me?' the woman asked. She was wearing a Countess Cruises ID. 'I'm Lorraine Miles. Head of Entertainment.'

Jane took her new friend to meet Kirsty.

'You were really great up there tonight,' Lorraine told her. 'I saw you earlier in the cruise as well – that night that you sang the Adele song. You were good then too. What do you do back in the real world?'

'What? For my job? I work as an office admin for a firm of accountants.'

'Do you like it?'

'I can't say it was always my dream.'

Kirsty smiled at Jane. Jane had heard all the stories.

'And what about singing?' Lorraine asked. 'Is that your dream?'

'It was,' said Kirsty. 'When I was a kid.'

'You're not that old now.'

Lorraine handed over her business card.

'I work for Countess,' she said. 'I'm responsible for all the original entertainment you see on board. Not just on this ship but across the fleet. I created some of the shows. Like *Mysterioso*. Have you seen that one since you've been on here?'

'Yes,' said Kirsty. 'It was amazing. It was like something you'd see in Vegas.'

'Thank you. I'm putting together another show now and I'm wondering if you'd be interested in auditioning in London next month?'

'Are you serious?'

'Don't get too excited. I'm offering you an audition, not a part. And if we did offer you a place in the show, you'd need to think long and hard. You'd be on ship for weeks at a time. It's not like being on holiday. And before that, you'd have to come and join rehearsals at the line's facility in the States. It's hard work.'

'Fame costs,' said Kirsty.

Lorraine grinned, recognising the iconic quote.

'Anyway, you've got my number now. Do think about it and give me a call if you want to ask anything at all. Enjoy the rest of your holiday.'

When Lorraine was out of earshot, Kirsty squealed with delight.

Chapter Seventy Two

Kirsty and Jane

There wasn't much of the holiday left. When the girls got back to their stateroom, they discovered that the housekeeping team had already laid out the plastic packing mats on the beds, a none-too-subtle hint that it was time to fill up the suitcases and prepare for disembarkation, which would be very early the next day.

Jane and Kirsty dutifully did their packing.

'Isn't it funny how even if you don't buy anything new, your clothes never seem to fit back in the suitcase you brought them out in,' Kirsty observed.

'That's because you don't fold them up properly,' said Jane, taking over. 'Look, I could get it all back in for sure. Let me do it.'

'There's no need . . .'

'It's the least I can do. I'm so grateful you came on this cruise with me, Kirsty. I know it hasn't been the best of holidays but you were so right that I needed to do it. Greg would have wanted me to. And I really feel like something has shifted. I know it's going to be different when I get back home.'

'Good,' said Kirsty. 'I'm going to be right there beside you.'

'Not if you ace that audition and end up working on here.'

'Do you think I should go for it?'

'You should.'

'I probably will.'

While Jane zipped up Kirsty's bag, Kirsty checked she'd left nothing in the drawers. She even checked under the bed.

'And the safe,' said Kirsty. 'We mustn't forget to make sure we take everything out of the safe.'

There had never been anything in the safe, except for . . . Once the ashes were in there, Kirsty had decided to keep her passport in her handbag instead.

'It's OK,' said Jane. 'The safe's empty.'

'Is it?'

'I gave Greg a burial at sea,' Jane admitted.

'When?'

'This afternoon, when you were by the pool. I was out on the balcony and the sea looked so beautiful. I decided it's what he would have wanted. I checked there was no one on the deck below in case I didn't throw it far enough but I managed it. Greg's urn is somewhere between here and the Azores by now.'

'Oh, come here,' said Kirsty. 'I hate to think of you doing that alone.'

'It was all right,' said Jane. 'I wanted to be on my own when I said goodbye.'

Kirsty embraced her friend.

Jane was glad that she'd told Kirsty about casting Greg's ashes but she hadn't told her the whole story. Kirsty still didn't know about the ring or the way the loss of it had led to the meeting with Adam Baxter. That would remain Jane's secret. For now . . .

Chapter Seventy Three

Chelsea and Jack

The last night at sea was also the last night that Chelsea and Jack would share a bedroom for a while. Finding the packing mats laid out on the bed when they returned from dinner, Chelsea pulled her own case and Jack's colourful Dalek case out of the wardrobe and carefully repacked their luggage, while Jack treated her to a précis of the highlights of their trip.

'Can we do this again?' Jack asked. 'Next year? I like being on holiday with you and Adam and Lily.'

'I think it depends on Adam and Lily,' said Chelsea. 'They might have different plans. I might not be necessarily going on holiday with them myself.'

'Why not?' Jack asked.

'I don't know,' said Chelsea.

'Lily wants you to go on holiday with her again,' said Jack. 'I think she would like that. When she talked about her mummy to me, the one who isn't alive any more, she said it doesn't matter so much because now she's got you to love her instead.'

'Oh,' said Chelsea, feeling a catch in her heart. 'It's not quite the same.'

'But it nearly is. She said you could be her new mummy if you married Uncle Adam. She said he's going to ask you.'

'He hasn't asked me, Jack.'

'But Lily said he's going to.'

'He hasn't. He won't.'

Jack ignored her. 'The only problem is, Lily said if you're her new mummy, that makes her more important in your life than I am.'

'You'll always be important in my life, Jack.'

'That's what I said to Lily. Sometimes she's very annoying,' said Jack. 'But I think it would be nice if she was my cousin.'

'Oh Jack,' said Chelsea.

'Why are you looking sad?'

'Only because we've got to go home tomorrow,' Chelsea lied. 'And I will miss you and all your loveliness.'

If only life was a simple as Jack thought it could be.

When Jack was asleep, Chelsea lay awake and thought about the past couple of days. She'd told Adam that her sudden exit at dinner was due to a dodgy prawn but she knew that he knew otherwise. So did her mother and father and her sister and Mark. Nobody was fooled. And now Chelsea was actively dreading the next time she and Adam found themselves alone together without Chelsea's family or Lily to tape over the cracks that had appeared. The next private conversation they had must surely be their last.

Chapter Seventy Four

Granddad Bill

Back in the Midlands it was time to put Granddad Bill to bed in the guest room at Annabel's house for the last time. That evening, the various members of the Buchanan family, Bill and Sophie had all been absorbed in different activities. Izzy and Sophie were upstairs, watching a DVD. Well, half-watching it while they checked their numerous social media accounts. Richard was taking calls from the States in his home office. Annabel had been in the kitchen, sitting at the table with her cookery books, planning a dinner party for the following week. Humfrey was tucked up in bed, dreaming of bottles of formula. Granddad Bill was in front of the television in the family room. The television had been tuned to Sky Sports for pretty much the whole of Bill's visit.

Leander didn't know where to put himself. Having Granddad Bill around for the past fortnight had really tested the dog's loyalty at bedtime. Ever since Humfrey arrived, Leander would go to bed where the baby slept. At least, he would position himself at the bottom of the stairs. He wasn't allowed up them. He was like a sentinel. Ostensibly asleep but in fact alert to every tiny sound that might indicate a threat to the baby.

But now he had Granddad Bill to worry about too, Leander did not know what to do. With Humfrey upstairs and Bill in the family room or the downstairs guest bedroom, Leander's nightly routine was all over the place as he paced backwards and forwards between his two self-imposed charges.

Just as Annabel was putting her recipe folder away, Leander came into the kitchen. That wasn't so strange. If anyone at all were in the kitchen, then Leander would have to add that to his beat, on the off chance that someone might slip him something to eat. That evening however, he pawed Annabel's knee in a very different way from usual. And when she asked him what was the matter, he actually put his head on one side and gave the sort of low whimper that used to indicate he wanted to go outside, before they had the dog flap put in.

'You don't need me to open the door for you, silly thing. Use your flap.'

Annabel gave Leander a friendly scratch between the ears, but he wasn't budging. He pawed her knee again and repeated that strange little whine. This time, Annabel understood that he was trying to tell her something. She stood up. She felt a prickle of fear run down her spine, leaving her knees oddly weak.

'What is it?'

She followed Leander out into the hall. 'Richard!' she called up the stairs before she got there. 'Is Humfrey OK?'

Richard emerged from Humfrey's bedroom. 'I was just checking on him. He's sleeping like a . . . like a baby.'

Then Annabel noticed that Leander was heading on towards the family room. As she hesitated he stopped and looked back at her, giving an impatient little whine as if to hurry her up.

'Oh God,' thought Annabel as she followed her dog. 'Please don't let anything have happened.'

Annabel had never thought of Leander as some kind of Lassie before, but now she was following him at speed, hoping he hadn't brought her attention to what was wrong too late.

Seeing his wife's agitation, Richard followed her.

Leander pushed open the door to the family room with his nose. Granddad Bill was still in his chair by the television. The remote control, which rarely left his hand, was on the floor. Bill's arm hung limply.

Leander bustled in and licked the old man's hand urgently. There was not even a flicker of response that Annabel could see from where she stood in the doorway, hesitant and slightly fearful. Leander gave that little whine again.

Annabel put her hand to her mouth.

She knew what she would find when she was finally standing in front of her grandfather and she wasn't sure she could bear it. She began to cry softly.

'Oh Bill,' she said. 'Oh Bill, no.'

Richard joined Annabel in the doorway. He too saw the remote control on the floor and Granddad Bill's limp arm and didn't need to be told what was going on. He wrapped his arms round his wife and let her snivel into his chest.

'What are we going to do?' Annabel cried.

'It's OK,' said Richard. 'We can handle this together.'

Leander stepped back to let Annabel and Richard do their bit.

Annabel's worst fears were confirmed when she finally dared step into the room. Bill's head lolled against the William Morris print cushions. His mouth was open. His tongue looked desiccated. Richard gently closed his mouth. His eyes, thank God, were already shut.

Annabel stood in front of her grandfather and looked at him sadly.

'Oh Bill, I wish you could have made it until everyone got home.'

Richard wrapped his arms round her again.

Annabel continued. 'They're all going to be so upset. They'll miss you so much. I'll miss you. I'm just so glad we were able to have this time together. I wish we'd had longer. I should have looked for you all earlier. I would have loved to have known you back in the day, Bill. All those years we lost because I was too scared to reach out.'

Leander wagged his tail slowly, as if in agreement.

'Oh, I don't know what to do,' said Annabel to Richard. 'I've never been through this before.'

Annabel's adoptive grandparents and her father had all died in hospital.

'It's OK.' Richard stroked Annabel's hair. 'I'm here. We're going to do this together.'

'Who are we supposed to phone? The doctor or an ambulance? I don't know how I'm going to tell Sophie. And Izzy. Jacqui and Dave! Ronnie and Chelsea. They're all going to be devastated that they weren't with him when he passed. I wish we had known him for longer. Oh, poor Bill.'

Richard held her tightly. 'There's no need to be sad for him, Annabel. He died in his sleep, in a chair in front of a television tuned to Sky Sports. I can't think of a better way to go.'

'But why did he have to go today? Everyone will be back tomorrow morning. Why couldn't he just hang on?'

'He went because it was his time, my love. He was eighty-seven. He had a good innings. He lived surrounded by people who loved him. He had three beautiful granddaughters and four great-grandchildren and he got to know them all. You did get to know him, Annabel. You got to see the real him while he was here with us. He enjoyed his last few days. I know he did.'

'But what about the other night, when he thought he was back in the war?'

'Even that gave you the opportunity to find out more about his life. Think about the way Sophie came to see him in the morning and told him he was her hero.'

Annabel gasped. 'Jack will be devastated.'

'He'll have all of us to support him. The Bensons are a strong family, Annabel. They'll rally round.'

All the time Richard and Annabel were embracing and talking in low sad voices, Leander continued to stare at the old man. He put his head in Bill's lap, respectfully resisting rooting through Bill's jacket pocket for the last of the Trebor mints. He whimpered softly. He turned to look at Richard and Annabel. He turned back to Bill again and gave another, slightly louder, whine.

'Oh Leander,' said Annabel. 'You loved him too.'

'Everyone who knew Bill loved him. Think of all the adventures he had,' Richard continued. 'Think of the way he made everyone laugh with the spoons and the musical belching. He lived his life to the full. We should all try to be more like him. He even won the bloody lottery!'

Suddenly, Leander skittered backwards, banging into Richard and Annabel's legs. He wasn't whining now. He started barking – an excited, joyful bark. At the same time, Granddad Bill snorted his way into wakefulness, searching for the remote control even as he came round.

'Who won the bloody lottery?' he asked.

Breathless from shock, Annabel hugged her grandfather tightly.

'We all did, you lovely, lovely man.'

Chapter Seventy Five

Everyone

The ship docked in Southampton overnight. Disembarkation was early but it took a surprisingly long time to get three thousand passengers off the ship and onto dry land, especially because no one really wanted to go.

Jack and Lily were both distraught at having to leave their home of the past fortnight. There were tears over breakfast.

'Can we come on another cruise next year?' Lily asked Chelsea.

'You'll have to ask your dad,' Chelsea said.

The atmosphere between Adam and Chelsea had still not defrosted. Chelsea was busy digesting so many humiliations, both real and imagined. She was mentally closing down in preparation for the end of yet another promising relationship. Adam had almost certainly picked up on that.

The minibus Ronnie had arranged to take the Bensons to the port was there to pick them up and take them back to Coventry. Jack wrapped himself round his aunt, begging her to come back to Coventry with them 'Just for the night'. He couldn't bear that the holiday was at an end. Jacqui tried to entice Jack onto the minibus with promises of treats ahead.

'You can come with me to pick up Granddad Bill. You can see Humfrey and Leander. And Sophie!'

'Sophie!' said Jack. 'I forgot about her.'

Jacqui tutted. 'How can you forget your sister?'

Jack put on his most winning smile. 'I have missed her really.'

Chelsea promised she would see them all soon but for now she had to go back to London with Adam and Lily, wondering for the whole journey whether Adam would beg her to spend the night with them anywhere near as enthusiastically as Jack had.

After two weeks on the Med, the south of England was disappointingly grey. The passengers of the *European Countess* were being delivered back from their heavenly holiday to earth with a bump.

Chapter Seventy Six

Everyone

Having dropped off their cases in Coventry, Jacqui and Bill headed straight for Annabel's to pick up Granddad Bill and Sophie.

'It's been wonderful,' said Annabel. 'I have to admit that as soon as I waved you all off on the cruise, I started to worry. But it's been great.'

'Leander's definitely going to miss Bill,' said Richard.

Annabel embraced her grandfather with all the warmth and love with which Ronnie and Chelsea had embraced him as small girls. Then she gave Sophie an extra-tight hug.

'You can stay here whenever you like.' Annabel turned to Jacqui. 'Tell Ronnie that her daughter has been a wonderful help.'

'I will. But sweetheart,' Jacqui pulled Annabel to one side, 'there's something I've got to tell you.'

Though she had promised Jack that she would let Annabel know what had happened to Ted, for some reason Jacqui had not been able to bring herself to let Annabel know until now, when they were together in person. The grave expression on Jacqui's face as she prepared to make the admission made Annabel worry that she was going to hear something much, much worse than bad news about a cuddly toy.

'I've been so upset,' said Jacqui. 'Ted was . . . well, she was the last link between me and you as a baby.'

Annabel nodded but she didn't really understand. Then she cottoned on.

'Jacqui,' she said, 'do you still have all Chelsea and Ronnie's baby toys?'

'Well, no,' said Jacqui. 'They all fell to bits years ago.'

'Then it doesn't matter that we no longer have Ted. She did her job. Now she's gone to live with the monkeys. We don't need her to keep some sort of connection open any more.'

'Don't we?' Jacqui asked.

'No,' said Annabel firmly, giving her birth mother a hug. 'We don't.'

Later that evening, with Bill back in his chair in front of the television, it was as if the whole family had never been away. Ronnie and her gang popped round for tea. Jack presented Bill with the gladiator's helmet he'd chosen in Rome.

'That's just perfect,' said Bill. 'I've won the bloody lottery.'

Annabel had said nothing about Bill's trip back in time to the Coventry Blitz. There didn't seem to be any point worrying the Bensons just yet. Sophie would almost certainly tell Ronnie anyway.

Sophie did tell Ronnie, and everyone else, over tea, when she talked about the article she had written for *County Class*. Ronnie agreed that Annabel had done the right thing, the kind thing, by not worrying Dave and Jacqui while they were on holiday. She also agreed with Annabel's view that Sophie could not be blamed for Bill's trip back to the past. Jacqui concurred.

'Anything might have set him off,' she said. 'A sound. A look. A smell. It's the way he is now.'

Jacqui gave Sophie a squeeze.

'We can't wait to read that piece you've written,' Jacqui told her. 'I'm sure you'll make us all very proud.'

'Did you get in the bit about the shelter and the farting lady who always blamed her dog?' Mark asked.

'Our daughter has been asked to write a serious historical article for a proper magazine and all you want to know is whether she wrote about farting!' cried Ronnie.

'I did put the farting in,' Sophie confirmed.

'Excellent,' said Mark.

Ronnie frowned.

'Adds a bit of colour!' Mark protested.

'And I wrote about how lucky we all feel that Granddad Bill survived and how proud we are to be his descendants.'

'Am I a descendant?' Jack asked. He looked concerned.

'You certainly are,' said Jacqui.

With his hair slicked down and tidy after a bath, everyone saw the resemblance between Jack and Granddad Bill in a photograph of him as a child, standing at the entrance to the Anderson shelter where he'd spent that fateful night in 1940. Later Sophie took a photograph of Jack sitting on Granddad Bill's knee that she would use to illustrate her article alongside the older picture. The editor of *County Class* would love it.

The Great House was strangely quiet that night. Leander moped by the chair that Granddad Bill had made his own. The Buchanans ate dinner without any musical burping.

'Mum and Dad,' said Izzy. 'I've got something to tell you.'

Sophie wasn't the only one who had been doing some writing.

'While she was here, Sophie helped me write a letter, to the family of my kidney donor. I've asked if I can meet them.'

Chapter Seventy Seven

Adam and Chelsea

Adam, Lily and Chelsea travelled from Southampton to London in their own taxi. Chelsea sat in the back with Lily, who was horrified by the grubby state of the taxi's booster seat and tried to insist that, thanks to all the ice cream she'd eaten on the *European Countess*, she'd grown enough not to need it. Adam sat in the front with the driver, rather than squash all three of them in the back.

Lily kept the conversation going. She wanted to reminisce about the cruise and talk about planning another one.

'Next year, we can go to America!' she said. 'The lady in the kids' club comes from there – from Disneyland.'

'I expect she meant *near* Disneyland,' said Adam.

'No. Actual Disneyland,' Lily insisted. 'She said she'd look forward to seeing me. When can we go?'

There was also a little bit of sadness about Ted. Lily asked to see photographs of the bear on Chelsea's phone.

'Do you think the monkeys are being kind to her?' Lily asked.

'Of course they are.'

'Will she be happy, in Gibraltar?'

'I expect so. And perhaps she actually likes it better, living with monkeys rather than humans. She probably doesn't have to wear clothes, for a start.'

Lily could not see how that might be an advantage, even if Ted was covered in fur. Lily definitely believed in the power of fashion.

Adam had the taxi driver go to Chelsea's flat first. He had suggested that she go back to his place but in the end Chelsea said that she would rather go straight back to Stockwell. She wanted to know if the place had been burgled or burned down in her absence. Might as well get the worst over with.

When they got to Stockwell, Adam got out of the taxi to help Chelsea carry her bags to the door, while Lily watched anxiously from the back of the car.

'Don't come up,' said Chelsea. 'Lily looks worried to be in the taxi alone.'

'She's OK for a minute. I'll help you carry these bags upstairs.'

Chelsea refused to let Adam go from Lily's sight. 'No. I can manage,' she said.

Just like I've always managed, she thought. On my own. The conversation they'd had, right at the beginning of the trip, about the possibility of her moving in with Adam and his daughter, seemed like a very long time ago.

'I was serious, you know. When I said that Lily and I would like you to move in with us,' said Adam, as if he had read Chelsea's mind. 'It would make things so much easier.'

'I don't think making things easier is a good enough reason,' said Chelsea. 'Look, I'm really tired and I've got loads of laundry to do. Why don't you call me later, once you and Lily are settled in at home? We can talk properly then.'

Adam didn't argue with her. Lily had her face pressed against the passenger window now.

'OK,' he said. 'I'll call you later.'

Lily waved forlornly as the car moved off.

Back inside her flat – the flat she had been so looking forward to leaving at last – Chelsea sniffed back a tear. Who would have thought that the dream holiday would turn out to make things so difficult? Still, better that all the issues that remained were brought out into the open now, before Chelsea moved in. Chelsea hoped that her landlord hadn't already found a taker for her place so she could stay on in Stockwell.

She sat in the chair in the bay window, which had seemed like the height of romance when she first moved in.

Maybe it would still work out. Maybe this was just another road bump and not a blockade.

Chapter Seventy Eight

Adam

Adam and Lily went home and Adam put the first of many loads of washing on, but Lily was not ready to be back. She followed her father around from room to room, moaning that she was bored.

'But you're back with all your toys,' he said. 'Surely you can find something to play with. You could set up a show and have Melinda tell all the other dolls about her travels.'

Lily curled her lip to let him know that she didn't think that was such a great suggestion.

'Melinda misses Ted,' she said. 'And I miss Jack.'

'You saw him just this morning. It's only been half a day since we got off the boat.'

'I still miss him. I might miss him less later,' Lily conceded, 'but now I am sad and I'm bored. Do something to make me happy?'

Adam pulled a funny face.

'It didn't work,' she told him.

'Well, perhaps something to eat will cheer you up,' he suggested. 'There might be something in the freezer.'

Which was when Adam discovered that at some point, while they had been away, there must have been a power cut. He noticed as soon as he opened a tub of ice cream. It had clearly melted and reset. He couldn't risk feeding any of the food in there to Lily.

'Nando's?' he suggested.

Lily shook her head.

'I hate Nando's.'

'You love it!'

'Not today, I don't. Granny and Granddad's,' she countered.

'OK.' Adam texted his mother, hoping that she would be at home rather than out at the shops. He had never understood why retirees always wanted to shop on Saturdays when the stores were full of people who had no choice but to shop on Saturdays, but his parents, like so many others it seemed, preferred to wait until the stores were rammed. Perhaps it was to give them something to complain about, he always joked. And as it happened, his parents were in Marks and Spencer when they received his text. They promised to be home within the hour though and of course they would be delighted to give Adam and Lily some tea.

A short while later, Adam and Lily were in his parents' kitchen. They confirmed that there had indeed been a power cut while they were on the cruise.

'You'll have to throw everything away,' Adam's mother reminded him.

'Yes, Mum.'

After tea, Lily lay down on the sofa and was asleep within moments.

'Bless her,' said Adam's mother. 'She's had a very busy couple of weeks. And how did you get on . . .?' she continued a little gingerly. 'You and Chelsea . . . did you?'

Adam didn't want to tell his mother about the incident in Aix-en-Provence so he said, 'We had a lovely time,' and left it at that.

'But you didn't . . .?'

'No,' said Adam.

'Oh. OK. If you want to talk about it?'

'I don't want to talk about it. Look, while Lily's asleep, would you mind if I dashed back home and got a few chores done? I've got to throw everything out of the freezer for a start and find some new stuff to put in it.'

'Of course,' his mother replied. 'You know, Lily can stay here tonight if she likes? Her bed is all made up.'

Adam's parents kept a room specifically for Lily's visits.

'That would be great, Mum. If you really don't mind.'

'We've missed you both,' she said, giving him a hug. 'Now, go and do your chores.'

Adam got home, emptied one lot of washing and put another lot in. He got a bin bag and threw everything from the freezer away, even the bag of ice-cubes, which had melted and refrozen as a single big block of ice, suitable only for a giant's gin and tonic.

While the washing machine was humming and the tumble dryer was tumbling, Adam opened the backlog of post. There was nothing interesting. Paper bills exhorting him to go paper-free.

Adam felt as if he should be doing something. He picked up his phone and dialled a number.

'Jane, hi. It's Adam from the cruise. I hope you don't think this is weird, me telephoning, but you said that I should. I've been thinking about you quite a bit and . . . well, I just really wanted to hear your voice.'

Would Jane even be back home yet? She was probably still travelling with that friend of hers, the big girl who made such a contrast to Jane with her tiny frame and her wrist-bones so delicate and narrow you automatically wanted to wrap her in something soft to protect her.

Would she call back or would she just think Adam was a nut and delete his message without even listening to the end? Adam tried to remember exactly what he'd said. That bit about wanting to hear her voice wasn't right. It wasn't how he meant it to come out. She wouldn't call him back. But at least the fact he'd reached her voicemail meant he was sure she had given him her real number, so he could always try again. Next time he would withhold his number and then maybe, just maybe, she would pick up.

Adam stood by the French windows and looked out on to the garden. Another chore. It had been wet but warm while they were away. The plants were going wild. Adam leaned his forehead against the glass. He'd stood like this for a long time on the day that Claire died, looking out at the deckchairs they'd sat in just two afternoons previously, feeling the tectonic plates of his life shifting into their new position. That day, he could feel them shifting again. Everything could change if he would only let it.

At last, Jane called him back.

'I'm so glad you rang,' he gabbled. 'I didn't think you would. Are you back home? Did you have a good journey?' He didn't give her time to answer. 'I wanted to talk to you. See you, even. If I could. There's something I need to get off my chest and you're the only person who could understand. Is this too much? Is this too soon? Can we do this over the phone?'

'Calm down,' said Jane. 'Take a deep breath. I'm listening.'

Chapter Seventy Nine

Chelsea

Alone in her flat, Chelsea uploaded the last few photographs of the cruise from her camera to her laptop. She had intended to create a real album using the pictures. She was going to help Jack write the book of Ted's adventures, of course, but this one had been going to be for her and Adam to look back on when they'd been together for forty years.

Chelsea looked at the photographs for more clues. In Barcelona and Ajaccio he looked pretty happy to be with her. Did Adam start to look uncomfortable when they were in Rome? How about Florence? He definitely looked unhappy in the group photograph Jacqui had the waiter take at that little restaurant in Aix-en-Provence. Though he had his arm round Chelsea, it seemed as though he was leaning away from her at the same time. He wanted to be off.

Towards the end, there were some photographs that Jack had taken during the final dinner on board the *European Countess*. They were poorly framed and some were out of focus, but Jack had managed to get pictures of everyone. In those, Adam didn't look quite so keen to be away from Chelsea. She was the one who looked tense and anxious to be out of there. Maybe she'd misread his attempts to patch things up.

But then Ronnie phoned.

'Chelsea,' said Ronnie. 'I've got something I have to tell you. I didn't want to say anything while we were on the ship but I think you ought to know now you're back.'

'What?' Chelsea asked.

'Is Adam there?'

'No.'

'Good.'

'What's happened?'

'Yesterday afternoon, while you were in your cabin having a lie-down and Mark had Jack and Lily, I went for a walk on my own.'

'Yes . . .?'

'I went on that Sky Walk thing. You know, the bit with the glass where you can look all the way down to the waves.'

'Yes.'

Chelsea had taken the Sky Walk with Lily, Jack and Adam several times.

'I did it on my own so none of you could freak me out. Thing is, when I looked down, I saw something that really did freak me out.'

'A mermaid?' Chelsea suggested.

'I'm being serious. I saw Adam. He was with a woman. He had his arms round her.'

There was a pause. 'Are you sure it was him?'

'I am. I'm really sorry, Chels.'

'No . . . Thank you for telling me. When you say he had his arms round her, what exactly do you mean? Was it just a friendly hug?'

'Perhaps it started out that way but it went on for a very long time.'

'I see.'

'He didn't mention having met someone he knew on board ship? An old friend? Old girlfriend, even?'

'No,' said Chelsea. 'What did she look like?'

'Small. Blonde hair.'

'The only thing I can think of is that perhaps it was the girl who lost the ring. Though I didn't think he met her.' Chelsea had to tell her sister that embarrassing story now.

At the end of it, Ronnie exhaled like a plumber right before telling you the job is going to be three times as expensive as you thought.

'So, you ended up with an *anti*-proposal?'

'You could put it that way.'

'This gets worse. If that was the ring's owner, she was looking pretty grateful,' said Ronnie. 'And why did Adam tell you he just handed the ring to customer services? I think you ought to know. I would want to. It might not mean anything but if it does, then you should be able to ask about it, right?'

Chelsea agreed.

'Maybe it was the stress of having asked you to move in with him. Maybe he was trying to sabotage things. People do that, when they've got something really good. It's like they feel they don't deserve it.'

'Maybe he just changed his mind about me,' said Chelsea.

'Well, if he did, he's a bigger idiot than I thought. Are you going to have it out with him?'

'I don't know what to do. I suppose we're going to have to talk about it but maybe we never will. I might never see him again.'

The doorbell rang. Chelsea was expecting a takeaway. Feeling too down in the dumps to haul herself round the supermarket, she had gone onto Deliverance.com and ordered sushi instead. Not too much because right now she felt the way she used to before a binge. She had to keep control. She told Ronnie what was going on.

'I've got to go downstairs and open the front door,' she explained. 'The buzzer's broken.'

Chelsea carried her phone and talked to her sister all the way down the stairs and back up and down again when she realised she'd forgotten the front door key. She told Ronnie about the afternoon in Aix-en-Provence and how badly she had mucked up hearing about Claire and the candle.

'I'd have been the same. You're talking like you've got some reason to think this is all your fault,' said Ronnie. 'Don't think like that. Adam's lucky to have you. He better have a good explanation for hugging that woman. If you want me to be there with you when you ask him . . .'

'I don't think there's any need for that . . . Hang on!' Chelsea called to the person at the door.

Chapter Eighty

Adam

Adam was standing on the front step.

'Oh!' said Chelsea.

'What is it?' Ronnie asked.

'I'll have to call you back,' Chelsea told her.

'Who is—?'

To Ronnie's chagrin, Chelsea cut her off.

'I didn't know you were coming,' Chelsea said to Adam.

'I wasn't sure myself until I turned into your street.'

'Where's Lily?'

'With my parents. She wanted to see them. Mum said she could stay overnight. Can I come in?'

'Of course,' Chelsea said.

It had been a long time since Adam had asked to come in to Chelsea's flat. He had his own keys. Why hadn't he used them? Chelsea could only think of bad reasons why Adam wasn't treating her place like home any more. He was different once he was inside too. He didn't put his car keys on the console table or take off his jacket. In short, he didn't look as if he was planning to stay.

'Tea?' Chelsea asked. 'Or something stronger?'

'Tea.' He gestured back to the street.

Of course. He had to drive the getaway car.

Adam sat on the window seat where Chelsea had

perched a few hours earlier, feeling like the Lady of Shalott, watching life going on in the looking glass, doomed always to be set apart. Adam never sat in the window seat. He didn't look comfortable.

Chelsea made the tea. She put Adam's mug down on the side table closest to him. It was the mug he always used – a chipped old thing with a picture of Cartman from *South Park* on one side. She would have handed it to him but even passing a mug between them suddenly seemed ridiculously intimate and wrong.

The tension between them was palpable and Chelsea was sure she knew what was coming. Heaven knows she'd seen this particular show often enough to know what the overture sounded like. She thought she recognised from boyfriends past the worried look in his eyes that would disappear the moment he'd said what he'd come to say. What Ronnie had seen wasn't just a hug, it was a *coup de foudre*. Adam had fallen for the girl on the ship. He was coming to tell Chelsea that it was over between them. She knew it with a conviction that grew when Adam said, 'This is really fucking hard, Chelsea. I don't know what to do other than just come out with it.'

Adam looked sick. Even with his tan from the cruise, she could see that the blood had drained from his face and there was a slight sheen of sweat on his forehead.

Chelsea sank onto the sofa.

Adam sank onto the floor.

'What are you doing?' Chelsea asked.

Adam rearranged himself so that he was on one knee.

'Chelsea Benson, will you be my wife?'

Chelsea had always wondered how she would react if and when she finally got a marriage proposal. She was surprised to hear herself actually scream. Well, squeal. Then she laughed and then she burst into tears.

Adam was bewildered.

'Is that a yes?'

Chapter Eighty One

Adam and Chelsea

Adam had bought Chelsea a ring long before they boarded the *European Countess* and it had travelled the Mediterranean with them, hidden in Adam's spare glasses case, safely tucked inside the room safe, awaiting the big moment. Adam had been gutted when his refusal to go into the church in Aix where Claire once lit a candle had brought back those awful memories and made the holiday go sour. When Jane's ring ended up in Chelsea's champagne glass a couple of days later, it really seemed as though the Universe was conspiring against them.

The ring Adam had chosen was nothing like the ring that Greg gave Jane in Paris. Adam had made a close study of the jewellery Chelsea already owned in an attempt to get a good idea of her style. One morning, while she was in the shower, he had taken a measurement of the diameter of the ring she usually wore on the third finger of her right hand, hoping that it would be a close match for the ring finger on the left. He'd taken that measurement to Tiffany and picked out a subtle solitaire on a plain platinum band. Though the stone wasn't huge, it was flawless.

Chelsea gawped at the ring Adam had chosen for her. She could not have made a better choice herself. It was exactly the sort of ring she'd always dreamed of.

'It's beautiful,' she said.

She allowed him to slip the ring onto her finger.

'You promise this is really mine?'

'Yes,' he said. 'And so am I.'

Chelsea threw her arms round his neck.

'I'm the happiest woman in the world.'

With Lily at her grandparents' house, Adam was able to stay the night in Chelsea's little flat. He suggested that they go out to celebrate their engagement but Chelsea only wanted to be with him. So they ate the sushi she had ordered and opened a bottle of cava that had been in her fridge for months. It wasn't the flashiest of celebrations but as far as Chelsea was concerned, it was perfect.

Though the sea had been calm and kind for the last few days at sea, Chelsea had been through an emotional storm and she still wasn't quite ready to step out into the world and show off her engagement ring. There were questions to be answered first.

'Ronnie said she saw you in a clinch,' said Chelsea.

'A clinch?'

'She was on the Sky Walk. She looked down and saw you. Who was the slim blonde girl?'

Adam explained everything. He told Chelsea about how Jane had come to throw her engagement ring from the balcony and how their conversation the following day had been a turning point for him. He'd felt then that he was ready to move forward but later he'd become frightened. It was hard to leave even such an uncomfortable position behind. Jane had given him the courage. When he spoke to her on the phone earlier that evening, she had sympathised with all his lingering doubts about betraying Claire by loving Chelsea just as much. Jane had given him the opportunity to say all those things out loud without feeling guilty.

'That was why I hugged her on the ship. Because she needed it and so did I. I've never been able to open up like that before.'

'I wish you'd opened up to me.'

'I will now, I promise. I just needed to hear that I wasn't mad from someone who'd been through the same thing.'

'Why didn't you tell me when we were on the ship?'

'I don't know. I suppose I thought it would make things worse.'

'I knew something was going on. I was worried. Let's never keep anything from each other again.'

Adam agreed. This time Chelsea thought the resolution would stick.

'I'd like to meet Jane one day and thank her,' Chelsea said.

'I don't think we'll ever see her again,' said Adam. 'We were there at the right time for each other but who needs a friendship based on mutual sadness? She gave me the strength to move forward. I hope I've done the same for her.'

'I hope so too. I feel like I owe her a great deal.'

The following day, Adam and Chelsea drove up to Coventry to tell Chelsea's parents the good news. They'd been waiting to hear it, ever since Adam asked Dave for Chelsea's hand on that day at Annabel's house. Later, when Adam met up with Dave again as they boarded the *European Countess* in Southampton, he'd told Dave that he would propose while they were all on holiday. Jacqui and Dave had been terribly disappointed and worried when the happy couple didn't get engaged before the end of the cruise.

Ronnie and her family came over immediately of course. Ronnie squeezed Chelsea so hard she thought she might stop breathing.

Mark gave Adam a gentle punch on the arm. 'Welcome to the family,' he said. 'Abandon hope all ye . . .'

Ronnie gave Mark the look that said there would be trouble later.

'Adam,' she said. 'I'm delighted you're going to be my brother-in-law.'

She gave him a hug and a kiss.

Meanwhile Lily told Jack, 'Now we're going to be proper cousins! That means Chelsea will be my new mummy, which is better than her being your auntie.'

Jack wasn't sure about that.

'She's been my auntie for ever,' he said.

'And I'll be your auntie for the rest of my days,' Chelsea interrupted the spat. 'You'll just have to share me.'

'Just out of interest,' Ronnie asked Adam a little later. 'When were you really planning to propose?'

'Gibraltar,' said Adam. 'I was going to give Chelsea her rock on The Rock.'

Ronnie nodded. 'I like that.'

Adam was sure that Claire would have approved. She would have liked Chelsea. She would approve of the way Chelsea interacted with Lily. The little girl was absolutely thrilled. Adam didn't suppose Lily had put much thought into the long-term implications of having her father remarry. She was just delighted with the idea of a wedding.

'It needs to be a Christmas wedding,' said Lily. 'So I can wear my *Frozen* dress.'

'I'm sure we can find you something even nicer,' Chelsea said. 'If you want to be my bridesmaid.'

'I do want to be your bridesmaid!' said Lily. 'And Jack can be a pageboy. He can wear velvet trousers and a waistcoat and carry the rings on a cushion. And he'll have to dance with me at the reception. And kiss me.'

'Nooooo!'

Jack ran away screaming. Poor Lily looked crestfallen.

'He'll come round to the idea,' said Ronnie, giving Lily a hug. 'I think the best part of this wedding is that I will be getting a new niece,' she added.

Chelsea was happier than she had ever been. At last she was going to have a proper family of her very own.

Chapter Eighty Two

Kirsty and Jane

Kirsty and Jane spent most of the weekend after the cruise together. On Sunday night, Kirsty sighed. 'I can't believe I've got to go back to work tomorrow. That's the worst thing about holidays, having to come home at the end of them.'

'Yeah,' said Jane. She wasn't certain that she would be going back to work on Monday but it felt more likely than it had done for a long time.

'I'm really glad we went, though,' said Kirsty. 'It was one of the best holidays I've had in my life. I can't think of any way I'd rather have spent my thirtieth birthday than in the South of France with you.' Kirsty touched her new pendant. 'Thank you.'

'You made it brilliant,' said Jane. 'And you'll be cruising the high seas all the time once you get that singing job. Are you going for it?'

'Of course I am. If you and this old town can spare me.'

'I'm not sure I can,' said Jane. 'But I want you to get that job.'

Kirsty left to go back to her own flat at about five o'clock, leaving Jane properly on her own for the first time in over two weeks. The house seemed very empty without the presence of her larger-than-life best friend but Jane didn't allow that to send her into a funk. She put the television on for background noise. It was something she hadn't done in months, for fear that she'd hear something that reminded her of Greg. Now she welcomed the sound of other people's laughter.

Quite a bit of post had piled up on Jane's doormat while they'd been away. With Kirsty gone home, at last Jane got round to going through it, getting rid of the junk mail and putting the bills to one side. Bills, bills, bills. Most of the post contained demands for money but there were a couple of things Jane hadn't expected. One was an invitation to a wedding. Seeing only her own name on the invite from Greg's cousin brought a little pang of melancholy, but Jane knew that when the day of the ceremony came, in November, she would be there with an enormous smile for the bride and groom.

The other unexpected item also had a handwritten address label. Jane tore open the big brown envelope to find another, smaller envelope inside. There was a covering letter from Greg's mother. It explained that the smaller envelope contained a letter from one of the people who had received Greg's kidneys, which had come via the patient advocate. Greg's parents had both read the letter and found it helpful but they'd resealed it to give Jane the chance to throw it away without opening it. It was important to give Jane this heads-up, in case she didn't want to read it. Jane wasn't sure that she did.

She held the small cream envelope – expensive paper – in both hands and looked at the elegant handwriting on the front. Whoever had written to her had gone to the trouble of using a proper fountain pen. Jane turned the envelope over. Was she about to open Pandora's box? She decided she would. Even Pandora's box had a grain of hope at the bottom.

The letter began:

Dear friend,

I feel strange writing to someone whose name I don't know, when we've got such an important connection. My name is Isobel – my friends call me Izzy – and I received your loved one's kidney on Boxing Day last year.

It goes without saying that the kidney transplant saved my life. I am ashamed to have to tell you that I suffered kidney failure through my own actions. I went to my first festival last summer. Mum and Dad didn't want me to go – I was only sixteen – but I persuaded them I would be safe and I wouldn't get involved with any drinking or drugs. I let them down. I took my first ecstasy tablet and got very unlucky indeed. The tablet was a fake, containing ingredients that shouldn't have been in there. I passed out and started fitting. When I woke up in hospital, my kidneys were packing up.

Why am I telling you this? There's a risk that you might think I didn't deserve a new kidney – that's certainly how I feel when I think about your loss – but perhaps you'll understand why I feel so lucky and blessed.

This time last year, I thought my life was over. I'd gone from being a smug, entitled private schoolgirl to a dialysis patient in the course of a weekend. I didn't think I would ever be able to plan an independent life again. I thought the rest of my days would be spent shuttling between my bedroom and the hospital. I could no longer take it for granted that the dreams I'd had since childhood – uni, an exciting career, marriage and a family – would come true. Now the future is something I look forward to again. But that relief and happiness is tinged with the knowledge that my gain has come from your loss. While my dreams have been resurrected, you're without doubt mourning the end of some of your own. Nothing I say can bring your loved one back.

I think about you and your family every day and hope that you are happy and well and that knowing how much my life has changed for the better might be of some comfort. I would love to meet you if you think that's a good idea but if we never do meet, I promise you that I will spend the rest of my life trying to be a better person, living up to the man who gave me a second chance. He's my hero.

With thanks and thanks and very best wishes,
Izzy

Jane put the letter back in the envelope. She didn't know what to think. She looked at the fridge door, to which she had tacked a photograph of her and Greg taken right after they got engaged on the Pont des Arts. That dream was definitely gone for good.

What would Greg have thought if he'd known that one of his kidneys would end up in the body of a teenage girl who'd been silly enough to take drugs?

Jane had a sudden clear image of Greg giving her the thumbs up. Greg was no saint. He'd smoked weed and taken ecstasy in his time. If he could have told her anything, it was that he would have loved the chance to do it all again.

Chapter Eighty Three

Sophie

The night before her GCSE results were due, Sophie couldn't sleep. Fortunately, Izzy couldn't sleep either for her own reasons, so they spent much of the night on Skype, whispering about their plans for the future, whether or not Sophie got the results she needed to carry on and do her A-levels.

The following morning, hollow-eyed from lack of rest, Sophie picked at her breakfast like a condemned man faced with his last meal. She had a day off from her internship to give her time to pick up her results and digest what they meant. Ronnie and Mark tried to cheer her up but they could just about remember a time when they too had been waiting for the letters that would decide their futures. They knew how important a moment this was for their daughter. Mark, for once, laid off his very worst jokes.

'I'll drive you down to the school if you want?' Ronnie suggested.

Though Sophie's legs felt horribly insubstantial right then – as though they might snap in half if she tried to use them – she insisted that she would walk down to the school on her own. She would probably meet up with some of the girls from her class on the way. The last thing she wanted was Ronnie looking over her shoulder as she opened an envelope full of bad news.

The school gates were open. One of the teachers had hung a banner proclaiming 'GCSE Results Day. Congratulations, Year Eleven!' from the fence. It seemed a little optimistic. There were already throngs of people in the courtyard. Some were bouncing up and down – just like Jack when they heard Granddad Bill had won the lottery. There were others who looked a lot less pleased with themselves. A couple were crying.

Sophie bumped into Skyler, her former best friend, as she turned into the courtyard. Skyler had no intention of going back to school that September and she was bolshie when Sophie asked her how GCSEs had gone for her.

'Who gives a fuck anyway?' was Skyler's answer, which said everything Sophie needed to know. 'I've got an interview with a model agency in London next week.'

To underline just how little exams mattered to someone like her – whose future would be full of lingerie shoots and boob jobs regardless of whether she understood BODMAS – Skyler showed Sophie the envelope that contained her results, then she got out her cigarette lighter and touched the flame to the corner. It went up surprisingly quickly, so that Skyler had to drop it on the floor and jump up and down on it to put out the flames.

'Fuck!' she exclaimed. 'That nearly set fire to my extensions.'

'Are you OK?' Sophie asked her. Tears had sprung to Skyler's eyes.

'I got three E's,' she said. 'My dad's gonna kill me.'

'Doesn't he know about the modelling thing?' Sophie asked.

'Of course he doesn't. I'll be all right,' said Skyler, carefully dabbing at her eyes to make sure she didn't dislodge her false eyelashes. That done, she quickly regained the composure of a girl who was going to get ahead no matter what. 'You'll be all right too,' she told Sophie. 'You'll have done brilliantly. You always were cleverer than the rest of us. I don't know why you ever hung out with a thicko like me.'

Then Skyler risked her make-up and her extensions to give Sophie a hug.

'I'm sorry about the way things worked out with you, me and Harrison and everything. You were my best friend. I should have treated you better.'

'It doesn't matter,' said Sophie. 'Seriously. Swipe left.'

Skyler laughed. 'Yeah! Swipe left. Well, good luck, swot. I'll see you around, I expect.'

Skyler clipped away on her fake Louboutins.

Sophie took a deep breath. Skyler, Izzy and her parents may all have been expecting her to ace her exams but Sophie was still convinced that the next ten minutes would hold nothing but disappointment. She joined the queue of pupils still waiting to pick up their envelopes. Miss Johannsen, her class and German teacher, caught her eye and gave her the thumbs up but Sophie managed to convince herself that Miss Johannsen was giving everybody the thumbs up. It had nothing to do with the results they'd scraped.

Sophie got to the front of the queue. Miss Johannsen had her envelope ready. She said nothing to give Sophie a clue as to what might be inside, but her eyes gave her away. She couldn't keep the smile out of them.

Sophie held the envelope in both hands. She was ready to cry.

'Will you open it for me?' she asked her form teacher. 'I can't get my fingers to work.'

Miss Johannsen obliged. Sophie's eyes were swimming as she read:

English Language – A*
English Literature – A*
German – A*
Maths – A*

The list went on. And all of the grades were A*.

'I think that's what you call a full house,' said Miss Johannsen. 'First one we've had at this school in a decade.'

Sophie was so surprised she was shaking.

Miss Johannsen wrapped her in a hug.

'You should call your parents. I bet they're just as nervous as you were. Then you should go and celebrate.'

Sophie called Izzy first.

'Oh my God!' said Izzy. 'You are such a swot!'

But she meant it in a good way.

'Didn't I tell you? This is amazing. You can do anything you want. We've got to meet up. We've got to celebrate.'

Ronnie and Mark already had plans for celebrating their daughter's huge success. Ronnie had secretly made a cake earlier that week, icing it quickly while Sophie was on her way home from school with all those A stars in place.

Jack had bought Sophie a lottery ticket with the help of his father.

'It's still illegal for me to buy one,' he explained. 'But I did choose the numbers.'

This time, none of them came up, but as Sophie's Grandma Jacqui told her that weekend, as they finished the GCSE cake, you don't need so much luck when you're prepared to work hard. And when you're surrounded by love.

There was more good news. The day after Sophie's results, the postman brought a parcel to the Buchanans' house. Inside it was Ted. It was quite the miracle that after her monkey adventures, Ted was still wearing her label, and though she was minus an ear she was still recognisably the black-eyed grumpy bear who had gone around the Med on the *European Countess*.

She looked even sadder after she'd been boil-washed, which was the first of several measures Ronnie took before she would even think about letting Jack give the bear back to Humfrey. A short spell in the freezer seemed like a good idea too.

Thanks to his Auntie Chelsea's proficiency with iPhoto, Jack was able to hand Ted back to her rightful owner along with a book entitled 'Ted's Big Adventure'.

'She's going to need a sequel,' said Annabel.

'Great idea!' said Jacqui. 'We should have a family holiday next year as well!'

Epilogue

The past is always with us but it's up to us whether the ghosts are good or bad.

On Greg's birthday in September Jane visited the plaque in the crematorium that marked his official resting place. It was a very plain plaque. There had been more exciting options in the funeral director's catalogue but Jane tried to choose one with Greg's preferences in mind. He liked to keep things simple. He definitely wouldn't have wanted flowers or an eternally weeping angel.

Jane brought with her a little cactus. Greg wasn't the sort of man who would appreciate roses but she wanted to bring something that would let people know he was cared for long after she'd gone home. The cactus she'd brought with her a few weeks before was gone. Jane sighed at the thought of someone nicking something from a grave but decided that if people were that desperate, then good luck to them. Perhaps it had ended up gracing the plaque of someone who didn't have anything else.

She brushed a little dirt from the brass. Then she got a tissue out of her pocket and buffed the letters of Greg's name to a shine. As she did so, she imagined how she must look from a distance. She'd seen women doing this before but they were older women. Women who'd had time to enjoy their loved ones properly before they lost them.

Ah well. At least Jane had known Greg for three years. At least she had known him well enough to decide that she wanted him for the rest of her life. Some people never felt that sort of connection. And he would always be young to her. She would never know him with grey hair and a pot belly. Though even as she thought it, she reminded herself that she would have loved that pot belly too.

The cruise had changed her. Meeting Adam, and the letter she'd received from Izzy, the girl who received Greg's kidney, had shown her that moving forward did not have to mean you were betraying those who couldn't come with you. Jane had written back to Izzy and assured her that Greg would be very pleased to know his kidney was giving her the chance to live a normal life. She hoped that Izzy would live that life to the full and that it would include a love as great as Greg and Jane's had been. Perhaps one day, Izzy and Jane might meet and become friends. And perhaps one day, Jane would meet someone else who made her laugh almost as much as Greg had. Perhaps she would meet someone who made her laugh even more. Probably not. But at least once more she could see a future in which there would be nights out and holidays and parties with her mates. Greg would want that for her.

'I can't stop long,' she told him now. 'I'm meeting Kirsty. It's karaoke night at the Welsh Harp. I'm singing.'

A light breeze rustled through the rose bushes at that, as though they were shaken by Greg's loud and lovely laugh. She imagined him in the Welsh Harp with her, looking as he had done the very first night they met, lifting a glass and raising a toast.

To the future!

ACKNOWLEDGEMENTS

First and foremost, thanks as always to editorial wonder woman Francesca Best for getting this book from my desk to the shelves in double-quick time. Thank you to copy editor Zelda Turner for catching all my spelling mistakes and to Eleni Lawrence, Jenni Leech and Lucy Upton for their PR and marketing magic. I'm especially grateful to Sarah Christie for creating my brand-new cover look. Isn't it lovely? Thanks also to my agents Antony Harwood and James Macdonald Lockhart.

I was lucky enough to be able to research this book onboard Princess Cruises' wonderful new ship, MS *Regal Princess*. Huge thanks are due to Princess MD of UK and Europe Paul Ludlow, devilishly handsome Princess PR supremo David Sanders and the *Telegraph's* Teresa Machan for getting me on board the trip of a lifetime – *Regal's* inaugural Caribbean voyage. I'd also like to thank Kerry Lovegrove, Princess's inspirational manager of show productions, for giving me a taste of what goes into making the on-board entertainment so special, and travel journalists Bridget McGrouther, John Honeywell, Jane Archer and Dave Monk for being so kind to a cruise newbie.

I based my fictional ship, the *European Countess*, on *Regal Princess* (www.princess.com). What a magnificent ship she is. *Regal* really does boast the largest floating pastry shop in the world and the pizza on the lido deck is to die for. If you're reading this on the *Regal Princess*, please have a slice for me. If you're not, I can't recommend the cruising life highly enough. It really does have something for everyone. See you onboard next year?

Back on dry land, I'd like to express my appreciation to my family, the Manbys and the Arnolds, for always being there. To my great friends and fellow writers, Victoria Routledge, Alex Potter and Michele Gorman for cheerleading when I hit the mid-book blues. And to Mark, for putting up with my working on holiday again. And for always knowing when to put the kettle on.

Lastly, I want to thank you, the reader, for joining me on yet another journey. The warm response received by the last two Benson family books really lifted my heart. I can't tell you how lucky I feel to be able to do this writing lark as a job!

Lots of love,

Chrissie
xxx

Find out what happens next to the Bensons and their friends, in the brilliant new novel coming out in November 2015 by Chrissie Manby:

A WEDDING AT CHRISTMAS

It's a proper family occasion!

If you liked *A Proper Family Adventure*, catch up with the first two hilarious instalments following the lives of the Benson family and their friends:

A PROPER FAMILY HOLIDAY

Chrissie Manby

Could you survive a week-long holiday with your entire family? Newly single magazine journalist Chelsea Benson can't think of anything worse.

Your grubby small nephew torpedoing any chance of romance with the dishy guy you met on the plane . . .

Your eighty-five-year-old granddad chatting up ladies at the hotel bar . . .

Getting nothing but sarcastic comments from your older sister, who's always been the family favourite . . .

And all this is before your parents drop their bombshell.

Is a week enough time for the Bensons to put their differences aside and have some fun? Or is this their last ever proper family holiday?

Heartwarming and funny, this is the perfect summer read for fans of Sophie Kinsella and Lindsey Kelk. And provides a great excuse for ignoring your annoying family members . . .

KEEP CALM: IT'S ONLY A WEEK

Out now in paperback and ebook.

HODDER